A Wedding on the Riviera

A Wedding on the Riviera

Evonne Wareham

Where heroes are like chocolate – irresistible!

Published 2022 by Choc Lit Limited
Penrose House, Crawley Drive, Camberley, Surrey GU15 2AB, UK
www.choc-lit.com

A CIP catalogue record for this book is available
from the British Library

ISBN 978-1-78189-501-6

Printed and bound in Great Britain by Clays Ltd, Elcograf S.p.A.

Acknowledgements

Thank you first to the team at Choc Lit, the Choc Lit author family and the Tasting Panel, whose comments assist so much in the editing process: Alan Roberton, Alma Hough, Amy Nordon, Carol Botting, Emily Seldon, Carol Dutton, Haley Eyre, Carol Fletcher, Helen Maddison, Honor Gilbert, Melanie Russell, Monica Mac, Sally Pardey and Sharon Walsh.

Thanks also to all the people who have supported me in my writing and in my studies, particularly the Cariad and Marcher Chapters of the Romantic Novelists' Association, and to Janet and Susan, two of my longest friends, who incidentally provided the idea for concealing Nadine's identity from a fraudster.

Special appreciation to Brooklinde, fabulous Cardiff jewelers, who gave me the inspiration for Jake's cufflinks.

Credit to Sue McDonagh, fellow Choc Lit author, for the suggestions for Mickey's motorbike. This information will be even more relevant if and when he gets his own book. Can I resist a bad boy on a bike?

And thanks to all the readers who have enjoyed my books and have taken time to leave reviews. Your time and trouble are appreciated.

Chapter One

Coming back to Bath might have been a mistake.

There was an uneasy, prickly feeling on the back of his neck. As if someone in the congregation was watching him. Ryan Calder assessed the picture-perfect village church, full to capacity with the upper echelons of the Bath social scene and business community. Flower-decked hats and flirty fascinators bobbed and dipped in competition with the swathes of pale cream roses and gold ribbon that adorned the pillars and ends of pews.

He cast a careful look around. He didn't actually *know* that Jake McQuire and his wife were here amongst the guests, but it seemed a fair bet.

His neck prickled some more. He resisted the urge to rub it. Jake had paid him off, after the debacle on the Riviera, and had even added a bonus on top, so clearly he wasn't bearing a grudge. The whole thing about being watched was just his imagination. *Guilty conscience.*

What he really needed to be concerned about was the job in hand, who was standing next to him – Nadine Wells. He took a deep breath and turned slightly to the left. All he could see was the top of her wide-brimmed hat as she studied the heavily embossed order of service. Roses curled around the edges of the cream card. *No prizes for guessing the bride's favourite flower, then.*

As if she'd felt him move Nadine looked up. Ryan's heart did a strange sort of snatching thing against his ribs. It had started about two months ago and he couldn't seem to get rid of it. She was a *client*, dammit. His absolute best and favourite client of the D and D Agency – *all your 'plus-one' needs fulfilled with discretion and dignity.* Hovering in gorgeousness somewhere between Penelope Cruz and Jessica Alba, with a distinct but understated poise that came from her status in

1

the local business community, she was looking up at him now with a questioning half smile. Today her luxuriant dark curls were confined under an expensive and glamorous hat, but her deep brown eyes, marked by gently arched brows, still had the power to affect his breathing. Long lashes fanned softly against the creamy skin of her cheek, skin that he ached to touch. And the perfect fullness of her lips... That mouth. Soft... Pink...

He could have a million fantasies about that mouth...

No. No way. Stop right there, Ryan Calder. You are working *here.*

This day, like all the other days, was about Nadine, not about him. Her comfort, her convenience. *Discretion and dignity.*

His heart really had no business doing stuff, nor his mind *thinking* stuff.

Even as Ryan swallowed hard over the uncomfortable lump in his throat, a stray sunbeam caught the diamond glinting on Nadine's hand. Her left hand. Put there by the beloved husband she had lost so tragically five years ago. The husband she still loved and mourned.

'Is everything okay?'

Ryan couldn't really hear her words over the swirling organ music and the restless muttering and movement of a hundred or so guests, but he could lip-read.

'Fine.' *Concentrate. Smile.*

'Doesn't the church look incredible?'

Ryan could only nod in agreement. In an average month he attended two or three of these events, in a professional capacity. This one simply screamed money no object. Not surprising when the bride was the owner of a very successful chain of patisseries that had tapped into the beginning of the cupcake craze and expanded from there.

'I wondered... Oh—' Nadine broke off as a flurry of movement at the back of the church had everyone turning to look. The organ slipped smoothly into 'Here Comes the Bride'.

Ryan glanced quickly round, checking that Nadine was in the best place to see her old school friend walk down the aisle. A slight shift to the side would move her out of the distraction of a woman with a purple cartwheel on her head. He touched Nadine's arm, indicating with a nod. Understanding, she stepped sideways, smiling thanks before turning to concentrate on the bride – a vision in a slim floor-length gown of soft ecru lace – who was making her way, brave, alone and radiant, towards her husband-to-be. The light in her eyes said it all.

As she passed, smiling as she recognised faces in the congregation, attention automatically shifted to the front of the church, and a gap opened up in the crowd of guests as they craned for a glimpse of the bride – Karen, her name was Karen he remembered – giving Ryan his first proper look at the man standing at the front of the church, looking back with a welcoming smile.

The shock of recognition hit Ryan like a sudden punch in the chest. He'd seen the man in the sharp grey suit before. Just over a year ago.

Standing in the same position before the altar.

Waiting for his bride.

Chapter Two

What do I do? What do I do? What do I do?

The service had begun. Any minute now they would reach 'Speak now or forever hold your peace.' Could he stand up then? Draw all eyes on himself, on Nadine, bringing the whole elaborate, expensive day of dreams to a ghastly grinding halt?

How could he?

And how could he not, considering what came after?

But can you be sure it's the same guy? You saw him for, what, fifteen, maybe twenty minutes tops, from the back of a church, crowded just like this one. You weren't even really paying attention. And how the hell do you explain? You can't…

The service had glided on, and the moment had passed. Beside him Nadine must have sensed some agitation. She put her hand on his arm. Forcing himself to relax, he threw her a reassuring smile. She smiled back. His heart punched him. Again.

After the service. That was the moment. You can do something then. Then you'll know.

Relief washed through him. If this *was* what he feared, some backup would be good. Someone who could handle themselves and would cotton on fast. Surreptitiously he scanned the rows of guests seated around them. Now he *wanted* to find Jake McQuire in the crowd. There was a tall guy with dark hair towards the front of the church that could be McQuire. He couldn't see if the woman sitting next to him was a redhead. Her hair must be piled up under her hat.

Ryan rose and sat, sang and fell silent, following Nadine's body language rather than the service, his mind frantically forming a plan. It wouldn't happen immediately. There would be some time. He just needed to be prepared. Two would be better than one. Would McQuire be ready to help? *Will he even recognise you? And if he does…*

It was ending. The couple were kissing. In a few minutes

people would be spilling out of the church. They were coming back up the aisle now. Mr and Mrs, man and wife, with wide smiles.

You're wrong. You must be wrong. It's not the same guy.

Silently blessing that a side door to the church had been opened to ease congestion at the main entrance, Ryan navigated Nadine out into the sunshine, giving her his arm over the tussocky grass, letting her enthusiastic comments about the service wash over him. He had to get her somewhere where she would be safe and happy for a few minutes.

Guests were milling about at the front of the church, two photographers, with assistants, were attempting to organise groups to pose. Some guests were already heading off to reclaim cars to make their way to the reception.

A figure at the corner of the church caught Ryan's eye. It was McQuire, but no sign of Cassie. Nadine had found a friend in the crowd and was drawing him forward for introductions.

Automatically Ryan slipped into professional mode – smiling, charming and attentive. Seeing the avid interest in the other woman's eyes, he gave into an evil impulse, pulling Nadine close, before letting her go. She was looking up at him, awareness sparkling in her eyes. She knew what he was playing at, and was going along with it. He was tempted to do it again, to feel her, soft and warm, against his side, and to hell with protocol, but he was aware of movement behind them. Ryan turned slightly to watch, without drawing attention.

Excusing himself from his bride's side, the groom had extracted himself from the congratulatory press around them, walking easily but with purpose towards the path beside the church. Ryan's heart rate powered up.

It can't be happening. It doesn't make sense. But it didn't make sense the last time…

And then he heard it. The roar of a powerful engine, faint, but coming closer. 'If I can just leave you with… er… Gemma… for a moment?' He took a step back. Nadine looked puzzled, but trusting. Nodding and smiling, he made his way to the corner of the church. Past McQuire. Who recognised him.

'Well, fancy meeting you here.'

'There's something happening. With the groom. Back there.'

Ryan didn't relax his pace as he passed Jake and kept going. His quarry was only just in sight. If McQuire followed him, fine, if he didn't he'd just have to cope alone.

Behind the church was a small gravelled area, partly enclosed by outbuildings. In the middle of it a motorcycle sat idling, with a helmeted figure astride it, hands on the handlebars. Ryan speeded up, heart sinking. It was all turning out exactly as he feared... He could hear someone calling him and footfalls behind him, or thought he could, over the noise of the engine. He couldn't stop to find out. The groom was standing alongside the powerful machine, reaching for the helmet strapped at the back of the bike.

Ryan closed the distance and dived. 'Stop!'

The helmet went flying.

With the advantage of surprise, Ryan grabbed the man's wrist, forcing him away from the bike. They swayed together, the groom cursing and trying to kick, the woman rider on the bike, screaming invective. At the corner of his vision Ryan caught a glimpse of movement. Panting, still holding on, he shifted slightly.

McQuire was running towards them and behind him, Cassie, McQuire's wife, and beside her – oh God – was Nadine.

It was a distraction of only a second, but it was enough. With a massive effort the groom broke free, bringing up a fist that connected with the edge of Ryan's jaw. Ears ringing, Ryan went down hard, groaning as his tailbone hit the ground. The bike was already moving as the groom flung himself aboard. The driver hit the accelerator, forcing Jake to jump aside. Ryan saw Nadine haul Cassie out of the path of the bike as it flew around to the front of the church.

His adrenalin high abruptly slumping, Ryan let himself fall back onto the gravel, closing his eyes.

Chapter Three

Ryan swirled a generous measure of single malt in his glass and took a healthy swig. Normally, when he was working, he classed a twist of lemon in his mineral water as heavy drinking.

Today was not a normal day.

He shifted slightly against the sofa, aware of the dull ache at the bottom of his spine. He was going to have bruises in interesting places. Mostly places no one would see, thank goodness. Gingerly he pressed his fingers to the side of his jaw, testing the extent of the damage.

'Here.' Cassie Travers, now Cassie McQuire, shoved a linen napkin filled with ice into his hand.

'Thanks,' he said cautiously, as she gave him a hard stare. He wasn't surprised. First the thing on the Riviera – he wondered fleetingly if she knew about the bonus – and now this.

Abruptly giving up on the stare, Cassie kicked off her shoes, dropped into a matching sofa, twisted her feet up under her and shut her eyes, dropping her head back against the sofa's deep-filled cushions. She was a woman who turned heads and made waves. Long red hair, green eyes, dark, well-marked brows, and a small but pugnacious chin were enhanced by the confident air of a successful businesswoman.

Jake was out on the balcony of the hotel suite, muttering into his mobile phone. With his hard-edged good looks, dark hair and arresting blue eyes, McQuire could have made it in films or modelling. Instead he'd made money. Lots of money. Right now he was the man in charge. Ryan was glad someone was.

It seemed like no one wanted to make conversation. *Suits me just fine.* He scanned the room – the Bridal Suite. Flowers, champagne, probably rose petals strewn on the bed in the next room, luxurious but understated. Jake and Cassie's luggage, hastily repacked by the hotel staff, stood by the door. The swap had been made before they had even reached the hotel. So the bride – technically she was still a bride – wouldn't have to face all this. Now Nadine was with Karen in the McQuire suite, across the corridor, and he was… here. Trying to get his thoughts in order for the explanations that would have to come, once Nadine joined them.

A soft knock on the door made his heart give a disjointed stutter. It settled again as a tall blonde girl let herself in. Cassie opened her eyes, smiled, then closed them once more. With a curious glance at Ryan, the girl crossed to the balcony to give Jake a status report.

As far as Ryan knew, being a billionaire didn't give you magical powers but it could give a damn good impression. The scene at the church had predictably been chaos. McQuire had taken charge, proving, if anyone needed proof, that you didn't get to be big on Wall Street without knowing how to make things happen. He might be running a detective agency in Bath now, rather than a global empire, but the skill set was still there. Organisation and delegation.

In a remarkably short time the crowd, agog at the sight of the groom riding off at high speed, had been collected and dismissed. The shell-shocked bride had been dispatched to the waiting limo, and everyone else to their cars, with a quickly fabricated story of a family emergency.

Ryan shifted the position of his impromptu icepack. Those guests who were staying at the hotel were downstairs, eating what should have been the wedding breakfast, and probably speculating like hell about all the drama. He could imagine the conversations. He rubbed the bridge of his nose. Actually he couldn't. No one knew exactly what had gone on. *Except you.*

He had to get his thoughts in order by the time Nadine joined them. Nadine. Oh shit. Was this a mess, or was this a mess? Ryan nursed the ice against his sore cheek and sipped the whisky, letting its warmth drift through him.

Dutch courage.

Chapter Four

With her hat, her shoes and the bride's bouquet in her hand, Nadine closed the door softly behind her, crossing the corridor to let herself into the Bridal Suite. Jake and Michelle – the operative from Jake's office who had been keeping an eye on the wedding presents, and now swiftly pressed into service to sort out the aftermath of a runaway groom – were coming in from the balcony. Cassie was curled up, half swallowed by an enormous sofa, and Ryan...

Nadine's heart turned over. The sight of Ryan could always make her heart turn over. Tall, well groomed, with broad shoulders and easy charm, he was her perfect foil at public events, but now it wasn't the unruly dark hair, the hazel eyes, the gorgeous cheekbones or the appeal of his smile that was making her pulse thrum. It was anger that he was hunched so awkwardly in the corner of a second sofa, clutching an untidy bundle of linen to a rapidly darkening bruise on his jaw. He looked unhappy, uncomfortable, in pain.

Nadine gritted her teeth. That man – Hemingway – had *hit* him, then tried to mow them all down. If she could get her hands on the man, to slowly wring his neck would give her immense pleasure. Dumping her hat and shoes and the bouquet on a console table, alongside a shallow bowl of white orchids, she padded over to sit on the other end of the sofa from Ryan.

Cassie opened her eyes and leaned forward. 'How is Karen now?'

'Devastated.' Nadine bit her lip. The word she wanted to use was broken. All the lovely light had gone out of her old school friend. 'The doctor gave her a sedative. Her PA is with her.' Nadine nodded towards the bouquet. 'I brought her flowers. She couldn't stand the scent.'

Cassie leaned back again, shaking her head. Jake had

propped himself on the arm of his wife's sofa and Michelle, after quietly introducing herself to Ryan, had pulled forward a chair from a small table for two, no doubt intended for serving the happy couple their post-wedding-night breakfast.

Nadine narrowed her eyes. Jake, Cassie and Michelle were all staring at Ryan. Michelle simply curious, Jake with one of his enigmatically assessing looks, and Cassie with an edge of something that looked like hostility. *Cassie already knows Ryan?*

Abruptly the penny dropped. Ryan was an *actor*, and an actor had been involved in the assignment on the Riviera two years ago that had brought Cassie and Jake together again, after many years apart. They'd left Bath at daggers drawn, in an uneasy alliance to catch a thief, and had come back engaged. Cassie had never actually spilled all the details, but Nadine had gathered that the actor – Ryan, it had to be Ryan – had somehow been caught in the middle of hostilities between Cassie and Jake, before they finally fell into each other's arms.

And now he was in the middle of something again. Resisting the betraying impulse to reach for his hand, she straightened her back, looked Cassie in the eye, and waited.

Jake broke the silence. 'I think we'd all like to hear a bit more from Mr Calder about what happened today at the wedding.' Jake dropped his hand, resting it lightly on his wife's shoulder. Some of the fire went out of Cassie's eyes and the corner of her mouth turned up.

'I'd *love* to hear,' she agreed with a pussycat smile.

Nadine saw Jake's hand tighten. 'Cassie,' he warned softly. 'If you eat that canary whole, you'll choke on the feathers.'

For a second there was a prickly silence, and then Cassie started to laugh. 'All right.' She held up her hands. 'Pax. Tell your story, Mr Calder. You knew what was going to happen behind the church today. And you tried to stop it,' she added thoughtfully.

'I wasn't part of it.' Ryan wadded the napkin and stuffed it into his empty glass, standing on a side table.

'I believe you,' Cassie responded with a slow nod of her head. 'So tell us your story,' she invited.

Some of the stiffness had gone out of Ryan's broad shoulders, but he still looked awkward and unhappy. *Hunted.*

Abruptly Nadine understood the problem. He was trying to tell the story *and* do his job. *He's trying to protect you.* A rush of warmth swirled around her chest. Sweet, but unnecessary.

'I think it might help if I explain something.' All eyes turned on her now. This time she did reach out and briefly laid her hand on Ryan's arm. 'Ryan is from an agency. An escort,' she got it out quickly, before he could try to stop her. 'He accompanies me to events like this, when I need a plus-one.' She turned to give him an encouraging smile and got an unexpectedly scowling response. *Not happy at having his cover blown.* Too bad! 'We've had this arrangement for a couple of years. He's never been anything less than professional,' she said pointedly. 'I'm guessing that whatever he knows is as a result of attending another wedding, with some other client.'

She folded her hands in her lap. Cassie looked surprised. If anything Michelle's curiosity had increased as she regarded Ryan. Jake's expression was blank, but the corner of his mouth was twitching. Nadine didn't dare look at Ryan, but she felt the level of tension at the other end of the sofa subside a fraction, as he let out a huff of breath. 'That's exactly it.'

'So...' Jake intervened. 'Mr Hemingway has previous form as a fleeing groom, and today he was unlucky enough to encounter someone who knew about it.' He nodded to Ryan. 'The floor is yours, Calder.'

Nadine swivelled a little in her seat, so she could see Ryan without turning her head. He shot her a rueful glance and shrugged, then looked as if he wished he hadn't.

How bad are *those bruises?*

'Well...' He took a deep breath. 'As Mrs Wells has put my cards on the table...' He shot Nadine a disjointed smile that still managed to flutter something in her chest. 'It was coming up to Christmas, the year before last. I was working up north, near Sunderland. He was calling himself Orwell then. It was more or less the same as this afternoon – the ceremony went without a hitch – the church was packed, over two hundred guests. Afterwards, outside, while the photographs were being organised, he excused himself and disappeared round the side of the church. The next thing this motorcycle came roaring out. He was the pillion passenger. He had a helmet, but you could see his face, and there was the morning suit and the buttonhole, but he was actually waving – drawing attention to himself. The bastard even blew the bride a kiss. Then the woman driving put her foot down and they were gone.' Ryan paused, clearing his throat.

Michelle was on her feet before Nadine could move, pouring a glass of water from a carafe on a side table and handing it over. Ryan gulped gratefully.

'You can imagine the chaos,' he went on. 'You saw how it was today. But this was a whole lot worse, because there was no one taking charge.' He nodded to Jake, who shrugged and indicated Ryan should continue. 'Guests were just milling about. No one could understand what was going on. Everyone assumed at first that it was some sort of joke, and the bride tried to laugh it off too, even though it was obvious she was in shock, and only just holding it together. Then someone had the idea of phoning the guy, but the number was unobtainable. None of the guests he'd invited knew anything. There weren't that many. Most of them seemed to be acquaintances from local golf and tennis clubs, and they were pretty embarrassed about it all. In the end the vicar's wife took the bride and my client – her godmother – back to the vicarage. People hung around for a bit, but then when nothing happened... They just drifted away. No one knew what the hell it meant. It was just... bizarre.'

'It was a scam,' Cassie supplied quietly.

Ryan nodded. 'I got a few details afterwards from my

12

client—' He stopped abruptly, expression stiffening, as the implications of the disclosures he'd just made hit home. 'And I really should have kept all of that confidential.'

Nadine curled her hands into fists, to prevent herself reaching out to him.

'You could hardly have refused to tell us, in the circumstances. You've only given us the outlines, and you've mentioned no names. The circumstances *are* exceptional.' Jake's quiet intervention let her relax her fingers.

Ryan's stricken expression softened, but he shifted uncomfortably, then gave another awkward shrug. 'I suppose... There's not much more to tell. The guy had racked up all the expenses of the wedding – which were considerable, as everything was pretty lavish – without paying any of them, taken the money the bride had put into what was supposed to be a joint fund, and disappeared. It was about thirty thousand, I think. She'd paid most, as he was supposed to be funding a fancy honeymoon.'

He took another sip of water. Nadine dragged her attention back from the way his fingers were cupping the glass, to focus on what he was saying.

'Today... I didn't know what to do. I didn't think I could stop the wedding.'

He threw a swift glance at Nadine. Her heart twisted. *He didn't want to let me down.* She nodded, encouraging him to go on.

'I couldn't be sure, you see. I'd only seen Orwell for a few moments and this man – Hemingway – for just about the same amount of time. I hoped I was wrong. But when we were outside the church and I saw the groom walking away and I heard the motorbike – I knew that it *was* happening again.' He shoved a hand through his hair. 'What are the odds?'

'Long enough to take the chance,' Jake responded. 'But shortened somewhat by having a professional amongst the guests.'

'A professional who wasn't able to stop it.'

'You tried.' Nadine started a little to hear Cassie's voice chiming in with hers to protest. At the joint expression of support Ryan's tension relaxed a fraction. Something in Nadine relaxed too.

Michelle topped up Ryan's glass, looking thoughtful. 'It's all pretty weird. Why go through the ceremony? Much easier to simply leave the bride waiting at the altar? Just clear out with the money the night before?'

'Something to find out.' Jake looked around the group, eyes going from face to face. Nadine's heartbeat quickened as he reached her, and she saw his expression. 'I take it that we do intend to find out?'

Chapter Five

Ryan sat up straight, ignoring the protesting bruises. 'You mean go after the guy? Try and stop it happening again?'

Jake nodded. 'We might even be able to get some of Karen's money back. It's not just what he has presumably stolen – the bills for the wedding will still have to be paid.'

Ryan inhaled sharply as Nadine winced, biting her lip. 'I didn't think of that. Poor Karen...'

She sighed. Ryan couldn't help himself. He put out his hand to briefly touch hers.

When he leaned back he found Cassie watching him, bright eyed. 'Well, I for one would *love* to catch up with Orwell/ Hemingway or whoever he is. I wonder what other aliases he has? And how many other brides has he left at the church?' Her grin was thoroughly predatory. 'I'd vote for forming a posse or a hit squad, or whatever – but won't the police be looking?' She tilted her head enquiringly at Jake.

'If they are, there's nothing to stop us scouting around as well.'

'*If* they are?' Ryan frowned. He was still catching up with the implications of McQuire's proposal. 'Why wouldn't they be? It's fraud. Surely they must be involved?'

Jake shook his head. 'Not necessarily. I'm no expert, but I've been told that it can be tricky to prove a case when the people concerned are in a relationship. And there's Karen herself. Think about it,' Jake prompted. 'About her reaction. The hurt she's suffered.'

'Ahhh.' Cassie was already there. 'You mean Karen, and any other brides, might not want to face an official investigation?' Her face clouded as the emotional consequences of the wedding debacle registered. 'Hopes and dreams shattered, hearts broken... How humiliating can that be? Made to look a complete fool, conned and then abandoned in front of your friends?' She stopped, her thoughts clearly visible on her face, and gave a small shudder. 'To take all that to the police…'

'But once they're over the shock, wouldn't they want to go after the bastard,' Michelle objected. 'Get mad and get even?'

'Some might. But Jake has a point.' Nadine's voice was quiet. Ryan turned to watch her. Her expression was reflective, but with an echo of remembered pain. 'Presumably this guy targets mature, successful women, like Karen, who have built up careers and businesses – women who have maybe concentrated on that, at the expense of their personal lives? If Hemingway, or Orwell, or whoever he is, represented husband, home… children…' Her voice flickered slightly, so slightly Ryan wasn't even sure that he heard it. *That's what Nadine deserves. Home, husband, children.* 'If you're facing a pile of broken dreams you might just want to crawl away and hide. *Not* call in the police. Maybe no one *is* going after this man?'

'You might be right.' Now he'd had time to consider it, Ryan began to wonder. 'I don't think the woman in Sunderland went to the police. My client never mentioned an investigation. We haven't really talked about it, but I think she would have told me that. She did say that her goddaughter had accepted an offer for her business – it was designer shoes and very successful. She's bought a lavender farm in Provence and moved there to live.'

'Well…' Cassie's voice had an undercurrent of approval. 'If you have to nurse a broken heart, that sounds a good place to do it, but much better not to get it broken in the first place,' she finished tartly, with a glance at Jake, whose face was completely bland.

Michelle, on the other hand, was frowning. 'Maybe the brides would want to keep quiet – but what about all the guests? There were hundreds of people in that church today, and I'm guessing other weddings would have been the same to warrant the kind of expenditure we're thinking of. People are going to gossip, surely?'

'Probably. But who too?' Cassie threw the question around the group. 'Each other, certainly, but then what?'

'If the bride and her immediate circle closed ranks and refused to speak, or came up with a story...' Nadine was clearly thinking out loud '... then the whole thing would just dwindle into a nine days' wonder.'

'Gossip, speculation and hearsay,' Jake agreed. 'And confined to a local area, if, as we suspect, we are the only people who realise Hemingway/Orwell is a serial offender. There's an outside chance someone might pick it up on social media and run with it, but again, if it's not fed by anything from the person who has been wronged, or anyone acting on her behalf, where does it go? And, of course, it could be that the two we know about *are* the only two.'

'But you don't think so,' Cassie said softly.

'I don't think it's only two,' Jake confirmed. 'The whole thing is a very slick operation. If the Sunderland wedding was nearly eighteen months ago, and this guy came into Karen's life what – three months ago?' He checked, with a glance towards his wife.

'About that.' She nodded. 'It was certainly a whirlwind romance. Which gives him over a year to play with.'

'Plenty of time to leave several more brides at the church.'

They all sat for a moment, contemplating the idea. Ryan eased his position on the sofa a fraction. His back was killing him and his jaw felt stiff.

Nadine caught the movement and sent him a sympathetic smile. Suddenly the bruises didn't seem half so bad.

'I suppose you're right, that some women would keep quiet.' Michelle broke the silence. From her expression Ryan could see that she still wasn't entirely convinced on that one. 'But if he's conned a lot of women, surely *one* of them would be angry enough to do something about it?'

'Maybe they did – if so, it should be easier to nail the guy.' Jake nodded. 'That's your job, Mitch. See what you can find by digging.' He looked around the group. 'Do we go for it, people?'

Ryan raised his hand. 'I don't think Mrs Wells—'

He found himself being talked over.

'Count me in.' Nadine was leaning forward, concentrating on Jake, so Ryan wasn't able to shoot her a discouraging look.

And why exactly do you want to do that? Why shouldn't she be involved?

Because... Because... Hell, he didn't know why, he just wanted...

Something like panic fluttered for a second in his throat, before he brushed it away. Nadine's profile showed him her face was delicately flushed and her eyes bright. She wanted to be part of this. *So who the hell are* you *to say no?*

And no one is listening to you anyway.

'Right. Good.' Jake rubbed his hands together. 'Before we make any decisions, we need information. I suggest everyone puts out discreet feelers with whatever contacts they have, and we meet at the office next week to pool anything we've found. Is Wednesday afternoon okay?'

Everyone around the circle murmured assent.

Nadine turned to mouth, 'Okay?' at him.

Ryan managed to nod. He could handle a trip to Bath for few hours on a midweek afternoon. *And you get to see Nadine again in... four days.* He banked down the warmth the idea generated. The reason for the meeting wasn't anything to be glad about. But he'd have to be a saint not to feel it. *And you, Ryan Calder, are no saint.*

Jake was getting to his feet, consulting his watch. 'Michelle will text to confirm time and location. We'll have a better idea then how we go forward – *if* we go forward. However many others we suspect there may be, we can only work with what we have. The Sunderland bride has chosen her position, which leaves Karen. Her wishes must come first. We have to respect what she wants, even if we're not happy about it. Nadine, you know her best, will you talk to her, see what you can find out? If she's involving the police, that's fine. We can think if there's any help we can give with that when we meet on Wednesday.'

It was smooth and subtle, but McQuire was quietly prompting them to leave the suite. Ryan jumped when someone knocked on the door. *Your nerves are shot to hell!* A waiter was wheeling in a trolley with what was obviously dinner for two, followed by another with an ice bucket on a stand. Michelle had risen and Nadine was getting to her feet. Ryan hoisted himself up with an effort, glad that his back hadn't seized in the low seat and that Nadine was too busy retrieving and replacing her shoes to notice that he was moving like somebody's grandfather.

He hobbled over and held the door open for Michelle and Nadine, leaving Cassie and Jake to their dinner for two.

In the Bridal Suite.

Once the door closed behind their co-conspirators, Jake swept his wife into a close embrace and a very thorough kiss.

'Mmmm.' Cassie licked her lips. 'That was very nice, but what was it for?'

Jake laughed. He hadn't let go of her and wasn't planning too anytime soon. 'Does it have to be *for* something?' He kissed her again. 'Actually, it's a celebration,' he said, struck by sudden inspiration. 'Of us, being together, here in the *Bridal Suite*.' He waggled his eyebrows like a cheap villain in a comic opera.

Cassie laughed. 'I think I get the message.' She traced a pattern on her husband's chest with one finger. 'That was very nice, what you did, changing the suites over. And I guess you'll be paying Karen's bills, assuming he has scammed her.'

Now he grimaced. 'If she'll let me.'

'There is that.' Cassie was still fidgeting with the button of his shirt, her head bent. All he could see was the glorious red crown of her hair. *God, I love this woman*. The bone-deep knowledge blossomed from nowhere. *Like it always does.* She didn't look up. 'You don't think she'll go to the police, do you?'

'No, I don't.' He'd seen the blank desolation in Karen's eyes.

'Do you really think *we* can do anything – about Hemingway?'

Jake sighed. Cassie was fiery, but she was also tender-hearted. 'I don't know, my love. We can but try...'

Picking up his hesitation, Cassie tilted her head to look at him. 'What?'

'I'm not sure. It may be nothing.' He captured her finger and kissed it. 'I was thinking about what Calder said, about that other woman selling her company. This wedding scam, it may net the guy hard cash, but there's a lot of organisation involved – everything about him has to look, and feel, right – address, car, clothes. He needs different identities. Most of the expenses will be on credit and won't ever be paid for, but the set up is complex.'

'You're wondering if getting hold of businesses is part of the scam?'

'Crossed my mind. A distressed and humiliated woman, with a pile of debt, plus whatever the legal formalities and expenses are for unravelling herself from a bogus marriage? I don't know how you even get started on *that* one! She might be willing to take an offer that she wouldn't otherwise have entertained. These things can be organised through shell companies. She'd be unlikely to realise.'

'That's *nasty*. Even more nasty,' Cassie corrected herself.

'At the moment it's just speculation, and it may well stay that way, but it feels as if it might be right. The other thing that's occurred to me – the man is technically, if nothing else – a bigamist.'

Cassie nodded slowly. 'Bigamy is a criminal offence.' She sighed, chewing her bottom lip. Jake refrained from pressing it with a kiss while she was thinking. It took willpower, but he was learning. 'If we can find more, particularly something to connect the guy to other frauds, we would have something to start from.'

'We will try.' Jake held her away from him, so he could see her face. 'Are you okay with that – working with Calder, I mean? You've forgiven him for his part in my downfall?'

'Huh! Downfall indeed.' Now her finger drilled a hole in his shoulder. His wife had sharp, determined fingers. 'Marrying me is going to be the making of you, my lad, and don't you forget it. And your mother agrees with me,' Cassie pronounced triumphantly.

'Who am I to argue?' That boat had sailed some time ago. Jake managed to capture Cassie's fingers again, before she did damage. 'You're okay with Calder?'

'I'm okay with Calder.' Cassie looked thoughtful again. 'He was a bit of a surprise – I've never suspected that Nadine used an escort service. She seems to think highly of him, so I'm good. He *was* only doing a job for *you*.'

Jake wasn't planning on opening *that* can of worms. He kissed her instead. It worked. She was wrapped close to him and he was planting tiny butterfly kisses on her face. 'Is there anything on that trolley of food that's going to spoil?'

Cassie tipped her head back, letting him nibble at her throat and peering at him through half-closed eyes, before giving him a wicked grin and stretching up to whisper in his ear. 'I spoke to the kitchen. There isn't actually any food under those covers. I just wanted to give everyone the hint to leave. We can ring down when we're ready to eat.'

Jake let out a long contented sigh. His wonderful, irresistible, sexy wife knew him so well. It was a fabulous feeling. 'Then why don't we take that bottle of vintage champagne and test the bed in this very exclusive suite?'

He was already navigating her towards the door of the bedroom, pausing to lift the bottle out of the ice bucket beside the trolley. Pausing, then stopping dead.

'Lemonade?'

There was what seemed like a long silence before the penny dropped. Hope, elation, fear and confusion flooded through him. 'Cassie...' he began cautiously.

'Yes.' She was grinning, but there was a softness in her eyes. 'I planned for this to be happening after we'd celebrated the wedding of a friend, not an unholy alliance to find a fraudster. I suppose I ought to know by now that around you, things don't always go to plan.' She sighed, then looked up at him. The joy in her eyes was almost enough to blind him. 'On a day like this, we need something good.' She took his hand, in a gesture that was probably centuries old, and placed it over her abdomen.

'Brace yourself, McQuire. You're going to be a daddy.'

Chapter Six

When the lift reached the ground floor, Michelle peeled off, muttering something about retrieving the wedding presents. Nadine slanted a glance over at Ryan. He looked... at a loss. Not something she'd ever seen before. 'Are you hungry?'

'Oh! I suppose so.' He gathered himself together with a visible effort. 'Yes.'

'Good. Because I'm starving.'

He was looking around the opulent, and busy, hotel foyer. 'Do you want—?'

'Not here,' she cut in, taking a chance and taking his hand. 'I saw a place, back along the road a bit.'

He let her tow him out into the car park. Nadine worked to keep her step regular. A normal pace, when her feet wanted to hurry, hurry, hurry. *I'm a marauder. I have my prize and I'm not letting go of him.* Nadine squashed down the bubble inside that felt a bit like hysteria.

Her car was parked close to the exit. She piloted him gently towards the passenger side of the Mercedes Cabriolet. 'Keys?'

He focused. 'I'm supposed to drive.'

'I know, but not right now.' He still looked puzzled. 'Whisky?' She mimed the act of drinking. A flush came up along his cheekbones.

'Oh! God, yes. I'm sorry. I shouldn't have—'

'Not a problem.' He looked so woebegone she almost smiled. Driving or not, he never drank when he was working. Whether he was still on the clock at the moment was an interesting point. Theoretically, yes. 'Keys?' she repeated.

He fished them out of his pocket and they got into the car. He still looked guilty. Chauffeuring the client was part of the agency package.

She started the engine. 'It's fine. Just buckle up and enjoy the ride.'

He'd settled down by the time they reached the roadside restaurant – and drove past it.

Ryan craned his neck to look back over the seat. 'Wasn't that—?'

'I thought of something better.'

'Oh.' Now he was looking at the road signs. All pointing towards Bristol. 'Should I be ringing the office to tell them I'm being abducted?'

Nadine laughed. Her heart gave the funniest little trill. *Oh boy.* She steadied her breathing, along with the car, and risked a glance in Ryan's direction. He gave her a lopsided grin.

'You can tell them if you like, but there isn't a damn thing they can do about it.'

By the time she had tangled them in the clutches of the Bristol one-way system, Ryan had gone quiet. She suspected that he might be asleep. She slotted the car smoothly into a parking space and hopped out. When she came back ten minutes later, with a carrier bag, he hadn't moved. He surfaced with a start when she dropped the bag into his lap. 'Argh. Wassat? Damn, that's *hot!*' He peered into the bag. 'Fish and chips?'

'Best in Bristol. I didn't feel up to coping with a restaurant. Not after the day we've had.'

He went quiet again as she guided the car back into the traffic. Nadine bit her lip. Maybe he would have preferred a restaurant? He had to know she was taking him home. Her home.

Nothing has to happen. Just because you… just because…

She turned the car into her road. A fish and chip supper in the kitchen. Nothing at all wrong with that. Then Ryan would go off to the friend he stayed with on the other side of the city. So far, so normal. Just two friends having something to eat after a stressful day.

Nothing has to happen. Nothing will *happen.*

Miraculously one of her neighbours was nosing his BMW

away from the kerb opposite her house. He raised his hand to wave as Nadine prepared to reverse into the space.

'There.' Ryan was fumbling with his seat belt. She took the bag out of his hands. 'I hope this is still hot.'

He'd been to the house before – a dozen times, maybe more, but then just to pick her up or drop her off. Never further than the hall. She ushered him into the kitchen, opening cupboards and drawers to get out plates and cutlery.

He was hovering awkwardly by the door.

'Sit down.' She gestured to a chair, put a plate of food in front of him and slid into her own seat. Normally she would have changed out of her wedding finery into something a lot more comfortable as soon as she got into the house, but that wasn't fair when Ryan couldn't do the same. She'd racked her brains, but she had nothing to offer him. All Rory's clothes were long gone. She slid out of her jacket. Her shoes were somewhere in the hall. He was used to her kicking those off.

'If you want—'

'Do you mind if—?'

They both stopped.

'If you want to take your jacket off, that's fine.' He *always* asked.

'Thanks.' He hung it on the back of his chair. He filled out a dress shirt very nicely. She already knew that. She knew so much, and yet so little. He was eating, which was good.

She decided to just eat and see what happened.

'You were right.' He'd cleared his plate. 'They were very good fish and chips.'

Nadine smiled. 'Coffee?'

'Please. Then I'll call a cab and get out of your hair. I'm sorry—'

Nadine shook her head as she poured boiling water into a cafetière. 'You don't need to apologise again. Today was… exceptional.'

You're here. In my kitchen. For that she might just be ready

25

to kiss the absconding groom, wherever he was. *But I'd much rather kiss Ryan.*

The sudden hitch in her breath took her by surprise. His head jerked up at the sound. 'I splashed hot water.' She put her finger into her mouth to back up the fib. He was watching her. Intently. Finger. Mouth. Hope jerked her heartbeat up a notch. *It isn't just me. Oh please,* please, *don't let it just be me.*

She put two mugs of coffee down on the table. 'I should have asked – how are the bruises – do you need anything?' *Hot shower? Massage? A night in my bed?* She took a deep breath and a firm hold of the fantasies that were pinging around in her brain. She'd taken the first step, inviting him for supper. *Be content with that.* Next time she saw Ryan, in Jake's offices, she wouldn't be paying for his company.

'I'm fine – I've had worse.' His shoulders didn't seem so tense now. He was relaxing. He shoved his hand through his hair in a gesture that she knew so well. It did something in the pit of her stomach. *Every time.* 'Today was... crazy. Do you think that McQuire will be able to do anything about that guy?'

'If anyone can he will. He's a very determined man. And so is Cassie – a determined woman, I mean.' She smiled. 'And we're all involved. We should be able to come up with something.' An unwelcome thought crossed her mind. 'It will be okay, won't it, for you to take time off?' She tried not to sound too anxious.

'There's nothing in the escort diary for next week and I can fix my hours at the bar.' Nadine knew that when he wasn't working as a plus-one, he job-shared a bar manager's post. And went to auditions.

'No acting jobs?'

'Not at the moment.' He looked away, studying the kitchen. 'This is a lovely house.'

'Thank you.' Nadine inclined her head. 'I fell for it as soon as I saw it, and I love it here, but really it's a bit too big for one person. I've wondered about getting a dog.'

They talked about that for a while. Ryan favoured a Labrador. Nadine argued for something smaller.

Light, pointless conversation while they sipped coffee.

Nadine chewed her bottom lip, realised what she was doing and stopped. He would be leaving soon. She thought about offering him a tour of the house, but that would mean the upper floors too. Bedrooms. Erm… No…

Ryan was telling a story about working with a dog in an advertisement, making her laugh. She knew that advert. A kitchen, something like this one, a perfect family, wife, baby, dog. And Ryan – as husband and father. Chasing the dog, carrying the baby, hugging the woman. She had a recording. On repeat play.

'I should be going.' He was getting to his feet, lifting his jacket from the back of the chair. 'Thanks for this.' He was reaching into his jacket for his wallet. Nadine waved her hand. 'It's cool. And it's my treat,' she said firmly.

She rose too. She mustn't try to delay him. *One step at a time*. But there *was* something she wanted to say. 'What you did today – trying to stop that man. It was brave.'

He shrugged, colour coming up into his face. 'I had to try. I wish it had worked.'

'He's not going to get away. Not with Jake and Cassie on the case.' She hesitated. 'Er… I may have this wrong, but you and Cassie… the thing that went pear-shaped on the Riviera… before she and Jake were married?'

He nodded, resignedly. 'That was me.'

'Will it be okay… now, I mean?'

'Provided Cassie is ready to bury the hatchet. *Not* in my head.' He gave her a rueful smile. It tied a few knots in Nadine's insides. 'I never got the chance to apologise to her. It might be good to do that.' He shrugged into his jacket, skirting the table for a brief air kiss to her cheek. The knots tightened, pushing up her heartbeat. 'I'll see you on Wednesday.'

He looked slightly surprised to be saying that. *And pleased?*

'Wednesday. And we have homework. Don't forget. I'll try to see Karen tomorrow.'

He grimaced. 'Good luck. I hope you can persuade her to talk to you. I'm not sure that *I'm* going to find out anything that's useful, but I know it's important.'

Nadine stood on the front steps of the house while Ryan climbed into the waiting cab. When the taxi reached the corner and turned out into the main road, she went slowly inside and shut the door, leaning against it. She felt a little dizzy. A little breathless. *Make that a lot breathless.*

She padded back to the kitchen and poured herself another coffee. She'd be too wired to sleep. *But you'll be too wired to sleep anyway.* She carried the mug into the main room of the house and then through the French windows to the terrace outside.

At nearly nine on a May evening the shadows were just beginning to creep across the garden. The smoky scent of a neighbour's barbecue drifted over the high wall. From a distance there were bursts of laughter and music. She flopped onto a delicate wrought iron bench. Wrapping her fingers around the coffee mug, she looked up at the house and then around the enclosed garden with its lawn and flower borders.

Rory had never lived in this house. Did Ryan realise that? She'd sold the property at Filton, close to the factory and showroom making and selling niche market designer beds, and moved here to Clifton a year after her husband died. She was nearer to the centre of town, and this place was all hers. *Property of the wealthy widow.*

She looked down at the rings on her left hand, glinting in the remaining light.

Engagement. Wedding. Eternity.

Except we never had eternity.

She shivered slightly and tightened her grip on the mug.

Maybe it was time to put them away? Maybe? But what did that say? That she was ready... Ready for what? For Ryan?

And if she did... try to take *that* further... was she just going to embarrass herself and him? Was it real? And what was real? Was it simply a little crush? Because he's a good-looking male? *A very good-looking male.* And cute with it.

And he's *there*.

She'd been alone for five years. Except for a disastrous one-night stand with one of Rory's climbing buddies on the first anniversary of his funeral – which had taught her a lot, and none of it good – and a two-week, no strings fling on a holiday in Corfu, she hadn't been with a man in five years. *Does that simply make you desperate? But even if you are desperate, it still doesn't have to be Ryan.*

She could date. By now no one would think it was wrong. Hell, most of her girlfriends thought it was weird that she *didn't* date. She simply hadn't wanted to – not after the climbing buddy fiasco. And Corfu had never been more than a holiday thing.

That was why she'd started to use the plus-one agency – for social and business stuff, awards and charity events. It was just... less complicated. The first guy the agency sent had been fine – but he reminded her so much of Rory that she almost decided to cancel the arrangement. And then they'd sent Ryan, who was nothing like Rory. He was cute and kind and funny and treated her like the finest piece of porcelain.

And always, *always* as the boss. She couldn't deny that there was just the tiniest hint of a frisson in that. Okay, so what if she was a latent dominatrix, who was to know? They'd become... friends. She was sure she could go that far.

Now she wanted more.

A lot more.

She'd even had a wild idea – for about three seconds – that she might offer to *pay* him, which was mega stupid and completely demeaning to both of them.

Her face burned at the thought that she just *might* have been that stupid in a moment of madness. Her guardian angel had worked overtime on that day, making sure her mouth stayed firmly shut.

Keeping their relationship professional didn't alter the fact that she wanted Ryan. Sometimes she got a feeling that he might want more than friendship too, before the professional veneer closed up again.

Is that just wishful thinking? Are you interested in Ryan because he's there? Because he's safe?

She put her empty mug down on the floor and stretched. She didn't believe it had anything to do with being safe. He *did* make her feel safe, but he made her feel a lot of other things too.

But she couldn't really be *sure*. And she needed to be, because if she did make any kind of move and she got it wrong, they were both going to be hideously embarrassed. It would probably wreck what they already had, and she didn't want to give that up. If what she was feeling wasn't real – or didn't stand a chance of being real – she'd rather keep the crush, if that's what it was, and not take the risk. A crush would work itself out, eventually, and she'd still have a good friend.

But if there *was* something... She knew Ryan would never make a move, because of who she was, so it was down to her. She'd been racking her brains for something subtle, but she hadn't been able to think of a way out of the straitjacket of the employer/employee relationship.

Now she had it. Some good might come out of a disastrous day.

A thrill of anticipation threatened her breathing for a few seconds. Tonight she'd had an unscripted evening with Ryan. Now they would be working on something together. As equals. Could she persuade him to look at her as a woman, instead of just a client?

Chapter Seven

The door to the apartment opened as Ryan approached it. Will stood on the threshold, dressed for a night out.

'Hey, dude.' His friend raised his hand in greeting, then stared. 'Shoot – what's the other guy look like?'

Ryan flexed his stiffening jaw. 'That bad?'

Will inspected him. 'Nothing a layer of slap couldn't hide, but, hey – you have to stop wading in to break up fights. No one actually made *you* Sheriff of Dodge.' Will drilled a finger into Ryan's chest. Ryan bit down on a wince. *Bruises there too.* 'I'm serious, man.' He shook his head. 'One day someone is going to ruin that pretty face.'

Ryan shrugged, relieved. Will's assumption of a bar fight meant he didn't have to explain anything. 'Hasn't happened yet, but, hey, maybe then I'd get a few character parts.'

'Huh!' Will was looking at his watch. 'Your lady kicked you to the kerb before time tonight. Good thing, if it was getting rowdy. And your luck is in, mate. Nick is staying over at Sophie's, so you can have his bed, instead of the sofa.' He held up a key ring. 'And now I don't have to leave these with the porter. You know where everything is. Unless you want to change and come with me? The night is young. Lots of beautiful women waiting out there.' Will swayed his hips, miming getting down and dirty on the dance floor.

Ryan shook his head. 'I'm beat. You go on.' He gestured with his thumb to the bank of lifts behind him. 'Have a good one.'

'*That's* a given.' Will moved past, tapping him on the shoulder. 'See you in the morning.'

Glad he'd already retrieved his rucksack from his car, parked since that morning in the basement car park where he always left it to avoid hunting for parking spaces, Ryan dragged it over the threshold. He closed the door of the apartment, scrubbing his hands over his face. Exhaustion abruptly washed over him. He was stiff, sore, dog-tired and far too caffeinated to sleep.

Caffeine? Really? Well, if that's what you want to call it.

He lifted the bag and carried it into Nick's room, relieved that he had a bed for the night, and not the slippery leather sofa.

Unpacking his sleeping bag, he dug deeper, unearthing a towel and wash bag before stripping off his favourite Hugo Boss suit, now somewhat battered. Hopefully the dry cleaner could revive it.

A shower helped ease some of the stiffness out of his muscles. He rubbed steam off the mirror, and assessed the damage. There were bruises on his chest. *How?* His ass, when he craned his head to look, was coming up in some nice tones of black and blue. Despite Will's comments, his face wasn't too bad. He explored gingerly along the jawline. His teeth were okay. Will's conclusion that the damage came from dealing with a fight had precedent. When you managed a bar that sometimes went with the territory. Thankfully not often, but sometimes.

And Will had been in the bar the night a guy broke Ryan's nose.

Wrapping a towel around his waist, Ryan ambled out of the bathroom to the kitchen alcove. Nick's girlfriend, Sophie, kept a jar of decaffeinated coffee in one of the cupboards. Ryan found it while the kettle boiled, then put it back and went for the real stuff. If he slept he slept, if he didn't...

More time to think... about her.

Carrying the coffee back to Nick's room, Ryan pulled shorts and a T-shirt out of the bag, put them on, then dragged a chair over to the window. The apartment looked down over the Floating Harbour, in the heart of Bristol. It was a busy scene. The night was just getting started. Revellers were swirling around between the bars and restaurants – eating, drinking or just hanging out.

And somewhere up there – Ryan tried to orientate himself and gave up – he didn't know which direction Clifton was – *that* was a thousand miles away. Will's place, this place, was fine – financed from the proceeds of a role in a long-running TV show that was filmed in the city.

His own place – in Ealing – that was good too. Much smaller, but he didn't have to have a lodger. Didn't need one, as he owned the flat outright, paid for with money inherited from his parents. They'd died in a house fire while staying with old friends of his mother's. Memory of the shock still sent a shiver through him. It was assumed that they hadn't made it out because of confusion from being in an unfamiliar place. Ryan had wondered too about his father's stubborn nature. If he'd insisted that the fire alarm sounding was only a fault, so that they'd left it just that little bit too late? He'd talked it over with his brother. Sean, ever the practical one, had pointed out that they would never know, so there was nothing to be gained in guilty speculation.

Ryan forced his thoughts away from painful recollections.

Nadine's house... That was in a whole different league. He'd been there before, but it had never really registered until tonight. Like something out of an upmarket magazine. *And if that doesn't show you how far apart you are...*

He leaned back carefully in the chair. Nothing jabbed at him. The shower had helped. It had been a crazy day. He wished Nadine hadn't been caught up in it. *Why couldn't that bastard have found someone else to con?*

Tonight they should have been eating, dancing, celebrating a wedding. *But the heart of that would be fake. Nadine isn't yours.*

He rubbed his hand over his eyes. Now they were both tangled up in McQuire's plan to investigate the guy. And that made him edgy. He knew he was overprotective of Nadine – there was looking after a client and there was... well... overprotective. Sometimes, when he really overstepped she looked at him with that cool quizzical look she was so good at. He tried then to dial down, but he just couldn't seem to help himself.

It was all he had to offer her.

Now he'd be seeing her on Wednesday. *And it has nothing to do with the agency.* His chest tightened at the thought. He closed his eyes, fighting the buzz of anticipation. That was just... neediness.

She was a wealthy, beautiful, successful businesswoman who had been tragically robbed of her soulmate. *And you?*

Not quite the near loser that he'd once been. Two years ago. After the debacle on the Riviera and when he'd turned thirty, he'd taken a long hard look at his career as an actor and what he'd achieved. He'd made a list. A few weeks and a few lines in *Corrie*, some experimental stuff and five star reviews at the Royal Court, two straight-to-DVD movies. Odds and ends in pub fit-ups and small studio theatres in the provinces and a wet summer playing Oberon and Orlando in Regent's Park Open Air Theatre. Six months in the States. He'd made the last call to play megastar Dan Howe's younger brother in a film being shot in Arizona, only to lose out to an up-and-coming Australian actor. He'd had half a season and a bloody death in *Game of Thrones* – he still got recognised occasionally from that, even though he'd had to dye his hair and grow a beard for the part.

His career had been respectable but not stellar. The big Hollywood break had never happened. After some soul searching, he'd made his decision. He hadn't given up on the acting. His agent still sent scripts, he still read for parts. *Just not anything and everything.* Goodbye desperation, hello realism. The acceptance that however fierce your ambition, however much you *wanted* it – that *wanting* still wasn't always enough.

He'd signed on for more work with the escort agency and taken a promotion to bar manager, job-sharing with Stacey, who had a husband in the army and a toddler at home. He bought the flat. And maybe, just maybe, Hollywood still might call, now that he was looking the other way. But until that happened, when he summed up what he was and what Nadine was...

However much you wanted it...

He swigged the last of the coffee, stifling a yawn. He took the mug back to the kitchen, rinsing it and leaving it on the draining board, then headed back to Nick's room and his sleeping bag, turning away from the revellers in the streets below.

Maybe he wasn't too wired to sleep.

His last thought was of Nadine's dark eyes, looking up at him, full of laughter.

Chapter Eight

There were butterflies doing complicated aerial manoeuvres in Nadine's stomach. She pushed a strand of hair behind her ear. Normally she put it up for work, but today she'd left it loose around her shoulders. It was Wednesday. Nothing special about Wednesday. *Just keep telling yourself that. And while you're at it, tell the butterflies.*

It wasn't as if she'd tried on four different outfits before settling on the understated linen dress. Or that she'd spent twice as long as usual on her make-up, accentuating her eyes. Of course she hadn't. The butterflies were just imagination. Or indigestion.

She was at the factory, looking over new ideas with Glen, the designer, when her phone trilled. She forced herself not to pounce on it. 'That one's great.' She tapped a design for a child's bed that looked like a huge ammonite. 'I think the kids will love it. And this.' She pulled forward an adult design that seemed to be floating on a cloud. 'Work them up and we'll talk costings.'

She dug her phone out of her bag. The butterflies fluttered anxiously, convinced it was Ryan, calling to cancel.

Lunch? Cassie had texted. Before the meeting?

Nadine typed. Noon? Usual place? And pressed send.

The restaurant was filling up fast. Nadine and Cassie had a table under a white umbrella on the tiny terrace. Nadine looked around. Sunlight was spilling across the flagstones. Tulips in tall planters made splashes of bright colour at the edge of the paving. The butterflies in her stomach had quieted, settling down to an intermittent jitter of anticipation.

At a large table to their left a group of women, all wearing pink hats of varying degrees of frothiness, were arguing over lunch choices and flirting with the waiter. Prosecco was circulating freely.

'I think they're a book group,' Cassie whispered from behind the menu.

Nadine had a swift mental image of the worthy tome sitting on her bedside table. 'They look like a lot more fun than the one I go to. Maybe I'll ask about joining.' She turned her attention back to the information she'd just given Cassie. 'Will you be able to do anything with those names Karen gave me?'

Cassie nodded as she slipped her notebook and pen back into her handbag. 'I'll do a quick search before the meeting.' She smiled her thanks as a waiter put a plate of risotto down in front of her, then looked over to examine Nadine's order of goats' cheese tartlets and salad.

Nadine saw her looking and grinned. 'Want to try some?'

'Nah.' Cassie wrinkled her nose. 'Your lunch is safe. I don't like goats' cheese.'

'I, on the other hand, *do* like risotto.' They both laughed. 'So...' Nadine cut into the nearest tartlet. The pastry flaked apart in a buttery crumble. 'How was the Bridal Suite?'

'Very satisfactory.' Cassie grinned. Then narrowed her eyes. 'Did you have dinner with Ryan Calder?'

'Guilty.' Nadine wasn't about to admit *where* they had dinner.

At Cassie's prompting she filled her in on her client/escort relationship with Ryan. Cassie wasn't the only one with questions though. 'I know there's history between you and Ryan,' Nadine prodded. 'He was the actor involved in that thing on the Riviera, and you were mad at him and Jake. Ryan admitted it was him on Saturday, when I asked. You'd already told me some of it – he didn't tell me any details.' She tilted her head encouragingly.

'Huh!' Cassie made a face, then sighed. 'I suppose I'd better spill the beans.'

When she'd finished the story Nadine gave her a quizzical look. 'Sounds like Ryan was in the wrong place at the wrong time.'

'Yeah, maybe. He got caught in the cross hairs between me and Jake,' Cassie acknowledged, slightly reluctantly. '*You* like him.' Her eyes widened. 'Oh. My. God!' She bounced in her seat. 'You *like* him.'

'I don't think the whole of the restaurant needs to know.'

'Sorry.' Cassie put her hand over her mouth, but her eyes were sparkling. 'I suppose I'll have to forgive him then. He is kind of cute,' she conceded. 'Have you... you know?'

'No! He's always a perfect gentleman.'

Cassie made a face. 'Does that stop him being G.I.B?'

'It stops me from finding out. At least I think it does. Sometimes I'm convinced he's kind of... hovering, and then he remembers I'm a client.'

'But today, and if we go on with this thing, you *won't* be a client.'

'I've been thinking that too.' Nadine pointed a warning finger. 'No stirring the pot, mind! I'll sort it out myself, if there's anything to sort.'

Cassie pouted, then gave an elaborate sigh, when Nadine didn't back down. 'All right, I won't interfere,' she agreed. Her expression softened. 'If you get the chance, sweetie, go for it.'

Nadine rested her elbows on the table. 'I don't want to mess up what we have.'

'But it's not what you want.' Cassie studied her friend's face. 'What about Rory?' she asked. 'Is that an issue?'

'Yes. No. I don't know.'

'Well, that's a comprehensive list of options.' Cassie took in a deep breath. 'For what it's worth, I'd go with "no". It's been what... five years?'

Nadine picked up an unused spoon beside her plate and put it down again. 'I've thought about taking off my rings,' she admitted.

'Do it when you're ready. I think you'll know. Losing Rory...' For a moment Cassie's expression was stark. 'If I lost Jake...' She put her hand to the corner of her eye. 'I know it's a cliché, but I don't think Rory would expect you to be alone for the rest of your life. If things had been reversed, would you have expected it of him?'

'No, I wouldn't.'

'Then if the opportunity arises…' Cassie grinned '… go for it!'

The grin was infectious. Nadine smiled. 'I'll bear it in mind,' she said dryly as the waiter bustled up to remove their plates and present two dessert menus.

Cassie fell on hers with a moan of delight. 'Have they still got that thing with the strawberries?' She ran her finger down the list. 'Yes! And they have the to-die-for apple tart. Decisions, decisions.' She looked at her watch. 'Oh, to hell with it, we have time. I'm going to order both.' She grinned at the waiter, standing ready to take their order.

Nadine requested a mango sorbet and an espresso, then sat back and surveyed her friend with an interested smile. 'You wouldn't happen to be eating for two, would you?'

Cassie made a comical face. 'Oh, bum. It's supposed to be a secret.'

'The two puddings put the idea in my mind, although that's probably just greed.' She grinned, nodding at Cassie's glass of mineral water. 'But also, no wine. That might be because you're working, but there wasn't any wine delivered with your dinner in the Bridal Suite either.'

Cassie nodded, impressed. 'We'll make a detective of you yet.'

Jake had set aside the detective agency's conference suite as their war room. Nadine stood at the window, looking down at the steps of the graceful Georgian building that Jake had bought and established as his HQ when he took over the family firm. Cassie's concierge service occupied the building next door, with an interconnecting door between Jake and Cassie's offices on the top floor. She knew this because she'd seen inside Cassie's office, though not Jake's. While Cassie's building was all bright colours and quirky repurposed furniture, Jake's was hi-tech corporate sleekness. Chalk and cheese, and still they were in love. So much so that sometimes it was hard to watch.

You could have that. You want that.

Nadine shut her eyes for a second, then opened them and leaned forward for a better view of the approach to the offices. She'd been disappointed to find that Ryan had not yet arrived when she and Cassie finished their lunch and ambled up the hill. Michelle was setting up her laptop on the table. Jake was on his way and Cassie was in the next room, borrowing someone's computer. They would all be here in a moment. The clock was already ticking up to two.

Ryan was going to be late.

Even as she thought it, a cab pulled up in the street below. She couldn't deny the swirl of emotion that raced through her chest as Ryan alighted and paid off the driver. He looked… gorgeous. She'd wondered if he'd be more casually dressed today, but he was still wearing the customary suit. He took the steps two at a time and disappeared under the portico.

Chapter Nine

Directed by a scarily smart receptionist, Ryan sprinted up the stairs to the first floor, swallowing down disappointment. He'd hoped for some time with Nadine before the meeting, but the train had been late, inexplicably stopped just outside Bath Station as the minutes ebbed away. He could have had a courtesy car while his own car was in for a service, but the train had looked a better option. *Bad choice.*

The door in front of him was open, the sign on it said Conference Room, and Nadine was standing at the window. She turned as he reached the door. *Maybe you have just a moment…*

Ryan's disappointment ratcheted up another notch when he saw Michelle working on a computer at the table. Behind him Jake and Cassie were coming along the corridor. The meeting was about to start. At least he'd avoided an embarrassingly late arrival. *Yeah – look on the bright side.* He slowed his breathing and greeted everyone with a nod, before pulling out a chair opposite the one Nadine had chosen. He didn't have a lot to contribute, but he did have something. Enough to justify being here.

Nadine was wearing a simple blue linen dress, businesslike but feminine. Her hair was loose. Usually it was pinned in an updo, under an elaborate hat, or restrained in a knot at the nape of her neck. Now it curled on her shoulders and Ryan wanted to bury his fingers in it. Her face looked a little flushed.

As if feeling his eyes on her she looked over and smiled. Ryan's heart flipped over and then Jake cleared his throat and everyone looked at *him.*

Jake nodded to Michelle, who had stopped fiddling with the laptop and was waiting expectantly. 'Do you want to kick off?'

Michelle sat up straighter in her chair. 'Firstly I couldn't find any more wedding cons, so I switched to looking at

Karen's case. What I found are all negatives – but quite *interesting* negatives.' She smiled at everyone around the table, clearly enjoying the attention. 'Until three months ago John Hemingway didn't exist. He's a ghost – no records of any kind. He has no social media presence, which is quite surprising these days, although Karen doesn't either. Not for her personally,' she corrected. 'Only for her business. There are no usable photos of Hemingway – the three I was able to find are group shots on a Facebook page belonging to one of Karen's friends, at an event they must have attended together. In all three of them his head is either turned away or obscured by his hands, or something he's holding.'

'Clever *and* careful,' Jake put in thoughtfully.

'Both,' Michelle agreed. 'Which confirms that he's a pro. He has skills.'

Ryan shifted in his chair. He'd started this thing off, but he really didn't have much more to contribute. Michelle was clearly excited to be demonstrating her talent in front of her boss. She'd established that Hemingway was a professional, but so were Jake and Michelle and all his other operatives. He and Nadine should be bowing out now, leaving it to them.

There was a small catch in his chest at the loss of the excuse to see Nadine 'off the clock'. Hemingway's bridal scam was nasty, right to the core. Ryan hated knowing something like that had come anywhere near Nadine, but it had given him a few precious hours of private time with her. He mustn't kid himself. Next time they met it would be back on a business footing.

He raised his eyes to look at her, studying her profile. Her head was turned towards Michelle. He'd got used to seeing that profile, next to him in a church, at a dinner table, in the audience of a presentation. *That* was their real relationship. Any more was just a sad fantasy. Regret hovered in his chest. Michelle was still talking. He tuned back into what she was saying.

'... then I did some digging in the local papers in the Sunderland area. Ryan's first deserted bride.'

He tried to hide the wince. Neither of the brides was *his*. For a fleeting second he wished he'd kept his mouth shut and his head down when he recognised Hemingway in the church, instead of wading in.

But could you really have done that? Really?

He pushed his thoughts away to concentrate again on Michelle. The glance she shot around the table was definitely excited – and just a touch triumphant? 'I think I may have found out why our Mr Hemingway doesn't simply jilt his bride, but actually goes through with the wedding. Just over eighteen months ago the local papers in the Sunderland area had a major story – they ran it under the headline *The Runaway Groom*.'

Ryan saw Jake's frame stiffen as he focused his attention. He hadn't heard this before. Michelle certainly knew how to play an audience.

'Our man's first outing?' Jake questioned brusquely.

'I don't think so.' Michelle's grin was wide. 'I'm guessing Hemingway may change his appearance – but I don't think he would be capable of *this*.'

She twisted the laptop. Even in the slightly fuzzy reproduction of a newspaper photo it was clear that this runaway groom was in his late teens or early twenties, a skinny beanpole with a shock of blond hair. 'When she was left waiting at the church, his bride created an enormous fuss – police, hospitals, appeals on social media and the local radio station – it was a couple of days before it emerged that her intended wasn't lying unconscious and unidentified in a ditch or a hospital somewhere, but had done a runner with the deposit they'd saved for a house.'

'You think this provided the original idea? That Hemingway borrowed the concept of the runaway groom and took it to a whole new level? And the wedding that Ryan attended was his first attempt?' Cassie asked quietly. She was looking thoughtful. 'I can see your point that Hemingway would want to make it clear that he was leaving, to avoid that sort of hue and cry.' She nodded towards the newspaper reports. 'But still, why the very public desertion *after* the wedding? Why not simply send a goodbye note to the church? He could have used the excuse we put out, of a family emergency. No hullabaloo, much less tangling with official procedures – the bride probably wouldn't even know until the unpaid bills started to arrive.'

'Because that's not the kind of man he is.' There was something flinty in Jake's tone that sent a slight shiver over Ryan's skin.

'It's the thing, above everything, that ensures the complete humiliation of the bride.' Nadine's soft intervention kicked Ryan's shivers up a few notches. That, and the distress that was clear on her face. He wanted to sprint around the table to hold her, comfort her, feel the weight of her head nestled against his shoulder.

He caught himself up with a jerk. *Not your place.*

'I finally got to see Karen last night.' Everyone's eyes were on Nadine, as she continued the story. 'It was...' her jaw jerked, as she swallowed '... painful. Her PA was there – Corinne – she's angry, furious. She was the one who answered a lot of the questions, or prompted Karen. Karen is just... devastated. In fact...' Nadine hesitated. 'She's leaving. She's flying to Australia tomorrow. Jake was right. She just wants to put the whole thing behind her. As far as she's concerned we can investigate if we want, but she doesn't want to be part of it. She's not going to the police.'

Jake nodded. 'That's not really a surprise, having seen her on the wedding day. If that's how she feels then I doubt if any of us would be able to persuade her to change her mind. What else did she say?' He gave Nadine an encouraging smile.

A knock on the door had them all looking round. Two

of Jake's employees wheeled in a trolley with tea and coffee and mineral water and a couple of plates of glossy, chocolate covered biscuits.

A tension in the atmosphere that he hadn't fully noticed until now dissolved. Nadine was laughing, teasing Cassie over eyeing the biscuits after all she'd eaten at lunch. Michelle passed a cup to Jake. Ryan inhaled the scent of really good coffee and wondered how many biscuits he could take without looking a complete pig. He'd grabbed a sandwich on the train, but that was hours ago. He held his breath, hoping his stomach wouldn't rumble.

Nadine turned her head as Cassie rose to pour a glass of mineral water. She must have caught something in his face. Grinning she pushed the plate in front of him. He took two. They tasted as good as the coffee smelled.

Once everyone had filled and doctored cups of coffee and tea, Cassie tapped the table for order, looking at Nadine. 'You want to go on, hon?'

Chapter Ten

Nadine put down her cup. 'Karen wasn't ready to talk to me at all until last night. She is completely focused now on getting away.' She nodded towards Cassie. 'Cass suggested that I ask Corinne, her PA, to be there, as she'd helped organise the wedding. As I said Karen was... well, distressed doesn't really cover it. Maybe... desolate?'

Nadine took a hitching breath that echoed in Ryan's chest. Right now he'd like to strangle Hemingway with his bare hands. But Nadine was still speaking. 'She was in the middle of packing. That decision was already done and dusted, although Corinne wasn't too happy about it. She would like to go after Hemingway. Karen has agreed that I can talk to Corinne again if we need to.' Nadine paused, with a look across at Cassie. 'You asked me to find out if there had been any approaches from companies wanting to buy Karen's business?'

'An idea I had,' Jake cut in, to explain. 'We'll get to that.' He raised an eyebrow at Nadine. 'Had there been?'

'Yes, last month. Karen turned it down, and it went no further.' Jake was nodding. Nadine waited, but when he said no more, she carried on. 'With Corinne's help I got Karen to talk about Hemingway. It was a complete whirlwind courtship – three months from start to finish. The guy was total romance on legs – that was what Corinne called him, although she only met him twice. He was a very smooth operator,' Nadine continued. 'There was nothing tacky or obvious in his approach – just old-fashioned romance. Flowers, meals at fancy restaurants, gifts, treats and surprises.' Nadine inhaled. 'The words Karen used were, "He really got *me*. Who I was."'

Ryan swallowed. Was there a wistful look in Nadine's eyes, or was it a trick of the light? *Maybe she's missing her dead husband?*

Ryan picked up his cup and took a gulp of coffee. It was still hot. It burned on the way down.

'All in all, Hemingway gave the impression of a man totally smitten, who couldn't believe his luck – that was Corinne's view again. There was one surprise – they didn't sleep together. Karen wanted to – she admitted that – but Hemingway claimed that what they had was too special. He'd at last met the woman he wanted to marry, and he wanted to wait until they *were* married.'

'That's interesting.' Jake was clearly examining the implications.

Michelle looked sceptical, or maybe mystified. '*Really*? Surely Karen would want to... er... test the goods?'

'But she was convinced otherwise,' Cassie put in dryly. 'Mr Hemingway, or whoever he is, strikes me as the kind of guy who could sell sand in the desert.'

'And it possibly made Karen even keener?' Jake suggested.

'Wildly romantic and frustrating as hell,' Cassie confirmed, grinning at him. 'Certainly a good reason to hurry the wedding.'

Ryan felt a hot stab of anger at a man who could use a romantic gesture as a weapon against a woman he'd tricked into loving him.

Cassie nodded to Nadine to continue.

'He proposed after a month. It was something pretty special. Personal – Karen wouldn't tell me what.' Nadine's face clouded at the memory. 'She just teared up and refused to talk at all for a bit. She said yes to him straight away. They both put thirty thousand pounds into a joint account to cover wedding expenses. He brought in a top-flight wedding planner who'd been recommended to him and who proceeded to create the wedding of Karen's dreams.'

'With the groom of her nightmares.' Jake was stirring sugar into black coffee, vigorously. 'No doubt he encouraged Karen to have everything she'd ever dreamed about and then a little bit more – you can imagine the line – this was the first and last wedding for both of them, so she deserved for it to be perfect, et cetera, et cetera.' Jake was still stirring. Cassie caught his eye, frowning. He stopped.

Michelle leaned forward, with a question. 'You didn't say – how did they meet?'

'Supper club. People in the radius of a few streets of Karen's home take turns to eat at each other's houses. One of her neighbours introduced them.'

'Shit!' Michelle dumped her cup with a bang. 'Oh, sorry,' she apologised for the outburst, eyes wide with shock… and disappointment. 'They met in person? Seriously?' Michelle looked almost comically woebegone. 'I was sure that they'd have hooked up online – a dating agency or something.'

'Ah – they *were* introduced, but that's not the whole story.' Nadine's face was lit with excitement. 'Karen met Hemingway at the supper club just after he moved into the area, but before that she *had* been computer dating. Apparently, after a couple of false starts and dire dates, she tried a new firm, very select and expensive, and was matched with a guy called Lionel Christopher. They really hit it off. After the dire dates, Karen was hesitant about jumping into a meeting and apparently he felt the same, plus he was temporarily living in Scotland – something about his work – but they got on really well by email. No phone calls – supposedly the place he was living was too remote for a reliable signal. Finally they fixed a proper date – he was coming down to London and they were going to spend the weekend together. At the last moment he cried off. His elderly father, who was living in Australia, had been diagnosed with an aggressive form of cancer. Lionel was dropping everything to go and care for him. He didn't know how things would pan out, and he didn't want to stand in the way of a wonderful woman like Karen finding the happiness she deserved, so this had to be goodbye. Abrupt end of romance. A few days later Hemingway appeared on the scene and memories of Lionel got left in the dust. I wouldn't have known about it, if Corinne hadn't mentioned him – that it was a pity things hadn't worked out with Lionel, because then Karen wouldn't have been interested in Hemingway.'

Ryan almost felt the connection clicking into place. 'You think Lionel and Hemingway were one and the same?'

Nadine rewarded him with a smile that almost stopped his heart. He felt blindly for his coffee cup and found it was empty.

'That makes sense.' Michelle bounced back from her disappointment. 'Establish the connection through the dating agency, find out everything you can about the target, break off the budding romance in a flurry of tragic nobility and turn up a few days later in a new persona, armed with all you've already found out and good to go. And no connection or comeback on the dating agency.' She gave a low-pitched whistle, shaking her head. 'Clever! To all intents and purposes Karen would be a satisfied customer. Not anyone's fault that it didn't turn out. If it *was* ever discovered that Lionel Christopher was a fabrication – well, even the most careful agency must get a small percentage of liars.' A hint of unexpected sadness flickered over Michelle's face. 'You think Karen's gone to Australia to look for Lionel?'

'Crossed my mind,' Nadine confirmed. 'But I didn't want to say anything to bring her down even more. If he does exist, finding him would be a complete long shot, and she must know that. I'm hoping that while she's there she'll find someone really lovely and *real*.'

'I second that,' Cassie chimed in. 'For the record, Nadine gave me a few names over lunch and I checked them out quickly before we came in here. The dating agency is one hundred per cent genuine. Exclusive and expensive, with a strong reputation and a high success and satisfaction rate. *Exactly* the kind of set-up to attract the sort of women Hemingway wants to target. I'm sure they'd be horrified to know they had a bad apple in the barrel, if Lionel is a bad apple – and that isn't proven. I also checked on the wedding planner. No firm exists under the name Karen gave.'

'So what's with the wedding planner?' Jake mused. 'The

woman on the bike? And might she be girlfriend, or even wife, which is why he didn't sleep with Karen?'

'Makes sense.' Nadine was nodding. 'Karen said she had photo albums and catalogues and she also showed her stuff online. I suppose it would all be possible to fake.'

Ryan leaned forward. 'Maybe she has, or does, work in that industry. Experience is useful if you're trying to create a role. Or a good fake,' Ryan added. He could see Jake storing that one away, to think about later.

Nadine looked over at Cassie and Jake. 'What about the offer for Karen's business that you asked about?'

'That was Jake's idea.' Cassie rose to pour herself another glass of water, resting her hand briefly on her husband's shoulder as she passed.

'It's just that this is quite a detailed con.' Jake nodded towards Ryan. 'It was your information about the Sunderland bride selling her company. It made me wonder if there was more going on. A deeply distressed and humiliated woman, who was ready to run, might be open to an offer that she wouldn't otherwise entertain.'

'So, you were anticipating an earlier approach to Karen?' Nadine frowned, considering the idea.

'Let's just say it's not a surprise. Putting the idea out there. Karen may have been quicker off the mark than expected in making her getaway. She'll be gone before any further approach arrives. We need to keep in touch with Corinne to check.'

The darkness of what they were uncovering turned the after taste of fine coffee in Ryan's mouth to bitter aloe. He was just realising the depths of it. 'It makes humiliating the woman an essential part of the operation.'

Jake met his eyes, in perfect accord. 'This thing isn't just about greed, it's about power. He doesn't just want to con these women. He wants to break them – to take what's theirs, but also to show how clever he is.'

Chapter Eleven

Cassie had moved to stand behind her husband, holding her newly-filled glass. She put her hand on his shoulder again, this time letting it rest there. Jake raised his to cover it, without looking up. The simple intimacy of the gesture shivered through Ryan. It was something clean and clear, in the face of something dark and sickening. It also made him deeply, helplessly, envious. He raised his hand. 'I have a little more information. Some of it confirms what we've been thinking.'

'Go ahead,' Jake invited, as Cassie resumed her seat.

Ryan took a breath. Nadine shot him a quick encouraging smile that dispelled some of the chill he'd been feeling. 'I spoke to my client in Sunderland. She'd had to change some plans and cancel a couple of bookings, so it didn't look odd that I phoned her. I mentioned before that the bride – the one who sold up and went to France – is her goddaughter. That's how I knew about the move. It wasn't hard to get her on the subject of the wedding. She's still pretty raw about it, although the goddaughter's new business is doing well and she's met someone else, so it looks as if the fresh start has worked out for her. The story is pretty much the same as Karen's.'

He looked over at Nadine, hoping for, and getting, another quick fix of a smile, before carrying on. 'The goddaughter had been computer dating, then met this guy at the village cinema club – I didn't make the connection on that.' He glanced at Nadine, who was managing not to look smug. 'Orwell, as he was called then, had just moved into the area, renting a place while he house hunted, etcetera. It was a similar story – whirlwind romance, expensive wedding and then the crash. Her goddaughter was adamant that she didn't want the police involved or the man pursued – my client would have hired a detective agency, but the goddaughter vetoed it. Like Karen, she just wanted to let it go. I think it was a bit of a relief to my client when I brought the subject up. She *wanted* to talk about it.' He paused. 'I've broken a client's confidence, *again*, by passing all this on. It's not a comfortable feeling, but that's on me. I'm justifying it, because I'm sure that if she knew, she'd be glad someone was trying to do something.'

'Do you think we should involve her?' Cassie leaned forward to ask.

Ryan exhaled. 'I've wondered, but at this point is it just going to make things more complicated?' He shoved his hand through his hair. 'There's a big chunk of cowardice in there, by the way, as I don't want to have to admit to her that I've talked about her to strangers, but if her goddaughter is settled and happy is it worth stirring things up, when she didn't want that?' He hesitated. 'If the guy is brought down, then maybe it would be okay to share it.'

The general murmur of approval around the table was a relief. He hadn't realised how much breaking a confidence had been weighing on him. *Letting down another client to stay close to Nadine.*

Jake reinforced the relief by nodding. 'Given that we're not really sure what we're about, I agree – best not to involve anyone else.'

'And now we have to decide how we are going to bring the guy down.' Cassie's eyes gleamed with determination.

Jake steepled his fingers. 'It looks like we have a pattern.'

'Orwell/Hemingway's MO,' Cassie agreed. 'I put out a few feelers through contacts in the wedding industry, by the way. Got some gossip about large-scale unpaid bills in the south of England, which may or may not be our man.' She helped herself to a biscuit, looking around the table. 'Does anyone have anything more?'

Everyone shook their heads.

'We have a pattern, but what do we do with it?' Ryan asked, when no one else spoke. 'What about the authorities?

There must be other crimes here, besides fraud. What? Bigamy, falsifying official records, identity theft, maybe?'

'Yeah, all that, and maybe more,' Jake agreed. 'But I suspect, like the fraud, unless an injured party is willing to make a complaint, the machinery is going to be slow to kick into gear, if at all. Who's going to know what's gone on if no one complains?'

There were rueful glances and nods around the room, Ryan's included, signifying understanding – and frustration.

Jake leaned his open palms against the edge of the table. 'This whole thing is nasty. The guy deserves to go down for it.' The set of Jake's jaw and the sudden frost in the dark blue eyes sent a chill across Ryan's skin, even as he was storing the look away in the memory bank for possible future use. *What are you like? Oh yes. An actor.* Jake wasn't so laid-back when it was something that mattered, and this mattered.

'What *can* we do?' Michelle voiced what Ryan was thinking. 'This guy is a hustler – a really nasty con artist – but the two women we know about don't want to get involved in an investigation, and I can't see any obvious way for us to find out about any other victims. We can't exactly take out an advert asking for information.' Thwarted energy thrummed in her voice. 'All *we* have is hearsay and supposition. It hangs together, but there's no real proof. If we did hand it over to the authorities we'd have to bring in Karen and the Sunderland bride. If neither of them is willing to go down that road...' Her voice faded, on a slightly bitter note.

'What we need...' Cassie brushed biscuit crumbs off her fingers '... is a proper case. Evidence to hand over, and people who can testify to back it up.' She looked expectantly at Jake. 'If we want to do something about this guy, it has to be hands-on. Which means setting up a sting.'

Chapter Twelve

An unexpected sense of reprieve flooded through Ryan. He and Nadine had done their part. Now they were out of the picture. He wanted to see this guy, Orwell/Hemingway, brought down, but if there was to be some sort of sting, that was a matter for the professionals – the detective agency. He and Nadine had no role in this.

Looking around the table though, Ryan felt an unexpected pull of regret – to be part of a team, going up against a con artist – but the professionals in the room were the ones to do this. It had started with him, but now he would be walking away. And that was *good*. Nadine wouldn't be mixed up in this any more. These people were the team, not him and not Nadine.

You can leave it to them now. Say your goodbyes and go.

He had an hour before the next train…

Maybe if he left now…

If Nadine came too…

He looked over at Nadine, but she was looking at Jake. If he could attract her attention and they left together, he could suggest…

What? More coffee? A drink?

Only a flicker of curiosity about McQuire's reaction to his wife's suggestion kept him in his seat for a moment more.

Jake was leaning back in his chair, assessing his wife with obvious approval. 'We give Mr Whoever-he-is a bride he can't resist? I like it.' Jake inclined his head in a small bow of acknowledgement towards Cassie, who grinned at him.

Ryan *felt* the atmosphere in the room lift. Michelle actually punched the air. His own heart picked up as the sense of excitement washed over him again. To be part of this – to keep seeing Nadine.

'*Can* we do it?' Cassie's eyes were shining. 'Will it work?'

Jake gave a one-shouldered shrug. 'We can try – first step – create a profile to make him salivate and put it up on the dating agency site.' He shrugged again. 'There might be a million reasons why it won't work and we have to be prepared for that. Most obviously – he might have got too big a shock when he encountered Ryan behind the church to want to try again.'

'You think so?' Cassie queried

'Who knows? If he has any sense he'd cut and run while the going was good. My gut feeling?' Jake shook his head slowly. 'No. He won't run. He's a conman – gambling and risk come with the territory. The guy gets off on the buzz. He can't be one hundred per cent sure why Ryan went after him, but even if he guesses correctly, will he think it matters? All the levers he's put in to cover his tracks are designed to be foolproof. Why should he worry? Any investigation is going to be looking back – where he's covered his tracks. He's not going to be looking forward. He's not going to expect *us*.' Jake grinned. 'Is he going to imagine that someone is taking his scam apart and is prepared to take him on? No way! Even so,' Jake turned to Michelle, 'I'd like you to keep up the investigation side, in the hope of finding something we can use, in case a counter scam *doesn't* work.' He looked around the table. 'The first step in the sting is to pool what we know to create that profile. There again, if we are wrong about him using computer dating to suss out a target, or if he uses a different agency each time, it's not going to work. And we don't know about the timing. It may be too soon after Karen to start another scam. Or maybe he already has one started.'

'Now you're making it sound as if it's impossible.' Cassie made a face at him. 'The luck just has to be on our side, not his. And I think it *ought* to be, as we're the good guys here. I vote we try.'

'I vote yes, as well,' Michelle spoke up.

'So do I.' Nadine was leaning over the table. 'But what do we do if we catch him?'

'Take it as far as is sensible, then hand it over to the proper authorities,' Jake said firmly. 'Tempting as it might be, we are *not* vigilantes.'

The vortex of their enthusiasm was sucking him in. Ryan could feel it. He was supposed to be leaving, but instead he wanted to stay. *This is crazy, man.*

For a horrible second he thought he'd said it out loud, when four pairs of eyes turned towards him. 'What about you, Calder – you in?' Jake asked.

Ryan swallowed. This was the moment he should leave. *But if you do, Nadine won't be coming with you.* Hers were the only eyes that mattered, and he could see from the light in them that she was *way* into this thing. *Way in.*

'Er...' Resistance crumbled. 'Yes. I'm in.'

'Good.' Cassie was actually rubbing her hands. 'Now we have to make a plan.'

Michelle was looking thoughtful. 'I know that we're conning a con artist, and it's no more than he deserves, but if it works, could it be classed as entrapment?'

Jake's expression confirmed that the idea had occurred to him too. 'I think it's a risk,' he agreed quietly. 'But is it a big enough one to make us back off?'

When no one around the table spoke, he gave a hard nod. 'In that case, we go ahead, in the knowledge that we're walking a fine line, and that it could all go belly up.' He gave a lopsided grin. 'Hell – there are enough gaps in the thing for it to go belly up for a dozen reasons, we know that. We have to remember to be careful. We dangle the bait, but *he* has to make the running.' Jake looked around the table, a warning in his eyes. 'If we manage to hook him, no one helps things along with a little push, however tempting it may be.' Jake let the sentence hang. 'We offer him opportunity. He is the one that digs the hole.'

'The deeper the better,' Cassie said with satisfaction.

Jake shot her another warning look. She responded with her pussycat grin.

'We need to create a bride, as well as a profile.' Michelle was thinking aloud, tapping a pencil against her teeth. 'Pity Michael James can't do it. He's the best in the agency at undercover stuff.' She looked over at Jake. 'Maybe Maisie? With a backstory that will hold up?'

'Why do we have to create something?'

The hairs on the back of Ryan's neck stood up when he realised the interruption came from Nadine. She was sitting back in her chair, her eyes sparkling in a way that hit him under the heart with a near combustible mix of need and terror.

'The best fakes are as close to the truth as possible,' Nadine carried on, with a wave of her hand. 'Didn't Ryan just say that – or something like it?' She smiled across the table at him. Something in Ryan's chest was turning icy. 'Why not give Mr Hemingway a fake that is not a fake?' Her beaming smile now took in everyone in the room. It turned Ryan's gut to freezing. Then she put into words exactly what he had feared. 'Why make something up? I can be the bride.'

Chapter Thirteen

Nadine held her breath, waiting for the verdict. She let it out when she heard the general murmur of approval, from one end of the table at least. Ryan was sitting very still. Some of the colour seemed to have gone from his face. She'd guessed that he wouldn't be too happy – *but isn't that partly why you're doing this?*

'That's a great idea.' Cassie leaned forward to kiss her cheek. 'You go, girl,' she whispered. 'But you do know you're crazy, right?'

Nadine smiled as her friend sat back.

'Um...' Ryan's voice grated a little. 'I hate to throw a spanner in the works.'

Everyone shifted to look at him. Nadine focused on his face. His expression was bland, but his eyes suggested that he'd like to be throwing a whole bag of spanners, and maybe the toolbox after it. *Don't panic. You knew this might happen.*

'What?' Cassie tilted her head to ask the question. 'If you have a flaw to point out, Calder, go ahead. This thing won't work unless we make sure it's watertight.'

Nadine watched Ryan's chest rise and fall. She had a fleeting impression of a man holding in his triumph at playing a trump card. It was gone so fast she wasn't sure of what she'd seen. He spread his hands in a don't-blame-me gesture. *He's an actor.*

'Won't Hemingway or Orwell, or whoever he is, recognise Nadine as Karen's friend?' he asked softly. 'Plus he's going to know something about all of us. He's seen Michelle and me, and your names were on Karen's guest list. He'll know there's a connection. So none of us can be involved in the sting, right?' He was looking over at Jake for support. *Male to male. Huh!*

'He's got a point,' Jake agreed. 'The rest of us can stay in the background, but if he's going to remember Nadine—'

'Except that I never met him,' Nadine interrupted quickly.

'I've been travelling a lot in the last three months, visiting suppliers and looking at new sites for possible expansion. Once it got serious and Karen would have introduced us, the opportunity never came up. He doesn't even know my name – Karen and I were at school together. I was on the guest list, but as Nadine Clark – without thinking, Karen used my maiden name. She might have mentioned me to him, but I doubt it.'

'But there's still a chance.' Ryan's eyes were challenging her now. 'She could have talked about your business or something.'

'Yes,' Nadine agreed levelly. 'But I don't think it very likely.'

'But it is possible,' he insisted. 'He's going to research you, he's bound to. And what about the location?' He was appealing to the whole room now. 'Bristol is so close to Bath. Won't he be looking for his next victim somewhere further away?'

'He might,' Cassie chimed in. 'But Karen wasn't living in Bath – she moved to Cheltenham six months ago, before the computer dating and meeting Hemingway. She wanted to get married here because she has friends here and that church was where her parents were married. They're buried in the churchyard. She was planning to leave her bouquet on their grave. Now, when she visits…' She huffed out a breath. 'Something else that bastard has taken away from her,' she finished acidly.

Nadine bit her lip. The list of the hurts that were down to this guy just kept on growing. She tried to telegraph that to Ryan, and thought she saw hesitation in his face, but he wasn't giving up.

'It's still a chance, one we don't have to take,' he said.

'It is,' Nadine agreed. 'But if he has any doubts he won't take our bait. And it's not unreasonable that I could be using the dating agency on Karen's recommendation, as she hit it off so well with Lionel. He won't know that we suspect that he *is* Lionel.'

'You've got it all figured out, haven't you?'

Nadine's breathing eased a little. Now she could see reluctant admiration in Ryan's eyes.

'Probably not nearly enough.' She shifted her gaze from Ryan to the others. Michelle was watching with interest, Cassie with approval and Jake was in his inscrutable mode. 'I'm going to need all the help I can get – from all of you.'

'You have it.' Jake held up a hand. 'How about we go with a two-pronged attack? Michelle creates us an identikit bride, a total fabrication, so guaranteed to be unknown, and we go ahead also with Nadine, who has an unshakeable backstory because it's all true. Let Hemingway take his pick.'

'Or not pick either?' Cassie suggested.

'There is that,' Jake agreed. 'But if he takes the bait from Nadine and then does recognise her in some way, he's most likely to put it down to coincidence. They do actually happen. From what we know of him, he's much too arrogant to expect a sting.' He looked slowly around the room, engaging all of them in turn. 'If anything feels even slightly off, we close the thing down and try something else.'

'Which might not work,' Cassie grumbled.

'*This* might not work,' Nadine pointed out. 'I'm happy with that, Jake.' She could see by the slight relaxation of Ryan's shoulders that he was too. *Or happier. Marginally.* 'If anything doesn't feel right, or I don't think that I can bring it off, we pull the plug.'

'Exactly. Although, I can't imagine the guy will have the poor taste to pass you by.' Jake saluted Nadine with his coffee cup. 'And then we get to plan a wedding.' He paused. Nadine felt the stir of anticipation in the room as they waited for him to carry on. 'I suggest we do everything we can to make this one his pièce de résistance.' Jake grinned at his wife. 'I believe the Riviera is very pleasant for an autumn wedding.'

Chapter Fourteen

'The Riviera!' Michelle's eyes opened very wide. 'That's awesome.' Then her face abruptly clouded. 'But if we want to hand Hemingway over to the authorities—'

'We're cooperating at the moment on something in that area with other agencies and the French authorities,' Jake forestalled her. 'If we get that far, we can work something out. We need to pull out all the stops – the guy is focused on high-end services – venue, catering, flowers – things where payment can be delayed and siphoned off. We can make sure that everything is *very* expensive indeed, plus he will be working in an unfamiliar environment, which will put him at a disadvantage – although I doubt if that will deter him.' Jake smiled at Nadine. 'You're going to be a very demanding bride, my dear.'

'I'm looking forward to it.'

'It won't get as far as that though.' Ryan's objections sounded gruff in his own ears.

'Far enough for our man to commit himself,' Jake agreed smoothly. 'But that's for the future. First we bait our hook. Slick—' Jake stiffened, as if something had connected with his foot under the table. 'Er... Cassie, Michelle and Nadine – do you want to organise the profile? The two profiles – we mustn't forget he might still choose our identikit.'

Michelle was poised at her laptop. 'We can start straightaway.'

Cassie shook her head. 'I have stuff that I have to do this afternoon.' She turned to smile at Michelle. 'Why don't you go ahead with the fake bride, and draft something for Nadine that we can play with?' She looked over at Nadine. 'We'll get together later in the week,' she said firmly.

Nadine blinked, then got the message. Ryan would be leaving as soon as the meeting broke up, but now she wouldn't be delayed here. *Thank you, Cassie.* She turned to give Ryan an encouraging smile. He still wasn't looking too happy. *Which makes it even more important to talk to him.*

Cassie was regarding her husband assessingly, a glitter of mischief in her eyes. 'Remind me? What's your contribution to all this?'

'Master planner,' Jake responded smartly. 'Bringing the show together and putting it on the road.'

'Well.' Nadine had a brief flash of alarm as Ryan got to his feet. There was something dark and very final about his expression. 'I guess this is where I bow out. I hope you'll let me know—'

'No!' Nadine put out a hand. 'I mean...' She backtracked, hoping she wasn't going to blush. 'This all started with you, you have to be involved.'

'Of course he does,' Cassie cut in matter-of-factly. She gave Ryan the pussycat grin. 'If Nadine is going to pull this off, she's going to need an acting coach.'

Ryan stared at Cassie for a couple of beats.

Acting coach. She wanted him to help Nadine play at being in love with someone else.

Forget that. Stupid. You'll still be seeing Nadine. The inner voice was so loud and jubilant Ryan almost jumped.

'Oh... uh.' Nadine was smiling at him in a way that stiffened all his sinews, and a hell of a lot more. She *needed* him. And he could still be part of this, part of the team. 'Oh. Okay, yeah, if that's what Nadine wants.'

'It is.' She'd moved around the table to touch his arm. 'If you have the time.' Her smile was hopeful and slightly shy.

'Time?' God, he'd make time, even if he had to cancel *everything* to do it. 'Ah.' For Pete's sake – he was in danger of sounding like a complete idiot. 'If you want...' He swallowed. 'If you want... er... to talk now... my train doesn't leave for a while.'

His stuttering was mercifully interrupted by the alarm on Michelle's phone. She looked down at it.

'Oops, completely forgot that! Got to go, folks.' She picked up her phone and laptop. 'Duty calls.' She waved to everyone as she headed for the door. 'Ciao.'

'Actually, if you've got a minute, Calder,' Jake intervened. 'One of the guys who works here, undercover, has got hold of some fancy prosthetics he wants to use. I'm not convinced that'll be a good idea, close-up. I'd welcome your opinion, if you have time to take a look.'

'Oh, yes, sure.'

Nadine and Cassie were both on their feet. Nadine was smiling at him. *Meet you downstairs*, he lip-read, before following Jake out of the room.

'Jake won't let him get away.' Nadine turned at the sound of Cassie's voice. Her friend had perched on the end of the table. She was grinning. 'He looked ready to do a runner.'

'I think he was.' Nadine pushed her hair away from her face. Had Ryan noticed she'd left it loose today? *Of course he did. But does he* like *it loose?* 'Thanks for the intervention.'

'No thanks needed. Someone might as well get something positive out of this mess. And you're going to need support from all of us, if you're going to do this.'

'I am.' Nadine raised her chin. 'Ryan is not happy about it though.'

'And that's part of it,' Cassie said shrewdly

'It is. I want the chance... all right...' She gave in when she saw Cassie's sceptical grin. 'I want the *excuse* to spend time with him, but I also want him to know that I don't have to be protected all the time – that I *can* take on something difficult.' She swallowed, suddenly aware of what she *had* taken on. 'I hope I haven't bitten off more than I can chew.'

'Don't know until you try. Though I must say you've picked

a hell of a way to show Mr Protective that you can stand on your own two feet.'

'Haven't I just?' Nadine grinned ruefully, smoothing down her hair again. 'But it just seemed to jump into place. Let's face it, I'm everything our Slimeball wants.' She ticked off her fingers. 'Mature, established, own business, biological clock ticking, desperate.'

'Beautiful, smart, confident,' Cassie continued. 'And definitely not desperate.' She put out a hand to pat Nadine's shoulder. 'It is a big thing though, sweetie. If it works, you're going to have to play nice with Slimeball. More than nice...' she said thoughtfully.

'That's why I need an acting coach.' Nadine ignored the cold lump that was forming in her stomach. 'This is important, Cass. I want to do it. Life has got... Well, a bit too cosy and predictable. This, what we're doing, it's... exciting. And scary as hell,' she admitted on a wail. 'Oh, Cass, can I do this?'

'Hey!' Cassie slid off the table to hold onto her friend's shoulders. 'Beautiful, smart, confident – remember? We play it by ear, but you do *not* get into anything you're not comfortable with. Or at least not too uncomfortable,' she qualified. 'It's not going to be a walk in the park. But we're not looking on the bright side here. Maybe Slimeball will snap the bait on the identikit and you won't need to take the stage at all.' She grinned. 'And you still get to spend some quality coaching time with Ryan.'

'Definitely that.' Impulsively Nadine reached over to kiss her friend's cheek. 'Thanks, Cass, for everything.'

'All part of the service.' Cass waved the thanks away. She shrugged. 'None of this may work anyway. Hemingway might not take *any* bait.'

'I hope he does.' Nadine grabbed her handbag, feeling focused and feeling better. She'd settled, and the cold ball in her stomach had more or less gone.

'You're not going to wait here for Ryan?' Cassie's question came over her shoulder as Nadine headed for the door.

'I'm meeting him downstairs.' Nadine grinned. Now the cold ball was completely gone. Next up – to reassure Ryan that she *could* handle this.

Cassie was perched on the corner of the table again when Jake came back. 'Ah.' He looked around the room. 'Calder seemed to think Nadine would be awaiting him downstairs. It appears he was correct.'

Cassie nodded, hopping off the table and crossing the room to her husband, putting her arms around him. Jake looked surprised, but quite happy about the move. 'We are doing the right thing, aren't we?' She tucked her head against his chest, rubbing her cheek against the fine cotton of his shirt and inhaling citrus scented soap, and Jake.

'We can stop at any time. We *will* stop if Nadine changes her mind, or is in any way unhappy.' Jake held his wife closer. She felt him blowing on one of her curls. It was probably tickling his chin. 'Calder made what he probably considered to be a subtle attempt to get me to dissuade Nadine from going ahead, while we were looking at Mickey's false noses.'

'And I was doing the opposite to her.' Cassie lifted her head to look up at Jake. 'If she has to step in, she knows it's not going to be easy, but that she has our support. And that includes calling it off, even if she doesn't want to,' she decreed softly.

'That's a given,' Jake confirmed. 'Her and Calder? Something going on there that I should know about?'

'She likes him, and on the basis of your conversation over the noses, he appears to like her.'

'Protective.'

'*Very.*'

'So part of this is proving to Calder that she isn't a fragile flower in need of his strong arm to defend her?'

'I didn't marry a dummy, did I?' Cassie marvelled, grinning when Jake gave her as much of a bow of acknowledgement as was possible, considering he was still holding her. 'I think Nadine would quite like the strong arm, but in a different context. All that is classified by the way,' Cassie warned, although she knew that she could trust Jake's discretion more than she could her own. 'I said I wouldn't interfere.' She didn't mention the slightly crossed fingers she'd held under the lunch table. There was interfering, and there was… assisting. She settled her head on Jake's chest again. 'How were the noses, by the way?'

'Okay at a distance, probably not suitable close-up. It was useful to get a professional opinion.' Jake sounded thoughtful.

Cassie leaned back to look up at her husband, curious. 'You have something on your mind?' Jake shrugged and shook his head. Cassie let it go. She could wait. Sometimes.

Cassie stood quietly for a moment in Jake's loosened hold. 'We're going to have to hit all the right buttons to get Hemingway out to play, aren't we?' she asked softly.

'Yep,' Jake agreed.

'A woman with money and a successful business. Old enough to be aware of the biological clock, so thinking marriage and life partner,' Cassie mused. 'No close family ties to get in the way, someone who values her dignity and her privacy, who isn't going to be displaying trophy photos all over social media, because our boy doesn't want his face known. Busy and successful, so amenable to sharing the wedding arrangements. Independent but… vulnerable? Maybe just a little emotionally insecure under the competence, so capable of being crushed by being made to look a fool?'

'That's quite a list,' Jake endorsed, admiringly.

'It's a horrible list. Manipulative. He needs to be stopped.' She paused, grimacing.

'Something else bothering you, oh best beloved?'

Cassie huffed at the extravagant compliment. Her husband

knew her so well. 'If we're really going to get evidence against this guy, we're going to have to take it right to the wire, aren't we?' She jerked her head towards the door. 'The others haven't thought it through yet, but the *fraud* doesn't happen until the end – which is when? The day before the wedding?'

'About then.' Jake nodded, acknowledging his wife's reasoning. 'Which is one of the reasons I suggested the Riviera.'

Cassie's thoughts scrolled back to the complexities of their own wedding in France. 'If he takes the bait, and we have to take it all the way to the wedding day – no one is going to end up sort of half married this time.'

'Exactly. The formalities over there just won't allow it. I wonder how long it will take him to find out that the bride or groom or one of their parents has to have lived there for forty days before the ceremony.' Jake smiled. 'It was a bit of a shock when we found out.'

'We coped.' Cassie smiled back. She had some fond memories of the time she and Jake had spent in France before their wedding.

'He only needs to make up some story to reassure his bride, and have it in reserve if he needs it,' Jake suggested. 'A woman in love is not going to query anything her prospective groom tells her. Why should she?'

Cassie gave a sarcastic laugh. 'You're right. He'd find a way. He's nothing if not inventive.'

'This is true,' Jake agreed. 'But good to make him work for his money. The other thing about a wedding on the Riviera – we're going to have a lot more control if he's operating away from his usual hunting grounds.'

Cassie made a face. '*That*, I like.'

'Thought you might,' Jake said smugly.

'He's going to have to improvise quite a bit. Any chance that he'll simply cut and run, even if he does take the bait, when he finds out he can't operate the usual scam?'

Jake shrugged. 'Always a possibility.' He grinned. It was not

an open and friendly grin. 'We'll just have to offer him a few...
incentives.'

'Hah!' Now Cassie was answering the grin. 'Juicy carrots
to bump up the cost?' She tilted her head, considering her
husband. Jake waited. 'You're going to be footing the bill for
all this, aren't you?'

Jake waved the idea away. 'It will be worth it. I have a few
ideas in mind that I'm sure our bride is going to love that
will... keep things in-house, shall we say?'

'An extra set up.' Cassie nodded. 'Welcome to my
parlour said the spider to the fly. You really get off on this
Machiavellian stuff, don't you?'

Jake stepped close again, to tighten his arms around her. 'All
part of my irresistible charm.' He planted a butterfly kiss on
Cassie's nose. She pretended to sneeze, brushing him off.

'First the fly has to walk into the trap.' Cassie chewed her
lower lip. Now the plan was launching, unwelcome doubts
were coming with it. That they were unwelcome didn't mean
they shouldn't be voiced. 'And it *is* a trap. Jake... are we letting
ourselves get carried away with being clever? If push comes to
shove, even if Hemingway walks into it, *will* there be anything
we can use? A court case? Would it even get that far?'

Jake moved back slightly to look down at her. 'Honestly?
I don't know. But if we can do enough that the authorities at
least get the guy on the radar.'

Cassie took a deep breath, accepting that it *might* have to
be enough. Jake had contacts. Money like his certainly talked.
If all that resulted were words in a few, well-chosen ears...

She sighed. They'd gone into this on an impulse, a surge of
anger, to make a conman pay. *Nothing about that has changed,
but you know it's not that simple.* 'Everything about this has
consequences. Just because we are the good guys it doesn't
make *us* lily-white, or that there will be any justice.'

'We do what we do, and then wait.'

Cassie nodded, still thinking. 'What about the half-married

thing? With other brides, the UK ones? There has to be legal complications with that? Anything you can look into?' She caught Jake's eye. 'Already being done?'

'It is,' he confirmed. 'If we can join up some dots that way it would be good. It might be a way of bringing him down. I imagine other women he's scammed will consult a solicitor at some point, but if Karen is a pattern, it might not be the first thing they do. And it's the same problem – every case being looked at in isolation. Plus it's such a crazy situation. For all we know there might be lawyers up and down the country scratching their heads over how the hell you deal with it. I'd guess any lawyer worth their salt would put enquiries in hand, and involve the police, if they can persuade their client, but our man is a pro. He covers his tracks.'

Cassie nodded then shook her head again, freeing herself from troublesome thoughts, and clearing her lungs with a deep breath. At present everything was an unknown.

Moving her hands to rest on Jake's belt, she looked round. 'You know, I've always liked this room.' She focused on the conference table. 'Do you have anything urgent planned for the rest of the afternoon?'

Jake raised one eyebrow. 'No. But I thought you did.'

Cassie grinned, laying a finger on her lips, and then on Jake's. She nestled close to him, hip to hip, pleased with the reaction the movement provoked. 'Before we know it, I won't be able to see my feet, and then there will be the patter of *tiny* feet. I think we should make the most of opportunity.' She slid out of Jake's arms and around him to lock the door, then turned to back him gently against the table.

Luckily he had no intention of resisting.

Chapter Fifteen

They'd reached the pavement outside the office and Ryan hadn't managed to find a way of phrasing what he wanted to say. Nadine was looking at her watch. 'It's too early for dinner. But just right for afternoon tea,' she decided. 'You have time before your train?'

It wasn't even really a question. She was already navigating them towards an imposing building further down the street. Everything seemed to be getting away from him.

Except for the fact that you'll take any chance to be with this woman.

Except that you need to convince her to back off from a crazy plan that is making that happen.

His heart swelled with longing and hopelessness.

Inside the hotel foyer Nadine conversed briefly with the uniformed concierge, and they were ushered into an elegant lounge, dotted with sofas and low tables. Several groups were already established with teapots and cake stands. Their tea began to arrive almost as soon as they sat down, including what Ryan recognised as a glass of very good champagne. 'You come here with Mrs McQuire,' Ryan guessed.

'Yes.' Nadine selected a smoked salmon sandwich, admiring the array of pastries on the top of the stand. 'The cakes are out of this world. Jake has a very sweet tooth, and he's passed it on to Cassie.' Plate loaded, she settled back to the comfort of her armchair. 'Right. Now you can make your pitch.'

'Pitch?'

'You don't want me to be part of...' Nadine looked around. There was no one sitting near them. 'What we were just discussing,' she finished carefully.

'Was I that obvious?' Ryan sighed. 'I'm sorry.' He kept his voice low. 'But this man, he's a complete... crook. I don't want... I don't think you should be involved with him.'

Nadine was looking at him. A straight stare that set his

nerve ends and brain cells jangling. He always tried to avoid any suggestion of gazing into her eyes. They were a depthless dark brown, and a man could so easily drown. Now they were pure and clear, and he was on his way down for the first time.

'That's a very gallant sentiment, Ryan, but it's my choice to make.' There was something in the depths of those eyes. Several somethings. Amusement? Impatience? Expectation?

And he was on his way down for the second time.

He broke away from the look. Wrenched was probably the better word. 'But why?' His voice was hoarse.

'Because it suits me to.' Now there was definitely amusement in her face. She touched his ankle with the toe of a sexy dark green shoe. 'I'm a big girl, Ryan. I *can* take care of myself.'

'I know,' he admitted, letting out a deep breath. He *did* know. But that didn't stop... Didn't stop him wanting... Recklessly he took a deep swig of his champagne. Nadine was spreading jam on a scone. She topped it with cream and slid it onto his plate. He stared at it.

If it was a peace offering, he could sulk or he could eat. He ate.

Nadine dolloped cream on another scone. 'He might not even choose me you know.'

'I'm holding on to that thought.'

Nadine laughed. 'Always honest.'

The waitress had materialised to pour more champagne. Ryan hadn't realised that he had drained his glass. 'Look, I know that it might seem exciting...' His voice faltered.

It's just like that heady, sick making, exhilarating blast, when you step out on the stage. Exactly like that. He closed his eyes briefly over the rush. *That's why she's doing it. How can you say no to that?*

'Lighten up, Ryan. We're trying to do some good here.' Her mouth was soft with laughter. *So soft.* She was looking straight into his eyes again, and the water was threatening to close over his head. 'It might even be... well, maybe not fun, but satisfying.' She sipped from her glass. 'Whatever happens, all of you will have my back.'

71

Ryan looked down at his plate, depression settling abruptly around him, like a cold cloud. And with it realisation. That was a big part of the problem. *He* wouldn't be here. He wasn't going to be part of the team. Once he got on the train tonight, he'd be relegated to the sidelines. Maybe not even that. Nadine had agreed that she needed an acting coach, but he wasn't fooled. That was only going to amount to the occasional phone call, if he was lucky. *And you're desperate enough to hope for that, you poor sod.*

An abrupt trilling noise and a vibration against his chest that had nothing to do with Nadine's eyes, jerked him out of his thoughts. 'Oh hell! Sorry.'

He fished the phone out of his inside pocket. A well-dressed matron on the other side of the room was giving him the death stare. 'Sorry,' he mouthed, in her direction, stabbing at the phone to shut it up, and frowning at the display. 'It's my agent. I need to take this.'

Nadine, mouth full of macaroon, waved her hand to indicate he should go ahead.

He hauled himself out of the chair, pressing buttons as he crossed the foyer into the street. 'Molly?'

He was too late. Voicemail had cut in. He waited, knowing Molly wouldn't leave a message, then called her back.

She answered immediately. 'Ah, glad I got you.' He could hear paper shuffling in the background. He pictured Molly's cramped office in a side street in Soho. 'I had a call from that friend of yours.' More shuffling. 'He has a job. Here, in the UK. Stage. Not much money, but he's desperate and I know you're mates. I said you'd give him a call. Jordan Bright,' she finished triumphantly, having apparently found the paperwork. She reeled off a number, repeating it twice. 'Let me know if you want to take it.'

The line went dead. Ryan grinned. Molly never took time to say goodbye.

He stood for a moment, looking at the sunlit street and the warm glowing stone of the buildings. Jordan was a fringe director he'd worked with several times in the past few years. A decade ago they'd even won an award together at the Edinburgh Festival. Ryan looked at the phone. Molly had said stage, and not much money. Translation – industry minimum wage and a fit-up in a room over a pub somewhere at the end of a tube line. But he and Jordan *were* mates. He dialled the number, still looking at the sunny street. Traffic was moving at the end of the road but here it was quiet. He leaned against the hotel's railings and waited for the phone to be picked up.

'Jordan? It's Ryan.'

'Ry!' Ryan moved the phone swiftly away from his quivering eardrum at the delighted bellow from down the line. 'You, my friend, are just about to save my life.'

'I am?'

'You remember that three hander you did, with Louella and Troy, in New York? God, I hope you do, or I'm wasting my time here.'

'I remember.' An off, off Broadway gig, right at the end of a six month stint in the US, when he hadn't managed to set Hollywood alight before the money ran out. It was an experimental script, but Jordan had brought out hidden levels of pathos, humour and anguish that had got them five star reviews. Unfortunately they apparently hadn't been seen by anyone who was anyone, and they'd flown home when the run closed.

'I'm re-staging it, new cast, new everything, except...'

'What?'

'The guy who plays the stranger – his dad died. In Sydney. He's flying out tomorrow to sort out all the formal stuff, and bring his dad home. God knows how long it's going to take, and the run is only a four-week gig. Great exposure, but shoestring stuff, so no understudies.'

Ryan could see where this was going. *The stranger. Your part.* 'You want me to do it.'

'Well, yes, man.' There was an uncharacteristically apologetic note in Jordan's voice. Jordan was a never-apologise-never-explain kind of guy. 'I would have cast you again, Ry, but you know, small space, low pay, and I know you're kind of... moving on now.'

Ryan remembered a night a few months back when he'd had more than he should have to drink, in Jordan's company. Presumably he'd talked a lot more than he should have as well. 'You want me to do it,' he repeated.

'If you don't, then we have to cancel, and the space goes dark. Which will be very bad news all round.' There was a note of hope in Jordan's voice now. 'Molly said you didn't have anything on.' *Thank you, Molly*. 'Like I said, lifesaver. You can do it on the book, if you have to.'

Ryan sighed, resigned. Jordan *was* a mate and they'd done good stuff together. And that play, that part... Huh! He could almost smell the stale beer and old dust of a pub fit-up somewhere on the edge of London. 'When and where?'

'Previews next Thursday, Friday and Saturday, opening the following Tuesday. Er... it's a good gig, very good, but it's not in town.'

Ryan leaned more heavily against the railings. The mental picture of the room over the pub was getting clearer by the second. Only this time it was in Luton. Or maybe Stevenage?

'Where?'

'New studio space in an old industrial building. Mixed arts complex. One of those warehouse conversion set-ups – gallery, art cinema, bookshop, pub, restaurant – and the theatre space. The facilities are awesome.'

Ryan grinned, reluctantly. Jordan really *did* want him, to be selling the space so hard. It was probably in Hull, or Newcastle. That was not really a problem. It was *way* better than his foreboding about the pub.

'It sounds... interesting,' he offered cautiously.

'It's a great venue and attracting a lot of attention for cutting edge stuff...' Jordan hesitated. 'It's in Bristol.'

Ryan straightened up so fast he nearly dropped the phone. 'I'll do it.'

Chapter Sixteen

Ryan was coming back, and he was smiling. Something fluttered in Nadine's abdomen and curled lower. For a second she just let herself enjoy. Broad shoulders, emphasised by the well-tailored suit, narrow hips. Long legs, dark brown hair falling forward over his eyes. She wasn't the only woman in the room who was watching him approach. Even the waitress had stopped what she was doing to smile as he passed.

He folded himself into his seat, still grinning. She raised her eyebrows, returning the grin, unable to resist that look. 'Hollywood calling?' The words were out, light and jokey – and settling on her stomach like lead when the possibility hit her. *If you go away…*

'No, nothing like that. Just a favour for a friend.' He'd bent his head to pick up his plate. Nadine's fingers, on the champagne flute, trembled slightly. She wrapped both hands around the stem to hold it steady. 'Something good?' she asked brightly.

'A play I did a while ago in New York. One of the cast had to drop out. The good news is that it's here, in Bristol, starting next week.'

The flood of relief to her system was as potent as the champagne in her glass. Elation bubbled through her. She felt dizzy. 'That's… amazing.'

She leaned forward and the champagne in her glass slopped. She took a swig to lower the level in the glass. Maybe she should be pouring it out, as a libation to whatever god was in charge of coincidences. *But probably not on the hotel's expensive looking Persian rug.*

Ryan's head was still bent. He seemed very intent on choosing a sandwich from the bottom of the stand. A heady impulse flitted through her. 'You could stay—'

He looked up, just as the enormity of what was about to

come out of her mouth hit the rational part of her brain. Her tongue curled over the words, impulse floundering. 'Um… With your friend. The one with a place in the city centre?'

He was staring at her. Almost as if he knew what she had been about to say. That she'd been about to ask him to stay with her. She could feel the heat rising from the base of her neck. She pressed her hands even tighter on the stem of the glass and did her best to will away the flush. 'Tell me all about it,' she invited quickly. She shifted back in her seat, sipping her drink and watching Ryan's face as he told her about the play and demolished the rest of the food.

Finally it was time to leave. Nadine excused herself to go to the cloakroom, paying the bill on her way there. Whatever she did, it seemed as if she ended up paying for Ryan's company. She stared hard at the ornate carved mirror over the sink in the ladies. Her skin was flushed and her eyes glittered in the flattering overhead lights. Was her longing showing in her face?

She put up her hands to cover the blush. When she was around Ryan she blushed much too often. It was like being sixteen again. Gawky, shy and tongue-tied. She'd moved on, *way* on, but that sixteen-year-old was still in there, waiting to burst out and ambush her when she got too close to declaring herself. She was sure, well almost sure, that Ryan wanted to be with her as much she wanted to be with him – that it *wasn't* just about being a client – but neither of them seemed to be able to get past that stumbling block.

His reaction to her volunteering to be the bait in their sting – that had been real concern, and maybe even a little jealousy? A thrill of pure feminine satisfaction shivered through her. Then she caught her own eye in the mirror and her mouth twisted. She wasn't looking at a powerful woman, she was looking at a wimp. Opportunity had been handed to her – she'd almost got her tongue around that invitation to Ryan to stay with her while he was working in Bristol, only to fold at the last second. *Like a wimp*.

She put out her hand and with one finger traced the outline of a heart on the mirror. She'd volunteered for their crazy sting operation because of Karen, but also to give herself a chance with Ryan. For an instant her breath hitched, and another shiver, this time something much colder, rippled through her. What had she taken on? Was Ryan right to be concerned? *Are you up to it?*

She steadied her breathing and waited for her pulse to settle, tapping her finger on the spot where she'd drawn the heart. She'd grabbed her chance, and now fate seemed to be helping things along by locating Ryan in Bristol, at least for a few weeks. So – she had to go ahead and actually *do* something.

And if you don't, you really are a wimp.

Ryan was waiting for her in the foyer, chatting to the concierge. 'Can I walk you to the station?' she asked, as soon as he looked up and saw her.

'Oh.' He sounded surprised. 'Yes. If it's not out of your way.'

It took a disappointingly short time to reach the railway station. At one point, while waiting to cross the street, she'd nearly taken Ryan's hand. Then the lights had changed, and the opportunity with them. *Wimp.* Now they stood, slightly awkwardly, in the station lobby, with commuters swirling around them. 'I'll text you when I've seen Cassie and Michelle,' she promised. 'A progress report.'

'That would be good. I—'

The tannoy drowned out the rest of Ryan's sentence as the tinny voice announced, 'Due to emergency engineering works passengers for Swindon, Reading and London are advised to take the next train to Bristol Temple Meads for connections to Bristol Parkway, where they may continue their journey.'

Nadine took a sharp breath. 'That's your train.' *Now or never.* She reached up, putting her hands on Ryan's chest, not for their usual air kiss, but to press her mouth properly, quickly, against his. Her heart was thumping so loudly as she stepped back she could barely hear the disembodied voice insisting that the next Bristol train would be departing from platform one in four minutes.

Ryan was standing as if frozen, eyes wide and dark. 'Go.' She gave him a push towards the barrier. The ticket collector had opened the gates and was rushing a milling cluster of confused people through. 'This way please, ladies and gents. Connections for the London train. Platform one. Change at Bristol Temple Meads. Hurry along now, please.'

Ryan abruptly came to himself. 'Nadine—'

'Go,' she said again. 'You'll miss it.'

He raised his hands, then dropped them. 'I... I'll call you.' He turned and was swallowed in the hurrying crowd.

WTF. Ryan hunched in a corner seat, staring blindly out of the window as the train edged out of the station. He'd just kissed Nadine Wells. No. He'd just *been* kissed by Nadine Wells. Not a down-and-dirty-full-tongues-involved, but still a kiss. Not a brushing of cheek to cheek. Warm and soft and right on the mouth. Premeditated. Not an accident. Not a mistake. *A kiss.*

He could still feel the imprint.

He raked a hand through his hair, tugging at it until it hurt. He was awake. It had not been a dream. Or a hallucination. Hell, he was making lists here of all that it wasn't, but what the hell *was* it? Did she...? She must... Had she...?

His hand went up through his hair again. God, if he had any balls at all, instead of running for his damned *train* he'd have leapt back over the bloody barrier, backed her into a corner and kissed them both senseless. Just like the best big screen romances. Things in his body were starting to tighten and ache simply at the thought.

He tipped his head back and shut his eyes. What the hell did he do *now*?

Call her. He had to call her.

He hauled out his phone. His hand wasn't quite steady and

it wasn't the champagne. Champagne! Was that it? They'd both had champagne. *Oh, come on! No way are you blaming this on a couple of glasses of champagne.*

His heart was hammering – stage fright to the power of ten. There were spots before his eyes. If he was going to do it, it had to be now, before he passed out. He prodded buttons, praying that the train wouldn't suddenly dive into a tunnel.

'Hello?' Her voice. Muffled.

'It's me.' He swallowed, trying to get saliva into his mouth. 'Uh – where are you?'

'On the way to the car park. Where are you? Did you catch the train?'

'Yes.' He looked out of the window. 'I think we're just coming into Bristol.' Suddenly he knew what he had to do. 'I'm getting off. I'll come to your place and wait for you. What just happened…? We need to talk.'

Chapter Seventeen

The official at the barrier at Temple Meads let him keep his return ticket to London. The taxis were queuing in a slow circle in front of the station entrance. There was a flower stall tucked into a corner. The girl in charge of it was packing up but stopped with a smile when he approached, wrapping the pink and blue blooms he'd hastily chosen into a cone of paper. She grinned as she took his money. 'Hope she likes them.'

He heaved in a breath. 'So do I.'

His taxi wound up to Clifton, in a series of stops and starts, through the road works, one-way system and early rush hour traffic. Even so, he was going to be there before Nadine arrived back from Bath.

Fine. He'd wait.

And try to figure out what the hell he was going to say.

They'd arrived. The sight of her house got his nerves jangling again. He paid off the taxi and hesitated. He could walk up and down the street. *And risk being at the very end when her car finally pulled in?* Voting no to that, he laid the bouquet carefully on the top step, and sat down beside it. Was he imagining it or was a curtain already twitching in the house opposite? If there were neighbourhood watchers in the area he might well be seeing a patrol car before he saw Nadine's. *Do burglars bring flowers these days?*

Whatever. He'd wait.

The car engine faltered and died, just as the lights changed. Nadine scrambled out of her thoughts to get back into gear and moving – away from the indignant volley of horns behind her. She kangarooed into a side street, took a deep breath and concentrated on her driving, rather than the questions inside her head. It wasn't easy.

We have to talk. What did that mean? That she'd crossed a

line? That she'd got the whole thing horribly wrong and he'd be dropping her from his client list? Could she joke it away? Imply he was overreacting to a friendly gesture? Even if she did, lying by implication, it would still be *there*. Between them. Had she just done one of the stupidest things she'd ever done in her life?

Her hands were jittering on the wheel as she pulled into her road. There were cars lined on both sides. She saw the gap about ten houses down from hers and grabbed it, parallel parking without ramming a Range Rover and a silver grey Smart car that were bracketing the space.

She got out, straightening her shoulders. Jaw set, she began to walk. She could see him. Sitting on the steps. His head was turned away, watching something across the street. What did his body language say? Could she read it? He looked tense, muscles taut.

Her knees were turning to water. He turned slightly, shifted. There was something lying beside him on the step. A parcel? Pink? In a rush she decoded the shape. Flowers. He'd brought her flowers. Her breath caught and her eyes misted. She finished the last few yards at a run.

She was almost at the bottom of the steps before it dawned on her that the bundle of pink roses and blue scabious could be 'Goodbye' not 'Kiss me again'. She stilled to a ragged, clattering halt, stricken. Ryan swung round to face her and rose smoothly to his feet. He was smiling. Nadine's knees went completely numb. He nodded towards the house opposite, the way he had been staring. 'I think your neighbour is about to get me arrested for loitering.'

'Oh!' Nadine's breath came out in a puff of surprise. She turned and waved, in what she hoped was a reassuring fashion. Mrs Copeland, the local neighbourhood watch coordinator, was peering at them around the edge of her fancy ruched blinds. Nadine turned back to Ryan. 'You said we had to talk?' she asked carefully.

Ryan nodded. 'I think…' She saw his chest rise and fall in a deep breath. *Oh God… he's as confused and nervous as you are.* 'I need to know what you meant… At the station, when…' His voice faded, but his eyes were still asking the question.

She took a step forward. 'What did you want it to mean?'

He didn't answer, just held out his arms.

She was up the steps and into them in a half second. Raising herself on her toes, she put her hands on his chest and lifted her mouth to his. His arms settled more firmly around her, steadying her. His mouth was warm and firm and the feel of it sent spiky shudders of need through her. She parted her lips and let him in, and the shudders exploded off the scale – exploring, teasing, challenging, stealing her breath.

She clung on, sinking into the kiss, holding on to Ryan to keep her upright, as every thought in her head dissolved. All that was real was the contact, his mouth, his body – scent, taste, texture. She moved her hands to frame his face, whole weight tipped precariously against him. His grip tightened in response. She held him, pressing her tongue between his lips, taking the taste of him deep into her mouth.

When they finally broke apart, she had to shake her head to clear it.

Ryan planted a butterfly kiss on her forehead. He was laughing at something, over her shoulder. She turned. Mrs Copeland's blind hit the windowsill with a telltale crash. Ryan gathered Nadine up, so that she was standing beside him on the top step. 'I think we'd better take this inside.'

She managed to get the front door open, then shut, before they were back in each other's arms. Ryan was showering kisses on her eyelids, her face, the corner of her mouth, tormenting her lower lip with his teeth. She wanted—

The doorbell rang.

She leaned back against the door, looking up at Ryan's face, eyes wide.

The bell pealed again.

'Had you better answer it?' Ryan suggested. His hair was ruffled from her fingers and in the shadowy light of the hall his mouth seemed half bruised from the pressure of her lips. He looked so sexy, so edible, she could hardly bear to let him go, until he gently pushed her away.

She fiddled clumsily with the door, trying to remember how the lock worked. At last she got it open. Mrs Copeland was standing on the step.

'You forgot these.' She held out the flowers. 'It seemed a pity to let them wilt, after your *friend* bought them for you.'

Her neighbour was visibly craning, in an attempt to see around the door. A sudden gust of laughter welled up from the pit of Nadine's stomach. She had to grit her teeth to stop it escaping, as she took the flowers. 'Eurgh... Thank you,' she gasped.

Ryan pulled the door fully open behind her, leaning over her shoulder. His warmth caressed her back. 'That was very kind,' he offered.

'Oh. Hello.' Mrs Copeland looked up, eyes eager. 'Such a thoughtful gesture,' she said encouragingly. 'From a visitor.'

'I think we better see about putting them in water. Thank you again.' Somehow Ryan scooped Nadine and the flowers into the hall and shut the door, politely but firmly.

Nadine put a free hand to her face, laughter coming up in irrepressible giggles. Ryan rescued the flowers to let her double over, watching with obvious amusement. Nadine knew some of the laughter was coming out of stress and relief, but she didn't care. It felt good. Finally she got the giggles under control.

'How long, do you think, before the whole street knows you're entertaining a gentleman caller?' Ryan asked, grinning.

'About half an hour?' She reclaimed the bouquet. The laughter had died away now. She put up her hand to touch Ryan's cheek, burying her nose in the blooms. 'Thank you.'

He caught her hand and held it. 'Thank *you*... for this afternoon, and the station... I've waited so long... I didn't know if you felt...' He pressed a kiss to her palm. 'You've got more guts than I have.'

'You were in a more difficult place than I was. If you'd made a move and it had been wrong, it was your job at stake.' She shivered slightly. 'Driving over here... I was afraid you were going to tell me that I wouldn't be seeing you again.'

'No way!' He dropped his head a little. 'But it's going to be complicated ... That's what I was afraid of.'

'We'll work it out. We have time.' She smiled as the thought struck her. 'Now I don't have to act as bait for our sting in order to keep seeing you.'

She saw the confusion in his eyes. It took a second for him to make the connection. 'That's why you wanted to do it?'

'It was a way out of the client/employee thing. I'll call Cassie later and tell her I've changed my mind. I'm sure Michelle's identikit profile will do the job just as well.'

'I'd be a lot happier with that.' Ryan took the flowers out of her hand, laid them down on the hall table and pulled her into his arms to kiss her again.

The clock in the hall chimed the hour as he let her go.

'I can't stay, I'm relieving Stacey at the bar at nine—' He broke off abruptly. 'Ah... I didn't mean...' His eyes were wide with dismay, colour flagging his cheekbones. 'I wasn't assuming... That is if you wanted... shit, help me out here, before I dig this hole any deeper.'

'Stop digging.' She reached up, in a swift light kiss. 'And go to work. Like I said, we have time.' She looked around for her bag, which was on the floor beside the door. 'I'll run you to the station.'

'No, I'll call a cab. If you move the car now you'll never get another parking slot.' A wide, wicked grin curled his mouth. 'Mrs Copeland is going to be disappointed to see me leaving, though.'

Nadine leaned towards him to whisper in his ear. 'You know, she won't be the only one.'

Chapter Eighteen

Jake glanced at the clock. The office was officially closed and he was on the point of leaving, but he dropped his jacket back onto a chair when he saw the name that had come up on his phone. 'Yes, Michelle?'

'I've got him, boss.'

'That was fast.' He looked at the clock again. Three hours since the meeting broke up. 'Good work.' He frowned. 'Um – why do I think I'm hearing a *but* in there?'

'You are, and it's a big one.' Michelle's sigh was distinctly audible. 'Were you on your way out? Or can you come down to the basement?'

'I was, but not a problem. I'll see you in a few minutes.'

Jake ambled down to the lower ground floor, where all the geeks' special toys were kept in surroundings designed to ensure their optimum comfort and performance. He didn't know what half the kit down here did, and was quite happy that way. All he had to do was sign the cheques. In exchange the machines seemed to be able to turn up all the information the business would ever want. Like now.

Except for that but...

Michelle looked up when he entered the room, closing the door carefully behind him. The place was temperature controlled, a little on the cool side for his taste, but the geeks didn't seem to mind. *Boys, and girls, with their toys.* He dragged over a chair to sit beside Michelle, so he could see her screen. They were alone. Everyone else had already left for the evening.

'He's using the same dating agency. This time he's calling himself John Thackeray.'

Jake whistled softly. 'Well, I really didn't think he would be back on the market that fast.'

'He's escalating.' Michelle did not look happy. 'And that's not all. He's gone off-piste, big time. I reached out to Corinne,

Karen's PA, for information to help track him. Apparently Karen likes to keep personal stuff on paper.' She gave a thin smile. 'The word Corinne used was anal, but in this case it's useful. Corinne was able to access the information. She had that couriered over.' Michelle nodded to a blue envelope file on the end of the desk. 'It has Karen and Lionel's profiles. And there's this.' She pulled forward a copy of a photo. 'Corinne remembered, and did some digging. Apparently, very early in the relationship, Hemingway was Karen's escort to some sort of gala, where her sales team were picking up an award. Corinne was snapping pictures of everyone while they were milling about, claiming their table. When Hemingway saw what she was doing, he excused himself and stood aside – said that it was a night for Karen and her team – blah blah.'

'Thereby earning himself extra brownie points for courtesy and modesty.'

'Yep,' Michelle agreed. 'But before he did, she'd got this.' Michelle pointed at the photograph. It was an informal group shot, in the corner of a hotel ballroom, a dozen people laughing and gurning for the camera as they found their seats. And at the side of the group, settling Karen in her chair – 'John Hemingway.'

Michelle drew the picture closer, so that it was on the desk in front of them. 'It's not all that clear, but you can see his features well enough. Which is what suggests we may have a problem.' She clicked on the mouse, bringing up a dating profile on the screen. 'The new profile for John Thackeray is almost a match for the one for Lionel Christopher.'

'Why fix it, if it ain't broken?'

'Exactly.' Michelle nodded. 'He knows it brings in responses from the sort of women he wants to meet. But it seems like he's in a hurry. Corinne couldn't find the photograph that went with the Christopher profile, but was sure that it wasn't Hemingway. Probably just something pulled off the internet. But this time, as John Thackeray, he's using his own photo.'

Jake studied the picture on screen, comparing it to the print on the desk and his memories of a chaotic afternoon in an idyllic country church. Or what would have been idyllic except for what this man did. And it *was* this man. The goatee beard was gone and the hair was maybe a shade or two darker, but he didn't have any doubt. John Hemingway was now John Thackeray.

Michelle tapped the photo, chewing her bottom lip. 'Why is he appearing now as himself?'

'What do you think?'

'Short of time?' Michelle hesitated. 'Is this his swansong with this particular scam? Is he going in as himself because if the bride does go after the dating agency it doesn't matter, because he won't be using it any more?' She paused for a moment, still looking at the screen. 'He's not bothering with reconnaissance. This time he's going straight to the target.' Her voice strengthened as she thought it through. 'I mean, how much longer can he keep doing this, keep taking the risk? Every time he pulls it off, the odds must get shorter... We know they *did* get shorter. The episode with Ryan must've made him think. He has to be assuming that Ryan doesn't actually know who he is, but it must have shaken him just to have someone intervene like that.'

'Judging when to cut and run is part of the skill set.' Jake studied John Thackeray on the screen, modestly smiling at his prospective target. 'Couldn't resist one last go round though, could you?' he asked the image. Jake turned to Michelle. 'And for that, we have to be grateful. We got some luck. Now we have to hope for a bit more.' He looked back at the screen. 'Whatever the next scam is on this guy's programme, and I'm sure there will be one, it will be bigger and nastier.'

Michelle made a face. 'I can't imagine what – oh, I forgot.' She scrabbled amongst the papers. 'You were right – Corinne confirmed that there was another enquiry about buying Karen's company.' She tipped her head to look at her boss. 'What are you thinking? Maybe some form of money laundering?'

'Crossed my mind – which means that this might well be part of something very much bigger.' Jake shrugged. 'I don't know enough about the intricacies of moving dirty money to judge. That'll be for the proper authorities to find out, when we hand it over.' He looked thoughtfully at the screen. 'I'm not sure about this scam. It's complicated but it's not big. It *seems* relatively small scale, but *is* there something bigger behind it? If there is, and someone else is dictating operations, maybe *they've* decided it's time for him to stop?' Jake studied the picture of Thackeray. 'Has he already been called off, and this is something he's doing on his own account? A last flourish? If he's been told to wind things up, that might explain why he's moved outside his regular pattern.'

Michelle looked anxious. 'But we are going ahead, right?'

'I think so. Whatever this might be…' Jake gestured to the screen '… *that* is one arrogant bastard. Doesn't believe he can get caught. If we're right and it is a swansong, and he's short of time for some reason, he still can't resist just one more trick. Going out with a bang. Which is our luck, and hopefully, will be his undoing.' He let out a breath. 'We need to be careful, extra careful, just in case we do only have the tip of the iceberg.' He stood, pointing a finger at Michelle's screen. 'This was excellent work. I'm not going to ask how you achieved it, though.'

'Thanks, boss.' Michelle grinned. 'I finished an invented profile based on Karen's and signed on, to try it out live, with Maisie's photo. Three perspectives popped up straight away. He was one of them. I haven't started the draft for Nadine yet.'

'Let that ride for now. We'll go with Maisie. If he's this impatient, the deep background may not matter. Accept all the matches.'

Michelle raised her eyebrows. 'All of them?'

'We don't want to risk anything showing up that suggests

he's been especially targeted. Maisie can let the others down lightly when she contacts them.'

Jake looked back at the screen, knowing his smile was feral rather than pleasant. 'Let Maisie know, and set the thing in motion. We're going to offer *him* the ultimate in last performances.'

Chapter Nineteen

Ryan topped off a large glass of wine and reached for a new bottle, glancing at the clock and surveying the bar. They were busy, but not crammed. A dozen or so regulars, a solo guy with a briefcase and a miserable slump to his shoulders who might need a strong coffee and a hand into a taxi at the end of the evening, and a large hen do, which had staked out a group of tables at the far end of the room. Casting an experienced eye, Ryan guessed that the wedding was second time around. The bride was wearing a sash and a tiara, but mercifully that was the extent of the fancy dress. No wings, no horns, no naughty schoolgirls. The party had clearly come to enjoy a few bottles of seriously good wine and sample the tapas. José, the chef, had brought out one of the plates himself and was now sitting with the group, talking them through the components of the dishes.

'Keep an eye on things for ten minutes?' Ryan pushed the two glasses of red he'd just poured toward Shannon, the waitress, who was standing ready with a tray to deliver it to the table by the door.

'Sure.' She frowned slightly as she loaded the glasses. 'You okay?'

'Fine – I'll be out the back. Fag break.'

'But Ryan you don't…' Shannon found she was talking to an empty space '… smoke.'

Ryan propped himself against the wall in the alley behind the bar, avoiding treading in what looked like a decomposing pile of cabbage leaves, and fishing his phone from his pocket. 'Hi, it's me. Is it too soon to be calling you?'

'Too soon? You mean as in I only saw you a few hours ago?' There was a delicious thread of laughter in her voice. It buzzed him all the way down to his boots. 'What took you so long?'

'Oh, you know, work and stuff.'

'Where are you? I can't hear any background noise.'

'Alley behind the bar.' He looked up at the sky. 'I think it's about to rain.'

'You'll get wet.'

Her voice had softened and grown more husky and the buzz went up a couple of notches. It didn't sound as if she actually minded the idea of him getting rained on. Women had a thing, didn't they, about that whole Mr Darcy/wet shirt scenario? He filed the thought away for possible future reference, hauling his mind and his disappointed body away from where it wanted to go. He had to be back in the bar in five minutes and not in a state of arousal. 'Where are you?'

'In the kitchen, making tea. Cassie just phoned. Michelle's already got a bite on the fake bride. I'm off the hook.'

Ryan whistled softly. 'That was fast. I'm glad. Although now I don't have the chance to practice one-to-one acting lessons.'

'Oh, I don't know. A girl can never have too many skills. Uh... Next week – when you're at the theatre – do you want to stay here?'

'Thank you, but no.' He'd thought about it on the train, anticipating the offer and deciding reluctantly to turn it down. His hours would be erratic and he wasn't going to treat her home like a hotel. It was all too new.

He wouldn't stay with Nadine, but he'd made up his mind he wasn't going to be sofa surfing with Will either. 'I've fixed up to rent a place.' He turned as the back door opened, throwing out a rectangle of light – Eddie, the kitchen hand, taking a genuine cigarette break. 'I have to go.' Ryan dropped his voice. 'Good night. Sleep well.'

Nadine stood at the bedroom window, looking down into the street, nursing a mug of chamomile tea. She should be asleep already. Tomorrow she had a full day of meetings and, knowing Glen, he would already have designs worked up for her to see. She sipped the tea and watched one of her neighbours attempting to insert his vintage Jaguar into a space that was at least a foot too short. Across the road the teenage girl from number twenty-seven was saying good night to her boyfriend in the dense shadow of a hedge. They'd been there at least fifteen minutes. Nadine was trying not to look. *Envy is a narrow, petty emotion.* She stretched, feeling the muscles in her body tense and relax, and thinking of Ryan. Had he got caught in that shower of rain? Her imagination started to fizz. Soaking wet. How hot would that be?

And if you keep feeding that *image, good luck with trying to sleep.*

As it was Ryan's whispered good night was still reverberating around her system.

In the street the Jaguar driver finally accepted the laws of mathematics and headed off to hunt down a bigger space. The young lovers were still entwined, a single silhouette in the dark lee of the hedge. Nadine turned away from the window and went to sit on the bed. Putting down the mug and picking up the TV remote control, she flipped through channels, looking for something to divert her, and settling on an American cop show. She muted the sound and just watched the parade of beautiful people chasing bad guys through unbroken sunshine. Maybe she and Ryan could holiday together? Somewhere warm. *Hot sun, hot guy.*

Possibilities. She stretched out on the bed. There were so many possibilities.

'Your name in lights.'

'Hardly.'

Nadine laughed. 'Well it impresses the hell out of me.'

The tiny foyer of the studio theatre was displaying a small collection of rehearsal pictures for the play that was due to preview the next day. Ryan featured in all of them. Nadine tipped her head back and compared the shots to the real thing, standing beside her. Both were versions of Ryan she'd never seen before. The man in the photo – sharp, louche and dangerous, the man beside her delightfully scruffy in a well-worn, well-washed sweatshirt, tattered jeans and a couple of day's growth of beard. He looked exhausted. *But happy in his skin.*

'I think you're star-struck.' He gathered her in with one arm and planted a kiss on top of her head. 'Let's get out of here, before Jordan decides he needs a few *more* hours of rehearsal time.'

'Go on, you love it.'

'I think I'd better take the fifth on that.' He saw her sceptical look. 'All right, yes, I do.' He was holding the glass door open for her. She went through it and they headed around the block to the pub, another part of the redevelopment, which acted as overspill bar for the studio and semi-official staff canteen, with a small area on a dais set aside for the theatre personnel. Nadine selected a table, while Ryan greeted the barman, ordering drinks and collecting menus.

He dropped them onto the table and sank into the seat opposite her. 'Hungry?'

'Starving.' Nadine looked round appreciatively. The place had atmosphere – the restoration, in traditional pub decor, had been carefully done. She felt a bit like a groupie, sitting in the staff area. Ryan noticed her expression. He grinned. 'I'm with the band?'

'Something like that. Oh, thank you.' The barman had brought over their drinks. He took their food order. Ryan picked up his glass with a tired sigh. Nadine knew he'd pulled extra shifts at the wine bar, setting up for the handover to the relief manager, and then had gone straight into rehearsals here in Bristol. They'd managed one snatched meeting, the day he arrived, and a nightly phone call. She studied his face. Now she was free to really look at this man, who had meant so much to her for so long. The thought sent a strange shiver down her spine. It was early evening, in an hour or so the place would start to fill up, but now it was quiet.

'Sorry I haven't been around much. And this.' Ryan gestured to the sweatshirt and jeans.

Nadine shook her head. 'Working.'

'Yeah, like twenty-four seven.' He stifled a yawn. 'I'd forgotten Jordan's middle name was sadist.' He took a grateful pull at his beer, then set it down to take her hand and look into her eyes. This time Nadine's insides shivered. 'So,' he said softly. 'How have you been?'

They talked trivia for an hour. Sausage and mash was delivered and eaten. Nadine declined a second glass of white wine, laughing. Ryan's eyes kept closing and his conversation was getting more and more random. 'I think you need to crash. Come on.' She got to her feet. 'I'll walk you home. My car's parked that way.' They ambled down the street and round the corner to the building housing Ryan's rented studio flat. Nadine curled her hand into Ryan's and matched her step to his. 'I almost forgot – Maisie, the fake bride, has a first date with you know who tonight.' She kept her voice soft. 'Would you believe they're going to the theatre? The Old Vic – and a meal afterwards.'

'He isn't hanging around.'

'That's what Jake said.' She didn't know whether she was relieved or disappointed that the Slimeball had chosen Maisie. She suspected a little of both – but she and Ryan were together now. She didn't need an excuse to see him, and Maisie was a professional, so it was probably for the best. She pulled on Ryan's hand. 'I think this is your front door.'

'Oh!' He stared owlishly at it. 'Are you coming in?'

'Not tonight.' She softened the refusal with a brief press of her mouth to his. 'I think you need to sleep. *Alone*,' she emphasised, seeing the sudden glitter in his eyes. He opened his mouth to argue but it turned into another yawn.

'Ah... Sorry. I have to say that it will be good to get out of these clothes and into a shower.' He straightened up. 'Oh God.' He sniffed at his armpit. 'Do I smell?'

'You smell fine.' She snuffled her nose into his chest to prove it. Warm, male, Ryan. A perfect combination. She reached up and wound her arms around his neck, pulling his head down for a kiss. Soft and sweet and sleepy and full of promise. 'Call me in the morning.' She gave him a small push. 'Now go.'

Chapter Twenty

'Wow!' Michelle's eyes widened as Maisie dropped her handbag and a huge cellophane wrapped florist's bouquet of lilies and roses on her adjoining desk. 'Looks like I don't have to ask how the date went last night.'

'Apparently not.' Maisie was searching the wrappings of the flowers for the card. 'They arrived by taxi just as I was leaving so I brought them with me. Ah.' She located the envelope and flopped into her chair to read it.

'He must be keen.' Michelle leaned over to inhale the scent of the pale pink lilies, then looked up startled as Maisie let out a muted exclamation. 'Hey, what is it?' Her colleague's expression had dissolved from satisfaction to bewilderment. Maisie held out the note. Michelle took it.

'Dear Maisie,' Michelle read aloud. 'It was great to meet you last night. I hope you had as enjoyable a time as I did. You're clearly a lovely lady, but on reflection I don't think you're the lovely lady I'm looking for. Please accept these, as a genuine thank you for your company for a delightful evening. I wish you well in your search for the man who will live up to your dreams. John Thackeray.' Michelle looked up, eyes heated. 'Shit! I thought we had him.'

'So did I.' Maisie sighed, crestfallen. 'It seemed to be going well, *really* well. I must've done something—'

'It could have been something in the profile,' Michelle interrupted. 'And that was down to me.' She exhaled, feeling slightly sick. 'Walk me through the date, let's see if we can identify anything. Start when you were getting ready, getting into the part.'

They went slowly through the date, twice. When Maisie had finished the second recital, Michelle's huff of breath was frustration. She knew her colleague's recollection would be as accurate and honest as she could make it, no sliding over slips, or awkward moments. 'There's nothing there. I'm sure you would have picked it up if something had spooked him. The man has people skills and his choice of mark has to be just right. We don't know how much filtering he did before, when he was using the computer dating. Karen might have been the sixth, seventh – who knows how many – who got Lionel's profile, before he chose. Maybe he was even stringing along a couple of others at the same time, pretending to be Lionel. This time he's doing it in person.' She scooped a fall of blonde hair back from her face. 'God, I hope so. Let's go and run this past Jake. He'll be expecting a report this morning.'

She stood up, heading for the door. Maisie picked up the note and the flowers and followed.

'The profile was enough to attract him and the date was fine.' Michelle shook her head as they walked down the corridor. 'I'm not accepting that it was anything you did, or didn't do, that put him off. He's picky, our Mr Thackeray.' They'd reached the lift at the end of the corridor. Michelle thumped the call button. 'We'll get Jake's input, and Cassie's, if she's around. Then, I hope, we try again.'

'What?' Nadine rose from her desk to close her office door, so that she could concentrate on Cassie's phone call in private. 'Say that again.'

'He sent a stonking great bouquet of flowers with a "thanks but no thanks" note attached. Maisie is worried that it was something she did. Michelle and Jake think he's just *very* selective in what he is looking for. That could be wishful thinking, but having talked to Maisie I tend to agree with them. Somehow the fake bride didn't hit his buttons.'

'Bugger!' Nadine perched on the corner of her desk. 'What do we do now?'

'I was getting to that.'

'We're going to try again.' It wasn't a question.

'Jake wants to talk about it. Can you get over here now, for an hour, and bring Ryan? My office. Jake's conference room is in use. Benita's not working today, but she's arranged for Tony's cousin to send over lunch for us from the restaurant,' Cassie added persuasively. Benita was Cassie's childhood friend and her partner in their concierge business, which organised everything from dog walking to surprise parties. In marrying Tony, Benita had become part of a large Italian family that stretched to accommodate all her friends as well. Nadine had eaten a number of times at Tony's cousin's restaurant. The food was excellent.

'In that case, I'm on my way.' She already had her bag and jacket in her hand. 'Ryan – I don't know. His first preview performance is tonight. I'll call him.'

'You want to do this?'

Nadine shot a swift glance to where Ryan sat in the passenger seat, then turned her attention back to her driving. 'As plan B, it's a no-brainer. I know you're not keen, but I *can* take care of myself. And I know what this man is, which his other victims didn't.'

She sensed Ryan letting out a long breath. 'I tried to talk you out of it before partly because I was jealous.'

'What?' Startled, Nadine took her eyes off the road again. Ryan was frowning. 'I didn't want you to do it because I was afraid of you getting hurt somehow. I still am, because the man is a bastard, but I know you want to try.' He shrugged. 'Also I was jealous that you'd be with that Slimeball and all I could do was stand and watch.'

His eyes were fixed on her face. Luckily they were stopped at traffic lights. His honesty, and the light she saw there, did some serious stuff to her insides.

'And now?' she managed to ask, before the lights changed.

'Still worried. Still jealous, a bit.' A brief glance showed her a rueful grin. 'Maybe not so much now,' he admitted. 'But let's see what comes of the meeting, shall we?'

*

In the reception area of Cassie's office Nadine found that Benita had come in specially on a non-work day to supervise the unloading of lunch, making sure that her cousin-in-law had provided everything that was needed from the restaurant. She had a grizzling baby at her hip.

'Luca!' Nadine greeted both of them with a kiss, and introduced Ryan. Benita gave him an assessing look. Luca's cries got a little louder and more determined. 'What's the matter, sweetheart?' Nadine touched Luca's cheek.

'Teething.' Benita switched her son from one hip to the other, inspecting some foil wrapped parcels being removed from a travelling container. Satisfied, she turned her attention back to Nadine and Ryan. 'I don't know about "sweetheart". You could have had him as a gift at three o'clock this morning.' She looked at her son, still wailing in her ear. 'Or even now, for that matter.'

Ryan leaned in, holding out his hands. 'Want me to give it a try?'

With a sceptical look Benita passed the baby over. Luca gave a startled and indignant squawk and stopped crying. Pouting, he exchanged stares with Ryan for a long moment, as the two women watched. Then he closed his fingers on the collar of Ryan's shirt, gurgling up at him. With an apologetic grin that didn't convince either of the women, Ryan carried Luca over to the window to consider the finer points of Jake's shiny black Porsche, parked at the kerb outside.

'Would you look at that!' Luca's mother let out an exasperated snort. 'He's like that with Tony too. Male bloody bonding.' Then she laughed, as Luca nodded seriously, in apparent agreement with something Ryan was telling him about the car. Looking away from her son, she slanted an enquiring gaze across at Nadine, tilting her head towards Ryan.

'Early days,' Nadine replied to the question that hadn't been asked.

'Well, he looks like keeper material to me,' Benita declared, before turning to check the rest of the food and catering supplies. Once the lunch had been dealt with, Ryan brought a now smiling Luca back to the reception desk.

'Who are you, and what have you done to my son? Hypnotism?' Benita enquired.

'Practice. My brother Sean has twin boys – I'm default babysitter on date night.' Ryan grinned. Luca patted his cheek. Nadine knew she was in danger of melting all over the expensive tiles of the foyer floor.

Behind them a crash and a curse suggested part of the lunch arrangements had gone off course. Benita turned to deal with it, waving a hand at Ryan. 'If you'd like to keep my son for the afternoon, don't hesitate to ask.'

'Are you trying to get rid of my favourite godson?' Cassie came down the stairs to the reception area. She took Luca out of Ryan's arms, nuzzling noses with him. Luca crowed with delight.

'I give up.' Benita rolled her eyes in pretend disgust. 'I wash him, feed him, burp him—'

'Love him,' Cassie said softly, as she handed the baby back.

'There is that,' Benita admitted. She squinted at her son. 'Come on, sunshine, time to go.' She settled the boy on her hip again. 'Good to see you, Nadine. And to meet you.' She gave Ryan a considering look, before turning to Cassie. 'His Highness has to go to the clinic in the morning so I won't be in until two. Enjoy your meeting.' She shooed the loitering restaurant staff towards the door. 'Someone will be over to pick up the crockery later.'

Cassie, Ryan and Nadine joined Jake, Michelle and Maisie in the conference room on the ground floor. Cassie unpacked the food, including a large chocolate cake. She put that down in front of her own place. There was also mineral water and lemon cordial. 'I suggest we eat first and then Maisie can take us through her date.'

Once they'd eaten and Cassie and Jake had been persuaded to share the cake, Maisie went yet again through the evening she had spent with Thackeray. Discussion went back and forth across the table. Jake leaned back in his chair, hands behind his head, staring at the ceiling. Nadine glanced from him to Ryan. Jake was hands down sex-on-a-stick, drop dead gorgeous, a pleasure to look at, with a rear that could win prizes, but he didn't stir her senses the way Ryan did. Even factoring in that he was married to a friend, there just wasn't the chemistry. *Does that tell you something?*

She started out of her reverie when Jake dropped back into the discussion, putting his hands on the table. 'We've looked at it now from every direction. I don't think there was anything in that date that was wrong.'

'But there was something that wasn't *right*,' Cassie chimed in. 'The weakest link in the background of our fake bride is her supposed financial standing. It's in place, but it's not obvious. Maybe he likes obvious. I think we've been over the date as far as we can. As far as we *should*.' Cassie exchanged a quick glance with her husband. 'The question is now, do we try again?' She looked over at Nadine. 'I think we all know that in the end it's going to be Nadine's call, whether she still wants to put herself out there, but before we get to that, I think we need to step back a bit.'

Cassie's face was serious, unsmiling. She rested her hand briefly on her abdomen. 'We've had one try. It didn't work. Does that tell us we should stop? If we do go on, what does that make us? Determined, or simply vigilantes taking the law into our own hands?'

'But we're not going to do that, are we?' Ryan asked softly. Nadine swivelled to look at him, her stomach giving an unexpected flip. 'We want to catch the guy, yes, but as far as I know we're not planning on stringing him up, tempting as it might be. We're not going to lead him on, not any further than we have to. We're just putting temptation where he can find it.

We won't be taking the law into our own hands. Once we've got him, we hand him over.' He looked directly at Cassie. Nadine's heart was beating fast, watching the exchange between them. 'I do know what you mean,' he continued. 'There are elements of what we're doing that we've all wondered about, but if we stop everything now – what then?'

'He finds another victim,' Michelle supplied. Nadine shifted to look at her. 'We know he's looking. Maybe she will be the one to take him down. Or maybe she'll get broken.'

'While he goes on to some other con,' Jake capped the thought. 'I can totally see where Cassie is coming from on this. Okay – we had a try, but it was more or less through the agency. If we move outside that… If Nadine takes it on – then, it gets personal. I don't want to be throwing all that on her.' He looked over at Nadine. Her heart was thumping in her ears. *Anticipation and trepidation in about equal measure.*

She met his eyes before he moved to look around the group. 'It will be her decision whether she wants to go ahead or to walk away, and we will respect that. But first I think we confirm that we are all in this. We are all behind her, as a team.'

Nadine's throated thickened. Under the cover of the table she put out a hand to reach for Ryan's. His fingers closed around hers in a quick squeeze. Around the table there was general nodding and murmurs of affirmation. 'I'm not really part of this,' Maisie put in diffidently. 'I understand the issues – but I'd like to think you were going to have another shot.' She looked over at Nadine with a shy smile.

'I think we need to check where we stand.' One by one Jake went round the table. Everyone confirmed their part in the team, whatever. Nadine was last. The lump in her throat was even thicker now. Jake smiled at her. 'There you are. We're behind you, but as Cassie said, it's your call. If you've changed your mind it is not a problem. So… do you want to step into the bride's shoes?'

Involuntarily Nadine looked towards Ryan. His expression

was open. No influence either way. *Whatever you choose, he's in your corner.* Something clenched and then unclenched in her chest. She had no idea what. She looked around the table. Everyone here had her back. Her heart was thumping with trepidation, excitement, anticipation. *Being alive.* There was no way she could let this go. She took a deep breath. 'Yes.' She nodded, for emphasis. 'Yes, I do.'

Chapter Twenty-One

'Do you want me to drop you at the theatre?' Nadine checked the clock on the dashboard. 'Is it too early?'

'No. It will be fine, thank you.' Ryan was attempting to get something out of the pocket of his jeans. If Nadine hadn't had to concentrate on the road, she could have got nicely hot and bothered, watching him struggle. At last he pulled out a small slip of paper. 'It's a ticket for tonight. I know you're coming to the opening with Cassie and Jake, but I thought you might like to see the first performance.'

'I would, very much.' She shot him a quick mischievous look. 'Do I get to snog the leading man?'

'You get whatever you want.' She sensed an interesting tightening of his muscles. 'After a show I'm always a bit wired.'

'That sounds... promising.' She rested a hand briefly on his knee, suspecting that if she moved it higher...

'Nadine.' Her name was a low-pitched growl.

'Sorry, sorry, sorry.'. She put both hands penitently back on the wheel and concentrated on the traffic. Although the rush hour hadn't yet started, everything was moving slowly, stopping and starting at a succession of lights. 'Shall we talk about something else? Thank you for your support over Operation Bride.'

'There's no need. It's your choice. I get that. That you have to try. If we can stop him, then we should. But who knows, maybe you'll get a "Dear Jane" note and a bunch of roses too.'

'Not impossible,' she agreed, checking the rear-view mirror. The car behind was getting too close. She speeded up a little. 'Do you have any instant acting tips?'

He thought for a moment. 'I'd say that you have to believe in what you're doing. Your script is that you're looking for a serious relationship and you're hoping that you've found it with Mr Thackeray. He'll do the rest.'

For a second a qualm skittered up through Nadine's chest. She was about to embark on a bogus love affair with a malevolent stranger, when the man she really wanted was this man, sitting beside her.

As if sensing her unease, Ryan reached over and quickly brushed her hand as it rested on the wheel. Warmth and comfort melted through her bones at the brief contact.

'If you're not happy anywhere along the line, bail out,' he said gruffly. 'You know that you don't have to be unhappy or uncomfortable.' From the edge of her vision Nadine could see that he was looking out of the window, apparently reluctant to go any further. A movement told her when he had turned back. 'How long have you and Cassie been friends?'

Nadine accepted the change of subject without comment. 'Five years? We knew each other before that. She had a boyfriend who used to climb with my husband. After Rory died, she was a lifesaver – the concierge service, that is. I had to throw myself into the firm, to stop it from going under – I didn't want to let Rory's hard work die too.' She swallowed, clearing her throat.

The stillness from the passenger seat gave away Ryan's consternation. 'I'm sorry, I didn't mean to stir up anything painful.'

Nadine shook her head as she slowed for a junction. 'It hurts a lot less now – remembering. I had to get up to speed with the business – to step into Rory's shoes. And they were big ones. My husband was a workaholic,' she said matter-of-factly. 'And there was so much chaos around his death. Cassie held the rest of my life together. She was running her business part-time then, with some help from Benita, from her kitchen table. They stocked my fridge, arranged cleaning and laundry, waited in for deliveries – anything and everything I needed and had no time to organise for myself. If it hadn't been for them, I'd have been eating beans on toast for every meal – until the bread ran out. When I decided to sell the house and move to Clifton they organised that too. In the process they both became good friends.'

'I can see that they would.' She sensed his hesitation. 'Tell me to shut up, if you want, but when your husband died – you said it was chaos?'

'It was.' She sighed. 'You know how Rory died. He collapsed during a sponsored climb in Snowdonia. He had a heart problem that no one knew about. He'd been using Facebook and Twitter and a few other things with names that escape me to fundraise for charities. When he died...' She stopped, swallowed. The nightmare of shock, the formalities and complexities of bringing her husband's body home, the funeral. And she'd never expected... 'Donations just poured in, much more than he would have raised if he'd lived.' She shrugged. 'In those situations, it happens. The story... moves people. I'm glad the charities benefited. Rory would have been really made up to know about that. The friends he'd been with sorted it all out, the donations, got the Facebook page memorialised, all that.'

'And that's why...' Ryan was clearly feeling his way. He'd remembered something, seen something in her. *Body language? Actors would be good at that.* '... Why you don't have any personal social media?'

She nodded. 'Just for the business. I... It had too many associations. I couldn't see myself posting chatty updates of life going on, so I just walked away. And now that might be a good thing, as we think it's one of the plus points that Thackeray looks for.' She stopped the car. 'This is as close to the theatre as I can get.'

Ryan looked around, taking in where they were. 'Oh. Thanks. I'm sorry for raking up old pain.'

Nadine leaned over and put a hand to his lips. 'Every hurt fades.'

She dropped her hand and leaned in a little further. Ryan's mouth met hers and took it, slow and soft and heady. They broke apart with a jerk when someone thumped on the car's bonnet. A group of teenage boys were passing, jeering and gesturing. 'Get a room!'

'Little sods.' Ryan gave them the finger, which was returned with interest. 'Sorry.' He held up his open palms.

Nadine looked at him with amusement. 'I expect you'd have done the same sort of thing when you were young.'

'Possibly. Probably,' he conceded.

'With Sean?'

'Sometimes, but he had Katie, so we didn't hang out together so much.'

'Is he older or younger than you?'

'Younger – two years. He's been with Katie, his wife, since they were both sixteen. They've been married twelve years. The twins are nearly nine.' Nadine could see from his smile the deep-seated affection. 'Someone in the family had to be the steady, sensible one – turned out it was Sean.'

'You didn't turn out too badly.' She gave him a peck on the cheek and a shove. 'You'd better get out, before I get done for illegal parking. Go on,' Nadine instructed. 'I'll see you tonight. Do I get to be a stage door Jane and hang about waiting for you?'

He pushed open the car door. 'I'm counting on it.'

He got out and leaned in through the open window. 'You're going back to work?'

'Yes, and Michelle is going to email the profile for the dating agency for me to tweak. She wants to get it up as soon as possible, before you-know-who chooses somebody else.'

Ryan made a face, before straightening up and away from the car. 'Later.'

Nadine blew him a kiss and watched him walk away.

Nadine sat in tense darkness. By turns frightening, hilarious and heartbreakingly poignant, the three actors on the small, almost bare, stage wove a story of betrayal, loss and abandonment that ripped a hole in her heart. She could sense from the silence and lack of movement from the rest of the audience around her that they felt the same way. Good as the other two actors were, it was hard to keep her eyes off Ryan. When he was on it, he owned the stage. The stranger's descent from ambiguous, threatening predator to hollowed-out, guilt-haunted shell took her breath away. All this light and shadow, living inside the man she knew and wanted to know better. The applause at the end was deafening in the small space. The actors, taking their bows, looked slightly stunned at the reaction.

When Nadine edged her way out from the press of people in the small foyer-cum-bar, all talking excitedly about what they had just witnessed, and made her way to the stage door, Ryan was already there. He slid out from a cluster of well-wishers and came to join her.

'What did you think?'

'Brilliant. But you know that already, or you should.'

She heard him exhale, as if he'd been waiting for her judgement. She could feel the buzz coming off him, like wild electricity. It was intoxicatingly arousing. The air seemed to crackle between them.

They walked away from the stage door, hand in hand. When they reached a patch of shadow in the mouth of an alley, and Ryan backed her against a wall and took her mouth in a fiercely possessive swoop, she was more than ready. She grabbed two handfuls of fabric, to yank him closer, and heard a tearing noise. Whatever he was wearing was apparently toast, and she really didn't care. She tilted her head, asking, no, demanding more. Ryan responded, turning his attention to the line of her throat. Hip to hip she was quivering at the feel of him, hard against her. He had reached her collarbone before some sort of sense prevailed and he pulled away from her, stabbing his hands through his hair, then holding them up, away from his body, and more disappointingly, hers.

'Hell. I'm sorry. I should know better than to pounce like that.'

'I think I gave as good as I got.'

'Er, yes, but even so...' He looked down the alley. 'We shouldn't be here.'

She shook her head. Her whole body was reverberating with the fierce elation running through her. She hadn't felt like this since she was seventeen, thrilled and a bit scared and crazy hot for a boy. Everything about her wanted to be touched, kissed. She held out her hand. 'Then take me somewhere that we should be.'

Somehow he managed to get them back to the block housing his flat, without doing something that could get them both arrested. The studio he was renting was on the top floor. There was a lift. Remembering another tenant's warnings about CCTV, he put Nadine carefully in one corner, while he stood in the other. Her eyes were glittering like he'd never seen them before, promising him things he'd never dared imagine. There were flashes of colour on her cheekbones and he could see her pulse yammering in her throat. He put up a hand to check. So was his.

He had his keys out, the door opened and closed behind them in a time that would have made the Olympic squad. She was back against him, plastered to him, her hands framing his face, mouth on his, before he'd taken two steps. He buried his fingers in her hair, holding her slightly away from him. 'Hey! I'm the one who's supposed to be buzzed, remember?'

'It's catching.' She pulled away, her whole body taken by a shiver, then laughed and held up her hands. 'You're right. This is nuts.' Her chest was heaving. He liked the look. 'We have all night.'

All night. He just stopped himself swallowing his tongue. He could only nod. She was looking down at his body, eyes wide with shock. *What the hell?*

'I did that?' She pointed. His shirt was untucked from his jeans and the seam was split, almost to the armpit.

'S'okay.' He raised his head. 'Never liked the thing anyway.'

And suddenly they were both laughing. He held out his arms and she came into them, soft and warm and vibrating with laughter. He brushed away her hair and found an interesting place, just below her ear, nibbling softly. She squirmed. 'Tickles.'

'Good.' He nibbled some more, hand exploring under her jacket. An indrawn breath told him he'd found his mark. But even so.

He shouldn't ask, but he knew he had to.

'Tell me,' he murmured against her neck. 'Is it Stone doing this, or me?' Stone was the stranger character he was playing on stage.

Nadine stilled, raising her head. 'I hadn't thought – it's you. But they're both you.' She twisted, leaning her arms on his shoulders. 'Why?'

'Just checking. It's just… I didn't expect…' He tailed off as she rested her forehead against his.

'I'm supposed to be cool and inhibited?'

'Hell no! Well at least—'

'You were planning on having to seduce me?'

'Thought had crossed my mind.' He breathed out, slowly. 'I didn't know what you might want. What you might need. Whatever it was, I wanted you to have it.'

'What I want is you.' She moved her head, to nuzzle his ear, then bit.

'Shit! That does it, woman.' He hauled her unceremoniously into his arms. 'The sooner I get you naked, the better.'

'Yes, please.' The huskiness of her voice right in his ear made things that were already painfully hard ratchet up even harder. He was halfway to the steps and the overhead ledge that held the bed, when a phone trilled.

'It's mine.' She spoke against his neck. 'Ignore it.'

'No.' Stopping, he put her down. 'It's late.' *The phone ringing, late at night.* 'It might be important.'

'It's more likely to be Glen with some brilliant idea for a new design for a bed. He has no sense of time. Honestly,' she asserted as Ryan shook his head.

'It will only take a second to find out.'

She was clearly puzzled by his insistence, but he couldn't let it go. The cold breath of memory was whispering down his spine. Memory of the night his baby nephew, Ross, had been rushed to hospital with suspected meningitis. Occasionally a call in the night still turned his guts to ice and tonight it was happening again. Rationally he knew why. He'd poured himself out on stage and his nerves were close to the surface. 'Just a second,' he repeated. Then it would be all right. It was always all right. And the chill would go away.

Nadine pulled out her phone. 'It's a text. From Michelle. Oh. My. God.' She looked up, eyes wide. 'Thackeray has taken the bait.'

Chapter Twenty-Two

'He's invited me to a gallery opening, tomorrow.'

'At the Cloister? I saw the posters. It's that local artist who made it huge in America.'

Nadine's heart was thumping, but not in quite the same way as it had been a moment ago. She checked the phone again to be sure she hadn't made a mistake. No mistake. She had a date with John Thackeray. Exhilaration rushed through her. Plan B was working. She put a hand to her mouth, to control the sudden burst of laughter. 'What do I do? What do I do?'

'Say yes?' The quietness of Ryan's voice sent exhilaration scattering. She was suddenly aware of his stillness, and of an emotion in his eyes she couldn't decipher.

'Not... Not if you don't want me to.' She held out an uncertain hand, feeling a burst of relief when Ryan seemed to focus and took it.

'We talked about that. It's fine. *Really.*' He raised her hand to his mouth to kiss the palm, sending shivers up the inside of her wrist and all the way to her heart. 'You want to do it, so you do it. I was just...' He stopped. 'It's the right thing to do.' His features relaxed into a smile. 'I just wasn't expecting it to happen this fast.'

'Nor me.' Nadine looked down at the phone. 'I can still say no – tell him it's not convenient.'

'And lose him to the next woman on the list? No.' He let her go. 'Apart from anything else, tickets for that exhibition are like gold dust. You'll enjoy it.'

'I'd rather enjoy it with you.'

'I'm not the one with the tickets.' She thought she saw a brief spasm pass over Ryan's face, before his eyes narrowed with thought. 'Either the guy plans ahead, or he has quite a bit of influence – it's the artist's first exhibition in Bristol for about ten years. It's been a hot ticket for weeks. Go on, tell

Michelle to accept on your behalf.' He nudged her elbow. 'It's only a first date.'

'It is.' Rapidly she texted back. 'Done.' She smoothed her hair back behind her ears. 'I'll have to take over the profile so he's talking to me direct, not Michelle.' She shivered suddenly. 'Ryan... It's happening.'

He pulled her towards him, holding her against his side, kissing her hair. 'Don't panic. The man is a con artist. He's not Bluebeard.'

'But... It's not just a date, or even a few dates. I have to get him as far as proposing. And beyond that.' Suddenly the enormity of what she was doing was digging huge holes in the pit of her stomach. 'Ryan!' It was almost a wail.

'*Don't* panic.' He held her slightly away from him. 'You know you can tell him to take a hike at any time.'

She looked up into Ryan's face. 'But that's not how it has to be, is it? I have to... believe... or it's not going to work.'

'You have to be convincing. But how hard is that going to be? We know the guy has a huge ego, or he wouldn't be doing this. He's going to be rolling out the red carpet and he's going to *expect* you to be bowled over. Acting advice, remember? Go with the flow and enjoy yourself.'

'He's going to think I'm pretty stupid.' Now the surprise was abating, something else was stirring.

'He's going to think you've suddenly found what he's offering – the man of your dreams. And that you won't be able to believe your luck.'

'Stupid and desperate and gullible!'

Ryan laughed. 'Nobody's perfect. But I think you're right. He doesn't have a very high opinion of women. Which will work in your favour, because he won't be imagining that he is being set up.'

Nadine shook her head, dislodging her hair so that it fell back around her face. She tipped her head to look up at Ryan. 'You know, this is weird, talking to you about how I'm supposed to fall for another man. Pretend to fall,' she corrected quickly as something flickered briefly in Ryan's eyes. She put up her hands to grasp his shoulders and draw him close.

Gently he unlatched her fingers and pushed her hands down again.

'What?' Alarm shot through her at the look on his face.

'Don't take this the wrong way – *don't!*' He captured her chin and held her face still. 'While this is going on, I don't think we should be together... like this.'

'Like what?' She jerked out of his hold as the implications of what he was saying registered. 'You mean...' Her eyes flitted to the overhead ledge, like a balcony, that held the bed.

'Yes,' he confirmed quietly.

'Why?' Anger and something else – fear, she recognised with a surge of panic – swirled through her. 'Because you don't want another man's leavings?'

'No! Nadine...' She stepped away, he came after her. 'It's not that *at all*. I told you not to take it the wrong way.'

The back of her legs hit the back of the sofa. She couldn't go any further. Ryan stopped, close, but not touching her. 'It's not about what might be happening with him, or about jealousy.' He forestalled what was about to come out of her mouth, holding up his hands. 'Truth – I'm as jealous as hell. Green with it, but that's not the reason. This is not going to be easy, Nadine. I think we're just beginning to realise that.' The look in his eyes echoed a small cold jitter in her stomach that she had been trying her very best to ignore. 'It's just that...' he took a deep breath '... if we're sleeping together it's going to make it harder. A distraction.'

'Huh!' The anger flared again, fed by that cold jitter. 'You think you're so much of a stud that I won't be able to keep my mind on what I'm supposed to be doing?'

'Of course.' His mouth was quirked at the corner, in the way that always sent a shiver down through places – places she did not want to hear from right now. He was laughing at her, the bastard! He caught her hand as she raised it and she hadn't even decided if she was going to thump him. 'Don't get mad, *please*.' The laughter had faded from his face. There was warmth still in his eyes, but of a different kind. Deeper. Something very deep in her stirred in response. 'I think if we had made it to bed tonight, before you took that call… well, things would have changed. I'm arrogant enough to think that.'

Nadine pulled in a breath and let it out again, slowly. She understood. He was right. What he was saying did make sense. *You don't have to like it.*

'I don't like it,' he voiced her thought. Had he seen it in her eyes? 'Actually I hate it. But I just feel that what we have… us… it's just starting and I don't want it mixed up with Mr Bastard Slimeball Thackeray.'

'I see.' She stepped closer and raised her head, pressing a kiss to the corner of his mouth. 'Think you'll ruin me for all other men, do you?'

'Something like that.' Very gently he closed his arms around her. 'It's not a caveman thing. It's just… instinct? A feeling that something between us might get spoiled?'

'I understand.' And she did. Hard to get her head around, but at a level she couldn't define, it made sense. And somehow, inside her, something was at peace with that feeling.

There will be time for you with Ryan. There will *be time.*

'Forgive me?'

'Yes.' Her legs wobbled and she leaned against the back of the sofa, eyes flicking regretfully back up to the balcony bed. 'Are we going to be able to see each other?'

'That's not going to be easy either, if the rest of us have to stay out of sight.'

'It's not, is it?' She sighed. 'I'm beginning to regret getting into this.'

'Really?'

'No. I want to do it.' She rested her head on Ryan's chest.

She could feel his heart under her ear, beating strong and steady. 'It is not going to be quite the caper that we thought though, is it?'

'I don't know. It can't be bad, if we make it as far as the Riviera.'

But if we do, I'll be with the wrong man.

She eased back in Ryan's hold. 'Calls might be a problem, but I can text you.'

'That would be good,' he agreed. He dropped a light kiss on her forehead. 'As I've managed to take the bloom off the evening, if you're up for it, I'll walk you home.'

She considered for a moment. She had taken a cab to the theatre, not wanting to juggle with parking. 'I'd like that.'

He looked down. 'I think I'd better change my shirt first.'

It was a soft night, and unusually warm for the end of May. Nadine would never have thought of walking to Clifton instead of taking a cab. She hadn't been walked home by a boy since senior school, but as they started out she knew it was a sweet, inspired idea. At first the route took them through the crowded streets and bars of the city centre, but as they made their way up, past the cathedral, towards her home, noise and bustle gave way to the quiet of residential roads. A thick hedge of jasmine was in bloom, perfuming almost the whole length of a street. Nadine gave a small shiver.

'Cold?' Ryan adjusted his arm to hold her closer. 'Do you want my jacket?'

'No and no.' It wasn't the temperature that had prompted that shiver. She had just remembered the young Romeo and Juliet in the shade of the hedge, outside number twenty-seven. When they finally reached their destination Nadine stopped, drawing Ryan towards her. His mouth was warm, the pressure firm and sure. She had a fleeting pang for what might have been, where she might have been right now, then pushed it away. *Why waste what's happening here, this minute?*

At last Ryan let her go and watched as she let herself into the house. She hurried to the window to wave, then watched as he strode away. Tonight hadn't turned out the way she'd expected, and tomorrow she had a date with a stranger. But a walk on a warm spring night and a goodnight kiss in the shadows had its own magic.

The kind of magic she hadn't felt in years.

Ryan retraced his steps, back down to the city centre, wondering exactly what sort of a fool he was being. Had he cut himself off from something he'd never dreamed to get, for the sake of a warped, machismo fear of sharing? His body, and some parts of it in particular, was telling him that he had. He and Nadine could have been together now in his flat, her soft warm limbs wrapped around him... The groan he gave earned him a startled look from an elderly man walking a King Charles Spaniel sedately along the kerb. If this was his own crazy version of masochism, he was paying for it. Regret now, and fear for the future. Only a tiny speck, but there.

What if you've blown it? What if you can't get it back? By the time this is over will she have changed her mind? What if she finds she prefers him to you?

No. His mind skittered. *Not him, but the kind of man who can give her that lifestyle. What if she realises how far out of your league you're playing?*

The questions tumbled through his head, making his step falter. He'd almost turned to go back, to bang on her door, tell her that he'd been talking crap, when his mind caught up with the voice of fear kicking its way through his brain. Nadine needed space to do this. It was the best and biggest thing he could give her.

If they'd spent the night together...

However much he might be beating himself up now – and he was doing an excellent job – the decision had been right. To have started something, then have to put it on ice, would have been torment. Trying to juggle both, maybe even worse. He was jealous, but that was because Thackeray would have her time, her attention, her company. He had no doubts about Nadine. On one level his trust in her was rock solid. *Which doesn't mean she can't realise that she's made a mistake.*

Tonight could have been... He caught his breath as the image of what it might have been played behind his eyes – tangled sheets, entwined limbs, moonlight and shadow and heat. But how much worse would it have been if she'd opened that text *after* a night like that?

And maybe it won't get beyond a first date?

Chapter Twenty-Three

The exhibition was amazing. The excited chatter and plethora of red dots on the paintings confirmed that the artist had a hit on his hands. But even more than the paintings Nadine was drawn to the sculptures that were the work of the second artist on display – figurines of wild elfish figures, some dancing, some mounted on foxes and wolves, some holding swords and crossbows. They matched her fey, edgy mood. She consulted the catalogue. The statues were well within her price range, unlike the paintings. What would Thackeray think if she bought one? Was it the right thing to do on a first date? Wasn't this supposed to be about him? About them? If she'd been with Ryan, she wouldn't have hesitated. He would have helped her choose. *Mustn't think of Ryan. Mustn't compare.*

Unable to help herself, she took a quick phone shot of her favourite, an androgynous figure crouched beside a moon gazing hare, and sent it to him. Gonna buy this. He'd be on stage now, and wouldn't pick it up until later, but at least he would know, be part of her choice.

She'd made up her mind. She would buy it tonight. It would establish her as a woman with the money to indulge herself. *And isn't that what Thackeray is looking for?* He'd been the perfect date, so far. She'd been ready for nearly half an hour, pacing nervously by the time he arrived, exactly on time, to collect her, in a top of the range Audi. She, Cassie and Michelle had consulted exhaustively on what she should wear and where they should meet. They'd settled on a grey linen trouser suit by a local designer and a pick-up at the office, rather than her home. It was all supposed to look casual and easy.

Surprisingly, once she was ensconced in the passenger seat of the car, her nerves had subsided. She'd made enthusiastic conversation about the exhibition, researched by the inexhaustible Michelle. As they'd drifted around the exhibits

Nadine had relaxed, giving her honest opinions, and graciously expressing thanks when informed that the show would be followed by a late dinner.

Thackeray had excused himself a short while ago, heading to the bar to refresh their drinks. She'd spotted him a moment later, in conversation with a tall man in a sharp black suit, who was definitely 'someone'. A business acquaintance, or someone from the gallery? She slipped her phone into her bag as she saw Thackeray returning. He was ushering a woman, in a flowing embroidered robe, towards her. Nadine arranged her face into welcome mode and waited for them to reach her through the crowd, which was thinning, but still numerous enough to impede their approach.

Watching and waiting, she took stock of Thackeray. Tall, athletic build, dusty blond hair, dark eyes, clean-shaven. She had to admit to herself that he *was* good looking. Not jaw-dropping so, but enough to have two or three pairs of female eyes following his progress, besides her own. It was as much a matter of presentation as looks, she decided. Good grooming, excellent tailoring, expensive hairdressing and dentistry, but none of it ostentatious. There was a confidence in his stance and movements that some women would probably find appealing. A man who knew where he was going, and was ready to take you along with him. Disconcertingly he wore the same aftershave that Rory had favoured. For a moment the once-familiar scent had thrown her, but there was no way that he could have known *that*. It was just coincidence. *You're jumping at shadows*.

Thackeray and his companion had reached her. Nadine accepted the glass he was offering and directed an enquiring smile towards the woman. There was maybe an edge of smugness in Thackeray's smile as he introduced them. 'Nadine, this is Monique Collette. I've been telling her how much you admire her work.'

'You're the sculptor.' Nadine didn't have to manufacture

her enthusiasm. 'I think the statues are intriguing.' She pointed to the hare and its elf. 'In fact, I like that one so much, I'm going to buy it.'

Buying the statuette had been the right thing to do. Nadine settled herself into the stylish but uncomfortable seat that the waiter held out for her, accepting a menu. Thackeray was giving off the vibe of a man who had produced something special on a first date, and who was well satisfied as a result. Nadine shifted in the skinny metal chair that was already digging into her back. The place was full. She recognised several of the people she'd seen in the gallery. Obviously this restaurant, with its industrial brutal decor, was the venue of the moment. She hoped the food was less austere than the furnishings.

It was, but not by much. Small, exquisitely arranged portions in combinations she would have never imagined, which mostly worked, but in her view didn't really amount to 'dinner'. As her stomach was churning gently with the effort of making conversation, the fact didn't bother her too much.

Actually it was easier than she'd anticipated. She'd had plenty of practice, when Ryan had simply been her social escort, in looking like a couple without actually being one. It wasn't too difficult to draw on that experience, to talk about books and films and plays and the show they'd just seen. *Thank you, Ryan.*

Thackeray seemed to have read what he should, and seen what he should, and talked fluently and amusingly about it. He genuinely caught her interest when describing a couple of major art exhibitions that had just ended in London. He spoke easily, offering opinions, but mostly drawing her out, to talk about herself. Quite delicately, she had to admit. *But then, he's had the practice.*

Dessert arrived. At least, a plate of something that looked as if it might be found on a beach arrived – two pebbles, one brown, one silver, rested beside a green frond that resembled candied seaweed, circled by pale green foam. Was the seaweed for consumption or decoration? Shifting it to the side of her plate, Nadine made a mental note to warn Cassie not to let Jake bring her here on date night. It probably wasn't likely. Jake was more of a burger and fries and ice cream sundae kind of guy. Cassie had personally trained him on the ice cream sundaes.

'I hope this isn't an inappropriate question.' Thackeray was looking intently at her across the table. Nadine had just put part of a pebble in her mouth. It dissolved on her tongue in a burst of intense citrus and something herbal that made her want to sneeze. Her mind cartwheeled. *What is he going to ask?* 'I wondered,' he continued, 'are you seeing other people? That you've met through the agency?'

Her mind was still cartwheeling, but now it was the answer that was making it spin, not the question. Of course, it was logical that he might ask, but she didn't remember Maisie reporting that. *Does it mean that he's interested? Wanting to size up the competition?*

She swallowed the herbal pebble, deciding that there *would* be competition, but nothing too specific. She cast her eyes down, hoping it made her look discreet, rather than toe-curlingly coy. 'I have seen one or two people. And you?' *Ball back in your court, buddy.*

'One or two,' he echoed her. He was staring at her even more intently now, reaching across the table to take her hand. 'The thing is, Nadine, I've really enjoyed your company this evening. I hope you've enjoyed mine.' Nadine gave him what she trusted was an encouraging smile. It seemed to work. 'I'd very much like to see you again.'

Yes! Nadine hoped her mental fist pump and high-five didn't show in her eyes. Perhaps it didn't matter if they did. He'd take it as a compliment. She wouldn't have to wait for the note and the flowers tomorrow morning. He was hooked.

Well, at least enough for a second date. 'I'd like that too, John. Very much indeed.'

And wasn't that the truth? *Well yeah, sort of.*

Settled on her own sofa, with a large bag of Kettle Chips and the promise of Ben & Jerry's Phish Food to follow, Nadine reviewed the evening. She'd already texted edited highlights to Team Bride. Now her phone buzzed with the reply from Cassie – You go girl! and a grinning emoji. By the limited standard they'd agreed to start – securing a second date – things had gone well. She had been nervous in places, but probably no more so than on a genuine first date.

And you really should stop thinking that way.

She'd had a wobbly moment when they left the restaurant, wondering if Thackeray would expect to kiss her good night. He hadn't kissed Maisie, but he hadn't been planning to see her again. In the event a brush on the cheek had closed the evening, to her relief.

She prodded a little deeper into her feelings, looking down at her left hand and her husband's rings. If this thing happened, then she would have to remove them, to replace them with one from John Thackeray. In Karen's case, a classic solitaire diamond, for which the jeweller hadn't been paid. *If you take off your rings, will you put them back on again?*

Screwing up the top of the bag of crisps, Nadine dropped her head back against the sofa cushions, considering the man with whom she had spent the evening. There was nothing to indicate that he was not the person he represented himself to be. Slight hesitations and evasions could be part of any first date – two people trying to impress each other. She knew she was looking with jaundiced eyes, but if there was anything that was off, it was the feeling that Thackeray was just a little *too* well presented.

She sat up straight, shifting her thoughts. No more analysis. She was a woman who'd just spent the evening with a personable man, who might just be the one she'd been searching for.

Hold that thought.

Her phone buzzed again with a text. Ryan.

Did you buy it?

Going not for the details of the date, but the thing that mattered to her. She texted Yes and pressed send. The response came back within seconds – a single X.

Her real good night kiss.

'Am I going to enjoy this play, then?' Cassie threw Nadine a challenging glance over her glass of orange juice. They were standing in a corner of the tiny theatre bar. A glass of wine waited on the counter for Jake, once he'd parked the car.

'I don't know about *enjoy*,' Nadine said, considering. 'It's not that kind of play.'

'But it's good. He's good. Your boy?'

'He's exceptionally good, but he's hardly a boy. He's thirty-two.' *And am I certain he's mine?*

Cassie looked thoughtful. 'Even allowing for your degree of bias, if he's that good, why isn't Hollywood calling?'

'Right place? Right time? Luck?' Nadine knew her smile was rueful. 'Just because you have talent doesn't mean you get the breaks. And he's trying to go straight. He only agreed to do this for a friend.'

'Go straight – you mean as in get a steady job?' Cassie narrowed her eyes. 'Would that have anything to do with trying to impress you?'

'He should know he doesn't have to impress me.' Nadine sipped her white wine. 'But I think I come into the equation somewhere,' she admitted.

Cassie nodded, without speaking.

Earlier, when Nadine had told her about Ryan's decision to put their relationship on hold, Cassie had looked surprised, then expressed approval. 'He's got you taped, sweetie. Nice girls don't run two men at the same time, and whatever else you are, you are essentially a nice girl.'

'*That* makes me sound like twenty varieties of boring. Thanks a bunch.'

'Not boring,' Cassie reproved. 'Playing around just wouldn't suit you.'

A cool draft of air signalled the outer door of the bar opening. Nadine didn't need to look round to know that Jake had just come in. The way Cassie's face lit up told her. There was a pang near her heart that she recognised as envy.

'Don't worry, hon,' Cassie leaned forward to whisper in her ear. 'You'll be seeing your boy in ten minutes.' A wide smile curved her mouth. 'Then you can look, even if you can't touch.'

The applause was deafening, even louder than on the preview nights. Drained and wired at the same time, Ryan pasted on a smile as he bowed, yet again, hand in hand with Rachel and Steve, the other players. He squinted into the darkness surrounding the acting area. Nadine was somewhere in the blackness. In a few minutes she would be going home for supper with Jake and Cassie. He wouldn't have been seeing her tonight, even if Thackeray had not existed. Rachel had organised a first-night party at her digs, inviting a crowd of old friends, ex-students from the theatre school where she'd studied. She wasn't going to let him slide out of it. Not that he intended to. Loud music, greasy pizza, lukewarm beer. Student memories. It wouldn't have been the sort of place to take Nadine.

His world, not hers.

Nadine was having the time of her life.

Or would be if John Thackeray was really the man of her dreams.

Five more dates in ten days. Yesterday he'd turned up at her office in the morning in an open-top sports car, with a picnic basket, to whisk her off to a stately home that she'd casually mentioned she admired, but hadn't visited since Rory was alive. She had enjoyed prowling around the house full of antiques and then spending a sunny afternoon in the grounds, once she'd carefully hidden her irritation over Thackeray's assumption that she would drop everything to accompany him. If it had been a day out with Ryan it would have been different, but Ryan understood about work. He would have asked first. At least the picnic had been excellent, and plentiful. John had sheepishly confessed to his shock at the size of the offerings from their first date restaurant and they'd both laughed, and at that point she'd quite liked him. Tonight they were going to some sort of immersive theatre event at a secret location. Another exclusive ticket. Whoever Thackeray really was, he had connections.

This time she'd made the time and place she expected to be picked up quite clear. Their seventh date. Her heart started to thump as she checked off a couple of spreadsheets on the office computer. Had they gone beyond the point where he might drop her? Surely they had. *But he still hasn't kissed you.* Every evening she'd nerved herself and every evening he'd handed her out of the car with a brush to the cheek and a squeeze of the hand. She scowled at the screen. With him *and* Ryan she was in danger of developing a serious complex over her physical attractions. Not that she wanted to kiss Thackeray, but it would be nice to get it over with.

Catching herself, she started to laugh. Not the way Thackeray would expect her to feel over the prospect of kissing him.

Trouble is, girl, you've tasted the good stuff...

'Something wrong?' Dom, the Finance Director, put his head around the door, clearly alarmed that the boss had found the financial forecasts amusing.

'No. I just remembered a joke, that's all,' Nadine excused herself hurriedly and gave her attention back to the screen.

*

'The little fella looks quite at home.' Thackeray had turned up twenty minutes early, which had made it difficult for Nadine to avoid his request to see the newly-delivered sculpture in situ. She'd temporarily put it on an open shelf, in what Cassie jokingly referred to as the morning room, until she could decide on the best place to display it. According to Cassie that room was where Nadine should sit to do her correspondence, interview housemaids and make the final adjustments to the household menus and flower arrangements. It had a very nice view of the garden and some excellent original ceiling mouldings, plus the old partner's desk that Nadine worked at when she was at home.

'Nice room, this.' Thackeray prowled over to the French windows to peer out.

Nadine stood by the door. 'I'll just get my jacket and we can go.' She moved into the hall. Thackeray followed her. She was halfway to the hall closet when she realised that her suit jacket was still upstairs in her bedroom. 'Won't be a moment.' She changed direction for the staircase.

'Plenty of time.'

The jacket was on her bed. Nadine slipped it on, checked her make-up in the mirror and reached for her handbag.

No handbag.

It was downstairs, on the hall table, with her mobile phone lying beside it. When she reached the bottom of the stairs Thackeray was standing a few paces away, studying a portrait that had been a wedding present from Great-Aunt Claribel. Her great-aunt had always claimed that it was a Rosetti and that she'd had an affair with the artist. Nadine crossed to the table, eyes on her phone. She didn't remember leaving it lying there beside her bag, but then she didn't remember leaving her jacket upstairs either.

'There was a call.' Thackeray nodded to the phone. 'Text, I think.'

Nadine scooped up the bag and checked the phone. Miss U. R.

126

'Something important?'

'No.' The phone should have been in her bag. Had Thackeray seen the message? No blame to Ryan if he had, she'd been careless. And no real harm done. The conversation she'd had with Thackeray on the first night, about seeing other dates from the agency, surfaced. 'Just a guy I was seeing before…' She let the sentence hang, wrinkling her nose. 'He still seems keen.' She deleted the text, dropped the phone in her bag and turned on her best smile. 'Shall we go?'

The air was humid, dank, and smelled faintly of metal. The flaring light from wall sconces sent strange shadows around a recreation of the Roman Baths that had been constructed in a warehouse on an industrial estate on the edge of the city. The uncertain torchlight ramped up the atmosphere. The immersive theatre presentation was an ancient Roman murder conspiracy, with the audience moving from place to place, piecing together the story in a variety of ways, depending on the order of viewing the various tableaux disposed around the space. It was clever and intriguing, and very frizzy on the hair. Nadine could feel hers coiling into ringlets in the warm damp atmosphere.

She wasn't following the plot as well as she might. Tonight was going to be the night of 'The Kiss'. She was sure of it. There was nothing overt, nothing that couldn't be explained by consideration for the dimness of the setting and the unevenness of the floors, but John's grip on her arm, his hand at her back – small possessive touches – were more in evidence. *Or maybe it was just the darkness, the uneven floor and her nerves.*

Part of her mind was still on the incident of the phone. Had he looked at the text? He'd shown no sign, and not referred to it again. There really was nothing to worry about. She had every right to receive a text message from whomever she pleased. She'd been regretfully punctilious about deleting exchanges with Ryan as soon as she'd received them and they'd been careful over the messages they sent. *Nothing to worry about.*

And if the idea that there was another man interested in her moved things along...

Nadine dragged her mind away from twenty-first century technology and concentrated on what the Roman soothsayer, half hidden in a niche in the wall, was predicting in a bone-chilling whisper.

'I have to say, that was different.' Thackeray guided her towards his car. 'I got the tickets from someone at the tennis club. He was a bit vague about what to expect. Now I know why.' His laugh was rueful.

'I enjoyed it. It *was* different.' Nadine sensed him relaxing at her assurances. *Not the only one who has a few nerves – interesting.* 'I've never been to anything like that before. It was clever, even if we didn't manage to solve the mystery before the denouement.'

'Good.' Thackeray smiled, confidence restored.

Outside Nadine's house, they had to double-park. Thackeray got swiftly out of the car. Nadine waited for him to come round and open her door. Old-fashioned manners were pleasant sometimes. He followed her onto the pavement. Nadine turned towards him. She took a deep breath as he put his hands on her arms. She had been right. Her heart was hammering.

Come on. A woman who reaches the age of thirty-five without kissing a few frogs has led a very sheltered life.

'Nadine?' Just a hint of a question in his voice. Without speaking, she nodded, lifting her face to his.

John Thackeray was no frog. The kiss was everything it should be – pressure, technique, duration – all just right. Very nicely judged. A kiss that any woman would be pleased to receive. *It just happens to be from the wrong man.* They moved apart. John was looking down into her eyes, his own very dark.

The mood snapped abruptly as furious hooting erupted in the road. 'Oh God!' Thackeray turned, raising a placating hand to the motorist unable to get past three cars parked abreast.

'It's okay.' Nadine waved towards the car. 'You have to go.'

'I'll call you in the morning.' Thackeray sprinted round to the driver's side as another volley of hooting announced two more cars joining the back of the queue.

Nadine shut the front door and leaned against it. John Thackeray had kissed her. She pressed her hand to her mouth. She'd done her best to respond with the right degree of enthusiasm, and it seemed to have worked, but she was grateful to the impatient motorists. The relationship had passed the point of no return. She rubbed her hands up and down her arms, fighting the involuntary chill that ran through her. She was going to need all the acting skills she could muster. They'd been focused on the bait and the hook. But now...

The hall, lit only by borrowed light from the street, was full of shadows. She crossed slowly to the morning room, shedding her jacket, turning on lamps and sitting down at her desk to stare at the figurine – the hare and his eerie companion. A tremor of apprehension quivered in her chest. Now she had to carry this through. John Thackeray had to believe that she was really attracted to him. *But why wouldn't he? It's what he expects.*

Nadine tilted her chin and pursed her mouth. She'd come this far, and she was damn well going to see it to the end. All she had to do was act like she was falling in love. Thackeray's ego would be on her side. *You've got this.*

She sat still for a moment, contemplating the statue. The house seemed very quiet. Out in the hall, the grandmother clock whirred up and chimed the hour. Automatically she checked her watch. Eleven o'clock and all's well. Ryan would be offstage by now. Where was he? In the pub with the cast and crew?

On impulse she scrabbled in her bag to find her phone.

'Hi. It's me. Nothing wrong,' she said quickly. 'I know we said we wouldn't call, but I just wanted to hear your voice.' She couldn't distinguish any background noise. 'Where are you?'

'At the flat.' His voice was warm and husky and a shiver of a very different sort ran through her.

'Not gone to the pub?'

'For about ten minutes. I'm glad I didn't stay,' he said simply. There was a slight hesitation. 'How was your… date?'

He knew that there had been one. Cassie was keeping the team, including Ryan, in the loop. Nadine's hand had tightened on the phone. She loosened it and got up to move to the sofa.

'I think it comes under the heading of "interesting".' Briefly, she filled him in. 'You probably would have enjoyed it. A couple of the performers were very good. There was a soothsayer that was especially bone-chilling.'

'So, if it was bone-chilling, they weren't handing out any reassuring predictions.'

'Well, there might have been something about a tall dark stranger.' She emphasised the last word.

Ryan laughed. It flowed through her, like warm honey laced with brandy and chocolate. 'Don't all fortune tellers say that?' There was a pause, as if he'd changed position. 'Where are you?'

'Morning room, with the statue. Where are you?'

'Standing at the window, looking up at Clifton, or where I *think* Clifton would be if I could see it from here. Too many buildings in the way. Or I may be looking in the wrong direction entirely. Hold on.' There was another pause and a scuffling noise. 'That's better. I was dripping on the floor. I got out of the shower to answer the phone.'

'Ahhh.' Nadine let out a long sigh. 'So what are you wearing?' She undid a couple of buttons on her blouse and curled up into the sofa cushions.

'A bath towel and... well, that's about it.'

'Mmm.' She put as much throaty emphasis into the murmur as she could manage, and was rewarded by a satisfying intake of breath at the other end of the line. 'I'm sitting here, imagining it. I have a very vivid imagination. Do you want to know what I'm imagining?' She settled more comfortably into the chair, coiling one of her frizzy ringlets round her finger.

'Please,' he confirmed. The wicked heat in the single word sent goosebumps all over her skin. 'Tell me *everything.*'

Chapter Twenty-Four

Nadine waited until Cassie was at the office before calling to report on 'The Kiss'. Her friend sounded even more exuberant than usual, if that was possible. *Morning sex, lucky cow.*

'Yay! We have lift off!' Nadine could almost feel the air punch coming over the phone. 'Come on then,' Cassie encouraged. 'Marks out of ten.'

'Oh...' Nadine considered. 'Eight for technique, six for artistic impression... zero for emotional impact.'

'Ryan has nothing to worry about then?'

'No.' Nadine held the phone a little closer. 'I broke the rules and called him last night.' Morning sex trumped telephone sex, but she wasn't going to let Cassie have it all her own way.

'Ahhh.' Cassie's low purr confirmed that she totally understood. 'We all deserve a treat from time to time. Oh! Hold on a minute.' There was a short, muffled exchange, then the sound of a door closing. 'Sorry about that. Sophie, confirming her schedule. So... we can now assume things will progress in an orderly fashion to our desired conclusion?'

'Looks like it.' Nadine's sigh caught her unawares.

'Are you okay, sweetie?' Cassie picked it up. 'And is Ryan okay?'

'Yes and yes. It's just... Well, it's happening now, and it feels... strange, that's all.'

'Scary?'

'A bit. And yesterday...' Nadine hesitated, then decided to share. 'I thought I'd left my phone in my handbag, but I hadn't. It was on the table, and there was a new text from Ryan.'

'You think Thackeray read it?'

'Can't be sure. It wasn't anything much. I told him it was a man I'd met before him who was still keen, and he didn't press it. It was just... Well, a little bit creepy.'

'Mmm.' Nadine could picture Cassie chewing her lower lip.

'Probably nothing, and it sounds like you handled it. What's done is done. Now we just have to keep on trucking.'

'Riviera here we come.'

'We hope.' Cassie's voice softened. 'I know this is all down to you, hon, and it's no use *at all* telling you to imagine he's Ryan, because that's not going to work. If it gets to a point when you do have to bail, do it. Even what we've got so far would be a starting point in putting something together.'

'No, I'm not going to bail.' Nadine was pleased to hear how firm her voice sounded, and touched by Cassie's understanding. 'I'm all set for the whirlwind courtship.'

'The essential thing is just to live it. And if you need us, remember we've got your back.'

'Thanks. I'll give you the heads-up when you need to buy a new swimsuit for the Riviera.'

'Hah! One swimsuit!' Cassie laughed darkly. 'I'm gonna bend Jake's credit card but good. I have form in that area.'

Nadine laughed too. She knew the story.

'We have an excuse for a shopping trip.' She stopped. 'I could be buying my trousseau.'

'Oh my God. Oh. My. God. This is for real now, isn't it?'

'Getting that way. We will do this,' Nadine said decidedly. 'And thanks for all the support. Oh before I go – work. Are you going to that business breakfast tomorrow?'

'The woman's networking thing? No. I'm doing clients for a couple of days. Imogen is off.'

Nadine knew that Cassie liked to fill in for staff on the client-face from time to time, to keep in touch with the nuts and bolts of the services they offered.

'So it's a day of parcel deliveries and dog walking? Good luck with that.'

'It has its compensations. There's a rumour about a particularly sexy postman in the city centre. Does his round in shorts.'

'I'll expect details. With pictures, if possible.'

'What do I get in return?'

'A full report on the networking meeting,' Nadine said sweetly, and rang off.

It was just before noon. Ryan was finishing breakfast of toast and coffee, sprawled in front of the Juliet balcony of the studio. The air coming in from the partly open doors was warm and sultry. He eased up from the sofa, yawning, to open the doors wider, looking down to the street below. A woman was approaching briskly along the opposite pavement, crossing diagonally to aim directly for the entrance to the block. A tumble of red curls glinted, momentarily, as a few rays of sunshine burned through the late morning haze. Unless he was very much mistaken, the brisk redhead was Cassie.

Ryan stood quietly for a moment, then crossed to the door of the studio. Concentrating hard, he made out the faint sound of the lift doors opening and closing. He put his eye to the spyhole in time to see Cassie letting herself into the apartment opposite. Backing away from the door, he returned to the low table in front of the sofa, picking up his plate and mug and taking them through to the kitchen alcove to stow in the dishwasher. Then he stood still again, frowning. Memories of an hour on the phone with Nadine last night warmed him for a few seconds, before his thoughts clouded with the knowledge of what she *hadn't* said. *Let it go. It doesn't matter.*

Undecided, he looked over at the door. With a huff of impatience he picked up the keys to the studio, stuffed them in his pocket and went to call on the apartment opposite.

Cassie opened the door and looked him up and down, inspecting the well-worn RSC sweatshirt and loose tracksuit pants. 'Well, I may be wrong, but I don't think you've come to service the boiler.'

'Er... No.'

'How did you know I was here? I assume you did know that I was here?'

'I saw you come in, and Mac said there would be someone. I didn't realise that it would be you.'

Cassie tilted her head. 'I'm assuming, again, that this conversation is not one for the doorstep.' A tiny eye movement up to the CCTV camera surveying the hallway. 'You'd better come in. Technically concierges are not supposed to entertain visitors in clients' premises, but as I'm the boss, I get to make the rules.' She turned and walked along the corridor to the interior of the apartment.

Carefully shutting the door behind them, he followed Cassie down the hall to the main room of the apartment.

'Wow!' He looked around. This was the penthouse, occupying the same area as three studios on the other side. 'This is really something.' The high airy space ran the width of the building, with a long balcony filled with plants and an interior full of cream sofas and contemporary art. He caught a glimpse of a famous work by Banksy. *Serious money.*

'It is rather nice,' Cassie agreed primly. She'd set herself up with her laptop and a cafetière of coffee at the island unit that separated the kitchen from the living area. She snagged a fresh mug, filled it and pushed it towards Ryan. He nodded his thanks and slid onto a tall stool at the end of the bar.

'Nadine called me last night.' He looked up from the mug of coffee to meet Cassie's eyes, and saw the glint. 'She told you,' he said flatly.

'Some.' Cassie was grinning. A bolt of alarm clutched at his chest. *Women share that sort of stuff, right?* The back of his neck was getting hot.

'Don't worry,' Cassie reassured. 'She didn't give away any secrets.' She was still grinning though.

Ryan took a deep breath. *Man up. Do the crime, do the time.* Not that he thought talking dirty to Nadine, and having her talk dirty to him was a crime. Shit! He was tying himself in knots here, and the back of his neck was getting even hotter.

Cassie gave him a long look and abruptly dropped the grin,

giving up her so far successful attempts to make him squirm. 'Why are you here, Ryan?'

He shifted on the stool. The thing might be a fancy designer model, all leather and polished metal, but was damned hard to get comfortable on. Or maybe that was him? The small ball of misery in his gut, that he'd been trying to ignore since last night, was mixing with residual embarrassment. *Why are you here? Put up or shut up.*

He focused hard on the coffee mug. 'Nadine saw Thackeray last night. I didn't ask, and she didn't say, but...' He looked up at Cassie, wondering if she could see the warring emotions in his eyes, and suspecting that she could. 'I probably shouldn't ask you, but I couldn't ask her. He *finally* kissed her, didn't he?' For a moment his heart gave a sickening lurch. He really wasn't sure why he was doing this. *Do you really want to know? And are you* really *asking* Cassie? Before she could speak, he put up a hand. 'No. It doesn't matter. I shouldn't have said anything. Forget it.' He started to slide off the tortuous stool, ready to leave.

'Wait.' Cassie stopped him with a quick pressure of her hand on his arm. Her eyes were very cool and clear. 'You care for Nadine. A lot.' He heard the tiny note of surprise in her voice.

'I know she's way out of my league.'

'All women are *way* out of their man's league. I'm *certainly* way out of McQuire's.' Cassie's eyes glinted wickedly. 'If you realise that, it's an excellent thing.'

Reluctantly, Ryan grinned. 'I know you don't think much of me.' He held up his hands. 'No blame for that. I was an asshole.'

'*Jake* was an asshole,' Cassie corrected. 'You merely assisted. And I believe I'm revising my opinion.' She stretched out her hand again, to briefly cover his. 'You care about Nadine. I happen to believe that is a good thing. And, yes, Thackeray kissed her. Which means everything, and nothing at all.'

The quick spasm of pain was as great as Ryan had feared. *You knew it had to happen. It was just a kiss. Get over it.*

In a second, with a deep breath, he found he had. 'He's hooked.'

'That's the bit that means everything. There will be courtship, a proposal, and wedding plans.' Cassie held Ryan's gaze. 'But that's all. Nadine doesn't feel anything for Thackeray. Because (a) she knows what he is, and (b) she wants *you*, not him. That's the nothing at all part. *You* have no reason to worry. Or to doubt her.' Cassie's gaze sharpened. 'Nadine watched you making out with that very pretty actress on stage the other night. She knows there was nothing between you, right?'

Slightly shamefaced, Ryan nodded. Cassie braced her arms on the granite top of the island unit, leaning away from it. 'That said, I don't think any of us, Nadine included, properly weighed up how much this thing was going to demand of her. You probably knew better than all of us. She's got to act the part of a woman in love to the point of idiocy. And let me tell you, the idiocy is as hard as the love bit. But she knows she can back out. So far she doesn't want to.'

There was a long beat of silence. Cassie pointed a finger at Ryan. 'Are you good with that?'

'If she is, then I am.' A feeling of relief was creeping through him. 'Not happy, but...' He shrugged, then straightened up. 'We're really going to do this, aren't we?' He could hear the note of wonder in his voice.

'I really think we are.'

For a moment they stared at each other. Ryan knew that what he could see in Cassie's eyes was mirrored in his own. Satisfaction, concern, maybe a small edge of fear.

Cassie broke the contact first, holding up her hand. 'There is one thing. Thackeray may have accidently seen a text you sent Nadine yesterday.'

Alarm shot through him. 'Sod it!'

'She handled it – implied she'd met you first, through the

agency, and you were still hanging around. You need to keep being careful.'

'Or stop.' The ball of misery was spinning back.

'Your call.' She looked him over slowly, then picked up a Post-it from her makeshift office, scribbling an address. 'I probably shouldn't be doing this, but if you want to see her, and I think maybe you need to, she'll be here tomorrow for breakfast. We can assume Thackeray will be stepping up his attention, but this is a work thing – businesswomen networking over kale smoothies and avocado toast. Even so, be discreet,' she warned.

'I will.' Ryan stood up, stowing the note in his pocket. The misery ball was fading again. 'Thanks, Cassie. I owe you.'

Cassie made a dismissing gesture as the doorbell rang. She looked at her watch. '*That* had better be the boiler man.'

Ryan surfaced slowly from sleep to find the sun streaming in through the windows. He reached blearily for his phone. When he got it into focus he nearly dropped it like a hot coal. The alarm that he thought he'd set hadn't gone off. *Or maybe you just slept through it.* He had half an hour to get halfway across the city in time for the end of Nadine's breakfast meeting.

Two minutes in the shower, the first thing he could grab out of the wardrobe, and a mouthful of last night's cold coffee, and he was good to go. He was almost at the door when he realised he didn't have shoes. Stuffing his feet into the trainers parked under a chair, he set off at a fast jog.

The foyer was all modern metal, marble and plate glass. Once through the automatic doors Ryan slowed his step, and his breathing, focusing on blending with the hotel clientele, who seemed to be mostly business types. What he'd grabbed out of the wardrobe, blue shirt and black jeans, wasn't what he would have chosen if he'd had more time, his hair was still damp and he hadn't shaved, but he still looked reasonably respectable. *You hope.* Avoiding the concierge's desk, he checked out the signage. According to Cassie's note, the group had a large table set aside in the main restaurant. *Which is that way.*

As he walked towards the floor to ceiling glass barrier that separated the restaurant from the foyer, he saw her. She was sitting at an all but deserted table that still bore debris of breakfast, at the far end of the room. As he watched, the other woman who had been sitting with her rose, gathered up her things and bent for an air kiss, before leaving. They passed in the restaurant entrance, the woman giving him a sideways look. Ryan resisted the urge to adjust the tie he wasn't wearing. There was a waiter bearing down on him. 'Sir?'

'I just want a quick word with Mrs Wells.' He nodded to where Nadine was sitting, working on a notebook. Her head came up fast when she heard his voice. The smile that lit her face made his mad scramble worth it. *More than worth it.* The welcome in her eyes crunched a few things in his chest, and cast some warmth a lot further south. She was perfect, in a plain navy linen dress, with her hair loose and curling on her shoulders. He wanted to bury his hands in that hair and bend his head to kiss her mouth. The waiter, seeing Nadine's smile of recognition, softly excused himself. Ryan barely noticed him go.

'Ryan!' He'd almost reached her. He knew his face was split in the biggest grin. That his heart was pumping in overdrive was a given. He drank her in, like a man in the desert, finding an oasis. He put out his hand to take hers, and saw her expression change. The smile died and her eyes widened in shock. 'Ryan.' Now his name was an urgent whisper. 'John Thackeray. Behind you. Coming straight towards us.'

Chapter Twenty-Five

Icy disappointment, hot fury and a bolt of pure panic fought in Nadine's chest. She couldn't breathe. *Why? Why is he here? Why now!* Her eyes darted, frantically, but there was nowhere to hide. If she had seen Thackeray, then he had seen them.

She looked up helplessly into Ryan's face, wiped clean now of all emotion. He leaned forward to speak, close to her ear. 'Give me the brush off.'

He stared, intently, checking that she understood, before shifting away from her. Even as he straightened, his body language transformed. His stance, the stoop of his shoulders, even the gesture as he dropped his hand to his side, screamed defeat and rejection.

A wave of denial washed over her so powerfully that she had to fight the choke of tears.

Thackeray had almost reached them. He was looking from her to Ryan. Unable to trust her voice, she put out a hand in a repudiating gesture to Ryan, shaking her head. He took another step back.

'Nadine, darling. Is this man bothering you?' Face full of concern and outrage, Thackeray moved to stand behind her chair, reaching for her shoulders. It took every ounce of willpower not to duck away.

She shook her head again, swallowing to find her voice. 'He was just leaving.'

Ryan took his cue, the one he had given her. 'I'm sorry to have troubled you.' His voice was stiff and stilted, with an underlying thread of hurt that almost divided her heart in two. He was acting. She knew he was acting, but the pain came anyway.

'Mrs Wells doesn't need your apologies. Just go.' Thackeray gripped her shoulders possessively, squaring up to Ryan. A thrill of malicious satisfaction laced some of Nadine's distress.

Thackeray had to tip his head. Ryan was a good couple of inches taller, and a lot broader. Ryan shrugged and turned to walk away, passing the waiter, who gave him a puzzled look, before rushing to the table with a clean cup and offers of coffee.

He was probably bringing those for Ryan.

After a brief, freighted pause, when they both watched Ryan walk towards the exit, Thackeray sat down beside her, taking her hand. A strong desire to punch the self-righteous expression off his face sent a sobering shock through her. She sat up a little straighter.

'He was that other guy, the one you met before.'

Nadine nodded, relieved that Thackeray had added his own two and two and that she didn't have to explain. *You mean lie.*

'Good God, I can't believe he's still hanging around.' Thackeray's eyes narrowed and his jaw stiffened. 'He's got the message now.'

'He saw me and just came to say hello,' she protested softly.

'Well, he'll know not to do it again.' Thackeray sat back, with the satisfaction of righteous possession. On the pretext of asking the waiter to serve Thackeray and fill up her own cup, Nadine risked a swift glance into the foyer. There was a flash of blue, near the main door. Ryan leaving.

Thackeray leaned forward, drawing her attention back to him. He was sugaring his coffee, but clearly unable to let it go. 'I'm surprised the agency took him on. He looks a complete lout.'

'He saw me and came over, that was all,' Nadine repeated, resisting the urge to pour her coffee in Thackeray's lap, rather than sedately sipping it. *Lout! He thinks Ryan is a lout. And what the hell are you?*

Her heart had very nearly jumped out of her chest when she'd looked up to see Ryan walking towards her. His hair slicked back, damp from the shower, her favourite blue shirt and a pirate scruff of beard. Surprise, delight and longing had made her mouth water. She looked now at John Thackeray's bland good looks and well-barbered face and wanted to push his perfectly sculpted nose right through to the back of his well-groomed head. The simmering violence was slightly shocking. She took a deep shaky breath, working to get her emotions under control. Gritting her teeth hard, then relaxing, she managed a tremulous smile.

'It's shaken you, I can see, darling.' Thackeray leaned in to pat her hand. 'The man's no better than a stalker. It was a good thing I was here.' He turned to speak to the waiter, who was offering a basket of pastries.

Nadine shook her head at the waiter, declining more food, studying Thackeray as he selected a muffin. *Why is he still going on about it? Alright, he's showing off his machismo and his protectiveness, with which I am supposed to be suitably impressed, but could it...* Hah! Abruptly she saw the tension in the man's movements as he accepted a pastry and a plate. Underneath the smooth exterior, Thackeray was the one who was shaken. *He's not sure enough of you to trust the possibility of competition.*

The realisation sent a surge of power through her. She put down her cup. 'Why are you here? I was so surprised to see you.'

'Came in for an early business meeting with a chap, and spotted you as I was leaving.' Thackeray was making a storm of crumbs with the buttery pastry. 'If you've finished your coffee, I'll run you to work.'

'No need. My car is in the hotel car park.'

'In that case, I'll walk you to it.' He crumbled the last of the muffin onto the plate. 'Make sure there aren't any undesirables hanging around.'

'Ryan had almost reached the table, and then Thackeray suddenly materialised behind him! I wanted to throw something at him! Ryan was brilliant. He really looked as if I'd kicked him in the teeth.'

'Instead of wanting to kick *Slimeball* in the teeth,' Cassie sympathised. Nadine had shut herself in her office to ring Cass and let off steam, as soon as she'd reached work. 'I'm sorry my plan to give you some time with Ryan backfired.' Cassie had already confessed that she'd told Ryan where Nadine would be. 'But how did *Slimeball* know where you were?'

'Just bloody bad luck. He enjoyed telling Ryan to sling his hook though, so I suppose that will stroke his ego. He said Ryan looked like a lout,' Nadine remembered indignantly. *But at least he didn't recognise him from the wedding.*

Cassie gave a provocative little growl, low in her throat. 'A sex-on-a-stick lout.'

Nadine groaned. 'You don't have to tell me!'

'Frustration is a terrible thing.'

'You don't have to tell me that either!'

'Is everything cool now, with Slimeball? He didn't suspect anything?'

'I'm sure not. He invited me to his place tonight for a meal, but I couldn't take hours of just his company. I persuaded him that there's a film I want to see tonight and promised him tomorrow night for the meal instead. I'll have my temper under control by then.'

'Again, I'm sorry, hon. But remember, he's going to get what's coming to him.'

'Too right he is.'

When she'd put down the phone on Nadine, Cassie checked her watch, then crossed to the interconnecting door between her office and Jake's, knocked and opened it, to put her head around. Seeing he was alone, she skipped over and hopped onto his lap.

'Not that I'm complaining, you understand.' Jake settled her more securely on his knee. 'It's lovely to see you. Both of you.' He patted her stomach. 'But to what do I owe this unexpected pleasure? Given that it's the middle of the morning on a working day, I'm assuming your presence is more than an irresistible desire for my company.'

'Nadine just rang.' Cassie wrinkled her forehead, which obliged Jake to kiss it smooth again. After a short interlude, Cassie told him about the encounter at the hotel.

'You don't buy it?' Jake guessed.

Cassie exhaled. 'Nadine didn't seem to think there was anything wrong, and I'm sure Thackeray didn't know about Ryan, but it is quite a coincidence that he just happened to be there, exactly when Nadine was. Nadine had a bit of a scare the other day too. She thought he'd read one of her texts, which may or may not have involved removing her mobile from her handbag.'

Jake considered. 'Think there's a spot of gaslighting going on?'

'Dunno.' Cassie jiggled her head from side to side. 'It's not quite gaslighting, but it *is* a little bit creepy. It's just enough to make me wonder. Prickles on the back of the neck sort of stuff.'

'And you should never totally ignore a prickle. We'll keep an open mind and an eye peeled,' Jake decided.

Cassie planted a kiss on the tip of her husband's nose, before sliding off his lap. She looked at her watch. 'Argh! I have a pair of Borzoi to walk in ten minutes. I'll see you for lunch.'

The proposal had to come soon. Nadine aimed the hosepipe at a large pot of agapanthus standing on the edge of the terrace, trying to analyse how she felt about it. How should a woman feel, expecting the man of her dreams to ask her to marry him? Nervous, excited, blissful? She tried to think back, but she couldn't recall that Rory had ever actually proposed to her. They'd first met at university, been an item for a while, drifted apart after graduation, met again a year later at a friend's dinner party. After that everyone had simply *assumed*... including them. They'd bought a ring on a winter weekend in New York, but it hadn't been an *engagement* weekend.

But now... Thackeray would expect to do it in style, with all the bells and whistles – all part of his plan. She'd been seeing him for nearly seven weeks. At his home – a tall modern townhouse overlooking the Suspension Bridge, that Jake had confirmed was rented by the month – or at hers. They'd dated at recitals, cinemas, theatres, galleries, restaurants and stately homes. They'd spent two weekends away – both surprise trips – one to a boutique hotel on the Welsh coast with wonderful food, an aromatic gin garden and a reputation for a resident ghost. They'd occupied separate rooms.

Deeply uncertain what she should do, and with her heart in her mouth, she'd tentatively hinted that she might be ready to be persuaded...

She'd been gently and tactfully rebuffed.

If he'd wanted to seduce her, the Paris weekend would have been the time.

Turning off the water, Nadine perched on the painted metal bench on the terrace, and looked out over the darkening garden. The Paris weekend had been something special. Knowing she'd been reading American author Eloisa James's account of the year she'd spent living there with her family, Thackeray had put a lot of effort into making sure they visited restaurants, shops and museums mentioned in the book. Now Nadine understood Karen's remark about the man 'getting her'. Thackeray had done his research and followed it through. Just like the job of work it was.

She'd wondered, half in hope, half in horror, whether she'd find a diamond ring nestling in a spinach salad or a glass of champagne, and she'd been pretty sure that Thackeray had been aware of the hope, though not the horror. He was moving her strings like a puppet, and she was letting him. Hell, she was encouraging him. It was a game that she and Thackeray were playing. She was constantly watching and calibrating her responses. Should she act this way, or that? How would a woman falling in love behave at this point? Was it obvious how self-conscious she was, and did it matter? If she was genuinely looking for love and marriage through the assistance of an agency, wouldn't she be just a little self-conscious?

If this had been about Ryan, all she would have needed to do was to be in the moment. Her heart gave a soft bump as she rose to coil the hose. She hadn't seen him since that disastrous breakfast encounter, when Thackeray had squashed their chance of time together. It still stirred anger and regret.

His run at the theatre had ended and he'd presumably left town, without getting in touch. There'd been no texts and no phone calls, but there had been... the postcards.

The first had puzzled her – a jolly picture of a couple of cartoon sheep, the classic cliché message of wish you were here on the back and an indecipherable squiggle for a signature. There'd only been a blurred scrawl for the intended recipient too, although the address was clear. The second card had been a view of Tower Bridge, the third, intriguingly, a picture of the Bodleian Library, with an Oxford postmark. They continued to arrive, two or three a week. She'd kept them all, tucked securely into the small wall safe the previous owner of the house had installed in a cupboard in the master bedroom. She'd started to send them too. Publicity material from work, with pre-printed advertising messages, a picture of the *SS Great Britain*, a couple advertising new businesses in Bath and Bristol. It was a weird correspondence, but it gave her something. She thought it might be hope.

In the pocket of her tracksuit her phone buzzed, intruding on her thoughts. She hauled it out. John. He'd excused himself from a date tonight, pleading work. Did he have something going on, or was he just keeping her keen?

'Hello?' She could hear the huskiness in her voice. She was still remembering the postcards. Maybe it wasn't a bad thing

'Hi. I was thinking about you.'

'I was thinking about you too.' Not a lie, exactly.

'Where are you?'

'In the garden. Just finished watering.'

'Not in bed yet then?'

'Soon. And you?'

'I have some work still to catch up on. Calls to the States, you know how it is.'

'Don't work too long.'

'I won't. Good night. Sweet dreams.'

'Good night.' Nadine disconnected with a sigh. A short, sweet, thoughtful call.

From the wrong man.

Ryan considered the sleek facade of the new hotel. He'd made it as far as the second round of interviews for the post of deputy manager, which was something, even though he hadn't got the job. He looked down the empty road. He didn't have to go back to the car just yet. Plenty of time to walk into Oxford to send another card. Suddenly the sky looked brighter and the air felt warmer.

Cutting off communication with Nadine had seemed the right thing to do. *Yeah, like cutting off your right leg.* He clenched his teeth. It *had* been the right thing. Full-scale deception was tricky enough for Nadine to pull off, without him making complications. Slimeball couldn't stumble over what didn't exist.

With an effort Ryan relaxed his jaw. He'd schooled himself not to think about what was going on in Bristol. Much. And he was pathetically grateful for the occasional call from Cassie, to confirm they were still on track. She knew exactly how pathetic he was, but what the hell, as long as she called.

He'd sent the first card on impulse. He'd seen it in a stand outside a shop a few doors down from the bar. He'd been on a break, snatching lungfuls of wet air under the shop's awning, avoiding the pouring rain, after a fun morning of cleaning up vomit and unblocking toilets. The glamorous side of the wine bar business. Wet, miserable and bloody *lonely*, the two fat sheep in the picture had given him a smile. And he'd wanted to share it. He'd made the thing as anonymous as he could, and posted it. And then, of course, he'd done it again. And again. He'd promised himself that the one sent from Oxford at his first interview would be the last. And then the cards had started to come back in return. Pictures of beds, restaurants, publicity for Cassie's concierge service. He'd just about stopped himself from sleeping with them under his pillow. He thought he could detect her scent on them. *But you know that's imagination.* Maybe he'd send her something from the Ashmolean Museum? If he could go and choose another card, the trip to Oxford wasn't entirely wasted.

Chapter Twenty-Six

'Excited, darling?'

'Who wouldn't be, planning a wedding?'

She really hadn't seen it coming. The surprise weekend this time had been Italy. Florence, a city she'd loved when she'd visited it with Rory when they were students. She'd wondered whether the proposal would come as she stood with Thackeray on the Piazzale Michelangelo at twilight, looking down over the panorama of the city below, with the sun setting and the lights beginning to come on. She kept her eyes open for string quartets or flash mobs of opera singers who might be waiting to come out of the shadows, not quite sure if she was relieved when they didn't. The next day, Sunday, she'd been genuinely delighted to find they were booked into a one day cookery course, learning, with a dozen others, the secrets of real Italian cooking. It had been a fun day and she had been caught up in something that absorbed her whole concentration, in a keen convivial group.

And, of course, it was then, at the end of the day, when the class was preparing to eat the results of their labours at a communal table, that the quartet and the singer emerged. And a cake, with sparklers and 'Will you marry me?' iced in gold across the top. Once she'd said yes, there'd been laughter and congratulations and an impromptu engagement party. Watching Thackeray over her wine glass, Nadine had wondered about that public declaration. Relaxed, smiling, receiving toasts and good wishes – just how sure of her 'yes' had he been? So confident that he could risk the public show, or using it to apply subtle pressure for the outcome he needed?

Once they'd returned home she had removed and stored her rings – which had been easier than she'd expected – in the bedroom safe, on top of the postcards. She and Thackeray had chosen a new diamond together, at Bristol's most upmarket jewellers. *Which we know will never be paid for.*

Now she was sitting in Thackeray's drawing room – there was no other word for the formal setting of antique furniture and fine rugs – waiting for the wedding planner. She leaned back against the dusty pink sofa. Although the house was modern, the classic look suited the space. It was a restful room, and one calculated to impress. A lot of the furniture was supposed to be pieces inherited from family members. Thackeray was behind her, sorting through post that had been on the doormat when they entered the house. By a quirk in the positioning of a pair of ornate mirrors, on two different walls, she had a direct view of his bent head as he leafed through the envelopes.

'But, John, do we really need a wedding planner?' She leaned back further against the cushions. 'Wouldn't it be more fun to do it ourselves?' She waited half a beat. 'Or we could just elope. There are even companies who can organise that. I googled it.' She laughed softly. *Yay! Happy woman without a care in the world.*

Her intuitive dropping of that small bombshell was everything she'd hoped. At the word elope Thackeray's head came up with a jerk, mail forgotten. Alarm and unconcealed anger creased his features. And all visible to her in the double mirrors. He had control of himself in a second. 'Why would we want to do that?' She had to give him marks for recovery. His voice was easy, smooth, indulgent. 'I want it to be a special, perfect day for you, my darling. You deserve it.'

'It's a special day for you, too.' Her voice was commendably steady.

He smiled, ditching the post on a side table to sit beside her. 'The bride is the centrepiece. Neither of us have family – we only have ourselves to please. I want you to have everything you've ever dreamed about.'

'Things I don't even know I want?' She laughed, nestling

her head into his shoulder, so that she didn't have to look into his eyes. He seemed to have forgotten that she might already have had the day of her dreams with Rory. *But that isn't what this is about.*

'Exactly.' He was laughing too. 'This woman comes highly recommended. She'll have all the contacts. We're both busy – having someone to do the heavy lifting takes the pressure off. All you have to do is enjoy. You can have anything you want.'

Nadine's heart had begun to thump. This was it. Time for the bride's outrageous suggestion. 'Well, if we really are talking dreams—'

The doorbell interrupted. 'That will be her.' Thackeray dropped a kiss on Nadine's forehead, indicating that she should stay where she was. 'I'll go and let her in, then you can tell both of us about your heart's desire.' As he rose, the movement dislodged the letters he'd piled on the side table. 'Damn.'

'You go, I'll pick them up.'

Thackeray hesitated for a moment, as the bell pealed again. 'Thanks, darling.'

He hurried out. Nadine shuffled up the envelopes – junk mail and letters in assorted different names, which she presumed were for previous occupants of the house. Nothing interesting. She piled them up on the console table as she heard the front door open, and voices in the hall.

The woman was tall, blonde, well presented, with immaculate hair and make-up, brisk and, to Nadine's mind, a trifle cold. But if her relationship to Thackeray was what they thought it was... She had a large leather portfolio and a separate laptop case.

Introductions were made, with a brief, strong handshake. 'Please call me Penny.' The offer of coffee was declined, and then they were settled back on the sofas.

'Nadine was just about to tell me what she really *really* wants for the wedding.' Thackeray lounged back, his indulgent smile in place. Penny leaned forward – bright, enquiring and alert. *With maybe a touch of wariness in her eyes?*

'It's all been so fast...' Nadine put her hands together. 'But it's really happening. And if I'm going to have the wedding of my dreams.' She turned to Thackeray, with what she hoped was a melting look. 'Then I'd *really* like to be married in the South of France.'

'Well, darling, you are a dark horse.' Thackeray took her hand to lead her back into the house. They had just seen Penny on her way, standing on the steps together. *The perfect engaged couple.*

Nadine tilted her head as he pulled her into an embrace, going for the slightly coy prospective bride. 'Well, you *did* say I should have whatever I wanted.'

'Quite so.' He was laughing. Her request hadn't thrown him for more than a few seconds of surprise, although it had briefly discomfited Penny the planner. Whatever proposals she'd been primed to make had gone out of the window, but she'd recovered fast, listening and taking notes when Nadine outlined a totally fictitious dream day. By the time Nadine finished, she had recovered enough to talk about the planning for a large society wedding in a French chateau, and a celebrity affair in Monte Carlo, both of which had been heavily covered in the gossip magazines. Nadine realised she was supposed to assume that Penny had helped organise them, although she was obviously only repeating things she'd read. Nadine had stifled a wicked temptation to suggest bringing in a planner who was an expert on overseas weddings. That was a provocation too far. Interestingly, neither of them had tried to dissuade her in any way. Penny had handed over a list of websites for wedding dresses and made an appointment for later in the week, when she'd had time to research.

Oh to be a fly on the wall when John and 'Penny' next speak.

'I really hadn't thought about something so unusual,' Nadine admitted. 'But then I remembered. A friend of a friend was married on the Riviera about two years ago, and everyone said it was magical, and I realised, when you said... about a dream day... that's what I want.' Nadine pulled slightly on Thackeray's hands, feigning excitement. *Don't overdo the girlish coyness.* 'Thank you, darling.'

'My pleasure.' He raised her hand to his lips. 'How about we go out to dinner, to celebrate?'

Nadine was shrugging herself into her jacket and locating her handbag, when a quiet curse from Thackeray made her look up. 'Something wrong?'

He was sorting the pile of mail she had rescued. He held up an official-looking envelope. 'A summons for jury service, would you believe, sent on from an old address.' He huffed out an annoyed breath. 'I'll have to sort it out.' He stuffed the envelope into his pocket and held out his hand. 'I thought we'd take a run out to that gastro pub outside Bath.'

'Sounds lovely.'

'Hold on,' Cassie instructed. 'Jake's here, I'll put the phone on speaker.' Nadine heard shuffling and muttering, a muffled giggle and the sound of an overburdened chair squeaking in protest, and then Cassie was back. 'You met the wedding planner. Tell all.'

Nadine related the details of the meeting, including the kite she had flown over an elopement, and Thackeray's reaction.

Jake swore softly. 'Well now we know for sure the bastard is working a con.'

'As if we didn't before,' Cassie objected.

'Always good to have confirmation. We're weaving a web of lies, but so is he.' Nadine's grip on the phone relaxed a little. Jake's unspoken perception of her position was a reassurance she hadn't known she needed. 'How did the idea of the South of France go down with Thackeray?'

'Didn't bother him at all.'

'Thinks on his feet, our Mr Thackeray,' Jake supplied thoughtfully. 'Everything is in place in Nice. The venue you are going to choose is lined up. All you have to do is feed Penny the details, and find some inventive reasons to turn down *her* suggestions. We've made sure that there will still be scope for them to improvise on your choice.'

'Did you get a look at the woman's portfolio?' Cassie asked, curious.

'Yes. All very upmarket stuff, ideas about colour schemes and themes and such. It was impressive, so I think we might be right, she does have experience. She had a slick presentation on her laptop, but I'd rather stolen her thunder by wanting to take it all abroad. She slid over it quite well, turned it into, "This is what I do," but I think it was suggestions she would have made about venues and catering. One of the places looked familiar. She did make it clear that she was all about the wedding. My dress, and those of any attendants, would be down to me.'

'They're focused on things that they can avoid paying for up front, in which we will oblige them,' Jake observed. 'Did Thackeray float the idea of a joint account for expenses yet?'

'Yes, last night, over dinner.' When he'd plied her with most of the bottle of wine, on the grounds that he was the one driving. Nadine shivered, although the morning room was warm from the early morning sun. *Softening her up.* 'We're supposed to be arranging it tomorrow.'

'The start of the end,' Jake said, with quiet satisfaction. 'Once it's done, he's committed to something that we *know* is in a false name.'

'Talking of names, I got sight of a whole bunch of post. Junk mail to previous tenants. There was nothing that looked interesting, but he had another letter too. A summons for jury service. He told me about that one. He said it was forwarded from a place where he used to live, but I've been thinking back and I don't remember any official-looking envelopes in the pile I picked up, or on the table. It was all junk mail and circulars.'

'You think Penny gave it to him?' Cassie speculated.

'It's possible. They were in the hall together for a few minutes.'

'Interesting,' Jake commented. 'Sounds as if it might be genuine,' he added, thoughtfully.

'You think it might be for the real John Thackeray, whoever he is?' Cassie chipped in. 'He has to have a real identity somewhere.'

'But why did he tell me about it? There was no need. I didn't even see the envelope,' Nadine questioned, puzzled.

'Jury service isn't something you can easily turn down.' Jake still sounded thoughtful. 'Telling them that you're living in another part of the country, under an assumed name, isn't really going to cut it as an excuse. If he doesn't want to rock the boat wherever his real base is, maybe he's already thinking he'll have to go through with it. He might even want to, if it contributes to a respectable reputation he has somewhere else. If that's the case, why *not* tell you the truth? If he has to decamp in the middle of wedding plans, it plays a lot better than some fabricated business crisis,' Jake suggested. 'Don't be tempted to ask questions,' he warned. 'Best if we just wait and see.'

'And in the meantime, we have to make everything on our side look authentic,' Cassie took over the conversation. 'You mentioned a wedding dress—'

Jake growled an objection. 'If this is going to degenerate into a discussion about *shopping*—'

'— of course it is.'

Nadine could almost hear Cassie's grin over the phone. 'But I don't actually need a dress,' she protested. 'I have things in the wardrobe—'

'South of France,' Cassie said firmly. 'I think we should take a trip over to Cardiff, hit the shops in the St David's Centre.'

'Excuse me?' Jake interrupted. 'Bristol, Bath, shops?'

'I feel like a change. And Cardiff has a Victoria's Secret store,' Cassie pointed out sweetly.

Nadine drew a breath to point out that so did Cabot Circus, but the faintest warning hiss from Cassie kept her silent.

'In that case, ladies,' Jake was laughing, 'Cardiff sounds like an excellent idea.'

The back seat of the car was crammed with parcels. Nadine eased back in the passenger seat, glad that Cassie had elected to drive. She slipped off her shoes. Her feet were vibrating rhythmically, and her calf muscles were joining in the chorus.

Cassie's insistence on driving over the Severn for the expedition was explained when she disclosed a top-secret commission she'd placed with a manufacturing jeweller in one of the Victorian arcades that crisscrossed Cardiff. 'We went to a thing in London. Something about business funding for the film industry. I was only there for the scenery. And what scenery.' She rolled her eyes. 'Jake got chatting to Dan Howe – the one who makes all the action movies. I just stood there and tried not to get drool on my dress. He had some cufflinks that had been made for him when he was filming in Wales last year. Jake admired them, so that was his birthday sorted. They've designed and made me something similar, but not the same.' She grinned. 'They're very Jake. They would have posted them, but I said I'd collect.'

The cufflinks were indeed spectacular, and looking at the original designs in the shop, some from repurposed pieces, Nadine had the beginnings of an idea about her wedding and engagement rings.

She grinned. It had been a very successful day. Her friend's idea of a capsule wardrobe had elastic sides. There were four boxes of strappy sandals, two each, and two deep leather tote bags, dark blue for Nadine and acid green for Cassie, plus a figure hugging red dress that Nadine would never have looked at had she been shopping alone. *And, of course, you weren't thinking of Ryan at all when you bought it.*

There were bags with jeans, swimwear and slouchy tees in white and pastels, some with slogans and pictures. Cassie had navigated them to a shop in another arcade specialising in vintage, where they'd found two original 1950s cocktail dresses. Cutting through the covered market, Nadine had impulsively added two off-the-shoulder tops and a couple of scarves from a stall selling retro reproductions, using authentic patterns and fabrics. She planned to wear them with skinny white jeans. They'd had a makeover at Charlotte Tilbury and lunch in the food court and all that *before* hitting Victoria's Secret.

Cassie had gone in like a hunting hawk, swooping with a true predator's instincts. Nadine could feel her face getting warm at the recollection of the contents of the candy pink bags at the top of the pile on the seat behind her. Her feeble protests of 'I can't wear that' had been ruthlessly ignored. The wisps of red lace and satin that would go under the red dress were bad enough, but the dark green basque, the shocking pink teddy and the leopard print bra and panties...

'His eyes are going to pop.'

'What?' Nadine jerked back to the present to find they were stuck in traffic. Cassie was grinning at her.

'Welcome back. I said that Ryan's eyes are going to pop. And possibly other parts also.' Cassie gave a thoroughly dirty cackle. 'And don't try and pretend you weren't thinking about that underwear. Your ears have gone pink,' she noted smugly.

'I have no idea *what* you are talking about,' Nadine responded with dignity. 'Why have we stopped?'

Cassie waved a hand. 'Cars?'

'I can see *that*. But what's the hold up?' They were on the outskirts of Bristol. 'I know it's the tail end of the rush hour, but there isn't usually a bottleneck here.'

Cassie fiddled with the radio, getting the local station. '... pile up involving three cars and a motor cycle—'

'That might be it. Hello, we're moving.' She quickly slid the car in gear.

The crumpled vehicles and the twisted wreckage of a motorcycle had been shifted to the side of the road. Nadine drew in a sharp breath and looked away. 'Nasty. I hope no one was badly hurt.'

'Penny was the motorcyclist?' Nadine didn't have to pretend emotion; she could hear the shock in her voice and knew it was genuine. She leaned back in her chair, staring blankly at the mock-ups for a new brochure pinned to the corkboard on her office wall.

'Afraid so.' Thackeray's response over the phone was carelessly casual, but Nadine detected the thread of strain running beneath. *As there would be if the woman is his lover.*

'How badly is she hurt?'

'I gather it's a broken arm and various nasty cuts and bruises. She'll be in hospital for a day or two for observation.'

'I'm so sorry. What hospital is she in? Can we send flowers?'

'All taken care of,' Thackeray confirmed. 'I organised it as soon as I heard as I knew that's what you would want. I understand she's intending to go back to work when she's out of hospital, but it rather depends on what the doctors say. In the meantime we're on our own.'

'Oh... well, I'm sure we'll manage, until she's on her feet again. Actually I wanted to talk to you about the venue – only I think I might have found somewhere.' She launched into Michelle and Cassie's carefully crafted story about a recommendation from a friend of a friend from the business network. 'It's an Art Deco villa, on the coast, near Nice. A young couple just inherited it. He's British, she's French. They haven't really started to market it for events, so at the moment it's kind of unique. We'd be their first booking.' Nadine took a breath. She had to blend her apparent excitement with enough information to tempt Thackeray, without going over the top.

'They're not experienced, so they're feeling their way slowly at the moment. They don't even have a website yet. Apparently the place is fabulous. There's an old chapel in the grounds, and accommodation for guests to stay. It sounds wonderful. Do you think we could fly over and take a look?'

'I'm sure we could, if that's what you want. It does sound good, and Penny can pick things up when she's on her feet again.' *Was that relief in his voice?* 'Cool. I'd better let you get back to work – we'll talk some more tonight.'

Nadine replaced the receiver and tipped back her head, to stare at the ceiling. Michelle and Cassie had provided her with a complete backstory for the villa, which belonged to some American friends of Jake's. Supposedly just on the market as a wedding venue, immediately available, owners who were new and naive in business, upmarket, select, wildly expensive and, from the photographs which Jake had organised, completely stunning. Everything Thackeray would be looking for.

Nadine chewed her lower lip. It had taken intense concentration to convey all that subtly but clearly enough for Thackeray to get the point. Tonight she'd follow up with photographs, and private access to the website that was allegedly still under construction. She swung a little on her chair, wondering if she'd overdone the excited bride, but Thackeray hadn't shown any sign. And with the planner out of the picture, even if it was only temporarily, it was an easy solution.

She inspected the ceiling and reviewed the whole phone conversation. The biggest hazard was showing that she knew something about Thackeray that she *wouldn't* know. If she made a slip now—

With a start she realised that her fingers were locked on the arms of her chair. The strain was building. She would be glad when it was over.

Chapter Twenty-Seven

Nadine surveyed the heap of garments laid out on the bed. She'd taken the results of the shopping expedition with Cassie out of the wardrobe, to cut off price tags and decide on the things that she would wear together. It was quite a heap. Egged on by her friend's enthusiasm, she'd shopped for the pure fun of it – although she wouldn't deny that Ryan had been in her mind too. It had been one of those days when just the right choices seemed to leap off the rails for her. *And really, how often does that happen?*

Now she was considering what she might pack for the exploratory visit to view the villa on the Côte d'Azur. It was all part of Jake's plan – the chance for Thackeray to confirm that he could make the scam work. The flights were booked and arrangements made. Penny, although out of hospital, was too incapacitated to make that kind of trip. It would be just her and Thackeray. Nadine looked thoughtfully at the pile of clothes. They were props. Support for her role as eager, excited bride. And it *was* still the Riviera, even if she would be with the wrong man.

'Yay! Complete hottie at two o'clock! Go for it, girls!'

Ryan emptied a bag of change into the till and tried to look disapproving. Considering his current low mood, he ought to have been doing a better job of it, but it was hard to stay grumpy around Shannon, the waitress. She was currently leaning over the bar, heads together with two of her friends. They were perched on stools on the customers' side, taking advantage of the early evening two-for-one offer on Prosecco. They'd all craned to look towards the end of the room. The object of their not-very-subtle attention was sitting at one of the alcove tables.

Shannon's friend wrinkled her nose. 'He's a bit old. Even older than Ryan.'

Ryan decided to pretend he hadn't heard that.

Shannon rolled her eyes. 'Still hot. Still would,' she decided 'Oh, bum!' she exclaimed, crestfallen. 'Wedding ring.'

'Yeah, you don't want to mess with him.' Ryan kept a straight face as he grabbed an open bottle of red and two glasses and made to move out from behind the bar. 'His wife has a black belt.'

Shannon and Co's eyes were round with confusion as he carried the bottle over to where Jake was sitting. He hadn't been able to resist. Cassie undoubtedly had a black belt somewhere in her wardrobe. He sobered quickly as he slid into the seat opposite Jake. 'Something's wrong.' Ryan's heart had been beating in overdrive ever since Jake had called asking to meet, despite his assurances over the phone. As Jake was on his way home, after an event in London, he'd agreed to come to the wine bar.

Jake shook his head, accepting the glass of wine that Ryan poured and passed to him. 'No, everything is on course for the trip to Nice.' He sampled the wine, nodding his approval. *And so he should, considering it's one of our most expensive bottles.*

'So why are you here?'

'To tell the truth, I'm not exactly sure.'

Ryan relaxed slightly, letting his intuition lead. It wasn't anything that *had* happened. Not yet. 'Something's bothering you? About the trip to Nice.'

'Yes,' Jake agreed. He picked up his glass, frowning. 'I'm putting people in place to help work our scam, good people, who speak the language and are familiar with the area. I have complete confidence in my operatives, but Nadine doesn't know any of them. From her point of view she's going to be alone in a foreign country with a man she *does* know is a very unpleasant criminal.' Jake paused, giving Ryan a straight look.

Ryan was struck, not for the first time, with how unexpectedly empathetic Jake could be. And he was beginning to get an idea where this was going. Ryan's heart kicked up. 'You're thinking—'

'—that one of our "Team Bride" should be in Nice when Nadine is there.'

Ryan took an unexpectedly large gulp from his glass and just managed not to choke. 'You want me to go,' he realised.

'Can you?' Jake looked around the bar. 'If you need any help to square it with your employer—'

'No. It's what? A week? I can juggle shifts and put my leave and rest days together.' Anticipation and apprehension made his hand jerk as he put down his glass.

Jake didn't miss the movement. 'I have no reason to suppose that there will be any problems. Quite the reverse. I hope Thackeray will be more than happy with what he finds. And, as I said, I'll have people in place, but I just feel... I'd be more comfortable if Nadine had one of *us* closer than a plane ride away. Being, as my wife regularly assures me, a male chauvinist pig, I'd rather that the person be male, which means either you or me. I think Nadine would prefer that it was you.' He reached for his briefcase, standing beside the chair, to take out an envelope. 'Plane reservation, euros for expenses, car hire and a place to stay. Close, but not too close, to the wedding villa. And before you start with the objections, I have the resources to organise this kind of thing.'

Ryan blinked, a mix of emotions churning his chest. 'You were pretty confident of me.'

'She's your woman. And I never said that,' he warned.

Ryan pulled in a very deep breath and took the envelope. He wasn't sure how he felt about Jake funding the trip, but it certainly made the thing a whole lot easier. He shut down on pride and focused on practicalities, opening the envelope and leafing through the contents.

'Okay?' Jake was considering him, with an assessing look.

'Yes...' He put the envelope down. 'But...' He had to say it. 'I'm not a professional at this.'

'Neither is Nadine. That's why she needs support. As far as she is concerned, I trust your instincts. Keep a low profile – he didn't recognise you before, from the church, but no sense in courting potential trouble. Anything doesn't feel right, just get out. There's no reason to expect any difficulties, but I'll be happier with you in place. You'll be back-up and a bolthole, if needed.'

'And will fall in front of the bullets, if necessary.' Even as he said it, Ryan wasn't sure it was a joke.

Jake's face sobered. 'We both know that we would do that. In a heartbeat.'

'Some people are jammy buggers.' Shannon hauled a rack of clean glassware out of the kitchen dishwasher. 'Riv–i–era!'

'It's a job. An audition,' Ryan corrected. He'd decided that Jake's visit would be an invitation to try out for a film role. He shrugged away a frisson of memory of his last film try out in the South of France. The company had gone bust, even before they'd finished casting. Not that he would have expected a part, with the commotion he and Jake had made at the casting call. 'You'll get some overtime out of it.'

''Course.' Shannon's pixie face split into a wide grin. 'An' you can bring me back a sexy French millionaire. With a yacht.'

'I'll see what I can do,' Ryan assured her gravely, scooping up some of the glasses, before shouldering open the door to take them back into the bar.

The noise – music, laughter and conversation – hit him like a wave. He dumped the glasses and started setting up a tray with two bottles of Chablis for a party of six. Once Jake had left, Shannon had been all agog to know about the guy in the Tom Ford suit, with the Smythson briefcase and the Rolex watch. Shannon had always been knowledgeable about that kind of stuff. She could size up a potentially good tipper at twenty paces. She'd been well impressed that Ryan was mixing with that kind of money.

You are so *out of your depth, mate.*

Michelle hurried along the corridor, dodging two colleagues deep in discussion about last night's football scores. She might just be in time to catch Jake before his first meeting of the day. She was in luck. When she knocked, and put her head around the door, he was there. He was alone.

'Whadya got?' he said encouragingly. She went in, closing the door and sitting down, in response to Jake's waved invitation.

'I just heard from Corinne. There was a formal offer for Karen's bakery business made yesterday. Keenly priced, but not derisory.'

'And?'

'She's undertaken to pass it on to Karen, with the caveat that Karen is unobtainable at the moment. Which is true. She's gone off on some sort of bush safari. Corinne gave me what details she could about the company involved, and I'll do some digging, but I'm not expecting much. If it's dodgy, it will be well hidden.'

'If there's something to find, my money's on you,' Jake said.

Michelle tried to look cool and professional and all-in-a-morning's work, rather than displaying her sudden flush of pleasure at the praise.

'There's been an approach to Nadine too,' he added. 'Just a tentative enquiry through a contact at her bank, at present. No names, no pack drill. I'll let you know if and when there's anything more concrete.'

Michelle nodded in acknowledgement. 'Why would they do that though? Make an approach *before* anything goes down?'

'Laying the ground for later, presumably. Although it did cross my mind that a woman contemplating marriage to what she assumes is a wealthy man *might* be open to an offer. New direction, new life – home and family.'

Michelle wrinkled her nose. 'Would a woman who'd built up a successful business really feel like that?'

Jake grinned. 'In my experience? I'd say that's a definite no. But that's not to say some other woman, that we don't know about, might have entertained an offer. And Thackeray is certainly the type to expect that they might.'

Michelle weighed the possibilities. It made sense, given what they'd assumed about Thackeray's opinion of women. Which sort of fitted with something else she'd been thinking about.

'I've been wondering… Do you think that was what was wrong with Maisie's profile? The business part, I mean?' They'd set Maisie up as the owner of a small cutting-edge technology company, researching artificial intelligence, in which Jake had an interest. 'It didn't compare with what Nadine had to offer in the way of established reputation and assets.'

Jake was following her chain of thought. He nodded. 'You could be right. When Nadine's husband inherited the business it was struggling, but with Nadine's help he turned it around – created a strong identity in a niche market. Since he's been gone, she's built on that. It's an old family business, so there was always property – the factory, and a local showroom, but Nadine developed both, and added small showrooms in London and New York, in areas that were up and coming and have since arrived. The business has a solid pedigree and some modest but prime real estate.' He considered the idea. 'The same applies to Karen. The bakery was a family business. Successful, but not outstanding. Karen took it in a new direction and acquired the chain of shops.'

'Two strong and savvy ladies, prepared to do the work.' Michelle got to her feet. 'And what they've worked for makes them attractive to a predator like Thackeray, and whoever might be behind him.'

Chapter Twenty-Eight

Nice Airport was coming into view as they descended through the cloud cover. Ryan eased his grip on the arm of the plane seat. Air travel didn't bother him and the flight had been smooth – made smoother by the fact that he was seated in business class. *How the other half lives*. The tension in him was coming from the knowledge that Nadine was down there somewhere, alone with Thackeray.

My woman. Something extremely primitive stirred in the pit of his stomach. *He doesn't sleep with them.* Nothing was going to happen, except he'd have a few days in the sun, away from the London rain. Everything would be fine. Nadine would be fine. He'd assumed that she and Slimeball would be in one of the big fancy hotels on the Promenade des Anglais, but Jake had produced something better. The supposed wedding venue they were inspecting had a number of cottages in the grounds, which could be available for wedding guests as part of the package. What better way to check the place out than actually to stay there? Jake had arranged for two cottages to be available, one for Nadine one for Thackeray. *So she has her own front door and Jake's people close at hand, right?*

He set his teeth. *He* wasn't close at hand, and that mattered. *Oh, get over yourself. What the hell is going to happen?* Jake's vague sense of unease was getting to him. He braced himself for the bump as the plane hit the tarmac, before taxiing slowly towards the airport buildings.

Definitely how the other half lives. Ryan hefted his holdall onto his shoulder as he emerged into the arrivals hall. A uniformed chauffeur was waiting, displaying a sign with his name on. There would be a hire car available at the farmhouse where he was staying, but Jake had arranged this pick up for the initial journey up into the hills. He walked forward, raising his hand to acknowledge the chauffeur, one of Jake's local contacts, who responded with a grin and stepped forward, in character, to take his bag. Making up his mind to enjoy this, while it lasted, Ryan handed it over. It would take a better man than him to ignore the envious glances of other passengers, struggling with luggage in unfamiliar surroundings.

But remember, you're still only here to take the bullet.

The renovated farmhouse, reached by a series of narrow twisting roads, was a low-slung whitewashed building, fronted by a dusty gravelled area and partly covered in some sort of creeper. Inside was a series of white-walled rooms, with cool tiled floors. The furniture was sparse but looked comfortable, and the art on the walls was clearly from local sources. At the back, and curving around the building, was a low-walled patio, with a shady eating area – more creeper, on a rustic pergola – and a garden that plummeted abruptly into a series of flower filled terraces, set into the hillside. Swathes of plants, somewhere between a jungle and a riot, in eye-popping colours, descended alongside a steep flight of steps to a pool at the bottom. A dark blue BMW convertible stood under a rose covered carport at the far side of the building. Mickey James, Jake's operative, ran through its finer points, confirmed that the paperwork was complete and then scooted around the house, checking everything was in order, before leaving Ryan to it. He was clearly curious, but didn't ask questions. 'You need anything, you have my number.'

Ryan checked his phone. 'Yes.'

'Good. All set then.' Mickey raised a hand in a mock salute. 'Enjoy.'

Ryan dumped his gear in the smaller of the two bedrooms and went in search of the kitchen, where hopefully there would be beer. The place wasn't actually sparely furnished, he realised, as he wandered through the rooms, shedding his jacket and tie. It was minimalist. The rainfall showers and freestanding baths in both the bedrooms were easily big enough for two. He shut down on the ache that he *really* didn't need, that reminded him that he was flying solo. The furniture was overstuffed and oversized and the sheets high thread count Egyptian cotton. In the small, immaculate kitchen, a brief survey of the freezer revealed a cache of chef-prepared meals, ready for heating, and in the fridge cheese and salads, a punnet of strawberries and two bottles of very superior white wine. A small carafe of red was already breathing quietly on the counter. And there was beer.

'Everything you could need.' *Except the girl*.

Deciding to leave the beer for later, he took a bottle of water, and returned to the bedroom to change and grab a towel, before ambling down to the pool.

'It's beautiful.' Impulsively Nadine turned to Thackeray, putting her hand on his arm. 'Absolutely perfect.' And it was. The tiny stone chapel, smothered in jasmine and roses; the villa itself, sugar cube white, cool and pristine, and the stepped flagstone terraces where they were standing, spilling down to the sea with a faultless view of blue water and blue sky.

'I agree.' Thackeray moved to pull her close. 'The perfect setting for the perfect bride.'

He looked up at the 'owners', Hélène and Andy, hovering anxiously but trying not to show it, on the top terrace, nearest to the house, and nodded. Their well-bred delight was judged to a nicety. *Must remember to tell Jake these two are good. Really good.* Nadine leaned away from Thackeray's embrace. 'Do you want to go and talk business? I'd like to stay here for a bit and just look at the view.'

'Sounds good.' Thackeray dropped a kiss on her forehead and turned to bound up the steps. Nadine leaned on the balustrade and contemplated that sea and sky. He'd made all the right noises, but he hadn't really been interested in what they were seeing. *Except for the eye-watering price.*

She wondered if he was even now negotiating for 'extras', allegedly to please the bride. Like the speedboat that was bobbing gently alongside the small, decked jetty, reached from a set of steep stone steps that led down to the base of the cliff. The boat had been Jake's input, to replace the getaway motorcycle. Thackeray liked the boat. He liked it a lot. Andy, the 'husband' of the newly inheriting owners, had taken them out for a spin, letting Thackeray take the controls. The launch would, of course, be decorated on the day, with ribbons and flowers, and used to ferry guests staying at hotels along the coast to the ceremony. *And to transport fleeing bridegrooms away from the ceremony.*

A muffled pop from the terrace above suggested champagne was being opened to seal the deal. Nadine looked down at her watch. Ryan's plane would have landed by now. He was on his way to a farmhouse in the hills. Maybe he was already there. With a small sigh, Nadine turned and climbed to the top terrace, to accept a glass of champagne and another round of congratulations.

She'd taken her first sip when a mobile phone trilled. Everyone laughed as they all moved to check theirs.

'It's mine.' Thackeray frowned, stepping to the far side of the terrace to answer. Hélène and Andy laid down camouflage of wedding small talk, while they all strained to hear. The call was not going well. Thackeray had not raised his voice, but the irritation was clear. He ended the conversation with a snap and a muffled curse.

Nadine raised her eyebrows as Thackeray rejoined them. 'Problem, darling?'

'Unfortunately, yes.' The easy manner didn't quite conceal the tension in the man's neck and jaw. Nadine swallowed, wondering just how cold his eyes were, behind the opaque dark glasses. 'I'm afraid I'm going to have to fly back for a couple of days, sweetheart. It's that jury thing. It was supposed to be sorted, but apparently it isn't.' He turned down his mouth in an 'if you want a job doing, do it yourself' grimace. 'My assistant is getting me a flight. I need to leave now.' He looked at his watch. 'It's going to take a day or two to get things straightened out, and while I'm there, there's some other business I need to take care of.' He took her hand, raising it to his lips. 'Sorry about this, darling. There's no need for you to come back with me,' he forestalled an offer she hadn't thought of making. 'Take the time, as we planned, and really get to know this place. I'll be back on Thursday.' His smile was full of reassurance. He looked over at Hélène and Andy, hovering anxiously. 'I know I'm leaving you in capable hands.'

While Hélène and Andy were offering any assistance that Thackeray needed, Nadine's heart began to thump. *Two days.* Her smile was wide and genuine. 'That's a wonderful idea, darling. By the time you come back, I'll adore this place even more.' *And wouldn't* you *just love that.*

His mind clearly fixed on the inconvenience awaiting him back in the UK, Thackeray gave her a quick peck on the cheek and left. Andy hustled after him, to see him out. Nadine stood quietly with Hélène, waiting. *That was a slip, my boy – not giving me time to see you off, like a loving fiancé should.*

Thackeray was rattled.

And he most certainly didn't want you volunteering to go with him.

Andy was back in a few minutes. 'He's gone.' He looked curiously at Nadine. 'What was all that about?'

Quickly Nadine explained. 'Obviously someone was supposed to make the thing go away, and didn't manage it.'

Andy nodded. 'I know they're not keen on people trying to excuse themselves. But Thackeray has to act if he wants to protect another identity.'

'If he did somehow get connected to one of the wedding cons, he can produce it, all squeaky clean.' Nadine joined the dots. 'It's a complicated life.'

'You wonder if it's worth the effort,' Andy commented, shaking his head. 'Possibly that's part of the kick – the guy gets off on living on the edge.'

Nadine suppressed a tiny shudder. 'I think he does.'

'So what now?' Hélène asked, pulling them back to the matter in hand. 'You have two days of freedom. You're welcome to stay—'

Nadine looked down, over the tempting view of the sea, feeling a weight lift from her shoulders. 'I think I might have other plans.' Laughing, she found her mobile phone and fired off a quick text. Room at your place for an abandoned woman?

Hélène was grinning, guessing what the plan was. She nudged Andy, who was looking blank. 'We're not the only people here for this conspiracy.'

'Oh!' The penny dropped. 'Excellent idea. And we can cover for you, if necessary.'

'Thank you. Although I suppose I'd better talk to Jake first.'

They retired inside, so Nadine could use the villa's landline. She got the connection to Bath easily and Jake was in the office. 'He's going to track Thackeray from the airport to see where he goes,' she confirmed as she put down the handset. At the same moment her mobile pinged, announcing an incoming text.

How abandoned?

Very. On my way.

With a deep breath she slid the diamond ring off her finger, turned the phone off and dropped both into her handbag. 'You said there was a hire car for me?'

Ryan stared down at the phone in his hand. The text message wobbled slightly. His hand was shaking, he realised. On my way. Nadine was coming here. Why? What had happened? Had the whole thing gone sideways? Was she running? *What has that scumbag done?*

Retrieving his trainers from under the sun lounger, where he'd been half snoozing when the first text arrived, he shoved his feet into them. He'd already dragged on his clothes as he waited for a response to the short, guarded reply he'd sent.

And now Nadine was on her way. With an effort he controlled his breathing. Did it really matter why?

Slipping the phone into his pocket, he climbed the steps back to the farmhouse. There was a small paved area right beside the front door, with a rickety metal bench, surrounded by pots that were heavy with flowers and heady with scent. Leaving the front door open, he lowered himself carefully onto the elderly bench. It rocked a little, but held his weight. He checked the phone again, in case he'd somehow missed another message. He hadn't.

All he could do now was wait.

Nadine eased the open-top car around a sloping corner, following the directions of the satnav. The road was narrow and overhung with greenery and twining plants. She hoped the device wasn't planning to dump her off a cliff somewhere. She took another corner, carefully, frowning and gripping the wheel. She'd met a few cars coming down, and a farm lorry, which had required some finessing on both sides, but they'd managed it, and the lorry driver had barrelled off down the hill, with a wave as he passed. She hadn't stopped to think about whether what she was doing was a good idea. Probably not, but she was doing it anyway, and to hell with it. Jake hadn't said that she shouldn't and that was good enough. Living with Cassie, he'd know better than to argue with a determined woman.

The satnav suggested that she had nearly reached her destination. She had two days before Thackeray came back. She was going to spend that time with Ryan. She'd been sensible and careful and all the other boring stuff, but now she was on the Riviera, with a gorgeous man within her reach. She'd waited long enough. She wasn't going to wait any longer.

Ryan heard the car, labouring a little on the steep incline leading up to the farmhouse. Would it go straight on by? No.

It was pulling in. He stood up quickly as a small low-slung sports car nosed into the dusty space in front of the farmhouse door. Nadine brought it to a neat stop and the motor died. She was wearing a bright green scarf to tie back her hair and large dark lensed sunglasses. Ryan swallowed hard. In the classic red MG Roadster she was the perfect retro screen goddess, somewhere between Bardot and Loren. And she was *here*.

He'd reached the car and had the door open before she'd had time to move. 'What happened? Are you okay? What did the bastard do?' Questions were tumbling out. He couldn't stop them. Then his heart gave a huge bound when he looked, really looked, and saw Nadine's smile. Tense muscles relaxed in a nanosecond. He could almost hear the hiss as his shoulders lowered.

She rose out of the car, throwing the dark glasses onto the seat, shaking her hair loose from the scarf, and leaning into his arms, hand going up to touch his cheek. Her face had sobered to concern. 'I'm sorry. I didn't think about you being worried. There's nothing wrong.' Her eyes glittered. 'Thackeray had to go back to the UK, so I've come to you.'

'But...' The warmth of her body in his arms was making it difficult for his brain to focus. But focus it had to. Peeling her fingers away from his cheek, he made a huge effort. 'We said we couldn't be together, not until this was over...'

'I know.' Nadine pouted. It was such an un-Nadine look that he almost let her go. His body wasn't that stupid though, even if his mind was. She nestled closer. *God – she has to know what this is doing.* 'I decided that I'm finished with the sensible stuff – at least for the next two days.' The grin she gave was complete feminine evil. It went through his blood like a shot of pure adrenaline. Her hand was resting now on his chest. She must be able to feel the wild thumping of his heart. 'I'm not going anywhere, Ryan Calder, so get used to it.' Her smile lit up, even wider. 'I'm quite prepared to seduce you, if I have to.'

His reflex response for swallowing seemed to have stopped working. With an effort Ryan worked some moisture back into a mouth that felt like the Sahara. Nadine's body was still pressed close to his. She wriggled a little, getting closer still. *Oh God, is that even possible?* Parts of his body that he had absolutely no control over were reacting. Violently. And she was laughing, knowing exactly what she was doing and revelling in it.

In the back of his brain, something snapped. His common sense and resistance went with it. He hefted her off her feet, and into his arms. 'If there's anything in that car that you need, you'd better get it now. We're going to be otherwise engaged for a while.'

'Bag. Keys,' she responded, with a hitch in her breath. He'd caught her off guard. *Good.* He lowered her over the open car, so she could scoop up both, and then headed for the farmhouse. She was nuzzling his neck as he carried her through the front door and kicked it shut behind them. The bedroom he'd chosen for himself was to the left, but the master bedroom, with its king size bed, was dead ahead. *Dead ahead it is then.* Nadine was nibbling under his ear now. It was just about driving him CRAZY.

'What the hell has got into you, woman?'

He felt the laughter ripple through her. 'You?'

'Oh, God.' Now his breathing was shot. 'Soon,' he promised huskily.

'I hope so.'

He dropped her gently on the bed, following her down, to kiss her. Her mouth was the perfect fit. Her lips were open, welcoming him. The world swam and narrowed to taste and heat as he slid his tongue inside, and she responded. He buried his hands in the luxuriant dark hair, holding her head steady as they explored each other. Coming up for air, in a haze of pleasure and jumping nerve endings, he butterfly kissed the corners of her mouth, then the centre. Her skin was so soft, so warm. Her breathing was as erratic as his.

She was working on the buttons of his hastily donned shirt, stroking skin as one by one they slid open. He couldn't stop the low groan as her fingers made their teasing progress. She laughed when she reached the last button, in the wrong buttonhole. 'Someone dressed in a hurry.'

'I was minding my own business, down by the pool,' he protested. 'And then *you* were on your way here.'

'If you want me to leave again...'

This time she kissed *him*, mouth demanding, hands making heat trails on his chest, wherever she touched.

Nadine ran her hands over Ryan's skin, revelling in the contact. *To touch, after so long.* She could feel the banked tension in him, vibrating under her fingertips. She rolled to the side of the bed, standing quickly to pull her wide necked T-shirt dress over her head and let it drop to the floor. Ryan's indrawn breath spiked the need that was coiling inside her. He reached up to run a finger, almost tentatively, along the lace-trimmed edge of her bra, dipping down to the hollow between her breasts. 'You're beautiful.' The words were breath-soft as he cupped her, his thumb brushing over the slippery satin.

As Nadine knelt on the bed beside him, Ryan knew that he wasn't dreaming. It was all too real for that. His heart might have stopped a time or two, he couldn't be sure, but he was definitely awake. Awake and touching... but it wasn't enough. 'Too many clothes.'

'Agreed. I want to see you naked, Calder.'

It might have been the words that nearly made him swallow his tongue, or the exploring fingers that had already flipped the button of his jeans, running over his abdomen. Her hand pushed at the zipper, fingers slipping inside...

'Nadine!' He grabbed her wrist in panic. 'Please.' He wasn't sure exactly what he was begging for.

'No?' She tipped her head in a question.

'I've wanted you for so long... if you... I'm going to go off like a rocket,' he admitted raggedly. 'Give me a minute.' He lay on his back and started to count silently. 100. 99, 98... 98, 97, 96...

Her breath was warm on his cheek. She'd nestled close, so their heads were level on the pillow. 'Would that be so terrible?'

'Yes!' He opened his eyes, losing the next number. 'I want everything to be *right*.'

She was stroking one finger down his biceps, making patterns on his skin. She slid her hand up to cup his chin. Reluctantly he let her turn his head. Her eyes were dark and totally focused. 'Ry, I'm here, with you. That's all it takes to make it right.' She kissed the hollow of his throat. 'We have two days to work on making it perfect.'

Suddenly he found himself laughing. 'Are you going to let me out of bed at all for those two days?'

'Hmm.' She considered him. Now the dark eyes were wicked. 'Ask me again in an hour or two.'

Chapter Twenty-Nine

They were sitting on the terrace, drinking the red wine and eating nuts and olives. The sun was setting and Nadine had lit two large citronella candles to ward off insects. The fragrance was mingling with the scent of jasmine. She was feeling blissfully relaxed, happier than she had in weeks, and yes... satisfied. Ryan had gone very quiet.

'I can hear you thinking.' She pointed a finger. 'Do *not* say that this was a bad idea.'

'How could I?' He reached over the gap between their chairs to grasp her hand, lifting it to kiss her palm. 'It was amazing. You're amazing.'

'Thank you.' She dipped her head in acknowledgement. 'And the same applies to you. You were worth waiting for,' she added wickedly. All she got was a strangled grunt in response. She flopped back in her chair, looking at the sky. There were stars just coming out. Her bones had melted and her skin hummed with the memory of pleasure. 'Now you're thinking that you're such a stud, that when Thackeray gets back I'll be totally distracted and unable to look him in the face.'

'Umm... yes?'

Laughter bubbled. 'Well, you are, but I shall just have to cope.'

'Actually. I still don't know exactly where he's gone, and why you were able to come here.'

'Oh. No, you don't.' Quickly she explained.

'God bless the British justice system.'

'Amen to that.' She sat up, abruptly serious, to look at Ryan. 'Wanting you, wanting all this.' She waved her hand at the quiet terrace. 'It wasn't just self-indulgence. Being with him... I knew what I was doing when I volunteered. I still know, and I'm still a volunteer. I'm good with it, most of the time, but Thackeray... He's so clever at what he does. I can *see* the game he's playing, and how he's playing it, but not letting him know that...' She raised her hand to quell Ryan's immediate response. 'I'm doing okay, although it isn't easy. I didn't expect it to be, but playing the part, being the puppet he's created – sometimes I'm afraid I'm going to slip and show him how I feel, or worse, *tell* him!' She took a sip of wine. 'I need some time, to get my head straight.'

'So – I'm a sort of pressure valve?' His smile was so completely understanding that the anxiety she'd been holding, deep inside her, abruptly dissolved. 'I get it.' He nodded slowly. 'But he's not here now, and we shouldn't let him be. *I* shouldn't let him be. We won't mention him again.' He found her hand to pull her out of the chair. 'Let's go and see what we can find in the kitchen for dinner.'

Later, in the quiet darkness of the bedroom, Ryan took Nadine's mouth in a soft sweet kiss. Her response was immediate. Heat flowed between them. Right now, right here, the woman in his arms was all that mattered. He was in a place he'd only ever dreamed he would be, because of the craziest set of circumstances. His role in the crazy was as supporting cast, his job to give Nadine what she needed to get the thing done. They had two days. It was up to him to make them count, in every way he could. He was going to make the absolute most of it. For both of them.

He deepened the kiss.

Nadine stood on the terrace. Stretching her arms above her head, she drew in a breath of balmy, fragrant air. It was only ten thirty in the morning, but the day was already beginning to warm, the scent of the flowers and herbs of the garden permeating the air. She had a few aches and twinges in muscles that had not been used in a while, but otherwise she felt amazing. Ryan had gone out early and they'd breakfasted on rolls and croissants from the bakery in the tiny hamlet a few miles up the hill – a scatter of shops and houses around the

Michelin starred restaurant that had provided the food that stocked the freezer.

She turned as Ryan came out of the house. 'I'd love to own a place like this – something for the bucket list.' She gestured to the lushness of the planting, brushing her hands over the lavender and scented geraniums in pots fringing the flagstones. 'Isn't everything gorgeous?'

'Yes.' It was a few beats before she realised that Ryan was looking at her, not the flowers. He looked pretty gorgeous himself, fresh from the shower, in shorts and a brightly patterned shirt. She'd never seen him look this laid-back and relaxed. Something settled inside her. *Contentment*. He held out his hand. 'Shall we go down to the pool?'

They spent the day enjoying the sunshine and the warm shade beside the turquoise water, snacking on pissaladière, salty with olives and anchovies, also bought from the bakery, and on almonds and peaches, swimming and messing about in the pool.

'Not fair!' Nadine surfaced, spluttering, scooping her hair out of her eyes. Ryan had just ambushed her with a sneaky move that had taken her legs from under her. 'I'm coming for you, Calder!'

Ryan was still laughing when she upended him in the deeper end, and came up spitting water. When he could speak, he held up his hands. 'Truce.'

'Hah! You can dish it out, but you can't take it!' she taunted. In response he pulled her into his arms, and then they were both breathless for a while. He gave her his hand to help her out of the pool and handed her a towel that had been drying in the sun. 'Thank you, kind sir.'

He'd found his own towel and was rubbing his hair. It stood on end, making her giggle. She looked round, taking in the sun on the water, the bright local tiles that edged raised beds, the flower-filled pots and the pergola, smothered by a vine, which offered welcome shade. 'This place really *is* fabulous.'

They spent what was left of the afternoon snoozing on an extra wide sun lounger. Nadine snuggled into Ryan's chest. 'You smell good.'

'Pool water and suntan oil?'

'On you, it's irresistible.'

'Flattery will not get you anywhere.' He began to unwind himself from her koala hug. 'At least, not at the moment,' he corrected as she screwed up her face in protest. 'I'm hungry.'

She slid down the lounger and sat up. 'Me too.'

'There's plenty of amazing food in the freezer. Or we could order in,' he suggested, as she hesitated.

'Why don't we go out? We're miles away from Nice. No danger of meeting anyone. Come on.' She made up her mind as she slithered off the lounger and stood up, grabbing his hand. 'Let's do it.'

For a second doubt showed on Ryan's face, then it was gone as he drew her in, for a quick kiss.

'Shower.' She pulled on his hand, dragging him towards the steps. In that massive rainfall shower, this morning...

'One each.' Ryan burst her bubble of anticipation.

'Spoilsport.'

'You want to eat. I want to eat. We have to find a place. Two showers,' he decreed. 'There's a file with menus and directions to restaurants in the kitchen. You can choose.'

Ryan ambled down the hall to the master bedroom that Nadine had commandeered to get ready. There was a huge, ornately framed mirror hanging in a niche in the passageway leading to the bedrooms. From the look of the hazy glass, darkly speckled at the edges closest to the frame, it was old, probably antique, but still clear enough for him to check that his lightweight linen jacket over slim black trousers looked okay. He'd slipped a tie into his pocket, in case wherever Nadine chose had a dress code.

A movement behind him caught his eye, reflected in the

mirror. A vision was sashaying towards him. He turned slowly. The skinny red dress flowed from shoestring straps, down over soft curves. And there were shoes. They were red, too. High narrow heels, with one wide band holding it all together, and red tipped toes peeping through. And a bracelet, anklet, something glittering around one perfect ankle.

To hell with dinner. What's under that dress?

Hauling together all his willpower, he stepped forward, hoping his tongue wasn't lolling like Shannon's Labrador pup at the sight of a steak. What Nadine whispered in his ear, when she leaned up to kiss his cheek, nearly undid him completely.

'You do *want* to go out to eat?' His voice sounded as if he'd been chewing gravel. If a giggle could be evil, hers was. She pecked his cheek again. The scent of her hair brought him close to forgetting everything but dragging her back to the bedroom. With a monumental effort of concentration, he remembered he was a gentleman. He wasn't sure if he still remembered how to breathe.

'Of course I want to go out to eat. I'm *starving*!' She waved the keys of the BMW under his nose. 'You can drive.'

The place had been marked on the kitchen file with a star, apparently indicating that it was high on 'romantic ambiance'. The entrance looked like a scruffy hole in the wall, with a paint peeling door and a small chipped enamel sign that simply said 'Le Restaurant'. At the end of a dark, narrow entryway the place suddenly opened out into a wide light-filled room and an open terrace, with a glorious view of the cliffs stretching down to the sea.

It was early and only a few of the tables were taken. The patrons were all couples of various ages, with their heads close together or their hands clasped on the red and white checked tablecloths. It was Romantic, with a capital R. They sat out on the terrace, under the shade of a vine that looked as if it might be a hundred years old.

In the kitchen the chef was rattling pans and singing

snatches of *Carmen*. There was no menu. Food was brought and everyone ate whatever the chef had elected to produce that night. Stuffed vegetables and wafer thin slivers of ham, a bowl of salad nicoise, to share, with three different kinds of olives and even a few flowers along with the capers, grilled fish with a glistening side of ratatouille, local cheese, a soft lemon water ice spiked with tiny biscuits that tasted of almonds. Every mouthful melted on the tongue in a burst of flavour.

Ryan wouldn't have cared if they'd offered him bread and water. Nadine's eyes sparkled at him over her glass of an unnamed red wine that had simply arrived with the appetisers in a small earthenware jug. When she wasn't using them to eat, her hands found his across the table. It was perfect. Almost too perfect. There was a dull ache under his heart that felt like a kind of homesickness. This was too close to being a dream. He pushed the thought away.

Tonight is about tonight, and to hell with tomorrow.

When they reached the farmhouse again the building and the bedroom were bathed in the very last golden glow of the setting sun.

The clinging red lace that had been concealed under the red dress was everything he'd hoped it would be.

Chapter Thirty

The landline rang when they were having a late breakfast in the kitchen. Sleeves rolled up, Ryan was wrestling with a peach, attempting to eat it without getting juice down his arm and onto his shirt.

'I'll get it.' Nadine stood up, grinning. 'You've got your hands full.' Pausing briefly to admire those hands – *clever, clever hands* – and the lightly tanned forearms, she crossed to the retro style phone that hung on the wall. *Even the guy's arms turn you on.*

As she lifted the receiver a stab of apprehension punctured the moment.

What if...

'Hello? Oh, hi, Jake. No, everything is fine this end. You?' She saw Ryan's shoulders tense and mouthed, 'Nothing wrong,' then listened intently as Ryan leaned back, watching her. 'That's good. Fine. I'll tell him. Love to Cassie.' She hung up and came back to the table.

Ryan tilted his head questioningly. 'Updates?'

Nadine nodded as she sat down. 'Nothing to cause alarm, but Thackeray didn't leave from Nice Airport.'

Ryan had been leaning back, with his chair tipped on two legs. His feet and the chair hit the floor with a thud. 'He's still here?'

Nadine shook her head, reaching to top up her coffee. 'He wasn't on a scheduled flight. He went on a private charter into Manchester. Jake had Nice Airport covered, but he's mad at himself for not thinking of alternatives. They were planning to meet the plane he was on, and follow him, but it was too late by the time they realised what he'd done.'

'Who *would* have expected it?' Ryan was frowning. 'The guy has access to resources we don't know about.'

'But now Jake does know, and he's working on it.'

Ryan was still frowning. 'The idea of luring Thackeray with a fancy wedding on the Riviera doesn't look such a good one now.'

Nadine leaned over to rest her hand on his arm. 'What's done is done. No point in going back. Jake's on it.'

Ryan's muscles stayed tense under her fingers for a few seconds, then relaxed, nodding as he acknowledged what she said. *Not that he's happy about it.*

'This thing is a lot bigger than just a con operation.'

'It looks possible. But that's still our part of it, so we carry on and let Jake worry about the rest.'

She watched warily as Ryan shrugged and picked up his coffee cup. *Definitely not happy – but there's nothing to be done about that.* 'Michelle checked the balance in the wedding account. Thackeray has begun to move money out of it – just the funds he put in, for the moment. But we know it's not to pay suppliers.'

'I suppose if you queried it, he'd claim it was a deposit for Hélène and Andy.'

'Or that he's arranged some sort of big, secret surprise.'

Ryan swirled the last of the coffee in his cup, before draining it. 'So… the con has begun in earnest. And at the moment we don't know where Thackeray is, or what he's doing, but he's planning on coming back tomorrow. Which gives *us* one more day.'

'I can find out more when I turn my phone back on. He's bound to have left messages. I don't want to turn it on while we're here.' *And there are so many reasons for that.*

'In that case, we'd better head out.'

Nadine nodded. 'We can only count on having this one day. I want to make the most of it.'

They were in the BMW, making for Nice, before Ryan asked the question. 'What was it you were supposed to tell me?'

'Oh!' She'd been focused on the window, catching glimpses of the sea as the car wound down the hill. 'Jake just wanted to confirm that all the arrangements will carry on, so you can stay until I leave.' She took her eyes off the view, to study his profile. 'Is that OK? For work, I mean?'

'It's OK,' he agreed.

'I haven't actually said thank you.'

'You know there's no need.' He glanced over quickly. 'Jake didn't apply any pressure, if that's what you're thinking. If I couldn't do it, he'd have come himself.' He grinned. 'In the circumstances, I think it was a very fine idea.'

'Hmm.' She tried to sound unconvinced. 'You think I don't *realise* that Jake was organising a big strong male to protect me?'

Ryan laughed. She loved his laugh. 'You'd better take that one up with him.' He cast her another quick glance. 'He thought you should have "Team Bride" support, as well as Hélène and Andy, that's all. If Thackeray is in unknown territory, so are we. He wanted you to have help, and somewhere to go, if there was a problem.'

'All right. I understand.' She wasn't quite sure why she was making an issue of it. Jake was protective. Ryan was out of the same mould. Cassie worked around it, so could she. She was edgy, and would be until she'd contacted Thackeray. 'We're close enough to Nice now. Can we pull over somewhere, so I can put the phone on?'

Ryan guided the car into the empty car park of a small roadside creperie that still had the shutters up. Nadine found her phone, took a deep breath, and turned it on.

There were three text messages, two from Thackeray, the first confirming he had arrived, and hoping that she was having a good time, the second that his plans had not changed. See you on Thursday. The other message was from Hélène, confirming she'd fielded a call on the villa's landline, and attaching a picture of a huge bouquet of roses that had arrived for Nadine. Enjoying them enormously, on your behalf.

Nadine showed the picture to Ryan. 'Keeping the bride

sweet. Hélène said he seemed distracted. He accepted her excuse that my phone signal was poor, and that I was out visiting wedding suppliers and florists.'

Ryan looked thoughtful. 'He doesn't want you to know where he is, any more than you want him to know where you are.'

'It looks that way.'

She sat quietly for a moment, the phone in her hand. Ryan opened the car door and got out, ostensibly to investigate the menu of the creperie. Nadine knew he was giving her time to make contact with Thackeray. After a few more moments of thought, she composed a gushing text, apologising for her silence and full of praise for the roses, the villa and a proposed trip to a place that did wedding favours with a Provencal theme that Hélène had briefed her on. Until Thursday. X. She pressed send, and clicked off the phone. Andy would contact them on Ryan's if there was an emergency. The day was theirs, and she was putting Thackeray right out of her head.

Starting now.

She gave Ryan a glowing smile as he came back to the car.

Deciding she preferred sightseeing to the beach, they began by wandering through the Cours Saleya open air market in Nice – stalls with luxuriant displays of fruit and vegetables, deep buckets full of flowers, piles of glace fruits and olives glistening in the sun, and pungent trays of herbs and spices. Diverted by a table selling lavender products, Nadine looked up to see Ryan studying a laden flower stall. With a small pang she knew instinctively that he would have bought her flowers, but now he wouldn't. *Because of those roses.* Even though a bunch of sunflowers from Ryan would be infinitely better than half a florist shop from Thackeray. *Sod you, Slimeball. The sooner we take you down, the better.*

Remembering Cassie's recommendation, Nadine navigated them towards Menton. They spent the day prowling through galleries and museums and old narrow streets, and walking beside the sea. Finally, in the late afternoon, the lure of the farmhouse and the pool beckoned.

Sunshine and blue water and a beautiful woman – who was currently circling him like an eel, trying to pull him under the water. Abruptly he toppled, taking her with him. They both came up spluttering and laughing.

'Why are you so intent on drowning me, woman?' He hooked sodden hair out of his eyes.

'I like it when you're all wet.'

He could understand that. He brushed sparkling droplets off her skin, the intriguing cocktail of cool water and warmth under his fingers. He waited, knowing she'd pull him closer. His chest was tight with an emotion he didn't want to examine.

What more could a man want?

Later, in the kitchen, they put together their final dinner at the farmhouse. Ryan opened one of the bottles of white wine, pouring them both a glass. He handed hers to Nadine. 'To our last night.'

'To our last night *here*,' she corrected.

'To our last night here,' he repeated.

Her face was turned up to his, her mouth and her eyes inviting. He bent to kiss her, no more than a butterfly caress. He couldn't manage more. Words were hovering on his tongue. Words he knew he couldn't say.

I love you.

On the stove a pot of pasta boiled over, hissing and spitting. With a laugh, Nadine went to rescue it.

Nadine stood at the window, silk robe belted around her, arms leaning on the sill. There was a sliver of waning moon in a velvety sky, studded with stars. The recesses of the garden looked dark and mysterious. The air was still warm, and the fragrances of night drifted in through the open window.

Behind her in the bed Ryan was sprawled on his face, asleep.

She ran her hands up her arms and down again, remembering the stroke of his hands. She wouldn't have believed…

Ryan seemed to know exactly the touch she needed to stir her, and if he didn't he asked, which was arousing in a whole different way. And she was learning his skin, his shape, his weight and his scent, exploring his body, listening for the glorious hitch in his breath that told her, better than words, how he felt. But there were words too, soft and sweet, urgent and demanding, fragmented and nonsensical. The communication of lovers.

It had been a long time, but with Ryan everything was easy. He gave, and took, and everything just… happened. Sex with Rory had always been good, but with the demands of the business, and his growing commitment to establishing himself as a mover and shaker in the local community…

She exhaled, straightening away from the window. *No comparisons.* It was unfair to both men. Rory was then, Ryan was now, and she was a different woman too. A woman who could take on a conman…

She turned, watching Ryan in the thin moonlight. He'd rolled onto his side, a dark shape against the pale tangle of the sheets. *What happens when all this is over?* She put up both hands to brush her hair away from her face, then dropped them to the belt of the robe, studying the sleeping figure. Her heart picked up as she traced the rise and fall of his breath.

Whatever happens, you can't lose him.

He'd carried her bag out and stashed it in the MG. All she had to do was get in the car and drive. There was already a cold lonely gap opening in his chest.

'I could stay, just a little longer…'

He shook his head. 'Too big a risk.'

She sighed, accepting. 'You can call the villa, Hélène or Andy will pass on a message.'

With an effort he pulled his head back into the moment. 'If I talk dirty to Hélène, will she pass that on, too?'

'Don't even think about it!'

'Okay.' He held up his hands in surrender. 'Take care.'

'You too, and it isn't forever.'

'I know.' He cupped her face in his palms. 'You will be alright—'

'I will be *alright*,' she cut him off. 'We can do this. We just have to hang on a little longer.' She reached up, pulling him down for a last kiss. Ryan closed his eyes, imprinting her taste, her scent, the way she felt in his arms, on his memory. Then she broke away, turning quickly to open the car door and slide into the driving seat. He stepped back. 'Drive safely.'

The car was moving out of the shelter of the farmhouse and into the narrow gateway that gave onto the road.

Ryan stood watching as it made a smooth right turn, and disappeared.

With an effort Nadine loosened her hold on the steering wheel. This journey was a transition, back to her borrowed persona – unquestioning and besotted fiancée of a confidence trickster. She guided the car into the traffic of the coast road towards Nice. She must put those stolen days and nights behind her, but the time at the farmhouse had centred her. *You can do this.*

She indicated and overtook a swaying camper van with GB plates, to gain a stretch of open road. Now she had to really throw herself into her borrowed role.

When she emerged from the shelter of the trees that shaded the driveway up to the villa, there was another car parked on the forecourt. Blinking, she took in the decal on the driver's door. A taxi dropping off a fare. She rolled the MG to a stop. The passenger turned from paying off the driver. Nadine's heart gave a jerk of recognition as she got a clear look at the man standing beside the vehicle.

Thackeray was back.

Chapter Thirty-One

Ryan lingered, long after even the faint sound of the car's engine had faded, staring at the gateway. If anyone had been watching, it would look like a classic scenario – married woman leaving her lover to return to her husband. *And would that image be so wrong?* Okay, so no one in this scenario was married, or likely to be, but there was a principle in there somewhere.

Ryan turned towards the farmhouse, looking it over. *Simplicity, sophistication, luxury – money.* This was Nadine's world, not his. Ryan kicked a stone, watched it bounce, then kicked it again. No question, he'd just had the most amazing two days of his life.

Nadine was… perfect.

A hollow desolate chill settled around him, despite the warmth of the day. Nadine deserved better than anything he had to offer. A guy who didn't know whether he was an actor, or a bar manager, and not making it at either? He could see Nadine, in a few years time, with the man she *ought* to be with – the real version of John Thackeray – solid, successful, the type who had all Hugh Grant's easy style, and an impeccable pedigree and manners. They'd have that house on the Riviera that she'd talked of buying, and maybe a couple of kids.

Kids.

Abruptly the image of Benita, holding baby Luca, and of Cassie, with that glow of first pregnancy, rose in his mind. He'd never given it much thought, but yes, he wanted kids. He wanted kids with Nadine. *Never going to happen, buddy. Settle for what you have now, and move on when the time comes, with your self-respect intact.*

He kicked the stone again. Nadine had found a soulmate in Rory, her husband, and lost him. She deserved happiness, even if the next guy would never quite match up. *And what the hell makes you think the next guy could ever be you?*

190

He walked back slowly to the farmhouse, stopping inside the door. Everywhere in the house was going to hold Nadine's echo. There was even a faint lingering trace of her scent, still ghosting the air. *Or maybe that's just your imagination?* He thought about the pool, but she was going to be there too.

With an abrupt curse he headed for the kitchen and the keys to the BMW. Driving somewhere, anywhere, would be better than staying.

'It's an imposition and an irritation, but it seems there's no getting out of it. You know what bureaucracy is – like trying to reason with fog.' Thackeray spread butter and jam on a croissant. Hélène had put together a late breakfast for them, and they were sitting on the villa's top terrace, overlooking the sea. He made a wry face. 'In the end it just seemed easier to let it go. And it is a public duty. Keeping the wheels of justice turning, and all that.'

'So you have to be back for court on Monday morning.' Nadine sipped a glass of freshly squeezed orange juice. 'Let's hope you get an interesting case, but not something that goes on too long. You'll need a flight on Sunday.' She frowned. 'We'll have to change the tickets.'

'Ahh.' Thackeray gave her a half sheepish, half apologetic grin. 'Thing is, I've managed to hitch a ride. I ran into an old pal – old business partner actually – he runs a little two-seater from an airfield down the coast. He's flying back on Sunday afternoon and he's offered me the spare seat.' Another wry face. 'Not the most comfortable of rides, but it will get me back to Birmingham in good time – and you can fly back in comfort on Monday, as we planned.'

Nadine took a deep breath. 'Well, that sounds great. And very kind of him. Can we take him to dinner, or something, as a thank you?'

'That is a *lovely* idea, darling. I'll check with Don, and see if he can do it,' Thackeray said easily.

And won't it be a surprise if he can? And now move on.

'Mmm. This is good.' She put down her glass of juice. 'Hélène and I were talking about mimosas – for the wedding breakfast. Orange juice and sparkling wine, very light and summery.'

'Hmm, sounds great, but I'm sure we can do better than sparkling wine. I've got a contact in Paris. Runs a wine business. I'll get him to ship us some of his top range vintage champagne.' He raised his coffee cup in a toast. 'Nothing but the best for you, darling.' He smiled expansively. 'Now, tell me about all you've been up to while I was gone. The flower place you went to so early this morning. Any good?'

Nadine snatched a moment when Thackeray was down at the jetty, going over the finer points of the speedboat with Andy, to call Jake. She relayed the information that Thackeray had given her over breakfast. 'Not that any of it is necessarily *true*, but I thought it might be useful.' Jake confirmed that it was, and she rang off.

A moment later Thackeray came into view from the terrace, swinging the keys to the MG. 'Ready, darling? Do you have the list?'

They had agreed to spend the day visiting some potential wedding suppliers that Hélène had suggested, finishing with a trip to Grasse, and dinner. 'So that the day isn't all work and no play, darling.'

Nadine forcibly unclenched her teeth. Thackeray's new habit of punctuating every utterance with 'darling' was shredding her nerves. She forced a smile. 'I'm ready.' Her mouth almost framed 'darling' to end the sentence. She resisted. Thackeray probably wouldn't even notice. He was going through the motions with her, his mind clearly elsewhere. *After all, he's done all this how many times before?*

She actually quite enjoyed a lot of the day, when she forgot herself and relaxed, becoming engrossed in sampling menus and morsels of wedding cake, and looking at displays of flowers and table settings. All the suggestions were meticulous – the sort of things that might have thrilled her, if any of it had been real. And wherever they went, and whatever they saw, Thackeray nudged her subtly towards the most expensive option, or suggested embellishments. *His mind isn't entirely elsewhere.* He even managed to adroitly raise the question of increasing the contribution to the wedding fund, over a simple lunch of salad nicoise in an open-air café alongside the sea.

At last, after the final florist's shop, they headed towards Grasse. Looking round the perfumeries, Thackeray insisted on buying her a heavy floral scent in a fancy glass flagon. 'Something for you to wear on the big day, darling.'

Nadine nodded and smiled and felt slightly sick. Thackeray had come back from wherever his mind had been. *Made a plan, or reached a decision.* Now for two, maybe three hours, she would be sitting across the table from him, in a fancy restaurant, his attention focused solely on her. All she could think of was that she was with the wrong man.

Ryan was right after all, about keeping them apart. I don't know if I can do this.

In Jake's office in Bath he was speaking on the phone to his local operative, Mickey James, briefing Mickey on Nadine's report from that morning. 'He's come clean about using a private plane – but I doubt if there's any mate called Don, or a two-seater, and we know he didn't fly into Birmingham.'

'I'll check it out. Last time he used a professional charter from a local company, but I haven't been able to get any further with that.'

'Nothing on who arranged the hire?'

Mickey huffed in frustration. 'No. He could have done it for himself.'

'You don't think so?'

'I don't *know*. It all seems... a bit too... slick? Hiring a private plane is not the first thing you would think of.' Mickey groaned. 'Well, *you* would. And the Côte d'Azur is the kind of place that people do that sort of thing, so perhaps I'm looking for something that isn't there.'

'We'll find out, Mickey. Don't worry. In the meantime, there's something else I'd like you to do.'

The air conditioning in the restaurant was set too high, and she was talking too much, enthusing about the suppliers they had visited. Thackeray was sitting back, with an indulgent smile on his face. *If he knew how irritating that smile is...*

He leaned over the table to push a full glass of red wine towards her. In desperation she lifted it and drank.

'That's better.' Now the smile was closer to a smirk. 'Relax, darling. Enjoy the evening.' He raised her hand to his lips. Nadine thought she heard a sigh from a woman sitting at an adjoining table, whose companion had his head down, consulting his phone. *If only you knew...*

Thackeray was still speaking. 'I wanted to talk to you, about the actual ceremony.' He was all earnestness now. 'I don't have any close family. There are just a few people I'd like to ask. I want you to invite as many of your family and friends as *you* want. It should be your day, but there is one thing...'

He stopped, making sure her attention was all on him. Her breath hitched, wondering what was coming.

'I have an old friend,' he continued. 'Well, he was really a friend of my late father. By coincidence he's just retired here, to the South of France. When I was young, he always said... when I found the right lady...'

In the back of her mind Nadine was appreciating the performance. The diffidence and hesitation had her hanging on his every word.

'It would mean a lot to me, and to him... Would you mind if he – Reverend Ellis – was the one to marry us?'

It was a bravura performance. Nadine almost wanted to clap.

'Of course.' *What else was there to say?* 'It sounds lovely. I'd be very happy if he was the one to marry us.' She squeezed Thackeray's hand as the waiter bustled over to deliver their first course. 'It's going to be the perfect wedding.'

Ryan spent the day exploring the small and picturesque hill towns in the hinterlands behind Nice. Gradually the sunshine and the novel surroundings eased his mood away from the bleakness that had overwhelmed him in the wake of Nadine's departure. *Dial down the self-pity, why don't you?* He might not be what Nadine needed in the long-term, but he was what she *wanted* now. He could be proud of that, even if he couldn't bridge the massive gulf between them in everything else. *Why let stupid fantasies mess up something brilliant?*

There might be a ton of hurt to come, but he didn't have to run towards it. The realisation that he was in love with Nadine shouldn't have been any kind of surprise. He'd known it for months, just hadn't been ready to admit it. It had crept up on him, slowly and irrevocably, poised to ambush him when his defences were down. And really, did it matter? He wasn't about to tell her, and ruin what they had.

He turned the car into the small forecourt of the farmhouse. A tall figure was standing in front of the building, leaning against a sleek, powerful motorbike. As he brought the BMW to a halt, Ryan recognised the man, although now he was wearing jeans and T-shirt, not a chauffeur's uniform. Mickey James – waiting for him.

Chapter Thirty-Two

'Hi.' Mickey raised his hand in greeting as Ryan slid out of the car. 'Jake thought you might be at a loose end tonight.' His grin was a little too knowing about why that might be, but it was friendly.

'And?' Ryan returned Mickey's grin. The man's relaxed stance had dissipated Ryan's sudden stab of alarm when he recognised him, but he wasn't a complete sucker. McQuire wouldn't be *that* solicitous about his well being.

'And he thought we should talk.' Mickey's expression showed his appreciation at the speed of Ryan's understanding. 'Andy, the operative from the villa, is waiting for us in the local bar.' He thumbed a quick text into his phone. 'Do you want to follow me down?'

Andy was seated at a corner table, presiding over three cold beers and a platter of bread, cheese and olives. Introductions made, Ryan sat down and picked up his beer. Andy pushed the plate towards him. They drank and munched for a while.

'So, what is it McQuire thinks we need to discuss?' Ryan asked eventually.

Mickey made a face. 'Smoke and mirrors.'

Ryan raised his eyebrows. Andy gestured with a hunk of bread. 'What my colleague is trying to express, in his own unique way, is that something might be going on, but that we can't be sure that anything *is*, and *if* it is, we don't have a friggin' clue *what* it is. That about right?' he queried with Mickey.

Mickey nodded, scowling. Together they ran succinctly over the details of the private plane and Thackeray's disappearance and reappearance, adding in the new information on Don, the so-called friend.

'You think that Thackeray may be part of something bigger because he has access to unexpected resources?'

'It doesn't necessarily mean anything.' Mickey was still

scowling. Ryan recognised frustration. 'Thackeray could just be making use of contacts he's acquired along the way. He's slick, but he's not exactly a criminal kingpin. The wedding scam is relatively small beer, a self-contained long con. Nothing about it leads anywhere else.'

'Except for the offers to buy the businesses of the women concerned.' Mickey and Andy exchanged sharp glances, and Ryan felt a quick stab of satisfaction, knowing that he'd got it right, and that he'd surprised them. It didn't last, as realisation hit. 'Is Nadine in danger?'

'No.' Both men shook their heads, but it was Andy who answered. 'Thackeray will be gone on Sunday. In the meantime she's playing along with him just fine. Hélène and I are watching out for her, and keeping in close touch with Jake. Once Nadine is back at home, there's no more problem.'

Ryan wondered if his relief showed on his face. *As long as Nadine is safe.* He took a swig of his beer. 'So, why are we here?' He thought he knew. Jake was being super careful. *Which is fine by me.* 'We're talking about a back-up plan, right?'

This time he could enjoy the satisfaction of seeing acknowledgement in Mickey's expression. 'Jake's not expecting trouble,' Mickey confirmed. 'But he wanted us to meet and talk about how we extract Nadine, before Monday, if it should be necessary. Andy and I do what's needed at the villa, you're the one who gets her out.' Mickey's grin had a wicked edge. 'You'll have use of McQuire's private plane, if that happens.'

After half an hour they'd hashed out the plan, and the bar was filling up quickly with fans of a local rock band, which was setting up to play. Time to leave. Ryan was experiencing a mix of apprehension and relief. *Everything will be fine. Nadine will be free and clear.*

And then...

While they were in the bar the sun had begun to dip, splashing the evening with orange and gold. Ryan and Andy ambled over to admire the finer points of Mickey's BMW GS Adventure bike, before he swung himself onto it and accelerated away, with a muted roar.

Andy was fiddling with his phone. 'Taxi,' he explained, when Ryan stopped in the act of getting into the car. 'A friend dropped me off on the way over.' He squinted at the phone. 'Huh. Picked a busy time, nothing for half an hour.' He looked back at the bar. The noise of the band was already making itself heard in the car park.

'Can I give you a lift?' Ryan suggested. It wasn't yet nine o'clock. When he got back, the farmhouse would be very empty.

'It's miles out of your way,' Andy objected. 'I can wait in the bar.'

Ryan shrugged. 'Not as if I have anything else to do.'

Andy hesitated, then they both winced as the bar door opened and closed behind another departing customer. A burst of thumping rock pulsed into the evening air.

'Okay, you're on,' Andy agreed. 'If you drop me at the gates, you can loop back.'

The blue convertible climbed steadily. Even in the slowly fading light, with his main attention on the unfamiliar road, Ryan could see that everything in the neighbourhood was expensive. Quiet, select, very little traffic – glimpses of well-kept homes and immaculate grounds, seen through security gates. Here and there were snatches of the equally expensive view – lights emerging into the dusk, and a dark phosphorescent sea. *You can practically smell the money.*

He dropped Andy a few yards from an open set of gates, as directed, and turned the car, about to start back down, when he heard the sound of another vehicle approaching in the quiet night, and saw the flicker of headlights. An open-topped sports car was approaching. He took in a brief flash of the dark-haired woman driving, and the man beside her in the passenger seat, before he turned his head away.

The MG swept in through the gates, as his heart galloped into overdrive.

'Sod, sod, sod.' He thumped the wheel. *Bad luck, bad timing.* He steadied his hands, as his heart rate slowed. He was overreacting. *Just two cars passing in poor light. Nothing to see here.*

'Hey, did you see that?' Thackeray was craning his head to look behind them as Nadine turned into the short driveway, up to the villa. She bit back the sharp retort that she'd had her attention on the road, not on a blue BMW convertible.

'What was it?'

'The driver of that car. It looked like that actor guy – the one you said you couldn't shake off.'

'Really?' Nadine was proud of how steady her voice was, with just the right note of surprised scepticism. *What the hell was Ryan doing here? And how the hell could* you *recognise him in this light?*

'He must be looking for you! Stalking you!'

'In the South of France? Do you really think he could have followed me here?'

Thackeray turned around, settling back in his seat. 'I suppose not. Especially in a motor like that,' he admitted sulkily. 'Anyone bothers you, you let me know.'

'I'll do that.' She risked the quick gesture of patting his knee.

'I don't want anyone bothering you.' Three large glasses of wine, and a brandy, that had prompted her to offer to drive, were making him belligerent. He seemed to realise it as she brought the car to a stop at the front steps. He let out a gusty sigh. 'It's an important time, darling. I don't want anything to spoil it.'

'I'm sure it won't.'

Nadine had expected the matter to drop once they were inside, drinking coffee in the villa's main salon, but Thackeray was recounting his suspicions to Hélène and Andy, with demands for extra security.

'Darling, it was a quick glimpse, from a moving car, in poor light,' she said firmly. 'How would he have known where to find me?' She ignored Andy's quick guilty grimace, which confirmed that it had been Ryan in the car.

'It looked like him,' Thackeray persisted. 'I checked him out on the internet,' he admitted. His lip curled in a sneer. 'A complete loser – hadn't worked for months before that two-bit play in Bristol. Surprised he could afford the fees for the dating site. Probably a hustler, looking to hit on a woman with money.'

Nadine swallowed her shock at Thackeray's revelation, pulling herself together to smile. 'Well, he's not going to attempt that with *me*, darling. I really don't have any worries about the guy.' *Nothing but the truth.* She perched on the arm of Thackeray's chair, putting her arm around him. 'It's very sweet of you to be concerned, but I know that you're fretting about nothing.' She squeezed Thackeray's shoulder. 'Let's talk about something else.'

'That was a hairy moment.' Hélène was sitting on the end of the bed, as Nadine removed her make-up. 'Not helped by the fact that he was right. Andy wants me to apologise, by the way. He should have waited for a cab. It was sheer bad luck. But who would have thought—'

'Don't worry,' Nadine interrupted her. 'And tell Andy not to either. I'm sure that it's over now.' She gave her face a last swipe with a cotton pad, dropping it in the bin. The scene with Thackeray had unsettled her, along with the revelation that he'd gone as far as tracking Ryan, presumably through the publicity for the play. When he'd asked, after the hotel incident, she'd told him only that Ryan was an actor, appearing locally. She suppressed a chilling touch of anxiety. She'd seen a new and disturbing side of the man tonight. *Probably closer to the real one.* 'We'll only be here for a couple more days. If there's no sign of Ryan, it can't go any further. We'll just have to keep Thackeray busy, spending money on wedding preparations.'

Ryan stood nursing a mug of coffee, watching the morning sun creep slowly across the terrace. He breathed deeply, taking in scented air, trying to control the impulse to kick himself for last night's carelessness. He'd convinced himself, when he got back to the farmhouse, that there was no way that Thackeray could have recognised him, only to have the conviction shattered by an early morning warning call from Andy, full of apologies. The news that Thackeray had researched him, after their brief meeting, was an unexpected shock.

'This guy is trickier than we thought.' Andy still had the note of apology in his voice. 'And more insecure. He needed to be sure that you weren't a threat, and that he had ammunition to counter you, if it looked like you might become one.'

That had caused a cold tremor down Ryan's back at the thought that he and Nadine might have been seen together somewhere. He quickly replayed everything he could remember of the past few days. He hadn't noticed anyone paying particular attention to them in the places they'd visited – but with his eyes and his thoughts on Nadine…

Had someone been following her, watching the farmhouse—

'You don't need to worry about it,' Andy had reassured, understanding the sudden silence on the line. 'Thackeray was perfectly fine all day. He only kicked off when he saw you. On last night's performance, he would have tackled Nadine before that, if he'd thought there was anything going on.'

Andy had rung off with an assurance of vigilance from Hélène and himself.

Now Ryan was sifting through his memory yet again, and coming up empty. To imagine that Thackeray would actually have Nadine followed… *That way, madness lies.*

He still had to resist an almost overpowering urge to get in the car and drive over to the villa, to scoop Nadine out of harm's way. *Out of Thackeray's way.* The man's attitude had sounded... disturbing... despite Andy's assurances that Nadine had handled him to perfection. He knew the impulse to snatch her away was wrong, and that Nadine wouldn't thank him for it, but it didn't stop the gnawing need to be *doing* something.

The only thing he could do, as Andy had assured him, was lay low at the farmhouse until Thackeray was gone. That it was the right advice didn't make it any easier to follow. Ryan finished the last of the coffee, put down the mug and started down the steps to the pool, hoping to swim off the gnawing restlessness.

He swam until his muscles began to protest. Giving up on the attempt to kill the pool water by flailing it to death, he turned on his back to float, staring at the unbroken blue of the sky. Andy had repeated what Thackeray had said, about him being a hustler in search of a rich woman, and had been suitably indignant on Ryan's behalf. *But is the guy really so wrong?* The disadvantage of lying low, even in luxurious surroundings, was that it gave him time to think. *Too much time.* The growing ache in his chest was so heavy he wouldn't have been surprised to sink, until the azure water of the pool closed over his head. Even that brief glimpse of Nadine last night...

If he wanted Nadine – and there was nothing else on earth that he *did* want – then he had to be in a position to meet her, if not on equal terms, then at least with something to offer. Either that, or set her free to find the person she deserved.

But not yet.

Please, not yet.

Chapter Thirty-Three

Saturday night, and all's well.

Or it will be, when you see the back of your fiancé tomorrow morning.

Nadine bit her lip, hoping her thoughts were not showing on her face. They'd filled the day with samples and suppliers, with a complete walk-through of everything related to the wedding, and set the date – exactly six weeks time. It would, of course, cost a little more to achieve such a tight timescale. Nadine's face felt stiff from smiling. She'd channelled excited gratitude, stifled the desire to throw things when she caught sight of Thackeray's self-satisfied expression, and given her very best impression of a woman totally caught up in arranging her wedding. *And totally unaware that she was actually caught up in a trickster's web.* Once she'd settled back into her role, it actually hadn't been too hard to lose herself in the planning. The magic of a celebration, in a beautiful setting, under the unbroken blue sky of the Côte d'Azur, had taken hold and carried her along.

Abetted by Hélène, she'd opted for a retro vibe – the glamour of the Riviera, embodied in the films of the 1950s, with a finger food buffet to allow guests to wander the villa's extensive grounds, and a towering chocolate wedding cake embellished with edible gold leaf. Vintage champagne would be chilled for mimosas and Kir royale. The tiny jewel box of a chapel would be lavishly decorated with roses and orchids, with potted citrus trees lining the entrance and the terraces. There would be a harpist and a string quartet and a singer for the chapel. The bride and groom would depart for their honeymoon from the jetty below the house, in a chauffeured motor launch. It was all impossibly, unbelievably over the top.

Thackeray had shed his febrile mood of Thursday night,

and had been at his most expansive and indulgent. There had been no more talk of potential stalkers. Nadine suspected that he'd realised that he'd not shown himself in a good light, and was as anxious to let the matter drop as she was.

Now they were enjoying pre-dinner drinks on the topmost terrace. Hélène had suggested they take the opportunity to try out the exclusive and upmarket local caterers who would provide the wedding buffet. Nadine was simply grateful not to be spending another evening alone with Thackeray in some fancy restaurant. She leaned back, letting her mind drift for a few blissful seconds, as she considered the glass in her hand, appreciating the pale straw-coloured champagne from a tasting case that had arrived from Paris.

With an effort, she tuned back into the conversation. Hélène and Thackeray were talking about the on-site chapel, and the details of the ceremony, to be performed by Thackeray's 'family friend'. Hélène had warned her that she intended to steer the conversation that way. Nadine sat up straighter to listen.

Hélène was looking uncharacteristically tense, her fingers tight on the stem of her glass. 'About the ceremony – the formalities, that is – you do realise, here in France, as non-residents—'

Thackeray waved an expansively reassuring hand. 'All that will be taken care of in the UK, before we get here.'

'Oh, good.' Hélène's apparent relief was subtly conveyed by the relaxing of her shoulders and her grip on the champagne flute. 'I'm glad you have it organised. And Reverend Ellis will be able to perform a lovely blessing—'

'He's really looking forward to it,' Thackeray cut her off, turning to Nadine. 'I was hoping that he could have been here tonight, as a little surprise for you, but unfortunately he couldn't manage it. He's keen to meet the lady who's captured my heart at last.' Thackeray raised his glass in a toast towards her, as everyone murmured suitable regrets. 'You'll meet him at the rehearsal though. Ah—' He gestured as one of the uniformed catering staff appeared in the doorway. 'It looks as if dinner is about to be served.'

Nadine stood up, to answer the soft knock on the exterior door of her cottage. Hélène stood outside, bearing a tray, with two mugs. She held it up. 'Herbal tea – night-time blend, help you sleep.'

'Sounds good.' Nadine stood aside, to let her in. The tea was an excuse for the visit, but even so it was welcome, to combat the weird mixture of tiredness and nervous energy she was experiencing.

Hélène put down the tray. 'It all seems to be working.'

Nadine nodded, flopping into a chair and taking one of the mugs, inhaling the delicate herbal scent. 'We were totally in the moment today.'

'We totally were,' Hélène agreed. They looked at each other and laughed. 'I have to say, spending Jake's money is a lotta fun.'

'That's what Cassie always says.' Nadine sipped her tea. 'We couldn't have done it without him bankrolling it. None of the suppliers will lose out.'

'He's one of the good guys, although he would hate to admit it.'

'Cassie says that too.' She put down her mug. 'Great job over the ceremony, by the way. It really looked like you were nervous about possibly losing the booking, because you hadn't made the legal stuff clear.'

'Well, we were pretty sure he knew the situation, or he wouldn't have organised his friendly vicar, but we couldn't just let it ride. I was so glad he jumped in with something I could grab onto. Now it looks like I think you're having a civil ceremony in the UK before coming over.'

'And he'll tell *me* that his reverend has special dispensation, or something.' Nadine picked up her mug again, cupping it in her palms and leaning back in her chair. 'He really does think I'm a brainless brunette.'

'Besotted brunette,' Hélène corrected. 'There is a difference. And really, would a bride, besotted or not, think to question it? We've been banking on that – and the idea that Andy and I are too naive and inexperienced to know we're being cheated. It all fits with his image of himself as the smartest guy in the room.'

Ryan cast a last look around the main room of the farmhouse, checking that he'd left nothing behind. He looked at his watch. Just over three hours before his departure time. Mickey had rung yesterday, once they were sure Thackeray was on his way, with flight details and instructions of where in the airport car park to leave the car, to be collected later.

'Thackeray refused all offers to take him to catch the plane, but this time we were able to follow him. He did the same thing as last time – private plane with a flight plan for Manchester. Jake's arranging to pick up the tail at the other end. This time we will not lose him.'

Ryan downloaded the documentation, packed his bag and tidied up. He was ready to go. He carried the bag to the car, letting the door close behind him. Straightening up, he looked back at the house. It was the epitome of a lifestyle that was way beyond his reach, and probably always would be.

A couple of days thinking time, alone at the farmhouse, had thrown up just one inescapable idea – it was time to finally let go of old dreams. He'd been telling himself for too long that he'd done what was needed. In reality he'd just been marking time, taking a portfolio of jobs that still left a sliver of possibility for him to cling to. He saw that clearly now. *Just been going through the motions.* It was time to man up, and stop chasing fantasies. *Give up the acting. Get the kind of job that would have satisfied Dad – steady, solid and reliable.* It might not give him a future with Nadine, but it would give him some self-respect.

Nadine dodged around a man rolling two enormous cases that seemed to want to make off in opposite directions. All her formalities were done, and she had time to hit the airport shops.

She stopped in front of a store with an impressive display of sunglasses. She'd spent a quiet Sunday with Hélène's laptop, catching up with work. If her involvement with the scam had taught her anything, it was that things could actually go on very well without her. She could afford to ease her foot on the pedal, and nothing would fall apart. She had a good team, a few of whom were very good indeed. *Time to think about some appropriate rewards – new titles, bonuses, maybe, in the future, the offer of a partnership?*

Rory had always been totally hands-on, and when he died, she'd simply followed the same pattern, putting her life on hold to build up the company in the shaky days after the loss of its driving force and visionary. At university she'd always vaguely imagined herself doing something creative, once she graduated. She wasn't sure what an English degree qualified you to do, and she'd had a number of temp jobs before she married. She'd certainly never imagined herself running a family company making designer beds. That had been Rory's dream, and she'd just found herself tagging along.

And then she'd been left holding the precious legacy, in shaken, grieving hands.

Alone.

But things were different now. She genuinely loved her work, but she could afford to take some time for herself. Build a few dreams of her own. Travel. Study, maybe. *Marry again, and start a family?*

She realised with a start that a sales assistant was leaning into the window in front of her, seeing her abstracted gaze as rapt attention, and beckoning her into the shop. Nadine bit her lip, on a half laugh. Well, she did need a new pair of sunglasses.

After purchasing a smoky 50s style pair that seemed to suit her mood of the moment, she wandered the shops, picking up a magazine for the journey, a small carton of macaroons and a bottle of body lotion to match her favourite French perfume, that she'd not been able to source in the UK. All together a good haul. Now her flight was being called. Her return flight was to Heathrow, not Bristol. She made her way to the gate, documents in hand.

Ryan retrieved his bag from the security scanner, dodging a cluster of sun-tanned ladies whose colourful tote bags suggested they'd enjoyed a weekend visiting gardens. The traffic had been much heavier than he'd expected, running him close to the limit for checking in, but he'd just made it, after a hectic dash from the car park. Now he could get his breath back over a coffee until the time came for boarding.

Approaching the departure gate, after downing an excellent Americano, he could see a line forming for Business Class. Near the head of it a woman with long dark hair caught his eye. *Oh, God, was he so far gone he was seeing Nadine in every dark-haired stranger?* The woman turned slightly, so that he could see her profile. His heart gave a violent lunge. Not a stranger. It *was* Nadine. Mickey had somehow omitted to mention that they were booked on the same flight to Heathrow. *Does she know I'm here?*

He cast a hunted look round. Surely there was no way John Thackeray could have anyone watching them? Nadine was relaxed, her hands full of parcels. *She* doesn't *know I'm here.* There was only one safe way to play it. *As if you've never met each other.* He took his place at the end of the line and moved with the flow, onto the aircraft.

And, of course, they had adjoining seats.

Nadine was stretching up to stow her packages in the locker. She hadn't seen him. 'May I help with those?' He kept his voice flat and neutral. Just a polite offer from a fellow passenger.

The small start she gave would have passed for surprise at being addressed. She turned, her eyes full of questions. 'That would be very kind, thank you.' He took the bags from her hand. The barest touch of skin on skin made him swallow hard, before he reached up with the parcels. She was still staring at him. He gave her the tiniest of nods, the message in his eyes.

Strangers.

Relief flooded through him when he saw she understood.

'Nadine! Nadine Wells! I thought it was you. Hello! It's so good to see you!' The gushing greeting, and a blast of heavy perfume, made them both turn towards the woman tottering down the aisle on pencil heels. Nadine was engulfed in a scented embrace.

'Hattie. Fancy seeing you here.'

'Long weekend. Nigel and Grace, you remember them? Such a lovely couple. He's something in financial services.' She gave a wide-eyed grimace that Ryan interpreted as 'little me doesn't understand that kind of stuff', before ploughing on. 'They've just bought a place outside Antibes, and of course I just *had* to come over to help them settle in. It's so nice to see you, darling. Is that your seat? Can we sit together? Or are you...' Hattie looked enquiringly from him to Nadine, with avid eyes, clearly checking for a connection. Behind her a flight attendant was approaching, the professional smile covering a steely intent to get dilatory passengers safely settled as quickly as possible.

'Please, take my seat.' He gestured permission, turning away and making his face a courteous blank, to let the attendant shepherd him into an empty place in the row behind.

'Oh. Yes.' Hattie looked flustered, and a trifle put out. 'You're not—'

'I think we'd better sit down,' Nadine intervened. 'We're holding everyone up.'

'Oh. Yes,' Hattie repeated, apparently only just noticing the late-coming passengers trying to squeeze past her. 'Thank you.' She waved a hand in Ryan's direction and finally sat down, only to let out an excited shriek. 'Darling! When did this happen?' She'd picked up Nadine's hand and was turning it back and forth, so that the light sparked off the diamond engagement ring. 'You are *such* a dark horse. Who's the lucky man?'

'It was very recent. Not anyone you know,' Nadine said quietly.

'He must be very special, the size of that rock.' Hattie laughed, in a way that was probably meant to be described as tinkling. 'But then, he would have to be, for you to even *think* of putting him in Rory's place.' She heaved a sentimental sigh. 'Rory was so *very* special, wasn't he? And you and he, together – complete soulmates. The perfect couple. I've always said, if anyone ever mentioned the idea of you marrying again, that it would have to be an exceptional man. And now you've found him.'

'Er, yes... You could say John *is* exceptional,' Nadine agreed.

Hattie patted her hand, taking another look at the diamond ring. 'And we have the whole of the flight for you to tell me *all* about him. I'm *so* glad that you've finally met someone, darling, who could measure up to Rory. I really do want to hear *everything*.'

Ryan leaned back in his seat, closed his eyes and tried not to listen to Hattie singing Rory's praises and attempting to coax information out of Nadine about the man who was to take his place.

It was going to be a long flight.

Once they landed he couldn't help himself from following the women to baggage reclaim, although he hadn't checked a bag. Hattie's well-travelled designer suitcase had already arrived. She claimed it and, with a flurry of perfumed air kisses and promises to do lunch, tottered off to find the friend who was putting her up in London for a few days. Ryan moved quietly to stand beside Nadine, watching the parade of almost indistinguishable blue and black suitcases bump their uneven way around the belt.

'Hattie is an old friend,' he said softly. 'She's known you… since you were married.'

Nadine kept her eyes on the conveyer. 'Acquaintance, not friend,' she corrected. 'She's a semi-professional freeloader. Pays her way in gossip.'

'So news of your engagement will be all over Bristol once she gets back there.'

'I hope not. I didn't tell her enough to be interesting.' He heard the soft sigh. 'I would have preferred to sit next to you.'

He wasn't quite sure if that was a compliment or an accusation. 'I'm sorry.'

'Not your fault. You did right to offer her the seat. She would have made something of it if you hadn't. Of us being together. *That* would have been interesting.'

Now that Hattie was gone, he could smell the delicate scent of Nadine's perfume. He wanted to reach out, to take her hand. Instead they stood side by side, watching the luggage, like polite strangers.

'How are you getting back to Bristol?'

'There's a car service waiting. You?'

'Tube, I suppose.' *And doesn't that say it all.*

Her shift in position told him that the grey striped case that had just appeared was hers. He reached to heft it off the belt and hand it over.

She smiled and murmured her thanks, as she would to any helpful stranger, then turned and walked away.

Chapter Thirty-Four

Nadine was having coffee with Cassie in the small seating area in her office, when Jake came through the connecting door, with a slim bundle of papers and a triumphant expression.

He bent to kiss his wife's cheek, dropping the bundle on the low table and collapsing bonelessly into a vacant chair. 'Kyle Edwin Dickens, known to his erstwhile associates as Charlie.'

'Erstwhile?' Cassie gave him a mocking glance. Nadine ignored this marital byplay and reached for the papers, separating out copies of photographs.

They were clearly old and slightly fuzzy, reproductions of reproductions. Casual shots of groups of teenagers, snapped outside amusement arcades and pubs, and one clustered around a powerful looking motorcycle. It took her a moment to pick out John Thackeray, at the centre of the group, grinning cockily into the camera. The change from the teenager to the man, the man he was *now*, was massive, but the features were still identifiable, if you knew what you were looking for.

'It's definitely him.' She passed the photos to Cassie. 'He's what... seventeen, eighteen?'

'About that. Born in Carlisle, where those were taken, and where he is now, assisting with the dispensing of justice at the Crown Court.'

'So, the jury service was genuine?' Cassie put the photographs down.

'It was. He's drawn a big robbery case, so he'll be there for a while.'

'Hah!' Cassie grinned. 'The goddess who looks after justice has an ironic sense of humour.'

'Themis,' Nadine said absently, leafing through the papers. 'Goddess of Justice,' she explained, when Cassie tilted her head in enquiry. 'He rang me yesterday to say that the trial might take longer than he was expecting, but he didn't say what it was. Not allowed to talk about it.'

'Glad to know he's taking his duties seriously.' Cassie looked over at Jake, who was leaning back, hands behind his head. 'Go on then – life and times of John Thackeray – who is he really?'

'The gang he hung out with when those pictures were taken were small-time offenders – car theft, shoplifting, handling stolen goods. He was suspected of being involved, but never charged with anything. Not enough evidence.'

'Slippery customer, even then.'

'I think so.' Jake gestured to the photos. 'But easy to put it all down to youthful stupidity, getting in with the wrong crowd, etcetera, if he ever needed to.'

'But we know that Kyle graduated to greater things.' Cassie picked up one of the photos, shook her head and returned it to the pile.

'He clearly had ambitions that were bigger than Carlisle was offering him. When he hit twenty he disappeared off the radar. Cut his ties to the old gang and left town. His parents were still there, and he inherited the old family home after his mother died, about five years ago. It's a respectable little mid-terrace – which he still owns and which it seems he keeps up – hence the jury summons, as he's on the electoral roll, although he told Nadine it was a mix up over a place he'd once owned in Birmingham. He pays the rates and the bills, and an old neighbour goes in once a week to look the place over and collect the post, which is forwarded to a PO Box in London. According to the neighbour, Kyle has made it big, particularly in America, providing some sort of consultancy service to Hollywood and Silicon Valley. She gets postcards from L.A and San Francisco. He travels a lot, so doesn't have a permanent address. Lives out of a suitcase in hotels and rented apartments, sometimes in a client's mansion or beach house. But he still has a sentimental attachment to the old home town.'

'Hmmm.' Cassie drew the exclamation out, picking up one of the photos again. 'He *has* come a long way. But he still has a bolthole and an identity there, just in case.'

'Yes, but I'm guessing it's not one he'd particularly want to drop back into.' Jake looked enquiringly at Nadine.

'I don't think so,' she agreed. 'The changes in him...' She gestured towards the pictures. 'Unless you were really looking for it, or knew him really well in the past, I don't know if you'd recognise him. It's not just age. He's completely re-invented himself. John Thackeray is a thousand miles away from Kyle Dickens.'

Jake nodded in agreement. 'We don't know who, where, or what he's been doing in the last twenty years, but for our purposes, that doesn't much matter. He's using a false identity and false passport here in Bristol, which is enough. We were able to follow him from the plane in Manchester. The people who are watching him say that he's keeping a very low profile. He's staying in a budget hotel, having room service and only going outside in daylight hours to walk to the court each day. He's got the neighbour's son in at the old house, doing some decorating – disruption and paint fumes would be a reason for not staying there, if he needed one. If he has gone anywhere near the place, it's been after dark. We don't have twenty-four hour surveillance on him.'

Jake reached forward to draw a typed report out of the paperwork. It had another photograph attached to the back of it. He passed it over. Nadine drew in a sharp breath. It was a recent photo, probably snapped surreptitiously from a mobile phone, a slightly blurred image of a figure descending a set of shallow steps. This was more clearly John Thackeray, but the cheap suit and gelled back hair was not the John Thackeray she knew. The only thing that could be labelled designer *here* was the hint of stubble darkening his jaw.

Nadine let the picture drop. 'So... what do we do now?'

'We forget we've seen all this, for a start.' Jake gestured to the papers. 'And we carry on as we have been. The wedding plans proceed *exactly* as arranged. We don't want any suggestion that you're not expecting it to go ahead.'

Cassie was gathering the paperwork together. 'Absolutely the safest way to play this now – perfectly straight – which means that you and I have to do something about sourcing a wedding dress.'

Nadine wrinkled her nose. When John Thackeray had disappeared, Penny the planner had popped up again. *Keeping an eye on the bride.* She was ruthlessly liaising with Hélène over email and Skype and showing strong signs of corralling Nadine to escort her to a choice of wedding dress outlets. 'I suppose so.'

'Come on, it will be fun.'

'An outfit I don't need, for a wedding that is not going to take place.'

'That is defeatist talk, and dangerous.' Cassie waved a finger. 'You don't have to think like that.'

'Yes,' Nadine conceded, with a sigh. 'You're right. But I don't want trains and veils, or one of those puffy confections that Penny keeps trying to show me,' she warned.

'I was thinking vintage – something cool and classy.'

Nadine tilted her head, then nodded. 'That sounds good.'

'In that case, it's a date.' Cassie looked thoughtful for a moment. 'Buying a dress is one thing – you need it to head off Penny – and a dress is always a dress, you'll find somewhere to wear it, but it seems a pity about all the arrangements for the wedding going to waste.' She shrugged. 'Nothing to be done. We knew we'd have to carry on the deception almost to the finish.' She turned towards her husband. 'Anything new on that?'

'Not much yet,' Jake admitted. 'I'm going to have a quiet word with a few people before Thackeray comes back from Carlisle, to get something official on the move. I think it's time. Michelle hasn't had any success in tracking down any more wedding cons.' He shrugged. 'It was always a long shot. Without any extra evidence I think it's going to be difficult to go forward with anything related to the fraud. A case would rest too much on what we've done, and there would be too much weight put on Nadine's role in it. We do know that he's operating here under an assumed name. There's proof of that. If he's picked up at the airport, flying out to the wedding on a false passport, that would be a start. Nadine can simply fade out of the picture, and "Team Bride" will never even appear in the story. As far as Thackeray is concerned Nadine would just be his last con trick.' Jake leaned forward, to check the temperature of the coffee pot. Finding it still warm, he poured himself some, using his wife's cup. 'We may not have gathered enough to successfully pursue the fraud, but there are other offences the authorities can look into. We'll have to be satisfied with that.'

'That will be enough for me.' Nadine shrugged off a brief chill, relieved that she would not after all have to be part of a case against Thackeray. She stood up, looking at her watch. 'I need to be back at the office. Thanks for the coffee, and the update.'

'You're welcome.' Cassie rose to offer a kiss, and see her out.

When Cassie came back, her husband was still lounging in her easy chair, finishing his coffee. She dropped into the chair beside him.

'Nadine all right?' he queried.

'Yes – but I know she'll be thankful when it's all over. I'm glad Thackeray is safely in Carlisle, so she doesn't have to keep up weeks of pretence with him. You do think the authorities will take it up, on the basis of what we have?'

Jake shrugged again, without replying, but his steady look suggested confidence in his powers of persuasion.

Cassie hunched her shoulders, then relaxed them. 'I'm ready

to see the end of it too. It seemed exciting when we started, but it's not that way any more.'

'Intrusion of reality,' Jake agreed. 'We won't be having the big dramatic final scene that I think we imagined when we began this – the last reel where the plot is revealed, the good guys triumph and the villain is confronted by his crimes.' He shook his head. 'I'm not sure now if that was ever really feasible, but Thackeray should at least get some of what he deserves.'

'I'm sure he'll find a tap on the shoulder at the airport quite dramatic enough,' Cassie said soberly. 'If it works out as you hope, he won't have any idea that Nadine was involved.' She inclined her head towards her husband in a small salute. 'Thank you for that.'

Jake just shook his head again, with a quiet smile. 'Everyone played their part. We've all done the best we could.'

'We have that,' Cassie agreed. 'And some of it *was* fun.' She sighed. 'It's a pity about having to ditch the wedding arrangements, after all that planning. It would have been spectacular.' It was her turn to shake her head. 'Can't be helped. It was necessary.'

'And it *will* have been worth it,' Jake assured her.

Work, work and more work. Ryan checked off a wine delivery at the service door. It was drizzling with rain and the alley smelt pungently of garlic from the pizza restaurant at the end of the block. He'd run down his commitments to the escort service, refusing new clients and passing on existing ones, but the bar was doing good business and he was working extra shifts. Only the occasional joke about his 'jet set' lifestyle reminded him that the trip to the Riviera had ever happened. *That's if you don't count the constant cold weight in your chest.*

When she remembered, Shannon asked him if he'd heard anything about the audition he was supposed to have attended, commiserating when he said no, which added guilt to the cold weight. If she asked again, he would tell her that he hadn't got the part. He hadn't called Nadine, and she hadn't called him. Which was perfectly fine. Exactly what he wanted.

The longing, and the cold weight, would go away.

Eventually.

Yeah, you just keep telling yourself that.

The few days at the farmhouse had been a golden dream. The flight back had shown him exactly how much of a dream, listening to Hattie's breathless admiration of Rory and the relationship that he and Nadine had shared. *You really think you're going to compare with that?*

He didn't think it. He really wasn't that foolish.

He'd always known about Nadine's circumstances, and about Rory, but only in a general way. When she began to book him regularly, he'd googled – research for the job – and found out bare details, but Nadine rarely referred to her marriage, and he'd respected her reticence. He hadn't noticed at the time, but until Karen's wedding, he'd never escorted her that close to home. He'd accompanied her to weddings of old university friends, up and down the country, and once to a memorial service, and to a lot of business and trade functions, including a stop-over at a furniture fair in Milan, where she'd collected an award on behalf of the company. They'd met people who knew Rory from university days, and in business, but never anyone who'd known both of them recently, and up to the end, as a couple.

On the flight from Nice, listening to Hattie, the reality that he'd been trying to ignore had hit him like a wall of falling bricks. That was Nadine's world, and he had no business to imagine being part of it. It wasn't that he thought that Nadine was using him, or that she hadn't meant the things that were whispered in the heat and the dark – a shiver of longing went through him – it was just that real life wasn't composed of stolen nights on the Riviera. They were simply too far apart.

She'd try, he knew that she would, and they'd probably have some good times before the thing inevitably ran its course, but it wasn't enough. He didn't want to see the light in her eyes cool to indifference, and then embarrassment. What she needed, God help him, was a man like the one John Thackeray was pretending to be. *You've known that all along.*

He *was* going to get his life in order, but not with some forlorn hope that suddenly dreams would come true. He'd had a taste of magic, which was more than a lot of people got. It was time for him to step aside, even though making that choice hurt like hell. Nadine was never going to know that he'd fallen in love with her. He wasn't burdening her with that. *Everything dies, if it isn't fed.* The vulnerable places in his heart would eventually heal.

As he checked the last case of Sauvignon Blanc, his phone rang. Fishing it out of his pocket, he nodded to the van driver, who was waiting for the consignment to be signed off.

'Jean-Paul! Hello! Good to hear your voice. *Ca va?*' He tucked the phone under his chin to fingernail scrawl a signature on the outstretched tablet, releasing the driver to get back into his vehicle, then let the phone drop back into his hand. 'I'm fine. Absolutely fine. What can I do for you?'

Chapter Thirty-Five

Thackeray had chosen the hotel carefully. On the outskirts of Birmingham, with a spa for her and a golf course for him, the rooms were luxurious, the restaurant an award winner. *And it's a long way from Carlisle.* The court case was in its third week, and Thackeray was getting restive. The weekend was meant to be a pre-wedding break, for both of them.

'Chance for us to relax, and for you to get some pampering, darling,' Thackeray greeted her in the foyer, with a kiss on the cheek and the indulgent smile.

Nadine clamped down on the impulse to roll her eyes. His careless implication that the biggest thing on her mind was what colour to paint her nails grated on her nerves. *Does he even know he's doing it? Would some women feel they were being cosseted, rather than patronised?* She clamped down even harder on the thought that Ryan would never treat her like a brainless bimbo. Although he did sometimes tease her about her choice of hat. She remembered a large confection that *had* looked a bit like a pink meringue.

The sudden surge of longing almost overwhelmed her. She swallowed hard. She was going to enjoy the weekend. *It's probably your money that's paying for it – if the hotel gets paid at all.* She made a mental note to ask Jake to check, when the thing was done.

'I'm going to make the most of it,' she assured Thackeray. 'I did some research online.' She made her smile as arch as she could manage. 'The spa has a bridal package.'

'You go for it, darling. Whatever you want.'

As they walked together to the desk, to check in, Nadine surreptitiously studied him. Under the usual gloss, he looked... haggard. *The strain of being both Thackeray and Dickens – or something else?*

They'd completed the formalities – Thackeray had booked

a suite, two en suite bedrooms and a sitting room between – and were turning to follow the bell boy and their bags, when a tall, heavyset man crossed the foyer.

'John! Good to see you. Here for the weekend?' The man was looking her over with interest. 'Going to introduce me to the lovely lady?'

'Er.' Some of the colour had gone from Thackeray's face. Nadine was sure of it. 'My fiancée,' he stressed the word. 'Nadine Wells. This is... Kenneth Fletcher.' Just the tiniest hesitation over the name.

The man was nodding. 'Old business associates,' he explained to Nadine, then turned back to Thackeray, dismissing her.

'I wasn't expecting to see you here.' Thackeray's voice sounded strained. 'I... er... thought you were still in America.'

Nadine looked up at him, attempting to read his expression. Why did she have the impression that he was lying? *Did you really think Fletcher was in America or did you know he wasn't?* She couldn't tell. Thackeray was clearly uncomfortable, but trying not to show it.

'Got back two days ago,' Fletcher explained. 'Been getting up to speed about what's been happening in my absence. Are you going to be on the course tomorrow, John?' he asked abruptly.

For a second Thackeray looked completely blank. 'Oh. Golf. Yes.'

'We must play a round. I need to have a chat with you. About that thing we discussed, before I went to America.' He gave Thackeray a pointed stare.

Thackeray cleared his throat. 'Oh... yes. That would be...' His voice faded.

Fletcher gave him another hard stare, and then nodded, as if satisfied with what he saw. 'Good. I'll see you tomorrow then, after breakfast. Nice to meet you, sweetheart.' He turned back briefly to address her, with a confident leer, before striding off.

Nadine took a deep breath. The man was an ill-mannered boor. *And maybe something else?* 'That's good, that you can play golf with your friend,' she said brightly. 'Now I won't have to worry about you being at a loose end while I'm enjoying the spa.'

'No. It's great. Great,' Thackeray repeated, his eyes on the front of the hotel, where Fletcher was getting into the back seat of a large black SUV.

Nadine got the feeling that actually it wasn't that great.

Fletcher, if that was his name, wasn't staying at the hotel. He turned up in golfing gear the next day, just as they were leaving the dining room after breakfast. The black SUV could be seen through the open doors, pulling away from the front entrance. Nadine had wondered why Thackeray wanted to take this expensive break before the wedding, and assumed that he was using it to make sure of her, or possibly because he was bored, stuck in Carlisle. Was there something else going on? Had he been trying to avoid Fletcher?

She'd texted the name to Cassie last night, part of a gushing message about the wonderful weekend. Cassie would read between the lines. Nadine left the men to their game, and headed for the spa. She had the distinct impression that Thackeray was not looking forward to his day on the course. *Not my problem.*

The facilities of the treatment rooms were as upmarket as the rest of the hotel. Nadine opted for the full bridal experience, relaxing as the therapist lit scented candles and selected massage oils, chatting as she did so. The woman was impressed by both the weekend away and the plans for the wedding. 'Gosh, you are lucky. I wish my bloke did romantic stuff like that.'

Nadine just smiled, settling down to enjoy her day.

Relaxed, and knowing she was looking as good as the treatment rooms could make her, Nadine caught up with

Thackeray in the hotel bar for pre-dinner drinks. She accepted an Aperol spritz, slightly disconcerted to see that he was nursing what looked like a double whisky. There was no sign of Fletcher.

Thackeray took her hand, lifting it to his lips. 'Darling, you look absolutely wonderful.'

'Thank you. Did you have a good day?'

They talked for a few minutes about the features of the golf course and the spa. Nadine turned to put her glass down on the bar, in order to search in her bag for a handkerchief. When she turned back, Fletcher was walking towards them. He nodded to her, in a perfunctory way, his attention focused on Thackeray. 'Just on my way, John. It was good to chat today. I know you'll think carefully about what we discussed.' The man's eyes narrowed and hardened. 'You really do need to be moving on. I thought we had an agreement on that in May, before I went to the States. When you've been doing the same thing for a while and your face and the way you operate gets known... well, time for a change.' He nudged Thackeray's shoulder in a gesture that was meant to seem jocular. 'I'm sure you're not looking for a permanent retirement, but you don't want to take any chances with your health. Take my advice. Ease up for a bit. I think you'll find there are opportunities in *Carlisle* that you *wouldn't* want to miss.'

Luckily neither man was paying her any attention, so Nadine's start of surprise at the mention of Carlisle wasn't noticed. She leaned towards the bar to retrieve her glass, giving herself time to compose herself.

'I'll do that, Ken. Plenty to think about.' On the surface Thackeray's voice sounded confident and casual, but the words had a hollow undertone and his fingers clutching his glass had whitened, just for a second. 'I'll be sure to let you know.'

'Don't wait too long. I'll be expecting your call.'

There was a brief pause, before Fletcher spun on his heel and left the bar without saying goodbye.

There was another pause, before Thackeray collected himself and turned to her, with a rueful smile. 'Sorry about that, darling. Bit of a rough diamond, Ken. Not too many social graces.'

'I noticed,' Nadine agreed, with a wry grimace. 'But a good businessman?'

'Oh yes. Very single-minded.' Thackeray's praise sounded forced. 'He goes after what he wants.'

'I'm sure. Oh!' With some relief, she saw the maître d' at the entrance to the restaurant calling them to their table.

When they were seated Thackeray immediately ordered another whisky. Nadine made a fast decision not to notice his unease or to mention the 'business opportunity' in Carlisle, chattering in what she knew was an inane way about her day in the spa. Halfway down the fresh glass of spirit, Thackeray seemed to pull himself together. He reached over to take her hand. 'Darling.' He fingered her engagement ring. 'You are absolutely the best thing that ever happened to me. You know that, don't you?'

'John!' With a coy tilt of her head, she conjured up a smile. 'You say the most wonderful things.'

'It's true.' He was gazing at her, with a look she couldn't decipher. 'Absolutely the best thing. I don't think I realised—'

Whatever declaration he was about to make was cut off as the waiter brought their first course. Nadine surveyed the carefully constructed tower of seafood on her plate. How was it possible to get so tired of fine dining so fast? Right now she'd willingly swop this, and the courses to come, for scrambled eggs, an old horror film and a sharing tub of popcorn. *Don't go there. Don't think of Ryan.*

She considered Thackeray's down bent head as he addressed his plate. If their relationship had been for real, this would be her future life. *If you loved this man…*

Disconcertingly Thackeray raised his head, and saw her studying him. He put down his fork and reached again for her hand, pressing it with an unexpectedly firm grip. His eyes were fixed on hers, with an expression she'd never seen before. There was something urgent, raw, and... desperate?

'You look so lovely tonight.' His chest rose and fell in a deep breath. 'The wedding can't come soon enough, my... love. I wish... I wish we were on the Riviera now, that it was all happening tomorrow. I really want us to make a go of it. You do know that, don't you? I need you, Nadine.'

Nadine's breath caught hard in her throat. She stared, unable to speak, as his fingers continued to hold tight to hers. Need? That was a word he'd never uttered. A word she didn't want to hear now. The urbane veneer was fracturing and something else was breaking through.

'Is everything satisfactory, madam, sir?' The interruption was a blessed intrusion. The waiter stood beside the table, with an expression of polite inquiry.

'Oh, yes, perfect,' Thackeray responded, withdrawing his hand. Nadine simply nodded her agreement. The waiter moved to top up their wine glasses and replenish the bread basket, and the moment passed. Plates were removed and a main course of lamb was served. When Thackeray next spoke it was to comment on the quality of the food, to admire the colour she'd chosen for her nails, and to ask about progress in her search for a wedding dress.

'My friend Cassie has found me some things to look at in a vintage shop in Bath. We're going there on Monday.'

'Vintage.' Thackeray frowned. 'That means second-hand. Wouldn't you rather have something new?'

'Cassie has quite a talent for sourcing unusual things. I don't want a long dress, and I *really* don't want yards of satin and lace.' She wrinkled her nose. 'Cassie suggested an old style cocktail dress, something with a bit of character.'

'Well, if that's what you would like, I'm sure it will be delightful.' She could see doubt in his eyes, but he raised his glass to her. 'Don't leave it too long though, in case you do decide you'd prefer something new,' he warned.

'If I do, Penny will come to the rescue.'

'Ah. Penny.' His voice sounded clipped. 'I'm sure she would.'

The waiter bustled up to set down dessert menus. Thackeray waved them away. 'We'll both have the chef's special soufflé.'

'Certainly, sir, an excellent choice.'

Nadine opened her mouth and closed it again, as the man gathered up the menu that she hadn't had the chance to open. *It's only a soufflé.* 'I'm sure it will be delicious.' *And I am so glad that I am* not *marrying you.*

It was just before midnight. The sitting room of the suite had long picture windows, overlooking the golf course. They stood for a while, admiring a sky tinselled with stars. Thackeray was nursing a brandy. Nadine had opted for decaffeinated coffee. After a while she turned to put down her cup, stifling a yawn and excusing herself with a laugh. 'Being pampered all day is completely exhausting.'

They'd fallen into a routine of a simple brush on the lips or the cheek. Tonight Thackeray took her in his arms.

Have to kiss a lot of frogs.

When he raised his head, his eyes were very dark. 'Darling... the wedding... now that it's so close...' His voice was husky. His glance skittered towards the door of her bedroom.

'It's going to be a day to remember.' Gently she disengaged herself. 'Goodnight, John.'

Heart beating fast, she crossed the room. Entering her bedroom and closing the door behind her, she leant against it. Her legs were shaking. She stood silent, listening, until she heard the door to the other bedroom open and close. She let out a long wobbly sigh. Had she misinterpreted? She didn't think so. She knew what was being asked, although it wasn't put into words.

Thackeray had come close to shifting the game to a whole different level.

Why?

And why now?

Did it have anything to do with Kenneth Fletcher, the man who went after what he wanted, and had business opportunities in Carlisle?

She heard a distant clock chime two, before she fell asleep.

Chapter Thirty-Six

The clear night was followed by a sunny morning. The hotel had once been a country house for a local gentry family, and Nadine suggested a walk around the extensive grounds before Thackeray had to leave. He'd explained the need to be gone before lunch, with the excuse of a meeting with the agent who managed his property portfolio to sign some new tenancy agreements. *And because it takes longer to drive to Carlisle than to the other side of Birmingham? Or is he avoiding another encounter with Fletcher?*

'I'm sorry, darling,' he apologised when she'd made a token protest over his having to attend to business on a Sunday. 'The paperwork is time critical, I'm afraid, and with the court thing tying me up, it's the only chance of getting it done.' He pulled her close, dropping a kiss on her forehead. 'I'll find a way to make it up to you, I promise.'

Tomorrow there will be roses.

The walk was pleasant, skirting the edge of the golf course, where players were taking advantage of the sunshine. Nadine had her nerves of the night before well under control. When they paused to watch some of the play on the course, from a safe distance, and Thackeray commented on the excellence of the greens and the round he had enjoyed the previous day, the question rose before she had really thought about it. 'Is it a property deal that Mr Fletcher wants you to get involved in?' Property was how John Thackeray was supposed to make his living, along with the occasional sideline of import and export. There might even be an element of truth in it.

'What?' Thackeray started slightly, drawing his eyes away from the golfers. 'Oh, er… yes. But I don't think it's something I want to pursue. I'm going to have to persuade him to take no for an answer.' He gave her an unconvincing smile. 'Shall we start heading back?'

After waving goodbye, half an hour later, Nadine walked thoughtfully towards the front doors of the hotel. She hadn't missed the sudden stiffness in Thackeray when she'd asked about Fletcher, or that during their walk her fiancé had been subtly quizzing her about assets of her company that might be rapidly realised. She certainly hadn't missed the black SUV that had fallen in behind Thackeray's car, when it pulled out from the hotel drive and into the main road.

Ryan sprawled on the elderly swing seat on his brother's patio, nursing the last inch of a beer. The sounds and scents of an early Sunday evening in suburbia drifted over the fence. Lawn mowers and cut grass, teenagers playing a noisy game of cricket, a barking dog, the bass thump of a music track that he couldn't quite identify, the acrid smell of barbeque firelighters.

They'd run the twins around the garden for over an hour, in a hectic game of football. Now his sister-in-law, Katie, was supervising baths, prior to bed. Later he'd be hounded to read a story. Both boys were proficient readers, but still clamoured for him to read, because 'Uncle Ryan does all the voices.' *The acting skills still have some use.*

From the sound of laughter from the upstairs bathroom window, the boys still had plenty of bounce. Uncle Ryan, not to put too fine a point on it, was knackered. *Which might have something to do with the fact that you're not sleeping too well?* He pushed that thought aside as his brother came out of the house, with two more beers.

Sean nudged his feet out of the way, to plonk down beside him, giving his brother an amused glance. 'Can't take it any more, old man?'

Ryan made a rude gesture, accepting another beer when Sean held it out to him. 'Shit, did we ever have that much energy?' He took a swig of the fresh bottle. 'Hughie's getting good. Too bloody good.'

'He's in the school team.' Sean grinned with paternal pride.

'And Ross for rugby. As like as two peas, yet they totally go for different things. Whereas we—'

'— did the same things and were as competitive as hell.'

Sean's face clouded. 'There was a reason for that, and it wasn't just that I wanted to be as good as my big brother.'

'Dad.' Ryan heard the flatness in his voice. It was always there when he spoke about the old man. *Still carrying the bloody baggage.*

There was a loud crash from the bathroom window, followed by a wail and Katie's voice, issuing orders.

'Er... Do we need...' Ryan jerked his head towards the house.

'Nah.' Sean shook his head. 'She'll yell if it's life threatening.'

They both sat silent for a moment. Katie didn't yell.

Ryan let out a breath, feeling his tension dissipate. 'Right. I'm assuming you didn't invite me over here just to let your demon sons half kill me, and then feed me supper?'

'What makes you think you're getting supper?'

Ryan didn't bother to answer that. The enticing scent of whatever Katie was cooking for the grown-ups was wafting gently from the kitchen. He sipped the beer, and studied Sean. He knew when his kid brother had something on his mind. He let out a long sigh. 'What?'

'Just – you're not happy, Ry. I know that. Can I help?'

'No.' Ryan shrugged. 'It's just the usual things – stuff, the future, what I'm doing with my life.'

'Making a career in something you love?' Sean asked softly. 'This is about Dad, isn't it?'

'It's about a reality check.'

He could hear his father's voice, *'You're never going to make it at that acting stuff. Needs proper talent, that does. Past time you grew up, lad, found yourself a real job. Finally make something of yourself.'*

'Yeah, well, Dad had a lot of opinions to share. Doesn't mean he was right.' Sean shoved at Ryan's shoulder, making him turn to look at him. 'It's *your* life, Ry.'

'But what if he *was* right? That I've been wasting my time all these years?'

'So what? It's *your* choice to make,' Sean reiterated. 'Dad was stubborn and self-opinionated and he liked to try and run everyone's lives for them. Just because *he* thought you were wasting your time, doesn't make it true.' Ryan shut his eyes. Sean could always put his finger unerringly on the source of the pain. 'You have a *right* to your own life, Ryan. But you're planning to give it all up, aren't you? Letting him win.'

'It's not a matter of winning!' Ryan sat up with a jerk that made the old swing shudder. He scooped his hand through his hair. 'I just... I need to make changes.'

Sean let out a long breath – tiredness and an edge of satisfaction. It told Ryan, without any words, that his brother had got the admission he'd been looking for – that he was finally turning his back on his acting ambitions. *It's always been like that. He reads you like a bloody script.*

They sat in silence for a while, looking at the rapidly darkening garden. *My brother, savouring his victory.* Ryan picked up his beer and took a swig.

Sean slanted a sideways glance at him. 'Why? Why do you have to change? And why now?' He waited for a beat, then answered his own question. 'It's a woman, isn't it?'

Ryan waved the question, and the answer, away. 'It's just time, that's all. Putting away childish things, and all that.'

'There's never been anything childish about your ambitions, bro, or your talent. And if she wants to change you that much, then she might not be the right one.' Sean shifted on the swing to study his brother. 'A woman. And for some reason, there's a problem. Is she married?'

'No! I'd never get involved with—' Too late Ryan realised what Sean had done. Manoeuvred him into giving himself away. He saw the knowledge in Sean's expression. He could still lie, but his brother knew him too well. 'Yes, alright.

That's not the reason I want to change, but, yes, I have met someone—'

'Wow! That's great.' Sean reached over to thump him on the back, Ryan fended him off.

'It's not going anywhere. We had… well, a thing, when I went to the Riviera. But it's not going any further than that. It's… complicated, and it's over.'

Sean was sitting back, looking sceptical. 'Really? Doesn't look like it from where I'm sitting, bro. Who is she… one of your escort ladies?' he guessed. 'If you've had a *thing*, then it's a bit late to have a dose of scruples about *that*, so there's another reason.' He studied his brother. Ryan squirmed inside. Sean was the only person who could see through him. 'Hah!' Comprehension dawned on Sean's face. 'You don't think you're good enough. What is she, bloody royalty?' he demanded gruffly. 'You're a good bloke, Ry. If she can't see that, then she's not worth your time. And certainly not worth grieving over.'

'It's not like that.' It cut him that Sean had so effortlessly identified the emotions that were tearing him apart. But that was Sean. Always. *And it is a form of grieving.* 'She's not married, at least not now. She's a widow. Her husband… well, he's a hard act to follow.' *Make that an impossible one.* 'She's way out of my league; she's got money, a business. The right sort of friends.' He could feel his face crumpling. When you recited it, like that, out loud. *You can hear how impossible it is.*

'You think you're not good enough for her,' Sean repeated flatly. 'What does she think?'

'She's… interested, for now. But it can't go anywhere, Sean.' There was desperation in his voice. 'We're just too far apart. And before you say anything, she's never done or said anything to make me feel that, and she never would. It's what *I* feel. We had… a few days, and it was magic. But I don't fit into her world, other than as a paid escort, acting a part. And

I can't, won't,' he corrected himself, 'I won't hang around to watch while she realises that. I don't want to watch while it all...' His voice faded and failed.

'Oh hell.' Sean stared into Ryan's face. 'You're in love with her, aren't you, you poor sod?' *That's my little brother, finger straight on the pain.*

'Yes.' Ryan hung his head. 'But I'm not going to do anything about it. Not with her. But it's made me think. About who I am and where I should be.' He looked around the garden, at the uneven grassy impromptu football pitch, the neat tubs of herbs that Katie tended, the dark pink rose, rambling over the fence. 'I want something like this, Sean, a home, and a family. It won't be with Nadine, but I hope it will be with someone, and for that I have to change the dream. It can't be acting any more. I've given it long enough. I've known it for a while, but I wasn't ready... I can't keep clinging on, neither one thing nor the other. I have to choose. She's given me that, and I'm grateful for it.' He cleared his throat, which was suddenly thick. 'I've had the offer of a job, an old friend put me on to it – you remember Jean-Paul, from exchange visits to France when we were in school? It's a good opportunity, better than I might have hoped for – as a deputy manager in a new hotel. I'm going to take it.' He saw his brother's expression. 'It is *not* letting Dad win.'

'I wasn't thinking that.'

'What then?'

'That the apple doesn't fall far from the tree. You can be just as stubborn and bloody-minded as he was.'

Chapter Thirty-Seven

'It was all... well, a bit creepy,' Nadine confessed to Cassie, as they set out dress hunting. She was still going over the events of the weekend, although she'd already filled Cassie in on the details. 'All that stuff in the restaurant, and then later... If I'd given him any encouragement, I'm sure he'd have made a move to share my bed, and then there was the business about Kenneth Fletcher.'

'He was frightened of him?'

'I don't know. I don't think Fletcher was there by accident, or that he was just a man looking to do a lucrative deal with an old friend. I think Thackeray was shocked to see him, although he covered it well. Fletcher was threatening him, I'm sure. And Thackeray was certainly rattled, but I don't know that he was going to give in. He said he was going to try to change Fletcher's mind,' she said doubtfully. 'It sounded as if Kenneth Fletcher is the one behind the wedding scams, and intended to pull the plug, but Thackeray isn't willing to give it up. He's being sidelined, and he's not going quietly... But all that stuff about retirement, and his health.' She gave a small shudder. 'Fletcher was telling him to go back to Carlisle.'

'And Fletcher has the power to make him go.'

'Which makes Fletcher his boss, and the real force behind the scams and whatever else might be going on.'

'Jake will check it out,' Cassie said reassuringly. 'And you won't be seeing Thackeray again until the jury service is over. Maybe he'll have made his peace with Fletcher by then. I think you can safely put it all out of your mind for the moment.' Cassie gave her a brisk hug. 'Come on, we have a dress to buy.'

The tiny jewel box of a shop, stuffed with all manner of vintage clothing, was tucked away in one of Bath's narrowest backstreets. When they arrived, Julie, the owner, flipped the sign on the door to show the shop was closed. 'Now we can have some fun!'

Cassie and Julie disappeared through a door at the back of the shop. Nadine prowled amongst the shelves, uncovering a heavily beaded evening bag, which looked as if it might have been carried by a flapper in the roaring twenties. Even if she didn't find a dress, she'd already decided the bag was going home with her.

'Very Daisy Buchanan,' Cassie approved when she came back. 'We have three possibilities, but there's one... Well, I'll let you see for yourself.' She moved a pile of frothy net petticoats off a small chaise longue, putting them gently on the floor, and tapped the seat next to her. Nadine obediently sat.

The first two dresses were lovely – a blush pink chiffon creation and a rather more slinky number in a pale coffee colour, but it was the third that made Nadine's heart beat faster. She hadn't had any idea of what she wanted because – not a real wedding – but when Julie brought out the last outfit...

It was a simple sleeveless sheath, in a dark cream heavy silk, and a short matching jacket, with a wide stand-away collar. Cassie laughed at Nadine's small intake of breath. Julie was grinning.

'I think we may have a winner,' Cassie said, still laughing. 'Go and try it on.'

The dress slid up over her hips as if it had been made for her. The label sewn into the pristine lining bore the name of an old French fashion house that she thought she dimly remembered. It appeared that it had never been worn. The back was fastened with a row of smooth, mother-of-pearl buttons. With an effort Nadine did them up without asking for help, standing back when it was done, to see herself in the mirror of the miniscule changing room. She hadn't known what she wanted, but she knew now that *this* was perfect. *Perfect for a non-wedding dress, or a dress for a non-wedding?*

'It's perfect,' Cassie echoed, with a purr of satisfaction, as Nadine emerged into the shop. 'Am I good, or am I good?'

Julie slipped the jacket off its padded hanger. 'Try this?'

Nadine shrugged it on. Here the three buttons fastening it were larger, shaded subtly with gold. The wide neckline fitted snugly, standing away to frame her head and shoulders. She walked up and down the shop, viewing herself in two strategically placed full-length mirrors. She felt as if she had stepped outside herself, into something magical.

Cassie was regarding her, eyes slightly narrowed. 'Totally classic. With your hair up, I don't think you'll need a hat, but maybe some sort of headband – and white cotton or lace gloves, to match the mood? A red lipstick, and red roses in the bouquet,' she decreed.

Nadine studied her reflection, and the cut of the neckline. 'My mother's pearls. It's a single strand choker, and earrings.'

'Cool.' Cassie nodded approval. 'Completely sorted,' she said with satisfaction. 'It makes you look every inch the bride.'

'It really does,' Julie confirmed. 'Genuine 1950s and never been worn. It was a small design house that flourished for a couple of decades after the war, then faded away in the sixties when denim jeans and miniskirts came in. I think it may have been used as a showroom model.' She grinned. 'Once he gets a look at you, you're going to rock the groom right down to his socks.'

Nadine unbuttoned the jacket, handing it to Julie to be bagged.

Well, that's not going to happen.

Hanging her purchase in her wardrobe when she got home, Nadine ran her hand down the dress, enjoying the texture of the silk. Cassie was right. Her friend knew her so well. It really was the perfect wedding dress. Even though it would never be worn, she didn't regret buying it.

Never be worn? Do you want to wear it?

Yes. I want to wear it for Ryan.

The voices in her head made her sit down with a thump on the bed. Concentrating on Thackeray and the scam, she hadn't allowed herself to think too much about Ryan. About what might be in *their* future...

The sudden shocked tightness in her chest suggested that while her mind was hanging on to that resolve, her heart might not have been paying attention. The way it was thumping against her ribs now, she was sure of it. Her head was ringing with the stupidest, most obvious realisation. It had come down on her like an avalanche. *How dim could you be?* What she had with Ryan wasn't just a casual fling – a few days in the Riviera sun.

Did you ever really *think that's all it was?*

Without knowing, without recognising it for what it was, without even *being* with him, she'd fallen in love with Ryan Calder.

Chapter Thirty-Eight

Coming back to Bristol had definitely been a mistake. Ryan let out a long sigh. Somehow he'd let himself be talked into this weekend festival to showcase the new arts complex, and raise much-needed funds.

Somehow? You know why you're here. And *why you shouldn't be.*

One of the highlights of the festival was two special performances reprising the studio theatre's biggest success to date – the play he'd done for Jordan, the three-hander with Rachel and Steve. The tickets, for gala performances on Friday and Sunday evenings, had been snapped up within two hours. Saturday evening would be taken up with a one-man show by a renowned theatrical knight, which had sold out even faster.

Knowing that Nadine was so close, and so far away, was messing with his head.

And your heart. He pushed away the voice in his mind. He hadn't had any contact with her since she'd walked away from him at Heathrow. And that was how it had to be. At least if Thackeray somehow found out that he was in town, he had a legitimate excuse.

It didn't make him feel any better.

And to cap it all, Cassie's concierge service was doing the event organising for the festival.

Now it was Saturday morning, he'd just come out of a lively 'meet the cast' question and answer session, and Cassie was standing in the foyer, waiting for him. His already persecuted heart jumped.

'Is everything all right? Nadine—'

'Is fine. She's working this morning at the showroom. Our friend is still in Carlisle.'

'Still?' Ryan's heart settled, as far as it ever did around Cassie.

'Probably back next week.' Cassie jerked her head, towards a quiet corner of the bar. 'I want to talk to you.'

But I don't want to talk to you.

Ryan ignored the whining four-year-old in his head, and followed her. When they were far enough away from anyone who might overhear, she turned to face him, leaning against a table. He kept his distance, just in case. The green eyes were boring holes in him.

'What's going on, with you and Nadine?'

'Nothing,' he replied in perfect truth.

Cassie subjected him to a slow, head-to-toe stare and back again.

Nothing to see here, lady. Move along now, please.

'You're leaving her, aren't you?'

'Ahh.' *Now what? Lies, confusion, playing dead? Stalling might be an option.*

'What makes you think there's anything to leave?' he asked carefully.

Cassie's eyebrows, *her eyebrows*, told him not to give her that. *She's been consorting with McQuire too long.*

'We had a few days together.' He didn't know what else to say.

'And now you're in love with her.'

'What!' His voice spiked, causing a few people to look round. He waited a couple of beats for them to look away again. Was there really much point in a fencing match with an expert? *And who, exactly, are you trying to kid?* 'Is it that obvious?'

'Takes one to know one,' Cassie responded cryptically. 'And you don't think you're good enough for her, right? That the escort thing makes you shop-soiled?'

That made him take a step forward. 'Nothing ever happened, with any woman, that I'm ashamed of.'

'Glad to hear it.' Cassie gave him a half smile, as if he'd scored some sort of point somewhere. He was too distracted to work it out. 'But you still think you're not good enough.'

Ryan paused, took a breath. *Honesty.* 'Cassie, you're her friend. Look at me – part-time escort, part-time barman, failed actor. And look at... what she had.'

'This is about Rory.'

'Of course it's about Rory.' *Loving husband, soulmate, successful entrepreneur, charity fundraiser, mentor, inspiration.* 'How can I expect...' His voice faded.

Cassie tilted her head, studying him again, before looking at the poster for the play on the wall next to them. A bright red slash proclaimed 'Sold Out' across it. 'I'm not so sure about the "failed actor" part.'

Ryan shrugged, dropping his eyes. *That* was messing with his head too, being on stage again, when he'd made up his mind...

When he didn't speak, Cassie exhaled. 'You could ask Nadine how *she* feels.' Ryan opened his mouth to protest, and shut it again when she pointed a finger. 'You've already admitted that you love her.'

'I'm just not—' He shoved his hand through his hair. 'Look, you *know* I can't come anywhere near the man she was married to. And I don't want to be there when she finally realises that. I've had the offer of a new job. An old mate put me on to it. Deputy manager at a boutique hotel that's just opening. In Paris.'

He had the brief satisfaction of knowing that for once Cassie was wrong-footed. It didn't feel as good as it should, and it didn't last.

'I suppose Paris is far enough.' She looked at him coolly. 'But if you are leaving Nadine, don't ghost her. You owe her that. And you have more guts than to just disappear.' She raised her hand to make a 'just coming' gesture to someone behind him, straightening away from the table. 'It's your decision.' She stepped past him. 'You're right, though. You're nothing like Rory.'

It was surprising how much that hurt. *Even though you already know it.*

Ryan found the turn off for the industrial estate on the second attempt. Once there, he flagged down a security guard for directions to the unit occupied by Nadine's company. After Cassie had left him he'd wandered around the arts complex, looked at some exhibits, signed a few autographs, had a coffee. In the end he'd given in and admitted that Cassie was right. He owed it to Nadine to say goodbye. And there would never be a better opportunity. He was here and Thackeray wasn't. *Maybe it was meant.*

Now the showroom, with its unique display of designer beds, looking like something out of a fairy tale, was in front of him. At the guard's suggestion, he drove to the back of the building, where the entrance to the office was. Locking the car he crossed the car park to the rear door and climbed the stairs.

Chapter Thirty-Nine

Nadine was sorting out her desk, tidying up things she'd let slide while Thackeray was taking up her time. It gave her a chance to think. She wasn't sure that was a good thing. Her mind was tumbling over itself with questions. Ryan was in Bristol. Should she go to him?

It was a risk, on so many levels. She wasn't really worried about Thackeray finding out, but he was a consideration. There were still several weeks to go before the wedding. She had a respite while he was in Carlisle, but once he was back she'd need all her acting skills to maintain her pose as a besotted bride. Would seeing Ryan make that even more difficult? Could she open a discussion on *their* future in what would inevitably be a snatched meeting? Was that fair to either of them? Was she ready to meet him, now that she knew she was in love with him? Could she protect her pride and dignity? Did she need to?

She hadn't seen him since the flight home from the Riviera. He hadn't contacted her. He was being ultra careful, protecting her. She knew that, but there was still a tiny cloud of doubt, hovering at the corner of her mind. For him, *had* it just been a summer fling? Would she embarrass herself by showing that she wanted more? If she didn't go to him, would he think that was how *she* regarded it?

The questions were still tumbling around in her head, without any answers, when there was a knock on the outer door of the office suite. She jumped a little, frowning. They didn't get many casual callers up here, and not on a Saturday. Maybe someone had taken a wrong turn from the showroom, or a customer wanted to discuss a special order and one of the sales staff had sent them up, knowing she was in her office, but hadn't rung to warn her.

Picking up her phone and checking the speed dial for the

estate security, just in case, she dropped it into her pocket, walked to the door and opened it.

'Ryan!'

He looked tired, with fine lines of strain around his eyes, yet still unbelievably, mouth-wateringly gorgeous. She drank him in, unable to get beyond that first amazed exclamation. And he was looking at her the same way, as if he wanted to imprint her face in his mind for eternity.

Realising with a jolt that her thoughts were running away in crazy circles, she put out her hand to draw him into the office. For a disturbing second she thought he flinched as she touched his arm. The lines around his eyes were worry, not fatigue, she saw with a sudden burst of clarity. 'Ryan?' she said again, hearing the uncertain wobble in her voice.

'Cassie said I should come.' His expression was curiously blank. 'I saw her, this morning.' He stopped, swallowed. 'I just wanted to let you know... I have a new job.'

'Oh, that's awesome. Where? What is it?' *Why doesn't it actually feel awesome?* Confusion washed through her like a cold wave. He was looking at a point over her shoulder, not meeting her eyes. He swallowed again, as if his words were sticking in his throat. Some emotion flickered across his face that sent alarm coursing through her. *What is this? What's happening?* Now he was trying to smile.

'It's a great opportunity. An old mate put me onto it. It's a hotel. In Paris.'

'A hotel? Paris?'

All she seemed able to do was repeat what he'd said. Her mind was foggy, struggling to understand. *He's leaving?*

Abruptly his eyes came back to lock onto hers. His expression now was bland, a fixed social smile. All she could see in his eyes was... pain?

He reached forward, taking her hand, raising it to his lips. 'It's... for the best. It's been... wonderful. The farmhouse. The Riviera. Thank you.' His breath seemed to hitch. As if it was a struggle to get air. 'Once the scam is over I know that you'll meet someone. Whoever he is, he will be a very lucky man.'

She felt the feather-light brush of the kiss on her knuckles.

He was turning away, and her phone was ringing, loud and demanding.

'Ryan, wait, please!' She hauled out the phone, frantic to silence it. She stabbed at it, unable to make it stop. And Ryan was walking down the stairs, without looking back.

Chapter Forty

Ryan powered down the stairs, mentally cursing Cassie for sending him here, and himself for disjointedly stumbling over what should have been a calm and dignified goodbye. *Words are your stock in trade, for heaven's sake!* He could still feel the warmth of Nadine's hand... see the confusion in her face... Thank God for the phone call that had interrupted before she could say something that might have made him take it all back...

In a headlong rush, he'd reached the bottom of the stairs. He'd put out his hand to push open the glass door when he realised that there was now another car in the almost empty staff car park. There was a man leaning against it, head down, speaking into his phone.

For a second Ryan froze, hand still outstretched, unable to believe what he was seeing, but there was no mistake. It was John Thackeray, not safely in Carlisle, but here. And phoning Nadine to let her know he was waiting?

Following blind instinct Ryan moved to the side, into a narrow corridor that probably led to the showroom at the front of the building. He could hear hurrying footsteps now on the stairs. He moved further into the corridor, alongside an open window that gave him a perfect view of the car park, as Nadine plummeted down the last few steps towards the door.

Nadine raced down the stairs, mind churning in panic. *Thackeray... and Ryan!* Reaching the bottom, she wrenched open the door, and almost fell into the car park.

And there was Thackeray, standing beside his car... alone. She skidded to a halt, looking frantically around. Ryan's car was still there, but there was no sign of Ryan. Somehow he'd managed to disappear. Relief shuddered through her.

Thackeray stepped forward to take her in his arms. 'Darling, you're shaking. I know I said it was urgent, but I didn't mean to frighten you.' He put up a hand, to smooth her hair.

'Oh!' She drew in her breath, pulling herself together. 'It was just… I was so surprised. I didn't expect you. Of course it's lovely to see you.' She stepped back, looking up into his face. He looked dreadful she realised, with a shock – heavy eyed, unshaven, hair flattened to his head. 'But why are you here? Last night when you rang, I thought you were staying in C— in Birmingham.' She swallowed hard on what she'd been about to say. *Be careful!*

He let out a pained exclamation. 'Long story.' He shook his head. 'We need… I need you to trust me, darling.' He slid his hands to clasp her arms. 'We have to go away, and we don't have much time. I went to your house first – your neighbour across the way said you'd be here.'

'Mrs Copeland.' Nadine nodded. They'd spoken briefly that morning, as Nadine was getting into her car. Her neighbour was just back from a trip to New Zealand to see her daughter. She didn't know Thackeray, but he must have convinced her that what he wanted was urgent. 'I don't understand.' Nadine frowned, feeling her way. 'Has the court case finished? I thought you were there for a while longer.'

'Ahh – yes. Change of plan. I need you to trust me,' he said again.

'Yes, of course.' The reassurance was automatic, although the words echoed uneasily in her chest. 'What is it? What's the matter… darling?'

He didn't answer immediately. He'd closed his eyes, his grip tight on her arms, almost as if he was drawing on her for support. His eyes flicked open. 'It's so good to see you, my love.' His expression now reminded her of the evening at the spa hotel.

Desolation.

'Darling! What *is* the matter?' Her heart was pumping uncomfortably against her ribcage. On a Saturday morning this car park was very quiet – no admin or warehouse workers coming and going. The silence and stillness around them had begun to feel unnerving. *But Ryan is here, somewhere.* The thought steadied her. She stared up into Thackeray's face, seeing the dark smudges under his eyes and the lines of strain around his mouth. The confident gloss was dimmed. *He looks... hunted?* 'What is it?' she asked softly, willing her voice not to shake.

'Oh, God, I'm so *sorry*, darling.' Thackeray put up a hand to cover his eyes, then dropped it quickly. 'A business project I was involved in... it's... gone bad. Kenneth Fletcher. He's made me one of *those* offers.' His mouth quirked in the semblance of a smile. 'You know – the ones you're not supposed to refuse.' He swallowed. 'I'm so sorry, my darling, but we can't go through with the wedding... not on the Riviera. We need to leave...' His grip on her arms tightened again, as if it was a reflex, then he seemed to recollect himself and let her go, stepping back. 'I love you, Nadine. I know you love me. You *have* to trust me. I have to get away, *now*, today. I want you to come with me. I can't leave you behind. I *need* you, and... I'm afraid it would be dangerous for you to stay,' he finished, with an air of desperation.

'John!' She didn't have to feign alarm. Fear was flooding through her. She couldn't leave with him. Somehow she had to stall him, to buy time... 'Is it really as bad as you think?' She forced her voice to sound level, reasonable. 'I have friends – maybe someone can help?'

'Maybe. Later. But not now.' A shudder ran through him. She heard him draw in a deep breath, gathering himself together. 'I'm sorry,' he repeated. 'I don't want to do this, but I *have* to get away. I don't know how long we have.' His voice had dropped, sounding firmer. He had his emotions in check. *For how long?* Panic was clawing in Nadine's chest. 'You have to come with me,' he reiterated. Now she could see the shadows of grim despair in his eyes. 'I *need* you, Nadine. It won't be the Riviera as we planned, but we'll be married as soon as we can, I promise. I know a place, an island. You'll love it. Our own hideaway – the beach, the sea, palm trees—'

'It sounds wonderful, but to leave everything... Can't we—'

'You said you wanted to elope, remember?' For a second the old indulgent amusement flickered to life in his voice. 'We can have a wedding on the beach. Something really romantic. Everything you want.' Now the promises sounded hollow. 'You just have to *trust* me. I can't leave you... Fletcher...' His head jerked. 'I just have to get away for a while. I want you to be safe, and I want us to be together. It will all work out. I'll *make* it work out. But we *need* to go. *Please.*'

The broken plea in his voice made emotion catch in her throat. The slick, self-assured John Thackeray was gone. This was a frightened man. *A man on the run.* And she had no idea what to do.

She was looking up into his face, mind whirling desperately, when the black SUV glided into the car park.

Chapter Forty-One

Ryan could only hear snatches of speech through the open window. Thackeray was trying to persuade Nadine to go away with him – but this wasn't a surprise weekend trip. Something had happened. *Something big.* For a few moments he'd thought that Thackeray had discovered their scam, but there was no anger in his body language. The guy looked rough. *Desperate.*

Ryan stood watching, undecided what to do. Nadine must know he was still around. He hoped that helped. Should he intervene? Would that blow their scam out of the water, if there was still anything left to blow? Could Nadine handle it alone? She seemed to be doing okay, calming Thackeray and getting him to talk – but Thackeray still looked desperate. *If he tries to force her into his car...*

Ryan was tossing up between moving closer to the outside door and giving up his vantage point at the window, when a large black car slid into the car park and stopped, blocking the entrance. The driver's door swung open...

Ryan had no idea who the man was who was uncoiling his bulk from the SUV, but Thackeray and Nadine clearly did. The guy was big, with the face and build of a prizefighter. Thackeray seemed to have shrunk, his shoulders sagging. *You're looking at fear.* Nadine was fumbling in her pocket, but her back was stiff, braced for something...

Whatever this is, it is not good.

The newcomer had moved forward. He was smiling, but there was no warmth in it. 'John.' His voice was loud, assertive. 'Glad that I've caught up with you. I thought we had an agreement to meet last night.'

Thackeray was mumbling something about a misunderstanding. The man made the exaggerated, mocking gesture of cupping his hand to his ear. 'I can't hear you, John.'

Thackeray straightened up. 'I didn't choose to meet you, Ken.' Now his voice was stronger. 'I'm not going to accept your offer.'

There was a long beat of silence.

On some instinctive level Ryan understood that Thackeray had made the wrong decision in standing up to this man. Something in the way Ken shifted his stance indicated that a judgement had been made.

'I don't think you quite understand, John. It wasn't an *offer*. I told you what was supposed to happen. I wasn't giving you a choice.'

Thackeray shook his head. 'I'm leaving. You can't stop me.'

'I think I can.'

The big man reached into his pocket.

Something metallic glinted in the sun.

Ken was holding a gun.

Chapter Forty-Two

Ryan gulped down a rush of fear. He started to edge towards the door. He needed to get outside. He had to get to Nadine.

The guy doesn't know you're here. Somehow you have to be able to use that.

He made it to the door in soft hurried steps. No one saw him. Thackeray and Ken were intent on each other. Nadine had her back to him, all her attention focused on the two men. Ryan dragged in a deep, steadying breath, concentrating on the scene in the car park. *It's a stage set. An improvisation. You just have to decide the best place to make your entrance.*

'You're not going to shoot me, Ken.' Thackeray sounded unexpectedly confident. 'What *profit* would there be in that?'

'No profit, but it would send a message to all the other toerags. No one messes with Kenneth Fletcher and walks away.'

For a second Thackeray's body seemed to sway, then he stiffened, standing his ground. 'Is it worth murder, just for a message?'

'Oh, John... John.' Fletcher sighed, shaking his head in mock sorrow. 'You should know. Remember Pat Dawson?'

Ryan couldn't be sure, but he thought Thackeray's face paled.

Behind Fletcher, a small movement caught Ryan's eye. One of the site security guards had slid quietly alongside the SUV, his radio held close to his mouth. Even from this distance Ryan could see the disbelief and horror on the man's face, but he hadn't panicked – and he'd noticed Ryan, standing just inside the glass door. Unseen by the two men just a few feet from him, ducking down so he was partially shielded by the bulk of the car, the guard raised his hand with a question, mimicking the shape of a gun. Ryan nodded to confirm and jerked his head in a gesture that said leave. When Fletcher had produced the firearm, everything had changed. *No gain in drawing someone else into this mess.* Understanding, the man opened his hand in salute and melted away. Ryan closed his eyes in a brief prayer of thanks. Help was coming. *But how long will it take?*

'Although, now I come to think of it—' Fletcher's voice dragged Ryan's attention back to the scene in front of him. 'Maybe I don't need another message. Everyone still remembers poor old Pat. No call to be too obvious. Don't want the coppers asking questions. But you…' He gestured with the gun. 'You're a loose cannon, *Charlie*. And I don't like those. I need to get shot of you.' He pointed the weapon at Thackeray, a fat, satisfied grin creasing his face. 'Shot? Get it?'

The bastard's enjoying himself.

'You can't mean to shoot both of us,' Thackeray's voice rasped.

'Well, I'm not leaving any witnesses.' Fletcher glanced over at Nadine. She was standing motionless, as if she was frozen. Ryan's heart twisted. 'Sorry, sweetheart.' Fletcher was still grinning. 'Wrong place, wrong time and all that.' He stepped back a little, clearly sizing up the situation.

Very faintly, in the distance, Ryan could hear the sound of a siren.

'It'll be a real tragedy,' Fletcher decided. 'Murder/suicide. Beautiful widow killed by deranged boyfriend. I can just see the headlines.' Abruptly the grin dropped away. 'It's not as if I haven't done it before.'

The way Thackeray's shoulders jerked told Ryan that he knew exactly when it had been done before. The realisation seemed to bring him to the point of collapse. He stooped, head bowed, hands braced on his legs and sliding down.

When he straightened again, another gun, a smaller version of Fletcher's, nestled in his hand.

He had an ankle holster.

'Well—' Fletcher sounded amused. 'That's a pretty little thing. Do you have any idea how to use it?' he asked conversationally.

'I know enough.' Thackeray jerked his head. 'Do you want to risk it?' He held out his hand to Nadine. 'We're leaving now.'

'I don't think so.' Fletcher turned away from Thackeray, pointing his gun at Nadine.

The noise of the sirens was getting louder. No one else seemed to have heard them.

But still too far away.

With a deep breath, Ryan stepped through the door. 'Am I interrupting?'

'Ryan!'

'Calder!'

'What the fuck!'

Three voices collided in shock.

Ryan didn't hesitate. He threw himself towards Nadine, desperate to get between her and the guns. Her body, as he grabbed her to push her behind him, was stiff with fear, but her voice was low and steady as she protested, 'Ryan, no!'

Half turned towards her, still shielding her and expecting at any minute to feel the thud of a bullet in his back, he urged her towards the door. 'Get inside. Go!'

'No! Look!' She held out a trembling hand to point.

Ryan turned again towards the two men. She'd seen what he hadn't. In the few seconds' diversion he'd made, Thackeray had taken his chance, leaping towards Ken Fletcher. The two men were locked together, struggling over the weapons.

The noise of sirens was very loud now, but not loud enough to drown out two gunshots.

Ryan gathered Nadine into his arms, ready to drag her to safety, as the men fell away from each other.

Fletcher was on his back, cursing and clutching his thigh as bright arterial blood spurted. For a long second Thackeray remained on his feet, swaying slightly, looking down, as if confused, at the red stain spreading across the front of his shirt

Then, almost in slow motion, he folded to his knees, toppled sideways, and lay still.

Chapter Forty-Three

It was getting dark when Nadine unlocked her front door, with a hand that visibly trembled. After hectic hours of armed response units, ambulances, interviews, confusion and questions, they'd finally been let go. John Thackeray, alias Kyle Dickens, had died at the scene. Kenneth Fletcher was still in surgery, with an armed guard standing by. Jake had turned up, accompanied by a high-ranking police officer, to take some of the burden of questions. Cassie had followed him later and had driven them home. Both their cars were currently part of a crime scene. It hadn't occurred to anyone that she would drop them anywhere but at Nadine's house.

Once through the door, Nadine turned into Ryan's arms, burying her face in his shoulder. He stroked her hair, murmuring broken phrases of comfort. She'd held up well during the aftermath and the questions, but now she was shaking. If he was honest, so was he.

'It was...' She swallowed and tried again. 'I wanted to bring him down. I didn't want it to end like *that*.'

'No one did.' He held her slightly away from him. 'We said a lot of hard things about him, out of anger and disgust, but when it came down to it, we only wanted some sort of justice. Not...' He took a breath. 'The thing was bigger than just Thackeray. Jake suspected there was more, but he didn't *know*. Fletcher was a wild card. There was no way of foreseeing what he was going to do,' he reassured her, looking into her eyes. 'Fletcher was the boss. Thackeray crossed him, but it wasn't anything to do with our scam. Neither of them realised that they'd been set up.' Ryan was sure of that. Thackeray would not have begged Nadine to go with him if he'd known he was being tricked, and Fletcher would have thrown the failure in Thackeray's face, as another reason to dispose of him.

Thackeray – he couldn't think of him as Dickens – was

arrogant and egotistical, confident of his own skills and eager to use them. He'd started the scam with Nadine when Fletcher was out of the way in America. He'd known the risk in defying the man, and had done it anyway, dragging Nadine in with him.

Ryan went cold at the memory of how Fletcher had planned to kill them both.

They would never know if Thackeray had any real feeling for Nadine, or if she'd simply been a convenient meal ticket, to be abandoned like the other brides when he'd got whatever he could scavenge. *She doesn't need to be burdened with that.* 'They both had guns and they were ready to use them.' Ryan put up a hand to lightly touch her face. 'You have to remember that.'

'I do. I will.' In the dimly lit hall borrowed light from the streetlamps showed the trace of tears on her face. 'And I have to... thank you... You pulled me away. You put yourself in front of me.'

A rush of emotions powered through him. Too complex for him to identify the individual components, they spilled out in words he couldn't control. 'You don't have to thank me. You'd never have to thank me. I *love* you.' The desperate admission hung, huge, in the dark hallway. The words he'd promised himself never to say.

'Ryan!' She was staring up at him, eye wide and shadowed in a pale face.

'I'm sorry. I shouldn't have said it. Forget it, please, forget it.' Now the words of denial were spilling out, falling over each other. 'I know I can't... that you—'

Nadine pressed her fingers against his mouth, to stem the flow. 'I love you too.'

'I... Nadine...?' His voice was muffled behind her hand. He wasn't sure he was hearing correctly. His brain was scrambled with the trauma of the day.

'I love you,' she said it again. 'But you were walking away

from me.' Her voice was soft, but there was accusation there. She dropped her hand to let him speak.

'I thought it was the right thing to do, that I couldn't be good enough...'

'You put yourself in front of me,' she said simply. She shook her head, intense weariness visible in the small movement. 'We can't talk now. It's all too...' She shuddered. 'Let's go to bed.'

She took his hand to draw him towards the stairs.

All he could do was follow.

She guided him to her room, both too shattered by events to speak. Ryan registered that the bed was a fantasy of leaves and flowers, carved in pale wood, before they shed their clothes and collapsed into it. Nadine curled into his arms, burrowing, seeking comfort. He held her close, soothing away the horror of how the day might have ended in the warmth of her skin and the scent of her hair.

Sometime in the dark of the early hours, they came together, making love with gentle heat, soft, slow and life-affirming, before falling back into the heavy sleep of exhaustion.

Chapter Forty-Four

Ryan woke up alone in a bed to end all beds. A fairyland fantasy of flowers, leaves and vines, spiderwebs and raindrops that curved above him, all carved in pale, gleaming wood. *A bed where Titania might make love to Oberon.* He lay on his back for a while, simply looking. A soapy, scented drift of warm air, from the en suite bathroom, suggested that Nadine had already taken a shower. A pile of fresh towels on a chair seemed to be an invitation for him to do the same. He got up, retrieved his clothes and padded to the bathroom.

Twenty minutes later, clean, but lacking a shave, he followed the scent of coffee to the kitchen. Nadine was making toast. Dressed in a pale blue tracksuit, damp hair piled in a messy knot on the top of her head, the sight of her made his heart stutter. Her face was still pale and her eyes shadowed, but she handed him a mug of coffee and gave him a kiss. They ate mostly in silence, with a local radio station playing softly in the background. The shooting at the industrial estate was the major news item at the top of the hour. Kenneth Fletcher, who was only referred to as a casualty, had apparently made it through surgery, but his condition was still critical.

By unspoken consent, when breakfast was done, they moved into a small sitting room, with a large desk and a view of the garden. Ryan crossed the room when he saw the sculpture on a shelf. 'This is the one you bought...' He hesitated.

'On my first date with Thackeray.' Nadine nodded. She crossed the room to stand beside him. 'I think I might put it away for a while.' He saw her bite her lip. 'He was a conman and a thief, and heaven knows what else besides, but he still shouldn't have died like that.'

'I don't think it's wrong to... mourn him... as a human being.' He held out his hand, when Nadine turned to him, he pulled her close. She settled against his shoulder. He felt her body relax against him.

'Is there anywhere you need to be today?' she asked, head still bent.

He thought for a moment, trying to decide what day it was. He remembered the sound of church bells when he got out of the shower. It was Sunday. 'The theatre, this evening. The second gala performance.'

'Will you stay here with me, until then?' she asked quietly.

'As long as you want me to.' *Forever.*

He guided her to a sofa and they settled together onto the wide cushions. They sat in silence for a while, Nadine curled into the crook of his arm. Then she straightened up, away from him. 'Why were you trying to leave me yesterday?'

'Ah.' He knew the question had to be asked, and answered. 'I thought it was the right thing.' *Maybe it still is?* He exhaled. 'I'm in love with you. I knew it when we were at the farmhouse, but, if I'm honest, it started a while before that, when you were still a client. Those days at the farmhouse were magical, but… I felt that I couldn't give you what you'd had before. What you deserved. I couldn't match up to your husband. I couldn't match up to Rory. That hasn't changed. I still can't.'

'Oh, Ryan.' She punched him gently on the arm. 'That's crazy.'

'Is it?'

'Yes.' She sighed. 'But I suppose I can see…' She was clearly thinking. 'We should have talked about him.'

'Not if it was painful for you.'

She shook her head. 'Some of the truth is painful, but there are things you need to know – you deserve to know.' Her dark eyes were fixed on his face. 'The first is that I'm not looking for a replacement for Rory. If I'd wanted that – the same sort of man, I could have had one any time in the last five years. There were plenty of men who thought they could step into his shoes. You're actually the first who *didn't* think so.'

Her mouth twisted. Ryan's muscles tensed as she went on. 'People have this image, because of the circumstances when my husband died... that somehow our relationship was so perfect that it can never be matched. That he was my... soulmate. It wasn't like that. I loved Rory, but when he died... we were drifting apart. We'd been together since university and we weren't the same people. I'm not saying that we couldn't have got past that... I don't know. Neither of us was looking elsewhere.' She smiled, but it was a sad smile. 'I know Rory had offers, subtle and not so subtle. As did I. But that wasn't it. He was a workaholic, focused on the business, more and more concerned with his public image. He wanted to be someone in the community. We never made the time we should have to talk about where our marriage was going. And then he died. Climbing. Doing something that he loved, but was also part of that public image – fundraising for good causes. And I was left – angry and guilty, as well as shocked and grieving.'

She stopped. Ryan could see the hurt in her eyes.

'My husband died a local hero. Money for the causes he was supporting flooded in. And my role was the tragic young widow of a wonderful guy. Which he was. He just wasn't the guy I'd married. There's a lot of romantic stuff written – "I want to die in your arms," and all that – but it doesn't take account of the one that's left behind. I was angry, because we never got the time to work things out. And guilty *because* I was angry. Eventually I came to terms with it – part of the grieving process. But there's still this image in people's minds, because it was so tragic.'

She leaned forward, arms resting on her knees. 'That's it. The whole thing. What I had with Rory will always be precious, and he *will* always have part of my heart. That's the baggage that comes with me, but I'm not still living in the past. His ghost is not standing between us. I *know* he wouldn't want it to. When I look, I see *you*, Ryan. No one else. So...'

She exhaled, a long breath. 'Can we give what's between us a chance?'

'I think...' His throat had closed. He wanted to just say yes and pull her back into his arms, but there was still the echo of a familiar voice in his head. *Not good enough*. 'It wasn't just about Rory. I felt you deserved better than me. I was trying to leave because I was afraid... that in a few months you'd realise you'd made a mistake... when your friends...' He tailed off when Nadine made a protesting huffing noise that sounded like 'Hattie.'

'You heard her, didn't you, on the plane? I was hoping it was too noisy.'

'Yes, and what she said—'

Nadine cut him off with a rude word. 'She is not a friend. She is a freeloading social climber who had an unrequited crush on Rory.'

'Oh.' He blinked, reading Nadine's expression. 'Was she—'

'Yes. She was one of the unsubtle offers.'

Ryan digested this. 'Even so—'

'If you want to talk about my friends, then Cassie is a much better example, and she seems to approve of you.' She reached out her hand. Ryan couldn't do anything else but take it. 'I'm not that special, Ryan. I inherited the business from Rory – you could call that luck.' She motioned for silence when he would have protested. 'I've worked hard, that's all.' She shrugged. 'I don't think you're a gold digger, Ry.' Suddenly she grinned. 'I wish you were a Hollywood megastar, because I know that acting is who you are, and then *I'd* be the gold digger.' Her face sobered and her fingers tightened on his, warm. 'Can we try? Just us – no one else. No history. Just two people, starting from the same place. Moving on together?'

Chapter Forty-Five

She'd laid it all out – the truth, and the hope. Now it was up to Ryan whether he picked it up. Nadine studied his face. Despite his declaration that he loved her, she couldn't tell if she was looking at joy, or heartbreak. She knew he *could* cope with the things some people would say – that *they* could. But that didn't really matter. It was what Ryan felt, inside, that counted. His opinion of *himself*. She could see he was struggling, and her heart lurched painfully. When he spoke, it wasn't what she expected.

'My father – I didn't have a comfortable relationship with him.' He dug his hand through his hair. 'He was... he had decided opinions.' Ryan's hand had slipped down, nursing the back of his neck. 'He shared them, generously. He was a hard man to please.' He looked up, a flash of alarm in his eyes. 'I don't want to lay all the blame on him. A lot of it's down to me.' He gave a half rueful laugh. 'Sean says I'm like him – stubborn and bloody-minded.'

'Sean.' Nadine risked a response. 'Your younger brother. I remember you telling me about him.' When Ryan nodded she took another risk. 'I'd like to meet him.'

'I'm sure he'd like to meet you.' It wasn't exactly a promise, but her heart lifted a little. 'Dad didn't think much of acting as a career, so he didn't think much of me. Kept on that I should get a proper job, leave the "nonsense" behind. It got that it was easier to avoid him. But it did eat into me. The voice in my head, telling me that I was never going to be good enough. And acting – maybe that voice is right.'

Nadine could have pointed out the awards and the rave reviews, but this wasn't about them, or her. It was about a man whose opinions had deep roots – another ghost.

She counted a few long beats, letting the air settle around them, before speaking. 'We both have things in our past...

people… that affect what we are today. But what we are *now* is our choice.' She gave him a long, steady look. 'Can we give it a go? Love is scary, but we're grown-ups. We can both be brave.' For a brief second an image flickered behind her eyelids; Ryan, standing between her and a man holding a gun. This man was brave. And she wanted him. But she had to give him time.

Ryan stood at the French windows, staring out at the rain – a steady, soft summer downpour. After he'd rung to apologise for not showing up for the sofa last night, Will had dropped off Ryan's rucksack on his way to Sunday lunch with his new girlfriend's parents. In a hurry, Will hadn't asked questions, just reminded Ryan that he'd see him at the after-show party that would close the festival that evening. The rucksack had provided clean clothes and a shave, and now Nadine was in the kitchen rummaging in the freezer for something they could eat later. He turned towards her as she came back into the room.

'I found a fish pie. I can heat it before you have to go.'

'Sounds good.' He hesitated. 'There's a party tonight, after the show. Will you come with me? I'll have to be there, but if you'd rather not…'

'No, that's okay. I'll come with you.'

She held out her hand and they settled back onto the sofa, dozing and watching the rain.

Ryan looked down at Nadine, stretched out asleep, with her head pillowed on his knees. Gently he traced the contour of her cheek with one finger.

The pain came in a quick stab, hard under the ribs, as sharp as any gunshot. Yesterday he could have lost her to a bullet. The horror of the thought, of the gaping blank that would have replaced the rest of his life, was almost enough to stifle him. *You love her. She loves you. What else do you need to know? Do it. When she opens her eyes, do it.*

'Nadine?'

'Ryan?' A glorious smile curved her mouth, before her eyelids flickered up.

'Will you marry me?'

'Yes.' She gave a long, contented sigh, and went back to sleep.

Nadine woke slowly. The desolate stress of yesterday had seeped away. She felt relaxed, at peace and ravenously hungry. She'd also had the most glorious dream. She opened her eyes to find Ryan studying her.

'You're properly awake now.'

She laughed. 'Properly awake,' she assured him. 'Oh!' She sat up, swinging round to face him. 'I was dreaming. Was I dreaming?'

'Um…. I don't know. I… er… asked you to marry me?'

'Then I wasn't dreaming. What did I say?'

'Well… you said yes, but I wasn't sure—'

'I'm properly awake now,' she repeated, coiling her arms around his neck. 'Yes, yes, yes!'

They were finishing the fish pie and celebrating with ice cream and a decadent glass of lemonade, as Ryan had a play to perform in a few hours, when his phone rang. 'Cassie?'

'You'd better get down here to the theatre, Calder. There's someone waiting to see you.'

'Who is it?' Nadine frowned at Cassie, totally confused. On the phone her friend had refused to say any more, except that they needed to get a move on. Nadine had changed into jeans and a soft cotton sweater as swiftly as she could, stuffing her hairbrush and her make-up into her handbag, As soon as they'd reached the theatre Cassie had hauled Ryan to the manager's office. Nadine heard the deep rumble of a male voice, that seemed oddly familiar, as Cassie pushed Ryan inside and firmly shut the door.

'Dan Howe.'

'Dan Howe?' Nadine knew her eyes had gone wide. 'The "drool down the dress" Dan Howe? The film star?'

'That's the one,' Cassie confirmed happily, shepherding her back to the foyer, where tea was being served after an afternoon concert.

'What does he want with Ryan?'

'What do you think?'

'No!' Nadine sat down with a thump in the nearest chair and earned an indignant look from an elderly lady who was clearly saving it for a companion. She apologised, getting up quickly. Cassie was grinning like a Cheshire cat. She pointed to a door that led to a small patio area that the foyer shared with the café. The rain had only just stopped and the tables and benches were still dripping, so the space was deserted.

'Tell me!' Nadine demanded, as soon as they got outside.

'Howe is making his first film as a director next year. Most of the action is set in Wales, with a few scenes in London and Monte Carlo. He explained all this to Jake in the pub, while he was waiting. He wants the casting to be predominantly British, and new talent. He remembered Ryan from some screen test he did in America, saw the publicity for the festival and the reviews of the play, and came looking. He's serious, hon. He's starring, and his wife, Nevada Shaw, will have a cameo part as well, to keep the money men happy, but he wants to offer Ryan second lead.'

'That's... that's...' Nadine found herself stuttering.

'Incredible, amazing, awesome,' Cassie suggested.

'All of those,' Nadine agreed, knowing that there was moisture on her face that she couldn't blame on the rain. 'Cass, it's his big break, at last.'

'And he doesn't have to go to the States for it. It's all good.' Cassie narrowed her eyes to give her friend a critical once-over. 'But how are you holding up, after yesterday? You look like you're hanging in there?'

Nadine nodded slowly. 'I'm doing okay.'

'No bad dreams?'

'No!' Nadine shook her head emphatically, unable to keep her smile inside. 'Very good dreams, in fact. I was asleep on the sofa. And when I woke up, Ryan proposed.'

'Honey!' Cassie threw her arms around Nadine's neck. They stood leaning together, laughing. Attracted by the noise, a few people came to peer out of the windows at them, also starting to smile, although they didn't know why. 'Come on.' Cassie tugged at her friend's hand. 'Let's go and find Jake. This calls for a celebration.' She stopped suddenly, in the act of pulling open the door. 'And I've just thought of the perfect wedding present.'

Chapter Forty-Six

'This place really is perfect.'

'It is, isn't it?' Nadine moved closer, to rest her head on Ryan's shoulder.

They were standing on the lowest terrace of the wedding villa, looking down at the sparkling blue of the Mediterranean.

'Happy, Mrs Calder?'

'Very,' Nadine confirmed softly.

Life could change so much in a short time. *You know all about that*. This time the changes were good. Ryan had given up the escorting and his bar job and was working temporarily for Jake, at the detective agency, while his ecstatic agent negotiated the contract for the film deal. His flat in Ealing was on the market, and they'd talked about buying a house together in Bath.

But now they were back on the Riviera again. *And this time you're with the right man*. They'd completed a brief formal ceremony, necessary to be legally married, at the Register Office in Bristol, the day before yesterday. The service of blessing in the tiny old chapel and the reception afterwards, here at the villa outside Nice, were the icing on the cake. As Cassie was involved, there were three cakes – a tower of gilded chocolate, a delicate creamy confection, dotted with edible flowers and a croquembouche – a pyramid of caramel covered profiteroles – the traditional French wedding cake.

Cassie's and Jake's wedding present – the wedding on the Riviera – had assumed epic proportions under Cassie's direction. It was going to be a party to end all parties. She'd embellished the decisions that Nadine and Hélène had made until only traces remained.

Even so, there were traces.

Ryan heard Nadine's soft sigh. 'It is alright? Being here?'

Cassie had checked and double-checked, before she'd gone ahead, but now they were actually *here*.

'Yes, it is. Before, all the planning, it was magical, but it was never real. This is.' Nadine turned in his hold to look around. 'Strangely enough, I don't think Thackeray, Dickens, whoever he really was, would have begrudged us this.' Her mouth twisted ruefully. 'He seemed to like weddings.' She turned again to Ryan. 'I don't feel his ghost anywhere here.'

She leaned back against Ryan's chest, so that they could both look out over the sea. He settled his chin against her hair and held her close. 'Good. We don't need to think about it any more.'

They'd managed to put most of the hurt and chaos that Thackeray had wrought behind them. The authorities in Bristol were still piecing together the events leading up to the confrontation at the industrial estate, a process made more opaque by the fact that Kenneth Fletcher had not, in the end, survived his injuries. Jake was fairly tight-lipped about the whole thing, but they knew he also had people investigating. The wedding scam was indeed the tip of an iceberg. Jake had confirmed that Fletcher was one of the heads of a sprawling crime network. Thackeray had been a front man for a small part of it. Cassie told them, in confidence, about a much bigger investigation, into art and jewel thefts, that the detective agency had been working on for some time, with colleagues in France. There was a disturbing possibility that Fletcher's organisation was involved. Fletcher might be gone, but someone else would take his place. Even so, the loss might cause cracks that could now be exploited.

Nadine and Ryan had no trouble promising Cassie not to speak of any of it. Neither of them wanted to remember what had happened, much less talk about it. Ryan dropped a kiss on Nadine's hair. He could hear the sound of hammering and snatches from a radio playing Europop coming from the direction of the villa. 'Shall we go up and see what's going on?'

The 'wedding' was two days away. Guests would start arriving in the next few hours, flown in on Jake's private plane, some to stay in accommodation in the grounds, some at hotels in the city. Nadine and Ryan had escaped to the farmhouse for a not-quite honeymoon, although Nadine would be back at the villa early on the day, for the attention of the various experts that Cassie had arranged. When Ryan suggested that his bride was entirely beautiful as she was, he'd only earned a pitying stare.

On the way up to the villa they diverted to check out the chapel. The interior of the small building, constructed against the slope of the cliff, was cool and dim compared with the brightness of the sunshine outside. It had already been substantially dressed for the wedding. The colours of the standard roses and massed orchids subtly echoed tones in the stained glass windows, sunlit behind the plain stone slab that served as an altar. Despite the abundance, there was also simplicity. The skill in the creation was impressive. The chapel provided the setting for the ceremony, but wouldn't upstage it. Nadine guided Ryan to sit for a while in one of the pews, just absorbing the peace and the beauty.

Up at the house, Cassie had used her events organising skills to the maximum. The villa had been lovely before, the gardens lush with plants and blooms. Now the place looked spectacular. All the noise and activity was currently concentrated at the front of the house, where a small army of contractors worked, under supervision from Hélène and Cassie. Temporary surfaces were being laid for car parking. A stylish awning decorated the main entrance, miles of fairy lights were being strung and solar battery candles positioned. Vintage 1950s crockery and cutlery were being unloaded and checked by the catering staff.

The house was cool and light, the walls of the public rooms draped with pale hangings that gave the ground floor the illusion of being one flowing space. Buffet tables were set up, waiting to be loaded with food that would be housed in a refrigerated lorry, to supplement the kitchen. Crates of drinks filled an anteroom. Chairs and small side tables covered in white linen had been set out in the rooms that gave onto the gardens. On the terraces white umbrellas, trimmed with coloured ribbons, shaded larger tables from the sun. In the room set aside for dancing, which opened onto the garden, romantic clips from 1950s films would be projected high on the back wall. There would be special spotlight performances from the harpist, opera singer and string quartet that would provide the music for the ceremony in the chapel. A baby grand piano had been expertly manoeuvred onto the top terrace, where a pianist friend of one of Cassie's Bath clients, celebrated for his interpretation of Cole Porter and Gershwin, had been persuaded to play. There would be a jazz band and a well-known local group for dancing later in the evening.

There were elaborate floral displays, and the terraces were heady with the scent of potted jasmine. On the day itself vaporisers would subtly lace the air in the front hall with a fragrance especially created by a designer perfumery, establishing the wedding mood for guests as they entered the house and passed through. Scented candles in the same fragrance would be presented to guests as they left, along with small boxes of designer chocolates. Even the cloakrooms had been decorated with sophisticated old film posters and supplied with baskets containing all the emergency items guests might need, from packs of sheer tights, in a range of shades, to cards of safety pins.

Displays of huge foliage plants, small potted citrus trees and banks of ferns lined terraces and steps, with vintage vases and urns waiting to be filled on the day with fresh flowers. The most delicate blooms would be dropped into position at the very last minute, along with those that would decorate the tables. There were even containers with umbrellas and parasols, dotted among the exterior displays, ready to cope with hot sun or unexpected showers. The whole thing was amazingly over the top. It almost felt as if the place was holding its breath.

The stage was almost set, and it was perfect.

In a few hours she would be walking down the aisle.

'Do you know this isn't at all bad?' Cassie helped herself to another glass from the jug of non-alcoholic pregnancy friendly mojito cocktail that the caterer had mixed especially for the bride's suite. Nadine grinned, careful not to move her head too far and disturb the work that the hairdresser was doing, piling her hair on top of her head in loose curls, secured with a band that perfectly matched the silk of her dress and jacket. *The* dress and jacket.

'You can pour me one now,' she instructed. Her freshly-painted nails should be dry, so she was ready to risk it.

'And me, please.' Bella, the make-up artist, was rummaging in her vanity case of goodies and setting out what she would need on the dressing table. Cassie did as she was asked. Nadine picked up the glass carefully and took a sip, savouring the sharp fresh taste. Later there would be champagne, but for now, this was just right. She looked around the room. Cassie was lounging on a sofa in a flamboyant silk dressing gown, patterned with tigers. Her hair and make-up, apart from her lipstick, were already done. She only had to slide into her dark green lace dress, for her role as matron of honour. Andrea Bocelli was playing softly in the background, singing about love. The sun was spilling in through open windows, the curtains moving in the slightest of sea breezes. Outside the sky was clear unbroken blue.

Nadine had walked alone through the gardens when they'd arrived at the villa before breakfast, drinking in the peace and the scent of the flowers. A bubble of happiness, mixed with a tiny sprinkling of nerves, welled up inside her.

There was a soft knock on the door. Cassie looked at her watch. 'If that's the florist with your bouquet, she must have finished the table displays earlier than we expected.' She uncurled herself from the sofa and went to answer. Nadine heard her laugh. 'Nadine, you have gentlemen callers.'

With a muttered apology to the hairdresser, Nadine turned to see. Ryan's twin nephews, already dressed in their smart ushers' suits, stood on the threshold, bursting with importance.

'Special delivery for the bride,' Hughie, or maybe it was Ross, announced, proffering an envelope.

'From Uncle Ryan,' the other twin explained. 'He can't come himself, Dad wouldn't let him. He said it was unlucky *and* he'd be in the way.'

Cassie was still laughing. 'Your dad is a very wise man.' She took the envelope, and after being suitably thanked, the boys retired in good order to report back to the groom's HQ in one of the bungalows in the grounds. 'Those kids are great.' Cassie put her hand to the swell of her stomach. Nadine was sure she wasn't aware of the telltale gesture. She and Jake had decided not to find out in advance if the baby was a boy or a girl, which had surprised Nadine. She'd thought her friend would be impatient to know. The baby would be welcomed and loved, however things turned out.

With a tiny sigh, she opened the envelope when Cassie brought it to her, sliding out the card inside and smiling when she saw a familiar drawing of two fluffy sheep. She turned it over, to read the Shakespeare quotation that Ryan had written on the other side.

'Hear my soul speak; the very instant that I saw you did my heart fly to your service.' And below that, 'I love you.'

Nadine sniffed, glad that she hadn't got to the mascara stage.

It was going to be a wonderful day.

It didn't matter if he'd just been cast in a potentially blockbuster film, alongside Hollywood megastars, Ryan knew *this* was the most important role of his life. He was just a little nervous, he had to admit to that. *But nervous in a good way – I think*. This was the lifetime commitment – the one that mattered. Sharing vows with Nadine in a setting like this – it was going to stay with him for the rest of his life. The party that Cassie had organised, for after the ceremony, was going to be amazing, but now Ryan was standing in the little chapel, with Sean beside him, as his best man, waiting for the bride.

In a few moments, it would be happening. Scent drifted in the air, from long stemmed roses in tall metal vases. The harpist was ensconced in a corner, playing a selection of romantic show tunes as guests were escorted to their seats by Ross and Hughie, unusually solemn and exceptionally tidy in their first grown-up suits. A restless murmur of gasps and whispers ebbed and flowed, like a small sea, behind him. The gasps were justified. The chapel, and the whole setting, looked awesome. Ryan had been to more than a few weddings and this was by far the most spectacular – and probably the most expensive – he'd ever seen.

Behind him the congregation had gone abruptly quiet. His heart started to beat a little faster. There was a small stir at the back of the church and the harpist slid effortlessly into something slow and stately. The bride had arrived. Ryan took a deep breath, and turned to watch.

Coming towards him on Jake's arm, Nadine seemed to float. She looked amazing – as if she'd stepped off a 1950s film set – in a perfectly fitting vintage suit and carrying a small tight bunch of dark red rosebuds. Something punched hard on Ryan's rib cage, then stood on it. Beside him Sean was muttering something about breathtaking. *Something's taken mine*. With an effort he got his lungs working again, before he blacked out in an undignified heap on the altar steps. When she finally reached him, the familiar scent of her perfume almost felled him again. Love – and deep gratitude that his love was returned – danced around his heart.

'You look beautiful.' He mouthed the words under cover of the final swell of the music. Nadine's smile could have melted snowdrifts.

The ceremony that had been crafted especially for them by the celebrant was a feast of words and traditional music. The soprano sang 'Ave Maria'; the string quartet played something sumptuously romantic. Ryan's friend Will read Shakespeare's 'marriage' sonnet.

Then the people and even the beauty of the church faded away as Ryan took Nadine's hands in his, first to exchange their vows, and then to recite Elizabeth Barrett Browning's Sonnet 43 together. 'How do I love thee?'

Nadine's face, looking up at him as they spoke that declaration of total love, would be imprinted in his mind until the day he died.

The last song came too soon. Ryan drifted slowly back to awareness of his surrounding as the silver notes of 'Panis Angelicus' spilled into the air. Then the whole thing was over. He was walking back down the aisle, this time with Nadine on his arm, to cheers, applause, and laughter.

This is what real love feels like.

The party was, as expected, amazing. The food was spectacular and the buffet arrangement, with tables in the villa and on the terraces, let guests mix and mingle. Cassie accepted compliments like a cat lapping up cream. Ryan took Nadine's hand for their first dance as the sun went down over the sea in a flourish of orange and gold. He held her close as they rotated around the floor and Elvis Presley crooned, 'Falling in Love with You'.

Much later they stood together in the darkness of the lower terrace, looking out over the water and watching the stars and the lights of passing boats. Nadine snuggled against Ryan's chest. *Her friend, her lover, her husband.* The lights had given her an idea. 'You know, Cassie missed a trick – there should have been fireworks to end the evening.'

'You think?'

With a low chuckle, she shook her head. 'No, not really. And don't tell her I said it!' she warned. 'Not after everything she and Jake have done. It's all been... magical.' She tilted her head to look up at him. 'I never imagined having a wedding like this. A wedding on the Riviera. It's well... the stuff of dreams... and memories. But it wouldn't have mattered if we'd only had the Registry Office in Bristol. What matters is that we're together.' She put out her hand. Ryan twined his fingers into hers. Two new wedding rings gleamed softly in the light of a solar lamp next to the steps.

'Are you ready to leave, Mrs Calder?' The note in Ryan's voice sent a little shiver down her back.

She stepped away, to look up at the house. It seemed as if the party would go on for some time yet.

'Yes. I'm ready.'

The red MG was waiting at the farmhouse, but Jake had arranged for a chauffeured car to take them back there tonight. They could slip away whenever they liked. There would be brunch around the villa's pool in the late morning, when they could say their goodbyes, before their guests left for home and they drove the MG down the coast to San Remo, for the last few days of their honeymoon.

Ryan looped his arm around her waist, and she dropped her head on his shoulder as they walked slowly up the steps. Her heart was thumping gently, with hope and promise. *This is the future. Together we can make this work.*

Ryan stopped, as her step slowed. 'What?'

'Just this.' She reached up to kiss him. *They had this, and they had a future.* She reached to kiss him again. 'I love you.'

Thank You

Hello

I hope you have enjoyed spending time with Nadine and Ryan on the Riviera and, of course, meeting up with Cassie and Jake again. When *Summer in San Remo* was published (the story of Cassie and Jake's romance) I had such fun writing it that I knew I wanted to make it the first of a series, based on the exploits of Jake's detective agency. Completing my doctorate meant that the second book took much longer to make an appearance than anyone anticipated, but my patient publishers were willing to wait, and I have my fingers crossed that you will agree it was worth the wait too. As always, I had a ball watching a brand new couple getting entangled in mayhem, and falling in love, in one of my favourite holiday locations, as well as catching up with characters from *Summer in San Remo* to find out how their lives have moved on.

If you have enjoyed *A Wedding on the Riviera*, it would be great if you could leave a review on any or all of your favourite sites, or mention the book on Twitter or Facebook. You can follow me on both and read my blog to keep up with my news. I really would appreciate a review, if you have a few moments to post one.

Thank you for reading *A Wedding on the Riviera* and here's to our next trip to the Riviera sunshine.

Evonne

About the Author

Evonne Wareham was born in South Wales and spent her childhood there. After university she migrated to London, where she worked in local government, scribbled novels in her spare time and went to the theatre a lot. Now she's back in Wales, living by the sea, and has just completed a PhD in history. She still loves the theatre, likes staying in hotels and enjoys the company of other authors through her membership of both the Romantic Novelists' Association and the Crime Writers' Association.

Evonne's debut novel, *Never Coming Home* won the 2012 Joan Hessayon New Writers' Award, the 2013 Colorado Romance Writers' Award for Romantic Suspense, the Oklahoma National Readers' Choice Award for Romantic Suspense plus was a nominee for a Reviewers' Choice Award from RT Book Reviews. Her second romantic suspense novel *Out of Sight Out of Mind*, was a finalist for the Maggie Award for Excellence, presented by the Georgia Romance Writers' chapter of the Romance Writers of America.

For more information visit:
Twitter: www.twitter.com/evonnewareham
Facebook: www.facebook.com/evonnewarehamauthor
Blog: www.evonneonwednesday.blogspot.com

More Choc Lit

From Evonne Wareham

Summer in San Remo

Anything could happen when you spend summer in San Remo …

Running her busy concierge service usually keeps Cassie Travers fully occupied. But when a new client offers her the strangest commission she's ever handled she suddenly finds herself on the cusp of an Italian adventure, with a man she thought she would never see again.

Jake McQuire has returned from the States to his family-run detective agency. When old flame Cassie appears in need of help with her mysterious client, who better than Jake to step in?

Events take the pair across Europe to a luxurious villa on the Italian Riviera. There, Cassie finds that the mystery she pursues pales into insignificance, when compared to another discovery made along the way …

Visit www.choc-lit.com for details.

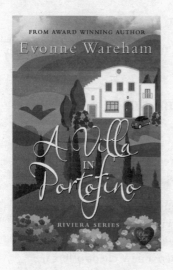

A Villa in Portofino

From chambermaid to "got it made" …

When hotel cleaning temp and poetry academic Megan Morrison finds out she's inherited an Italian villa and small fortune from her estranged great-great aunt Olwen, she doesn't quite know how to react. That is, until she travels to Portofino to see Il Giardino delle Rose for herself. Then she knows exactly what she has to do: live there!

Enchanted by the beauty of the house and gardens, fascinated by the history, and more than a little intrigued by handsome hired landscape gardener Gideon West, Megan can immediately see the villa's potential as a dream home.

But having long-lost relatives sometimes means long-lost secrets – and it seems that Olwen had plenty of those. Could these secrets and a jealous obsession be powerful enough to drive Megan out of the house that she's already fallen in love with?

Visit www.choc-lit.com for details.

Never Coming Home

*Winner of the 2012 New Writers'
Joan Hessayon Award*

All she has left is hope.

When Kaz Elmore is told her
five-year-old daughter Jamie
has died in a car crash, she
struggles to accept that she'll
never see her little girl again.
Then a stranger comes into her
life offering the most dangerous
substance in the world: hope.

Devlin, a security consultant and witness to the terrible
accident scene, inadvertently reveals that Kaz's daughter
might not have been the girl in the car after all.

What if Jamie is still alive? With no evidence, the police
aren't interested, so Devlin and Kaz have little choice but to
investigate themselves.

Devlin never gets involved with a client. Never. But the more
time he spends with Kaz, the more he desires her – and the more
his carefully constructed ice-man persona starts to unravel.

The desperate search for Jamie leads down dangerous paths
– to a murderous acquaintance from Devlin's dark past, and
all across Europe, to Italy, where deadly secrets await. But as
long as Kaz has hope, she can't stop looking …

Out of Sight
Out of Mind

*Finalist for the Maggie
Award of Excellence*

**Everyone has secrets. Some
are stranger than others.**

Madison Albi is a scientist
with a very special talent –
for reading minds. When she
stumbles across a homeless
man with whom she feels an
inexplicable connection, she
can't resist the dangerous impulse to use her skills to help
him.

J is a non-person – a vagrant who can't even remember his
own name. He's got no hope, until he meets Madison. Is she
the one woman who can restore his past?

Madison agrees to help J recover his memory, but as she
delves deeper into his mind, it soon becomes clear that some
secrets are better off staying hidden.

Is J really the man Madison believes him to be?

Visit www.choc-lit.com for details.

What Happens at Christmas

Kidnapped for Christmas?

Best-selling author Andrew Vitruvius knows that any publicity is good publicity. His agent tells him that often, so it must be true. In the run-up to Christmas, she excels herself – talking him into the craziest scheme yet: getting himself kidnapped, live on TV.

But when the plan goes ahead and Drew is unceremoniously thrown in the back of a van before being dragged to a hut in middle of the Brecon Beacons, it all starts to feel a little bit *too* real.

Meanwhile, not far away, Lori France and her four-year-old niece Misty are settling in to spend the holidays away after unexpected events leave them without a place to stay. Little do they know they're about to make a shocking discovery and experience a Christmas they're not likely to forget …

Visit www.choc-lit.com for details.

Introducing Choc Lit

We're an independent publisher creating
a delicious selection of fiction.
Where heroes are like chocolate – irresistible!
Quality stories with a romance at the heart.

See our selection here:
www.choc-lit.com

We'd love to hear how you enjoyed *A Wedding on the Riviera*. Please visit **www.choc-lit.com** and give your feedback or leave a review where you purchased this novel.

Choc Lit novels are selected by genuine readers like yourself. We only publish stories our Choc Lit Tasting Panel want to see in print. Our reviews and awards speak for themselves.

Could you be a Star Selector and join our Tasting Panel?
Would you like to play a role in choosing which novels we decide to publish? Do you enjoy reading women's fiction? Then you could be perfect for our Tasting Panel.

Visit here for more details…
www.choc-lit.com/join-the-choc-lit-tasting-panel

Keep in touch:
Sign up for our monthly newsletter Spread for all the latest news and offers: www.spread.choc-lit.com. Follow us on Twitter: @ChocLituk and Facebook: Choc Lit.

Where heroes are like chocolate – irresistible!